Jasper Fforde

One of Our Thursdays is Missing

HODDER

First published in Great Britain in 2011 by Hodder & Stoughton
An Hachette UK company

First published in paperback in 2011

1

A CIP catalogue record for this title is available from the British Library

B format paperback ISBN 978 0 340 96309 8
A format paperback ISBN 978 0 340 96310 4

Typeset in Bembo by Palimpsest Book Production Limited,
Falkirk, Stirlingshire

Printed and bound by Clays Ltd, St Ives plc

Hodder & Stoughton policy is to use papers that are natural, renewable and
recyclable products and made from wood grown in sustainable forests. The
logging and manufacturing processes are expected to conform to the
environmental regulations of the country of origin.

Hodder & Stoughton Ltd
338 Euston Road
London NW1 3BH

www.hodder.co.uk

04736569

For Tif Loehnis
To whom I owe my career
and by consequence
much else besides

Author's Note

This book has been bundled with **Special Features** including:
The Making of . . . wordamentary, deleted scenes, alternative
endings and much more.

To access all these free bonus features,
log on to: **www.jasperfforde.com/features.html**
and follow the onscreen instructions.

Contents

I

The BookWorld Remade

'**The Remaking was one of those moments when one felt part of literature, and not just being carried along within it.** In less than ten minutes, the entire fabric of the BookWorld was radically altered. The old system was swept away, and everything was changed for ever. But the group of people to whom it was ultimately beneficial remained gloriously unaware: the readers. To most of them, books were simply books. If only it were that simple . . .'

Bradshaw's BookWorld Companion

Everyone remembers where they were when the BookWorld was remade. I was at home 'resting between readings', which is a polite euphemism for 'almost remaindered'.

But I wasn't doing nothing. No, I was using the time to acquaint myself with EZ-Read's latest labour-saving Narrative Devices, all designed to assist a first-person protagonist like me cope with the strains of a sixty-eight-setting five-book series at the speculative end of Fantasy.

I couldn't afford any of these Devices – not even Verb-Ease™ for troublesome irregularity – but that wasn't the point. It was the company of EZ-Read's regional salesman that I was interested in, a cheery Designated Love Interest named Whitby Jett.

'We have a new line in Foreshadowing,' he said, passing me a small blue vial.

'Does the bottle have to be in the shape of Lola Vavoom?' I asked.

'It's a marketing thing.'

I opened the stopper and sniffed it gingerly.

'What do you think?' he asked.

Whitby was a good-looking man described as a youthful forty. I didn't know it then but he had a dark past, and despite our mutual attraction, his past misdeeds could end in only one way: madness, recrimination and despair.

'I prefer my foreshadowing a little less pungent,' I said, carefully replacing the stopper. 'I was getting all sorts of vibes about you and a dark past.'

'I wish,' replied Whitby sadly. His book had been deleted long ago, so he was one of the many thousands of characters who eked a living in the BookWorld while they waited for a decent part to come along. But because of his minor Designated Love Interest character status, he had never been given a backstory. Those without any sort of history often tried to promote it as something mysterious when it wasn't, but not Whitby, who was refreshingly pragmatic. 'Even having no backstory as my backstory would be something,' he had once told me in a private moment, 'but the truth is this: my author couldn't be arsed to give me one.'

I always appreciated honesty, even as personal as this. There weren't many characters in the BookWorld who had been left unscathed by the often selfish demands of their creators. A clumsily written and unrealistic set of conflicting motivations can have a character in therapy for decades – perhaps for ever.

'Any work offers recently?' I asked.

'I was up for a minor walk-on in an Amis.'

'How did you do?'

'I read half a page and they asked me what I thought. I said I understood every word so I was rejected for being overqualified.'

'I'm sorry to hear that.'

'It's okay,' he said. 'I was also offered a four-hundred-and-six-word part in a Horror last week, but I'm not so sure. First-time author and a small publisher so I might not make it past the second impression. If I get remaindered I'd be worse off than I am now.'

'I'm remaindered,' I told him.

'But you were *once* popular,' he said, 'so might be again. Do you know how many characters have high hopes of a permanent place in the readers' hearts, only to suffer the painful rejection of eternal unreadfulness at the dreary end of Human Drama?'

He was right. A book's life could be very long indeed, and although the increased leisure time in an unread novel is not to be sniffed at, a need to be vigilant in case someone *does* read you can keep one effectively tied to a book for life. I usually had an understudy to let me get away, but few were so lucky.

'So,' said Whitby, 'how would you like to come out to the Smellies tonight? I hear *Garden Peas with Mint* is showing at the Rex.'

In the BookWorld, smells were in short supply. *Garden Peas with Mint* had been the best release this year. It only narrowly beat *Vanilla Coffee* and *Grilled Smoked Bacon* to the prestigious Noscar™ 'Best Adapted Smell' award.

'I heard that *Mint* was overrated,' I replied, although I hadn't. Whitby had been asking me out on a date almost as long as I had been turning him down. I didn't tell him why, but he suspected there was someone else. There was and there wasn't. It was complex, even by BookWorld standards. He asked me out a lot and I declined a lot. It was kind of like a game.

'How about going to the Running of the Bumbles next week? Dangerous, but exciting.'

This was an annual fixture on the BookWorld calendar, where two dozen gruel-crazed and indignant Mr Bumbles yelling: 'More? MORE?!?' were released to charge through an unused chapter of *Oliver Twist*. Those of a sporting or daring disposition were invited to run before them and take their chances; at least one hapless youth was crushed to death every year.

'I've no need to prove myself,' I replied, 'and neither do you.'

'How about dinner?' he asked, unabashed. 'I can get a table at the Inn Uendo. The maître d is missing an apostrophe and I promised to give her one.'

'Not really my thing.'

'Then what about the Bar Humbug? The atmosphere is wonderfully dreary.'

It was over in Classics, but we could take a cab.

'I'll need an understudy to take care of my book.'

'What happened to Stacey?'

'The same as happened to Doris and Enid.'

'Trouble with Pickwick again?'

'As if you need to ask.'

And that was when the doorbell rang. This was unusual, as random events rarely occurred in the mostly predetermined Book-World. I opened the door to find three Dostoyevskivites staring at me from within a dense cloud of moral relativism.

'May we come in?' asked the first, who had the look of someone weighed down heavily with the burden of conscience. 'We were on our way home from a redemption-through-suffering training course. Something big's going down at Text Grand Central and everyone's been grounded until further notice.'

A grounding was rare, but not unheard of. In an emergency, all citizens of the BookWorld were expected to offer hospitality to those stranded outside their books. I might have minded, but these guys were from *Crime and Punishment* and, better still, celebrities. We hadn't seen a celebrity this end of Fantasy since Pamela from *Pamela* stopped outside with a flat tyre. She could have been gone in an hour, but insisted on using an epistolary breakdown service, and we had to put her up in the spare room while a complex series of letters went backwards and forwards.

'Welcome to my home, Rodion Romanovich Raskolnikov.'

'Oh!' said Raskolnikov, impressed that I knew who he was. 'How did you know it was me? Could it have been the subtle way in which I project the dubious moral notion that murder might somehow be rationalised, or the way in which I move from denying my guilt to eventually coming to terms with an absolute sense of justice and submitting myself to the rule of law?'

'Neither,' I said. 'It's because you're holding an axe covered in blood and human hair.'

'Yes, it is a bit of a giveaway,' he admitted, staring at the axe, 'but how rude am I? Allow me to introduce Arkady Ivanovich Svidrigaïlov.'

'Actually,' said the second man, leaning over to shake my hand, 'I'm Dmitri Prokofich Razumikhin, Raskolnikov's loyal friend.'

'You are?' said Raskolnikov in surprise. 'Then what happened to Svidrigaïlov?'

'He's busy chatting up your sister.'

He narrowed his eyes.

'My sister? That's Pulkheria Alexandrovna Raskolnikova, right?'

'No,' said Razumikhin in the tone of a long-suffering best friend, 'that's your mother. Avdotya Romanovna Raskolnikova is your sister.'

'I always get those two mixed up. So who's Marfa Petrovna Svidrigaïlova?'

Razumikhin frowned and thought for a moment.

'You've got me there.'

He turned to the third Russian.

'Tell me, Pyotr Petrovich Luzhin: who, precisely, is Marfa Petrovna Svidrigaïlova?'

'I'm sorry,' said the third Russian, who had been staring at her shoes absently, 'but I think there has been some kind of mistake. I'm not Pyotr Petrovich Luzhin, but Alyona Ivanovna.'

Razumikhin turned to Raskolnikov and lowered his voice.

'Is that your landlady's servant, the one who decides to marry down to secure her future or the one who turns to prostitution in order to stop her family descending into penury?'

Raskolnikov shrugged.

'Listen,' he said, 'I've been in this book for over a hundred and thirty years, and even I can't figure it out.'

'It's very simple,' said the third Russian, indicating who did what on her fingers, 'Nastasya Petrovna is Raskolnikov's landlady's servant, Avdotya Romanovna Raskolnikova is your sister who threatens to marry down, Sofia Semyonovna Marmeladova is the one who becomes a prostitute, and Marfa Petrovna Svidrigaïlova – the one you were *first* asking about – is Arkady Svidrigaïlov's murdered first wife.'

'I knew that,' said Raskolnikov in the manner of someone who didn't, 'so . . . who are you again?'

'I'm Alyona Ivanovna,' said the third Russian with a trace of annoyance, 'the rapacious old pawnbroker whose apparent greed and wealth lead you to murder.'

'Are you *sure* you're Ivanovna?' asked Raskolnikov in a worried tone.

'Absolutely.'

'And you're still alive?'

'So it seems.'

He stared at the bloody axe.

'Then who did I just kill?'

And they all looked at each other in confusion.

'Listen,' I said, 'I'm sure everything will come out fine in the epilogue. But for the moment, your home is my home.'

Anyone from the Classics had a celebrity status that outshone anything else, and I'd never had anyone even remotely famous pass through before. I suddenly felt a bit hot and bothered and tried to tidy up the house in a clumsy sort of way. I whipped my socks from the radiator and brushed off the pistachio shells that Pickwick had left on the sideboard.

'This is Whitby Jett of EZ-Read,' I said, introducing the Russians one by one but getting their names hopelessly mixed up, which might have been embarrassing had they noticed. Whitby shook all their hands and then asked for autographs, which was embarrassing.

'So why have Text Grand Central ordered a grounding?' I asked, as soon as everyone was seated and I had rung for Mrs Malaprop to bring in the tea.

'I think the rebuilding of the BookWorld is about to take place,' said Razumikhin with a dramatic flourish.

'So soon?'

The remaking had been a hot topic for a number of years. After Imagination™ was deregulated in the early fifties, the outbursting of creative alternatives generated huge difficulties for the Council of Genres, who needed a clearer overview of the how the individual novels sat within the BookWorld as a whole. Taking the RealWorld as inspiration, the CofG decided a Geographic model was the way to go. How the physical world actually appeared, no one really knew. Not many people travelled to the RealWorld, and those that did generally noted two things: one, that it was hysterically funny and hideously tragic in almost equal measure, and two, that there were far more domestic cats than baobabs, when it should probably be the other way round.

Whitby got up and looked out of the window. There was nothing to see, quite naturally, as the area *between* books had no precise definition or meaning. My front door opened to, well, not very much at all. Stray too far from the boundaries of one's book and you'd be lost for ever in the inter-book Nothing. It was confusing, but then so were *Tristram Shandy*, *The Magus* and Russian novels, and people had been enjoying them for decades.

'So what's going to happen?' asked Whitby.

'I have a good friend over at Text Grand Central,' said Alyona

Ivanovna, who had wisely decided to sit as far from Raskolnikov and the bloody axe as she could, 'and to accomplish a smooth transition from Great Library BookWorld to Geographic BookWorld, the best option was to close down all of the ImaginoTransference engines while they rebooted the throughput conduits.'

This was an astonishing suggestion. The ImaginoTransference engines were the machines that transmitted the books in all their subtle glory from the BookWorld to the reader's imagination. To shut them down meant that reading – *all* reading – had to stop. I exchanged a nervous glance with Whitby.

'You mean the Council of Genres are going to shut down the entire BookWorld?'

Alyona Ivanovna nodded.

'It was either that or do it piecemeal, which wasn't favoured since that way half the BookWorld would be operating one system and half the other. It's simple: all reading needs to stop for the nine minutes it requires to have the BookWorld remade.'

'But that's insane!' exclaimed Whitby. 'People will notice. There's always someone reading *somewhere*.'

From my own failed experience of joining the BookWorld's policing agency, I knew that he spoke the truth. There was a device hung high on the wall in the Council of Genres debating chamber that logged the Outland Read-Rate – the total number of readers at any one time. It bobbed up and down but rarely dropped below the twenty million mark. But while spikes in reading were easy to predict, such as when a new blockbuster is published or when an author dies – always a happy time for their creations, if not their relatives – predicting slumps was much harder. And we needed a serious slump in reading to get down to the 'under fifty thousand' threshold considered safe for a remaking.

I had an idea. I fetched that morning's copy of *The Word* and turned to the week's forecast. This wasn't to do with weather, naturally, but trends in reading. Urban Vampires were once more heavily forecast for the week ahead, with scattered Wizards moving in from Wednesday and a high chance of Daphne Farquitt novels near the end of the week. There was also an alert for everyone at Sports Trivia to 'brace themselves', and it stated the reason.

'There you go,' I said, tapping the newspaper and showing it to the assembled company, 'right about now the Swindon Mallets are about to defend their title against the Gloucester Meteors, and with live televised coverage to the entire planet, there is a huge potential fall in the Read-Rate.'

'You think that many people are interested in Premier League croquet?' asked Razumikhin.

'It *is* Swindon versus Gloucester,' I replied, 'and after the Malletts' midhoop wingman Penelope Hrah exploded on the forty-yard line last year, I would expect ninety-two per cent of the world will be watching the game – as good a time as any to take the BookWorld offline.'

'Did they ever find out *why* Hrah exploded?' asked Whitby.

'It was never fully explained,' put in Ivanovna, 'but traces of Semtex were discovered in her shin-guards, so foul play could never be ruled out entirely. A grudge match is always a lot of fu—'

Her voice was abruptly cut dead, but not in the way it is when you suddenly stop speaking. Her voice was clipped, like a gap in a recording.

'Hello?' I said.

The three Russians made no answer and were simply staring into space, like mannequins. After a moment they started to lose facial definition as they became a series of complex irregular polyhedra. After a while the number of facets of the polyhedra started to diminish, and the Russians became less like people, and more like jagged flesh-coloured lumps. Pretty soon they were nothing at all. The Classics were being shut down, and if Text Grand Central were doing it alphabetically, Fantasy would not be far behind. And so it proved. I looked at Whitby, who gave me a wan smile and held my hand. The room grew cold, then dark, and before long the only world that I knew started to disassemble in front of my eyes. Everything grew flatter, and lost its form, and pretty soon I began to feel my memory fade. And just when I was starting to worry, everything cleansed to an all-consuming darkness.

```
#shutting down ImaginoTransference Engines,
  46,802 readers
#active reader states have been cached
#dismounting READ OS 8.3.6
#start programs
#check and mount specified dictionaries
#check and mount specified thesauri
#check and mount specified idiomatic database
#check and mount specified grammatical data-
  base
#check and mount specified character database
#check and mount specified settings database
Mount temporary ISBN/Bisac/Duodecimal Book
  category system
Mount ImaginoTransference throughput module
Accessing 'book index' on global bus
Creating cache for primary plot development
  module
Creating /ramdisk in 'Story interpretation',
  default size=300
Creating directories: irony
Creating directories: humour
Creating directories: plot
Creating directories: character
Creating directories: atmosphere
Creating directories: prose
Creating directories: pace
Creating directories: pathos
Starting init process
#display ImaginoTransference Engine error
  messages
#recovering active readers from cache
System message=Welcome to Geographic Operating
  System 1.2
Setting control terminal to automatic
System active with 46,802 active readers
```

'Thursday?'

I opened my eyes and blinked. I was lying on the sofa staring up at Whitby, who had a concerned expression on his face.

'Are you okay?'

I sat up and rubbed my head.

'How long was I out?'

'Eleven minutes.'

I looked around.

'And the Russians?'

'Outside.'

'There is no outside.'

He smiled.

'There is now. Come and have a look.'

I stood up and noticed for the first time that my living room seemed that little bit more realistic. The colours were subtler, and the walls had an increased level of texture. More interestingly, the room seemed to be brighter, and there was light coming in through the windows. It was *real* light, too, the sort that casts shadows, and not the pretend stuff we were used to. I grasped the handle, opened the front door and stepped outside.

The empty inter-book Nothing that had separated the novels and genres had been replaced by fields, hills, rivers, trees and forests, and all around me the countryside opened out into a series of expansive vistas with the welcome novelty of *distance*. We were now in the south-east corner of an island perhaps a hundred miles by fifty and bounded on all sides by the Text Sea, which had been elevated to 'Grade IV Picturesque' status by the addition of an azure hue and a soft billowing motion that made the text shimmer in the breeze.

As I looked around I realised that whoever had remade the Book-World had considered practicalities as much as aesthetics. Unlike the RealWorld, which is inconveniently located on the *outside* of a sphere, the new BookWorld was anchored on the *inside* of a sphere, thus ensuring that horizons worked in the opposite way to those in Real-World. Farther objects were higher in the visual plane than nearer ones. From anywhere in the BookWorld it was possible to view anywhere else. I noticed, too, that we were not alone. Stuck on the inside of the sphere were hundreds of other islands very similar to our own, and each a haven for a category of literature therein.

About ten degrees upslope of Fiction I could see our nearest neighbour: Artistic Criticism. It was an exceptionally beautiful island, yet deeply troubled, confused and suffused with a blanketing layer of almost impenetrable bullshit. Beyond it were Psychology, Philately and Software Manuals. But the brightest and biggest archipelago I could see upon the closed sea was the scattered group of genres that made up Non-Fiction. They were positioned right on the other side of the inner globe so were almost directly overhead. On one side of the island the cliffs of irrationality were slowly being eroded

'Oh, brave new world, that has such stories in't!'

away, while on the opposite shore the sands of science were slowly reclaiming salt-marsh from the sea.

While I stared upwards, open mouthed, a steady stream of books moved in an endless multilayered criss-cross high in the sky. But these weren't books of the small, paper-and-leather variety that one might find in the Outland. These were the collected *settings* of the book all bolted together and connected by a series of walkways and supporting beams, cables and struts. They didn't look so much like books, in fact, but more like a series of spiky lumps. While some one-room dramas were no bigger than a double-decker bus and zipped across the sky, others moved slowly enough for us to wave at the occupants, who waved back. As we stood watching our new world, the master copy of *Dr Zhivago* passed overhead, blotting out the light and covering us in a light dusting of snow.

'What do you think?' asked Whitby.

'Oh, brave new world,' I whispered as I gave him a hug, 'that has such stories in't!'

2

A Woman Named Thursday Next

'. . . A major benefit of the "Internal Sphere" model of the Remade BookWorld was that gravitational force diminished with height, so it was easier to move objects the higher you went. You had to be careful, though, for if you went too high you would be attracted to the gravitational dead-spot right in the centre of the sphere, from where there could be no escape . . .'

Bradshaw's BookWorld Companion

My father had a face that could stop a clock. I don't mean that he was ugly or anything; it was a phrase that the ChronoGuard used to describe someone who had the power to arrest time to an ultra-slow trickle – and that's exactly what happened one morning as I was having a late breakfast in a small café quite near where I worked. The world flickered, shuddered and stopped. The barman of the café froze to a halt in mid-sentence and the picture on the television stopped dead. Outside, birds hung motionless in the sky. The sound halted too, replaced by a dull snapshot of a hum, the world's noise at that moment in time paused indefinitely at the same pitch and volume.

'Hello, Sweetpea.'

I turned. My father was sitting at a table behind me and rose to hug me affectionately.

'Hi, Dad.'

'You're looking good,' he told me.

'You too,' I replied. 'You're looking younger every time I see you.'

'I am. How's your history?'

'Not bad.'

'Do you know how the Duke of Wellington died?'

'Sure,' I answered, 'he was shot by a French sniper early on during the Battle of Waterloo – why?'

'Oh, no reason,' muttered my father with feigned innocence, scribbling in a small notebook. Once done, he paused for a moment.

'So Napoleon *won* at Waterloo, did he?' he asked slowly and with great intensity.

'Of course not,' I replied. 'Field Marshal Blücher's timely intervention saved the day. This is all GCSE history, Dad. What are you up to?'

'Well, it's a bit of—'

'—hang on,' said Dad, or rather, the character *playing* my book-father, 'I think they've gone.'

I tasted the air. He was right. Our lone reader had stopped and left us dangling in a narrative dead zone. It's an odd sensation: a combination of treading on a step that isn't there, someone hanging up the telephone mid-speech without explanation, and the feeling you get when you've gone upstairs for some reason but can't think why. Scientists have proved that spaniels spend their entire lives like this.

'I was *marvellous*,' intoned my book-father haughtily, the implication being that it was somehow my fault the reader didn't last until even the end of the second page, 'you need to *engage* the readers more, darling. Project yourself. Make the character come *alive*.'

I didn't agree that I was at fault, but wasn't going to argue. He had played my father longer in the series than I had played Thursday so he had a kind of seniority, even if I was the protagonist, and First-Person Player, to boot.

'Sometimes I yearn for the old days,' he said to Hector, his dresser, but obviously intending for me to hear.

'What do you mean by that?'

He stared at me for a moment.

'This: it was a lot better when we had the previous Thursday play Thursday.'

'She was violent and immoral, Dad. How could that *possibly* be better?'

'She might have been a shit of the highest order, darling, but she brought in the readers. I'll be in my dressing room. Come, Hector.'

And so saying, he swept from the café setting with his ever-present dresser, who pouted rudely at me as they left. My father had a point, of course, but I was committed to promoting the type of Thursday the *real* Thursday wanted to see in the series. The series had originally been written to feature a violent and disorderly Thursday Next who slept her way around the BookWorld and caused no end of murder, misery and despair. I was trying to change all that, but had met with stiff resistance from the rest of the cast. They saw my attempt to depict reality as damaging to the overall readability – and for a character, the only thing worse than being read badly is to be badly unread.

I sighed. Keeping everyone within my series happy and fulfilled and focused was about as hard a job as acting in the book itself. Some books had a Page Manager to do all that boring stuff, but for financial reasons I had to do it myself with only a defective Mrs Malaprop for assistance. Making us all readable were the least of my worries.

I walked slowly home through my book-version of Swindon, which was forty times more compact than the real one. Owing to the limited number of locations mentioned in my series, I could go easily from the café to my mother's house to the GSD church and then on to the SpecOps building in the space of a few minutes, something that would take the best part of an hour in the real Swindon. There were a few handy short cuts, too. By opening a door at the back of the Blessed Lady of the Lobster I could find myself in the mock-up of Thornfield Hall, and by taking the first door on the right past Jane's bedroom, I could be in the Penderyn Hotel in Wales. All told, the series covered about five acres on six levels, and would have been larger if we hadn't doubled up the east façade of Thornfield with the front of Haworth Parsonage in Yorkshire, and the Gad's Hill museum with the redressed lobby of the SpecOps building. Economies like this were commonplace in remaindered books, and helped us keep the cast at almost full strength. Doubling up characters *was* possible, but caused problems when they were in scenes with themselves. Some characters could handle it, others could not. On one memorable occasion Vronsky played *all* the parts in an abridged version of *Anna Karenina* when the rest of the cast were on strike for more blinis. When asked what it was like, he described it as 'like, totally awesome, dude'.

'Good morning, Pickwick,' I said as I walked into the kitchen, which served not only as the Command Centre of my series, but also where tea and toast could be consumed. 'Good morning, Mrs Malaprop.'

'Cod moaning, mist knocks,' said the defective Mrs Malaprop, bobbing politely.

'May I have a word?' asked Pickwick in a not-very-subtle aside.

'Is it important?'

'It is vitally *crucial*,' said Pickwick, rolling her eyes oddly.

We moved out to the hallway.

'Okay, what's the problem?' I asked, since Pickwick *always* had a grievance of some sort – whether it was the cold, or the heat, or the colour of the walls or a hundred and one other things that weren't quite right. Whitby and I referred to her as 'Goldilocks but without the good manners' – but never to her beak.

'It's Mrs Malaprop,' said the dodo in an affronted tone, 'she's becoming increasingly unintelligible. It would be okay if it was faintly amusing but it isn't, and well, quite frankly, there is the risk of infection and it frightens me.'

To a text-based life-form, unpredictable syntax and poor grammar are sources of huge discomfort. Ill-fitting grammar are like ill-fitting shoes. You can get used to it for a bit, but then one day your toes fall off and you can't walk to the bathroom. Poor syntax is even worse. Change word order and sentence useless that for anyone Yoda except you have.

'Now then,' I said, using an oxymoron for scolding effect, 'it is totally unproven that Malapropism is infectious, and what did we say about tolerating those less fortunate than ourselves?'

'Even so,' said Pickwick, 'I want you to tell her to stop it. And her shoes squeak. And while we're on the subject, Bowden referred to me as 'that bird' again, the baobab in the back garden is cutting out the light from my bedroom and I'm taking next Wednesday off to have my beak oiled, so you'll need to get a replacement – and not the penguin like last time. She didn't do justice to my dynamic personality and poetic sensibilities. Played it all a bit . . . *fishcentric*, if you know what I mean.'

'I'll do my best,' I said, making a mental note to *definitely* rebook the penguin.

'Good,' said Pickwick, 'have you the paper?'

We returned to the kitchen and I found *The Word* for her.

'Hmm,' she said thoughtfully, staring at the City pages, 'Metaphor has risen by seventeen pounds a barrel. I should dump some Metonym and buy into Synecdoche futures.'

'How are things going with Racy Novel?' I asked, since the political problems up in the north had been much in the news recently. A long-running dispute between Racy Novel, Women's Fiction and Dogma had been getting worse, and was threatening to erupt into a genre war at the drop of a hat.

'Peace talks still on schedule for Friday,' replied Pickwick, 'as if

21

that would do any good. Sometimes I think that Speedy Muffler nut-job wants nothing but a good scrap. By the way,' she added, 'did you hear about *Raphael's Walrus*?'

'No?'

'Got their eviction papers this morning.'

This wasn't surprising. *Raphael's Walrus* was a book six doors down that hadn't been read for a while. I didn't know them well, but since we were located at the Speculative end of Fantasy, the real estate was valuable. We'd have a new neighbour almost the moment they left.

'I hope it's not Sword and Sorcery,' said Pickwick with a shudder, 'goblins really drag down the neighbourhood.'

'Goblins might say the same about dodos.'

'Impossible!' she retorted. 'Dodos are cute and cuddly and lovable and . . . don't steal stuff and spread disease.'

People often wondered why my written dodo was such a pain in the arse when the real Pickwick was so cute. The reason was simple: lack of choice. There are only three dodos in Fiction. One was dangerously psychotic, the second was something big over in Natural History, which left only one: the dodo from *Alice* is the same bespectacled know-all in my series. Her name wasn't actually Pickwick, it was Lorina Peabody III, but we called her Pickwick, and she didn't much mind either way. She put down the paper, announced to the room that she would be taking her siesta, and waddled off.

'Mrs Malaprop,' I said once Pickwick had left, 'are you still attending your therapy sessions?'

Mrs Malaprop arched a highbrow. She knew well enough who had complained about her.

'Eggs tincture is too good for that burred,' she said in a crabby tone, 'but isle do as Uri quest.'

The average working life of a Mrs Malaprop in *The Rivals* was barely fifty readings. The unrelenting comedic misuse of words eventually caused them to suffer 'Post-Syntax Stress Disorder', and once their speech became irreversibly abstruse they were simply replaced. Most 'retired' Mrs Malaprops were turned out into the BookWorld where they turned ferrule, but just recently rehoming charities were taking note of their plight. After intensive Holorime Bombardment Therapy to enable them to at least *sound* right even if they didn't *read* right, people like me offered them a home and a job. Our Malaprop was an early model – number 862 to be precise – and she was generally quite helpful if a little tricky to understand. There was talk of using *Dogberry* stem-cells to cure her, but we didn't hold our broth.

I stared at the Diagnostics board that covered one wall of the kitchen. The number of readers on the Read-O-Meter was stuck firmly at zero, with thirty-two copies of my novels listed 'bookmarked and pending'. Of these, eighteen were active/resting between reads. The remainder were probably lying under a stack of other unfinished books. I checked the RealWorld Clock. It was 08.42. Years ago I was read on the train, but that hadn't happened for a while. Unreadfulness was a double-edged sword. More leisure time, but a distinct loss of purpose. I turned to Mrs Malaprop.

'How are things looking in the series?'

She stared at her clipboard.

'Toll rubble. Twenty-six characters Aaron leaf or training courses; all can be covered by eggs hastings characters. Of the settings, only Hayworth House is clothes bee coarse of an invest station of grammasites.'

'Have Jurisfiction been informed?'

'We're low prior tory, so they said eight hours.'

'How close is our nearest reader?'

'Nine teas heaven minutes' read time away.'

It wasn't going to be a problem. Our nearest reader wouldn't pick the book up again until this evening, by which time the problem would have resolved itself.

'If they start reading early for any reason,' I said, 'we'll use the front room of Thornfield Hall as a stand-in. Oh, and my father has a flea in his ear about something, so keep an eye on him in case he tries to do his own lines. I got a letter last week from Text Grand Central about illegal dialogue flexations.'

Mrs Malaprop nodded and made a note.

'Come harder hearing cold,' she said.

'Sorry?'

'Comma DeHare ring cooled.'

'I'm . . . still not getting this.'

Mrs Malaprop thought hard, trying to place the correct words in the correct place to enable me to understand. It was painfully difficult for her, and if Sheridan had known the misery that using *acyrologia* in a comedic situation would bring, he would possibly have thought butter of it.

'*Come hander hair-in culled!*' she said again in an exasperated tone, sweating profusely and starting to shake with the effort.

'Commander Herring called?' I said, suddenly getting it. 'What about?'

'A naval antecedent,' she said urgently, 'in evasion.'

She meant that a Novel had met with an accident in Aviation.

'Why would he be calling me after I blew it so badly last time?'

'It sea-reprised me, too. Here.'

She handed me a scrap of paper. Commander James 'Red' Herring was overall leader of the BookWorld Policing Agency. He was not only in command of the Fiction Police, known as Jurisfiction, but also Text Grand Central's Metaphor Squad and at least eighteen other agencies. One of these was Book Traffic Control – and as part of that, the Jurisfiction Accident Investigation Department or JAID, a department I occasionally worked for. The overhead book traffic, despite its usefulness, was not without problems. Fiction alone could see up to two thousand book-movements a day and the constant transportation of the novels across the fictional skies was not without mishap. I spent at least a day a week identifying sections that had fallen off books passing overhead, trying to get them returned – and if possible, find out why. Despite safety assurances, improved glue and updated safety procedures, books would keep on shedding bits. The loss of a pig out of *Animal Farm* was the most celebrated incident. It fell several thousand feet and landed inside a book of short stories by Graham Greene. Disaster was averted by a quick-thinking Jurisfiction agent who expertly sewed the pig into the narrative. It was Jurisfiction at its very best.

'Did Mr Herring say which book or why he was calling me?'

'Nasty mess, Walsall he said. You're to me Tim at this address.'

I took the note she'd handed me. Commander Herring calling me *personally* was something of a big deal.

'Anything else?'

'Your new understudy is waiting Toby interviewed.'

This was good news. My book was first-person narrative, and if I wanted to have any sort of life outside my occasional readings – such as a date with Whitby or a secondary career – I needed someone to stand in for me.

I walked through to the front room. My potential understudy looked pleasant enough and had even troubled to assimilate herself into my body-type and vague looks. She had a Thursday Next outfit on, too. She wanted this gig badly.

'The written Thursday Next,' I said, shaking her hand.

'Carmine O'Kipper,' she replied with a nervous smile, 'ID: A4-5619-23. Pleased to be here.'

'You're an A4, Miss O'Kipper?'

'Call me Carmine. Is that a problem?'

'Not at all.'

An A4 character was theoretically only three steps down from the Jane Eyres and Scout Finches. To be able to handle First Person you had to be an A-Grade, but none of the other understudies had been higher than an A9.

'You must be at least an A2, yes?' she asked.

'Something like that,' I replied as we sat. 'Do you know of the series?'

'I used to keep a scrapbook of the *real* Thursday Next.'

'If you're here to catch a glimpse of her, it's unlikely. She dropped in once soon after the Remaking, but not since then.'

'I'm really just after the work, Miss Next.'

She handed me her CV. It wasn't long, nor particularly impressive. She was from an original manuscript sitting abandoned in a drawer somewhere in the Outland. She would have handled loss, love, uncertainty and a corkingly good betrayal. It looked like it might have been a good gig. But after fifteen years and not a single reader, it was time to move on.

'So . . . why do you want to work in my series?'

'I'm eager to enter a new and stimulating phase of my career,' she said brightly, 'and need a challenging and engaging book in which I can learn from a true professional.'

It was the usual bullshit, and it didn't wash.

'You could get a read anywhere,' I said, handing back the CV, 'so why come to the speculative end of Fantasy?'

She bit her lip and stared at me.

'I've only ever been read by one person at a time,' she confessed. 'I took a short Third Person locum inside a *Reader's Digest* version of *Don Quixote* as Dulcinea two weeks ago. I had a panic attack when the read-levels went over twenty-six and went for the Snooze.'

I heard Mrs Malaprop drop a toecap in the kitchen. I was shocked, too. The Snooze button was reserved only for dire emergencies. Once utilised, a reverse throughput capacitor on the ImaginoTransference engines would cause the reader instantaneous yawning, drowsiness and then sleep. Quick, simple – and the readers suspected nothing.

'You hit Snooze?'

'I was stopped before I did.'

'I'm very relieved.'

'Me too. Rocinante had to take over my part – played her rather well, actually.'

'Did the Don notice? Rocinante playing you, I mean?'

'No.'

Carmine was just what I was looking for. Overqualified understudies rarely stayed long, but being severely readerphobic, the low read-rates would suit her down to the ground. I was mildly concerned over her eagerness to hit Snooze. To discourage misuse, every time the button was pressed one or more kittens were put to death somewhere in the BookWorld. It was rarely used.

'Okay,' I said, 'you're hired. One caveat: you don't get the Snooze button access codes. Agreed?'

'Agreed.'

'Excellent. How much reading time do you have?'

'Aside from my own book, I've got eighty-seven pages.'

It was a lamentably small amount. A single quizzical reader hunting for obscure hidden meanings would have her in a stammering flat spin in a second.

'Get your coat and a notebook,' I said, 'we're going to go and greet our new neighbours – and have a chat.'

3

Carmine O'Kipper

———

'. . . Outland Tourism was banned long ago, and even full members of Jurisfiction – the BookWorld's policing elite – were no longer permitted to cross over to the Real-World. The reasons were many and hotly debated, but this much was agreed: reality was a pit of vipers for the unwary. Forget to breathe, miscalculate gravity or support the wrong god or foot-ball team and they'd be sending you home in a zinc coffin.'

Bradshaw's BookWorld Companion

After taking a pager off the counter so Mrs Malaprop could reach me in case a reader turned up unexpectedly, we stepped out of the main gate and walked down the street. The Remade Geographic BookWorld was as its name suggested: geographic, and the neigh-bourhoods were set out like an Outland housing estate. A single road ran down between the books complete with sidewalks, grass verges, throughput hydrants and trees. To left and right were compounds that contained entire novels with all their settings. In one was a half-scale Kilimanjaro, and in another a bamboo planta-tion. In a third, an electrical storm at full tilt.

'We're right on the edge of Fantasy,' I explained, 'straight on is Human Drama, and to your right is Comedy. I'll give you Wednes-days off but I expect you to be on stand-by most of the time.'

'The more First Person time I can put in,' replied Carmine, 'the better. Is there anything to do around here when I'm off-duty, by the way?'

'If Fantasy is your thing,' I said, 'plenty. Moving cross-genre is not recommended as the border guards can get jumpy, and it will never do to be caught in another genre just when you're needed. Oh, and don't do anything that my dodo might disapprove of.'

'Such as what?'

'The list is long. Here we are.'

We had arrived on the top of a low rise where there was a convenient park bench. From this vantage point we could see most of Fiction Island.

'That's an impressive sight,' said Carmine.

There was no aerial haze in the BookWorld, and because the island was mildly dished where it snuggled against the interior of the sphere, we could see all the way to the disputed border between Racy Novel and Women's Fiction in the far north of the island, and beyond that, the unexplored Dismal Woods.

'That's the Metaphoric River,' I explained, pointing out the sinuous bends of the waterway whose many backwaters, bayous, streams and rivers brought narrative ambiguity and unnecessarily lengthy words to the millions of books that had made their home in the river's massive delta. 'To the east of Racy Novel is Outdated Religious Dogma.'

'Shouldn't that be in Non-Fiction?' asked Carmine.

'It's a contentious issue. They were removed from Theology on the grounds that the theories had become "untenable in a modern context" and "were making us look medieval".'

'And that island off the coast of Dogma?' she asked, pointing to a craggy island partially obscured by cloud.

'The smaller of the two is Sick Notes, and the larger is Lies, Self-Delusion and Excuses you can use to justify poor behaviour. South of Dogma is Horror, then Fantasy, with Adventure and Science Fiction dominating the South Coast.'

'I'll never remember all that.'

I handed her my much-thumbed copy of *Bradshaw's BookWorld Companion*.

'Use this,' I said, showing her the fold-out map section and train timetables, 'I've got the new edition on order.'

While we had been sitting there, the recently evicted book had been unbolted by a team of Worker-Danvers.

'*Raphael's Walrus* has been unread for over two years,' I explained, 'so they're off to the narrative doldrums of the suburbs. Not necessarily permanent, of course — a resurgence of interest could bring them back into the more desirable neighbourhoods in an instant.'

'How come your series is still here?' she asked, then put her hand over her mouth. 'Sorry, was that indelicate of me?'

'No, most people ask that. The Text Grand Central Mapping Committee keep us here out of respect.'

'For you?'

'No — for the *real* Thursday Next.'

A smattering of soil and pebbles descended to earth as *Raphael's Walrus* rose into the air, the self-sealing throughput and feedback conduits giving off faint puffs of word-vapour as they snapped shut. This was how the new Geographic BookWorld worked. Books arrived, books left, and the boundaries of the various genres snaked forwards and backwards about the land, reflecting the month-to-month popularity of the various genres. The Crime genre was always relatively large, as were Comedy, Fantasy and Science Fiction. Horror had taken a boost recently with the burgeoning Urban Vampire sector, while some of the less well-known genres had shrunk to almost nothing. Squid Action/Adventure was deleted quite recently, and Sci-Fi Horse Detective looked surely set to follow.

But the vacated area was not empty for long. As we watched, the first of many prefabricated sections of the new book arrived, fresh from the construction hangars in the Well of Lost Plots. The contractors quickly surveyed the site, pegged out strings and then signalled to large transporter slip-cases that were hovering just out of sight. Within a few minutes handling ropes were dropped as the sections moved into a hovering position thirty feet or so above, and the same small army of Worker-Danvers manhandled the sections into position with cheers and grunts, and then riveted them with pneumatic hammers. The first setting to be completed was a semi-ruined castle, then a mountain range, then a forest – with each tree, rabbit, unicorn and elf carefully unpacked from crates. Other sections soon followed, and within forty minutes the entire novel had been hauled in piecemeal from overhead, riveted down and attached to the telemetry lines and throughput conduits.

'It's a good idea to be neighbourly,' I said, 'you never know when you might need to borrow a cupful of irony. Besides, you might find this interesting.'

We walked up the drive and across the drawbridge into the courtyard. Notices were pinned up everywhere that contained useful directions such as: 'This way to the denouement' or 'No boots to be worn in the backstory' and even 'Do not feed the Ambiguity'. The contractors were making last-minute adjustments. Six were arranging the clouds, two were wiring up the punctuation to the main distribution board, three were trying to round up a glottal stop that wasn't meant to be there, and two others had just slit a barrage balloon full of atmosphere. The ambience escaped like a swarm of tiny midges, and settled upon the fabric of the book, adding texture and style.

'Hello!' I said to the cast, who were standing around looking bewildered, their heads stuffed unrealistically full of 'Best Newcomer' prizes and a permanent place in every reader's heart. They were about to be published and read for the first time. They would be confused, apprehensive and in need of guidance. I was so glad I wasn't them.

'My name's Thursday Next and I just dropped in to welcome you to the neighbourhood.'

'This is indeed an honour, Miss Next,' said the King, 'and welcome to *Castle of Skeddan Jiarg*. We've heard of your exploits in the Book-World and I would like to say on behalf of all of us—'

'I'm not that one,' I replied, before it all got embarrassing. I had denied I was the *real* Thursday Next more times than I would care to remember. Sometimes I went through an entire week doing little else.

'I'm the *written* Thursday Next,' I explained.

'Ah,' said one of several wizards who seemed to be milling around, 'so you're not Jurisfiction, then?'

'I got as far as a training day,' I replied, which was still a proud boast, even if I had been rejected for active service. It was annoying, but understandable. Few make the grade to be a member of Fiction's policing elite. I wasn't tough enough, but it wasn't my fault. I was written to be softer and kinder – the Thursday Thursday herself thought she wanted to be. In any event, it made me too empathetic to get things done in the dangerously dynamic landscape of the BookWorld.

They all returned my greeting, but I could see they had lost interest. I asked them whether I could show Carmine round, and they had no objections, so we wandered into the grand hall, which was all lime-washed walls, flaming torches, hammerhead beams and flagstones. Some of the smaller props were only cardboard cut-outs, and I noted that a bowl of fruit was no more than a Post-it note with 'bowl of fruit' written on it.

'Why only a Post-it?' asked Carmine. 'Why not a real bowl of fruit?'

'For economic reasons,' I replied, 'every novel has only as much description as is necessary. In years past each book was carefully crafted to an infinitely fine degree, but that was in the days of LRS.'

'LRS?'

'Limited Reader Sophistication. Today, with the plethora of experience through increased media exposure, most books are finished by the readers themselves.'

'The Feedback Loop?'

'Precisely. As soon as the readers get going, the Feedback Loop will start backwashing some of the readers' interpretations into the book itself. Not that long ago books could be stripped bare by over-reading, but since the invention of the Loop, not only do books suffer little internal wear, but readers often *add* detail by their own interpretations. Was that a goblin?'

I had just seen a small creature with pixie ears and sharp teeth staring at us from behind a chair.

'Looks like it.'

I sighed. Pickwick *would* have something new to complain about.

'What is Thursday like?' asked Carmine.

I got asked this a lot.

'You've heard the stories?'

She nodded her head. Most people had. For over fifteen years Thursday Next had worked at Jurisfiction, tirelessly patrolled the BookWorld like a narrative knight errant, bringing peace and justice to the very edge of acceptable prose. She was head and shoulders above the other agents – giants like Commander Bradshaw, Emperor Zhark, Mrs Tiggy-Winkle or even The Drunk Vicar.

'Did she really take Hamlet into the RealWorld?' asked Carmine, excited by my mentor's audaciousness.

'Among others.'

'And defeat Yorrick Kaine?'

'That too.'

'What about *The Great Samuel Pepys Fiasco?* Did they *really* have to delete two weeks of his diary to make everything okay?'

'That was the least of her worries. Even Thursday had occasional failures – it's inevitable if you're at the top of your game. Mind you,' I added, unconsciously defending my famous namesake, 'if Samuel Pepys hadn't set Deb up in a pied-à-terre in the backstory of *Sons and Lovers* with Iago coming in for half-costs for alternate weekdays, it would never have escalated into the disaster it became. They could have lost the entire diaries, and as a consequence, anything in Non-Fiction that used the journal as a primary source. It was only when Thursday changed the historical record to include a "Great Fire of London" that never actually happened did she manage to pull anything from the debacle. History wouldn't speak to the Council for months, but Sir Christopher Wren was delighted.'

We walked back out into the courtyard. The King and Queen invited us around for a 'pre-reading party' that evening, and I responded by inviting them around for tea and cakes the following day. Thus suitably introduced, we made our way back out to the street.

'So how do you want me to play you?' asked Carmine.

'You're not playing *me*, you're playing *her*. There's a big difference. Although I've been Thursday for so long sometimes I think I am her, I'm not. I'm just the written her. But in answer to your question, I try to play her dignified. I took over from the *other* written Thursday – long story, don't ask – soon after *The Great Samuel Pepys Fiasco* was deleted – even longer story, still don't ask – and the previous Thursday played her a little disrespectfully, so I'm trying to redress that.'

'I heard the violent and gratuitous-sex Thursday had a lot more readers.'

I glared at Carmine, but she simply stared back at me with big innocent eyes. She was making a statement of fact, not a criticism.

'We'll get the readers back somehow,' I replied, although I wasn't wholly convinced.

'Can I meet the real Thursday?' asked Carmine in a hopeful tone of voice. 'For research purposes, naturally.'

'She's very busy and I don't like to bother her.'

I was overplaying my influence. Despite overseeing my creation, the real Thursday didn't like me much, possibly for the very reason she thought she might be improved. I think it was a RealWorld thing: the gulf between the person you want to be, and the person you are.

'Look,' I said, 'just play her dignified – the individual interpretation is up to you. Until you get into the swing of it, play her subtly different on alternate readings. Hamlet's been doing it for years. Of course, he has twenty-six different ways of playing himself, but then he's had a lot of practice. In fact, I don't think even he knows his motivation any more – unless you count confusing readers and giving useful employment to Shakespearean scholars.'

'You've met Hamlet?'

'No, but I saw the back of his head at last year's BookWorld Conference.'

'What was it like?' asked Carmine, who seemed to enjoy celebrity tittle-tattle.

'The back of his head? Hairy,' I replied cautiously, 'and it might not have been him. In any event, keep your interpretation loose, and don't telegraph. Let the readers do the work. If you're going to explain *everything*, then we might as well give up and tell everyone to stick to television and movies.'

'Were there any goblins?' asked Pickwick as soon as we walked back in.

'I didn't see any. Did you, Miss O'Kipper?'

'No, no, not a single one.'

'Mrs Malaprop?' I said. 'We'll be having royalty for tea tomorrow. Better bake a cake and have the silver cleaned.'

'Very good, Mizzen Exe.'

'Here,' I said to Carmine, handing her the complete script for my part, 'I have to go out for an hour. I'll test you on it when I get back.'

She suddenly looked nervous.

'What if someone starts to read me while you're away?'

'They won't,' I replied, 'and if they do, Mrs Malaprop will point you in the right direction. Just take it smooth and easy. The rest of the cast will help you along.'

'What do I do with Skimmers?' she asked with a faint tinge of panic in her voice. All rookies feared Dippers, Skimmers and Last-Chapter-Firsters.

'There's no hard-and-fast rule. Skimmers move in a generally forward direction, and with experience, you'll figure out where they're going to land next. But the main thing is not to waste time with the nuisance reader – in a word, *prioritise*. Find the stable, methodical bread-and-butter readers and give them your best. Leave the Skimmers and Dippers high and dry if there's a crisis. When things die down you can pick them up later.'

'And students?'

'A breeze. They'll pause at the end of each sentence to think quasi-intellectual deep thoughts, so as soon as a full stop looms, you can be off dealing with someone else. They'll still be pondering about intertextuality, inferred narratives and the scandalously high price of the subsidised beer in the Student Union when you get back.'

She was quiet and attentive, so I carried on.

'You should show no discrimination with readers. Treat the lip-movers as you would the *Times Literary Supplement* critic. You might not be able to distinguish between the two at first, but you soon will. Yossarian said that you can get to know individual readers by the *way* they read you. Mind you, he's been doing it a long time, and *Catch-22* gets reread a lot.'

'You've met Yossarian?'

'He was just leaving the room after giving a talk. I saw his foot.'

'Left or right?'

'Left.'

'I met someone who wasp eaten about the headboy Sir John Falstaff,' remarked Mrs Malaprop in an attempt to show that she too hobnobbed with celebrities.

'I talked to someone who held Pollyanna's hat for three whole pages,' added Carmine.

'Small fry,' remarked Pickwick, eager to outdo us all. 'Sam Spade *himself* actually spoke to me.'

There was silence. This was impressive.

'What did he say?'

'He said: "Get that stupid bird out of my way".'

'Well, pretend to be a soldier and elope with my ward,' remarked Mrs Malaprop, her word choice rendered clean and clear by the sarcasm, 'you can dine out on that one for years.'

'It's better than your dumb Falstaff story.'

'The thing to remember,' I remarked to stop the argument before it got to the next few stages, which were insults, crockery-throwing, punches and then screaming, 'is that the more readers there are, the easier it becomes. If you relax, it actually becomes a great deal of fun. The words spring naturally to your lips, and you can concentrate on not just giving the best possible performance, but also dealing with any readers who are having problems – or indeed, any readers who are trying to *cause* trouble for you and change the book. You'll be surprised by how strong the power of reader suggestion can get, and if you let readers get the upper hand it'll be *Miss Smilla's Feeling for Snow* all over again.'

Carmine looked thoughtful. The 'Sea Worms' incident was a sobering lesson for everyone, and something that no one wanted to repeat.

'I'll be back as soon as I can,' I said, making to leave. 'I have to meet with Commander Herring. Mrs Malaprop, will you show Carmine around the series and do the introductions? Start with the Gravitube and the Diatryma. After that, it's all fairly benign.'

4

The Red-haired Gentleman

'**Despite the remaking of the BookWorld, some books remained tantalisingly out of reach.** The entire Sherlock Holmes canon was the most obvious example. It was entirely possible that they didn't know there was a BookWorld, and still thought they were real. A fantastic notion, until you consider that up until 11.06 a.m. on 12 April 1948, everyone else had thought the same. Old-timers still speak of 'The Great Realisation' in hushed tones, and talk of the glory days when the possibility of being imaginary was only for the philosophers . . .'

Bradshaw's BookWorld Companion

I stepped out of the front door and walked the eight blocks to the corner of Adams and Colfer. A bus arrived in a couple of minutes – they always do – and after showing my pass to the driver, who looked suspiciously like a Dr Seuss character on furlough, I took a seat between a Viking and a nun.

'I'm on my way to a pillage,' said the Viking, as he attempted to find some common ground on which to converse, 'and we're a bit lean in the "beating people to death with large hammers" department. Would you like to join us?'

'That's most kind, but it's really not my thing.'

'Oh, go on, you might rather like it.'

'No thank you.'

'I see,' said the Viking in a huffy tone, 'please yourself, then.'

And he lapsed into silence.

It was the nun's turn to speak.

'I'm collecting,' she said with a warm smile, 'for the St Nancy's Home for Fallen Women.'

'Fallen in what respect?'

'Fallen *readership*. Those poor unfortunate wretches who, through no fault of their own, find themselves in the ignominious status of "the less well read". Are you interested?'

'Not really.'

'Well,' said the nun, 'how *completely* selfish of you. How would you like it to be hardly read at all?'

'I *am* hardly read at all,' I told her, mustering as much dignity as I could. There was an unfair stigma attached to those characters who weren't read, and making us into victims in need of saving didn't really help, to be honest.

The Viking looked at me scornfully, then got up and went to the front of the bus to pretend to talk to someone. The nun joined him without another word, and I saw them glance in my direction and shake their heads sadly.

I took the bus across the Fantasy/Human Drama border, then changed to a tram at Hemingway Central. In the six months since the Remaking, the citizens of the BookWorld had learned much about their new surroundings. It was easier to understand, we had usable maps, a chain of outrageously expensive coffee shops known as Stubbs, and most importantly, a network of road, rail and river to get from one place to another. We had buses, trams, taxis, cars, and even paddle-steamers. Bicycles might have been useful but for some reason they didn't work inside the BookWorld – no matter what anyone did, they just wouldn't stay up. Jumping directly from book to book had rapidly become unfashionable, and was looked upon as hopelessly Pulp. But if you really wanted to be taken seriously and display a sense of cool unhurried insouciance, you walked.

'So what do you think?' asked a red-haired jowly gentleman

who had sat next to me. He was dressed in a blue double-breasted suit with a dark tie secured with a pearl tiepin. His hair was long but combed straight, and there seemed rather a lot of it. So much, in fact, that he had tied the bright red locks that grew from his cheeks into fine plaits, each secured with a blue ribbon. Aside from that, his deepset eyes had a kindly look, and I felt immediately at ease in his company.

'What do I think about what?'

'This,' he said, waving a hairy hand in the direction of the new BookWorld.

'Not enough pianos,' I said after a moment's reflection, 'and we could do with some more ducks – and fewer baobabs.'

'I'd like it to be more like the RealWorld,' said the red-haired gentleman with a sigh. 'Our existence in here is very much life at second hand. I'd love to know what a mistral felt like, how the swing and drift of fabric might look, and what *precisely* it is about a sunset or the Humming Chorus that make them so astonishing.'

This was a sentiment I could agree with.

'For me it would be the rattle of rain on a tin roof, or to see the vapour rise from a warm lake in the chill morning air.'

We fell silent for a moment as the tram rumbled on. I didn't tell him that I yearned for the most under-appreciated luxury of the human race – free will. My life was by definition preordained. I had to do what I was written to do, say what I was written to say, without variance all day every day, whenever someone read me. Despite conversations like this where I could think philosophically rather than narratively, I could never shrug off the peculiar feeling that someone was controlling my movements, and eavesdropping on my every thought.

'I'm sure it's not all hot buttered crumpets out there in the breathing world of asphalt and heartbeats,' I said, by way of balance.

'Oh, I agree,' replied the red-haired gentleman, who had, I noticed, nut-brown hands with fingers that were folded tight along the knuckle, 'for all its boundless colour, depth, boldness, passion and humour, the RealWorld doesn't appear to have any clearly discernible function.'

'Not that better minds than ours haven't tried to find one.'

The jury had been out on this matter for some time. Some felt that the RealWorld was there only to give life to us, while others insisted that it *did* have a function to which no one was yet party. There was a small group who suggested that the Real-World was not real at all – and was just another book in an even bigger library. Not to be outdone, the nihilists over in Philosophy insisted that Reality was as utterly meaningless as it appeared.

'What is without dispute,' said my friend once we had discussed these points, 'is that the readers need us just as much as we need them – to bring order to their apparent chaos, if nothing else.'

'*Who are you?*' I asked, unused to hearing such matters discussed on a number 23 tram.

'Someone who cannot be saved, Miss Next. I have done terrible things.'

I started at the mention of my name, and was suddenly suspicious. Our chance meeting was no chance meeting. In Fiction, they rarely are. But then again, he might have thought I was the *other* Thursday Next.

'Sir, I'm not her.'

He looked at me and smiled.

'You're more alike than you suppose.'

'Physically, perhaps,' I replied, 'but I flunked my Jurisfiction training.'

'On occasion, people of talent are kept in reserve in times of crisis.'

I stared at him for a moment.

'Why are you telling me this?'

'I don't have much time. I think they saw us talking. Heed this and heed it well: *one of our Thursdays is missing!*'

'What do you mean?'

'This: trust no one but yourself.'

'Which "yourself"?' I said with a frown. 'I have several. Me, the last me, the real me and Carmine, who is being me when I'm not me.'

He didn't get to answer. The tram lurched, and with a sharp squeal of emergency brakes, we ground to a halt. The reason we had stopped was that two highly distinctive 1949 Buick Roadmaster automobiles were blocking the road, and four men were waiting for us. The cars and their occupants were one of the more iniquitous features of the Remaking. The Council of Genres, worried about increased security issues with the freedom of movement, had added another tier of law enforcement to the Book-World. Shadowy men and women who were accountable only to the Council of Genres, and seemed to know no fear or restraint: the Men in Plaid.

The doors of the tram hissed open and one of the agents climbed inside. He wore a well-tailored suit of light green plaid with a handkerchief neatly folded in his top pocket.

I turned to the red-haired gentleman to say something, but he had moved across the aisle to the seat opposite. The Man in Plaid's eye fell upon my new friend, and he quickly strode up and placed a pistol to his head.

'Don't make any sudden movements, Kiki,' ordered the Man in Plaid. 'What are you doing so far outside Crime?'

'I came to Fantasy to look at the view.'

'The view is the same as anywhere else.'

'I was misinformed.'

The red-haired gentleman was soon handcuffed. With a dramatic flourish the Man in Plaid pulled out a bloodstained straight razor from the red-haired gentleman's pocket. A gasp went up from the occupants of the tram.

'This lunatic has been AWOL from his short story for twenty-four hours,' announced the first agent, 'you are fortunate to have survived.'

The red-haired gentleman was pulled from the tram and bundled into the back of one of the Buick Roadmasters, which then sped from the scene.

The first Man in Plaid came back on the tram and stared at us all in turn.

'A consummate liar, whose manipulative ways have seen two dead already. Did he say anything to anyone?'

The red-haired gentleman had admitted he had done terrible things, but that wasn't unusual. Out of their books, crazed killers could be as pleasant as pie.

'He murdered two women,' continued the Man in Plaid, presumably in order to loosen our tongues, 'he cut the throat of one and strangled the other. Now: did he say anything to anybody?'

I remained silent, and so did everyone else. In the short time the Men in Plaid had been operational, people had learned they were simply trouble, and best not assisted in any way.

'Are you a Man in Plaid?' asked one of the passengers.

The man stared at the passenger in a way you wouldn't like to be stared at.

'It's not plaid, it's tartan.'

The agent, thus satisfied that the red-haired gentleman had not spoken to anyone, stepped off the tram and the doors hissed shut. I shivered as a sudden sense of foreboding shuffled through the four hundred or so verbs, nouns and similes that made up my being. The red-haired gentleman had told me he thought that 'one of our

Thursdays is missing' and I took that to mean Thursday Next, the *real* Thursday Next. My flesh-and-blood alter-better ego. But I didn't get to muse on it any further, for a few minutes later we arrived at the border between Human Drama and Thriller.

5

Sprockett

'. . . The logic of cog-based intelligence is unimpeachable.** Unlike the inferior electronic-based intelligences, they cannot show error, for the constantly enmeshed cogs, wheels and drives never slip or jump. I think one can safely attest that there is no puzzle that Men of the Cog cannot solve, given sufficient oil, facts and winds . . .'

Bradshaw's BookWorld Companion

There was a queue to cross into Thriller. Bookpeople either being permanently transferred or on a Character Exchange Programme, designed in order to stop characters getting bored, restless and troublesome. There were a few travelling artisans, salesmen and a dozen or so tourists, apparently on a package 'Get Beaten Senseless by Bourne' holiday, which had just overtaken the 'Being Shot in the Leg by Bond' break for popularity, much to the Fleming camp's disgust.

As little as two months ago I would have been waved across with nary a glance, but the heightened security risk due to the potentially inflammable political situation up at Racy Novel had made everyone jumpy.

I took a TransGenreTaxi as far as the Legal part of Thriller, then continued on foot. I took a left turn by *The Firm* and picked my way along a weed-covered path and across a plank that spanned a ditch of brackish water, the best method to get into Conspiracy Theory without being waylaid by deluded theorists, who always wanted to explain in earnest terms that President Formby was murdered by Prime Minister Redmond van de Poste, or that Best-

Selling Author Colwyn Baye was far too handsome and clever and charming to be anything other than an android or a reptile or an alien or all three.

I took a left turn at the Single Gunman pub, and walked past a hangar full of advanced flying machines that all displayed a swastika, then entered a shanty town that was home to theories that lived right on the edge of Conspiracy owing to a sense of overtired outrageousness. This was where the Protocols lived, along with alien abductions, 9/11 deniers and the notion that FDR somehow knew about the attack on Pearl Harbor. I had hoped I might tread unnoticed within the genre, but I was mistaken. Despite avoiding eye contact, I was spotted by a wild-eyed loon with hair that stuck out in every direction.

'There's no such thing as time,' he confided with an unwavering sense of belief in his own assertions, 'it's simply a construct designed by a cabal of financiers eager to sell us pensions, life insurance and watches in their pursuit of a global-wide timepiece-selling agenda.'

'Really?' I asked, which is probably the only answer to anything in Conspiracy.

'Definitely. And the seal is not a mammal – it's an insect. The truth has been suppressed by the BBC and Richard Attenborough, who want to promote a global-wide mammal-centric agenda.'

'Don't you mean *David* Attenborough?'

'So you agree?' he said, eyes opening so wide I was suddenly worried I might see his brain. 'Would you like to stone a robot?'

'What?'

'Stone a robot. Just one of the first generation of mechanical men, designed to be placed among us in order to take over the planet and promote a clockwork, global-wide cog-centric agenda?'

'I'm not really into stoning anyone.'

'Oh well,' said the theorist as he picked a rock off the ground, 'suit yourself.'

And he walked off. Intrigued and somewhat concerned, I followed him to New World Order Plaza, where a small crowd had gathered. They were an odd bunch that comprised everything from small grey aliens to reptilian shape-shifters, Men in Black, Elvises, lost cosmonauts and a smattering of Jimmy Hoffa/Lord Lucan secret genetic hybrids. They were arranged in a semicircle around a tall man dressed in a perfectly starched frock coat, striped trousers and white gloves. Of his clockwork robotic origins there seemed little doubt. His porcelain face was bland and featureless, the only moving feature his right eyebrow, which was made of machined steel and could point to an array of emotions painted in small words upon the side of his head. From the look of him, his mainspring was at the very last vestige of tension – he had shut down all peripheral motor functions, and if his eyes had not scanned backwards and forwards as I watched, I might have thought he had run down completely.

'They banish us here to Fiction,' said a rabble-rousing grey alien, pointing his finger in the air, 'when we should be up there, in Non-Fiction.'

The crowd agreed wholeheartedly with this sentiment, and clacked their stones together angrily.

'And then,' continued the alien, 'they have the temerity to send robots among us to spy on our every movement and report back to a centralised index which holds the records of everyone in the BookWorld, all as a precursor to thought-control experiments that will rob us of our minds and make us into mere drones, lackeys of the publishing world. What do we say to the Council? Do we politely say: "No, thank you" or do we send their messenger home in a sack?'

The crowd roared. I didn't know much about Conspiracy, but I did know they were mostly paranoid, and tended to value conviction above evidence.

I was just wondering what, if anything, could be done to stop the needless destruction of a finely crafted automaton when the Mechanical Man caught my eye, and with the last few ounces of spring pressure available to him, he moved his eyebrow pointer between the array of emotions in a manner that spoke of fear, loss, betrayal and hopelessness. The last plea from a condemned machine. Something shifted within me, and before I knew what I was doing, I had spoken up.

'There you are!' I said in a loud voice as I strode into the semicircle of stone-wielding conspiratees. 'I *knew* I should have given you an extra wind at lunchtime.'

The aliens and Elvises and the alien-Elvises looked at one another suspiciously.

'Thursday Next,' I said as I searched the automaton's pockets for his key. The crowd looked doubtful and the ringleader blinked at me oddly, his large teardrop-shaped eyes utterly devoid of compassion.

'Thursday Next is too important to trouble herself with the fortunes of a mechanical man,' he said thinly, 'and she told me personally she would rather kneel on broken glass than ever visit Conspiracy again.'

This was doubtless true, and I could see why.

'You are an impostor,' said the alien, 'sent by the Council as part of a plan to destabilise our genre and promote your own twisted evidence-centric agenda.'

There was a nasty murmuring among the crowd as with fumbling hand I found the large brass key and inserted it into the socket located on the back of the automaton's neck. I gave him a quick wind to get him started, and I felt his body shift slightly as the gyros, motors, cogs and actuators started to reboot his mechanical cortex.

'. . . and with the last few ounces of spring pressure available to him, he moved his eyebrow pointer between the array of emotions in a manner that spoke of fear, loss, betrayal and hopelessness.'

'You're the *written* one,' said someone at the back, 'the dopey one who likes to hug a lot.'

The situation had just taken a turn for the worse. But since this was Conspiracy and facts weren't necessarily the end of an argument, I thought I'd try a bluff. I reached into my pocket and held out my JAID shield. From a distance it might be confused with a Jurisfiction badge. I had to hope no one would look too close.

'Read it and weep,' I said, swallowing down my nervousness. 'Make a move on me and I'll have Jurisfiction dump forty tons of Intelligently Reasoned Argument right on your butt.'

'So *you* say,' said the small alien. 'Elvis? Check her badge.'

The two dozen Elvises looked at one another and began to squabble as they tried to figure out which Elvis the alien was talking to, and once this was established, I had half-wound the mechanical man. If it came to a fight, I wouldn't be on my own.

'Steady on, lads,' said the Elvis after looking at my badge, 'she's not bluffing — it's her all right.'

'I am?' I said, then quickly added: 'Yes, I am. Now piss off.'

The small group hurriedly made some excuse about having to view some reverse-engineered alien technology hidden in a hangar somewhere in a desert, and within a few moments the clockwork man and I were entirely alone.

'Permission to speak, madam?' said the automaton once I had wound him sufficiently to reboot his memory and thought processes. He spoke with the rich plummy tones of the perfect gentleman's gentleman, but with a faint buzz — a bit like a bumblebee stuck inside a cello.

'Of course.'

'I am one of the older Duplex-5 models, so if madam would wind me only as far as twenty-eight turns, I would be most grateful. My spring will take a full thirty-two, but the last four winds have an *unpredictable* effect upon my Central Reasoning Gears that render me unable to offer my best.'

'I'll remember that,' I said.

'And if I might be so bold,' added the clockwork man, 'I would highly recommend that you do not let me fall *below* two winds as I fear I might become somewhat languorous in my movements, and may stray unforgivably into short-tempered impertinence.'

'Between two and twenty-eight it is.'

I finished winding him but, as requested, was careful not to go beyond the red mark on the mainspring tension indicator just under his chin. Once this was done, he turned to face me and his single expressive eyebrow quivered momentarily and then pointed to 'uncomfortable'. I knew exactly what he meant; that the winding of a manservant is a mildly embarrassing undertaking, and to preserve both employer and employee's mutual respect, should not be commented upon again.

'That's a very useful eyebrow.'

'It's a standard feature of the Duplex-5s. Since we have few genuine emotions, it helps to telegraph how we think we should be feeling, given the circumstances.'

'It works for me, Mr—?'

'Sprockett,' said Sprockett, 'ready and willing to enter your employ.'

'I'm not sure I need a butler.'

'In that you would be in error, ma'am. It has been long proven that *everyone* needs a butler. Besides, you saved my life.'

It was complex, but I knew what he meant. Because I had saved him, he was indebted to me – and to refuse him an opportunity to repay my kindness would leave him burdened by a favour unpaid. And if you had a potential life of a thousand years or more, you could be a long time fretting, and fretting increases wear on cogs. Clockwork life-forms could be annoyingly steadfast at times, but it was their saving grace, too.

'All right,' I agreed, 'but for a trial period only.'

'Very good, ma'am. Would you care for a cocktail? I do a very good Tahiti Tingle – without the umbrella if you think they are a bit passé.'

'Not now. I'm working.'

'In Conspiracy, ma'am?'

I pointed at the book traffic that was moving constantly overhead.

'One of those books came down last night, and I'm here to find out why.'

'I see,' said Sprockett, his eyebrow pointer nodding towards 'worried' as he looked upwards. 'I will assist in whatever capacity I can.'

We made our way towards the Regional Offices. Sprockett talked and thought well for an automaton, and aside from a slight limp, his empty features and a muted buzz when he moved or thought, he was reasonably lifelike. I asked him where he was from, and he told me he was from Vanity – a pilot book for a series entitled *The League of Cogmen*, and the many adventures that befall a series of mechanical men designed by an Edwardian inventor. A mixture of *The Admirable Crichton, Biggles* and *The 1903 Watchmaker's Review*. Sprockett was initially built as a butler, but soon transcended his calling to become a dynamic machine of action. When unemployment beckoned, he reverted to domestic service – butlers are more sought after than action heroes.

'What was your book like?'

'Uneven,' replied Sprockett, 'a fine concept but lacking in legs to carry it off. Sadly, I have too few emotions to be engaging as a principal character.'

'Because you were designed as a butler?'

'Not at all – because I'm only a Duplex-5. The empathy escapement was never quite perfected before we went into production. I can indicate a range of emotions through my eyebrow pointer, but that's about it. I can recognise your sorrow and act accordingly –

but I cannot feel emotions, nor truly understand what "emotion" or "feel" actually mean.'

'But surely you felt danger when you were about to be stoned and relief when rescued?'

'Yes, but only in the context that to be destroyed would deny me the opportunity to serve cocktails – and that would contravene the Second Law of Domestic Robotics.'

Sprockett told me his books were hastily printed, had not been read once in seventeen years and now, aside from a few copies in the circulation of friends and family, were sitting unread in a cardboard box in the writer's garage in Cirencester.

'And becoming damp, too,' he added. 'Sometimes rain is blown under the garage doors; there is mould and damp seeping up the print run – look.'

He rolled up a trouser leg to reveal a green patch of patination on his otherwise shiny bronze leg. His would be a long, lingering journey to unreadfulness. He would gradually look more tarnished and increasingly lost over the years until the last copy would be destroyed, and – unless picked up in another book – he'd suddenly wink out of existence.

'What's it like living in Vanity?'

'May I be candid?'

'I'd welcome it.'

'We tend not to use the term Vanity any more. It sounds derogatory. We regard it as Self-published or Collaborative, and you'd be surprised just how much good prose is interspersed with that of an uneven nature.'

This was true. Beatrix Potter, Keats and George Elliot had all been self-published, as was the first issue of *Alice in Wonderland*. I looked across to where the island of Vanity lay just off the coast beyond the Cliff of Notes. Even from here the high-stacked accommodation blocks could clearly be seen. The turbulent waterway between Vanity and the mainland was swept with dangerous currents, whirlpools and tidal rips. Despite this, many Vanitarians attempted to make the perilous journey to brighter prospects on the mainland. Of those that survived, most were turned back.

'I'd like to come out and see the conditions for myself,' I said, the unease in my voice setting Sprockett's eyebrow to flicker twice before pointing at 'Worried'.

'No, really,' I said, 'I would. You can't believe anything you read in *The Word* these days.'

Sprockett demurred politely, but his eyebrow said it all – of an entire genre kept marginalised, right on the edges of Fiction. The 'Vanity Question' was one of many issues that had dogged the political elite since the Remaking. The problem was, no published books like anything self-published in the neighbourhood. They argued – and quite eloquently, as it turned out – that the point of having similar books clustered in neighbourhoods and genres was for mutual cross-fertilisation of themes and ideas. Having something from Vanity close by would, they claim: 'lower the tone of the prose'. Liberal factions within the Council of Genres had attempted a cross-genre experiment and placed *The Man Who Died a Lot* right into the middle of McEwan on the basis that the localised erudition could only have a bettering effect on the Vanity book. It was a disaster. None of the characters within McEwan would talk to them and they even claimed that some descriptive passages had been stolen. It was then that McEwan and the nearby Rushdie and Amis threatened to go on strike and lower their Literary Highbrow Index to a shockingly low 7.2 unless *The Man Who Died a Lot* was removed. The offending book was gone before teatime, and no one had tried anything similar since. Vanity's contribution to Fiction in general was an abundance of cheap labour and the occasional blockbuster, which was accepted into Fiction with an apologetic 'gosh, don't know how that happened'.

We continued our walk through Conspiracy, past something odd that had been dug up on the Quantocks, and Sprockett asked me whether I conducted many accident investigations.

'My last investigation was in a book-club edition of *Three Men in a Boat* which had sprung a leak,' I told him, 'and lost forty thousand gallons of the River Thames as it passed across Crime Noir, where it fell quite helpfully as rain. My theory had been a sticky pressure-relief valve on the Comedy Induction Loops, probably as a result of substandard Metaphor building up on the injectors. I penned an exhaustive report to Mr Herring, who congratulated me on my thoroughness but tactfully pointed out that Comedy Induction Loops were not introduced until April 1956 – long *after* the book was built.'

'Oh,' said Sprockett, who perhaps had been expecting a story with a happier ending, 'so what had *really* happened?'

I sighed.

'Someone had simply left the plug out of the Thames and it had drained away.'

We walked on in silence for a moment.

'Ma'am, if you would forgive the impertinence, might I place one small condition upon my employment?'

I nodded, so he continued.

'I have an overriding abhorrence of honey. No matter what happens, it always seems to end up in my insides, and it is the very devil to remove. In my last employ my master insisted upon honey for breakfast, and a small quantity became lodged in my thought-cogs. Until steam-cleaned, I became convinced I was the Rajah of Sarawak.'

'No honey,' I said, 'promise.'

And so, fully introduced, we talked about the much-heralded and much-delayed introduction of the advanced Duplex-6 clockwork automaton. And after that, the relative merits of phosphor-bronze over stainless steel for knee joints. So it was that I arrived, thoroughly versed in the Matters of the Cog, at the regional Conspiracy offices a few minutes later.

6

The Bed-sitting Room

———

'. . . The ISBN security numbering system achieved little.
Thieves simply moved into stealing and trading sections of older
books. The Out-of-Print brigade were furious; after looking
forward to a long and happy retirement, they instead found their
favourite armchair pinched from under them as they dozed. Entire
books were stripped of all nouns, and in the very worst cases
large sections of dramatic irony were hacked from the books and
boiled down to extract the raw Metaphor, rendering once fine
novels mere husks suitable only for scrapping . . .'

Bradshaw's BookWorld Companion, 7th Edition

The local Genre Representative was sitting on a wicker chair on
the veranda of his office, a clapboard affair that looked much ravaged
by over-reading. The rep was described in what we termed UK-6
Aristocracy Dapper-12, which meant that he had a fine pencil moustache and spoke as though he were from RADA. I told Sprockett
to wait for me outside, which he unhesitatingly agreed to do.

The rep did not rise from his chair, and instead looked me up
and down and then said in a disparaging tone: 'You're a long way
from Mind, Body and Soul, old girl.'

It's true that I may have looked a bit New Agey, but I didn't
really need this. Bolstered by my earlier claim to be the real Thursday,
I decided to try the same here.

'The name's Thursday Next,' I said, waving my shield. The reaction was electric. He choked on his afternoon tea and crumpet, and
in his hurry to get to his feet nearly woke a large and very hairy
Sasquatch who dozed in a wicker chair a little way down the veranda.

'Good gracious!' exclaimed the Genre Rep. 'Please excuse me. The name's Bilderberg. Roswell Bilderberg. My office is your office. Hey!'

He kicked the foot of the Sasquatch, who opened one eye and stared at him.

'Thursday Next,' hissed Roswell, nodding his head in my direction.

The Sasquatch opened his eyes wide, and jumped to his feet.

'I was nowhere near the Orient Express that evening,' he said hurriedly, 'and even if I was, I had nothing against Mr Cassetti — isn't that right, Roswell?'

'Don't drag me into your web of deceit,' hissed Roswell out of the side of his mouth, still smiling at me. 'Now, how can we help you, Miss Next? Pleasure, or business?'

'*Official* business,' I said as the Sasquatch nonchalantly picked up a set of snow shoes and sneaked guiltily away.

'What sort of official business?' asked Roswell suspiciously. 'We've heard that the Council of Genres were planning on moving us across to Juvenilia as part of a secret cross-BookWorld plan to marginalise those genres than don't toe the official line. And if we didn't comply, we would all be murdered in our sleep by government assassins who can drip poison into your ear down a thread — if such a thing is possible, or even likely.'

As far as I knew, no such plans were afoot. But you didn't live in Conspiracy for long without imagining all sorts of nonsense. Not that Conspiracy always got it wrong. On the few occasions they *were* correct, a rapid transfer to Non-Fiction was in order — which threw those who were left behind into something of a dilemma. Being in Fiction meant a wider readership, something that Non-Fiction could never boast. Besides, a conspiracy theory that turned out to be real wasn't a theory any more, and the loss of wild uncorroborated speculation could be something of a downer.

'I'm working with JAID – the Jurisfiction Accident Investigations Department.'

'Ah!' he replied, suddenly realising what I was here for. 'The Lola incident. I believe Mr Herring is already up there. Can I stress at this time that we will afford Jurisfiction's representatives all possible help and assistance?'

It was all he could say, really. No one wanted to fall foul of Jurisfiction or the Council of Genres. This was Fiction. There were skeletons in everyone's closet.

'It came to earth nine hours ago,' he said as we walked past two faked moon landings, three UFO abductions and a grassy knoll. 'It bounced on a pamphlet on the notion that Diatrymas are being bred by the Goliath Corporation to keep people out of the New Forest, then landed on a book outlining the somewhat dubious circumstances surrounding the death of Lola Vavoom.'

With Sprockett following at a discreet distance, we took a short cut through a field of crop circles, a laboratory covertly designing infectious diseases for population control, moved aside as a white Fiat Uno drove after a black Mercedes, then entered the sub-genre of Lola Vavoom Suspicious Death. Roswell pushed open the swing doors of a concrete multi-storey car park which opened directly on to the tenth floor, and standing next to a large lump of tattered wreckage the size of a truck were two men. I didn't recognise the more dishevelled of the two but the older, wiser man, and clearly the boss, was someone I did recognise: it was Regional Commander 'Red' Herring of the BookWorld Policing Agency.

He was very much a 'hands on' type of administrator. He had no staff, carried all his notes in his head, and was one of the few people who still jumped from book to book rather than taking a taxi or public transport. He was a BGH-87 character type. Male, pernickety and highly efficient, but seemingly without humour. He was about fifty, was dressed in a short-sleeved white shirt with an infinite quantity of pens in his top pocket, and a garish tie. He wore spectacles, but only for effect. He was high up in the chain of command at the Council of Genres, and had access, it was said, to Senator Jobsworth himself. He was the most powerful man I knew.

'About time,' he said when I appeared. 'Places to be, people to visit – wheels within wheels.'

'Wheels within wheels,' echoed the man next to him.

'This is Martin Lockheed,' explained Herring. 'You'll answer to him as I am a busy man. After this meeting, he will be your point of contact.'

'Yes, sir.'

'Your *Three Men in a Boat* investigation didn't really impress,' he began.

'Yes, I'm sorry about that.'

'Apologies don't really cut it, Next, but I am a man loyal to friends, and the real Miss Next has always intimated in the past that you may show promise one day.'

'I'm very grateful to her, and you,' I managed to stammer.

'So I look upon you as an investment,' replied Herring, 'and a long-standing favour to a valued colleague. Which is why we are here now. Do you understand?'

'I think so.'

'Good.'

'That's good,' said Lockheed, as if I might not have heard what Herring said. The Regional Commander waved a hand at the wreckage.

'Easy one for you to cut your teeth on. It has all the signs of being another unprecedented event which, despite all expectations, has become repeatedly unrepeatable. Don't let me down, will you? Wrap it up nice and neat and don't get all showy or anything; Fiction has a 99.97 per cent book safety record, and the last thing we want is the residents of this fair island worried that the fabric of their world is prone to shredding itself at the drop of a participle, hmmm?'

'I'll do my very best to discover that it's an unrepeatable accident,' I told him, 'and with indecent haste.'

'Very good. Twenty-four hours should see you through, yes?'

'I'll see what I can do, sir, and I'd like to thank you for the opportunity.'

'No need. Lockheed?'

'Yes, sir?'

Herring snapped his fingers impatiently and the rather harassed Lockheed passed him a clipboard.

'These are the reported items of debris,' he said, handing the clipboard straight to me without looking at it. 'Not good, having narrative falling from the skies, so let's keep it simple, hey? Wheels within wheels, Thursday.'

'Wheels within wheels,' added Lockheed earnestly.

'Wheels within wheels, sir. Would you thank Miss Next from me when you see her?'

'When next I see her. She's very busy.'

He looked at Sprockett, who was standing off from the group, being unobtrusive.

'Who's that?'

'Sprockett,' I replied, 'my butler.'

'I didn't know you had a butler.'

'Everyone needs a butler, sir.'

'I have no argument with that. Duplex-3, is he?'

'Duplex-5, sir.'

'The Fives were prone to be troublesome without sufficient winding. I'll let you get on. You can call Lockheed any time you want for guidance. Any questions?'

I thought of asking him whether he had seen the real Thursday

Next recently, but decided against it. The red-haired gentleman had spoken of 'being able to trust no one but myself', and besides, I didn't want to look a fool if the man on the tram really *was* a murderous nut-job.

'No questions, sir.'

'Good luck, Miss Next.'

He gave me a half-smile, shook my hand and vanished.

'I'll be off too,' said Lockheed, handing me a business card and a folder full of health and safety literature. 'Mr Herring is a great and good man and you are lucky to have been given this opportunity to converse. He doesn't usually speak to people as low as you.'

'I'm honoured.'

'And so you should be. I was his assistant for three years before he deigned to look me in the eye. One of my proudest moments. If you need me the JAID offices are at Norland Park.'

And he walked off. Eager not to waste the opportunity I had just been given, I turned my attention to the wreckage.

The chunk of book had splintered off the main novel as it broke up. But this wasn't pages or ink or anything; it was a small part of setting. Despite the ragged textual word-strings that were draped across and the graphemes lying scattered on the ground nearby, the misshapen lump seemed to be a room from a house somewhere. It had landed on the asphalt covering of the car park and cracked the surface so badly the textual matrix beneath the roadway was now visible. The battered section had landed upside down just behind Lola Vavoom's Delahaye Roadster, which prevented Lola from reversing too quickly from her parking place, breaking through the barriers and falling eighty feet to her death. It had always been a suspicious accident, but nothing untoward was ever found to suggest it wasn't just that – an accident.

'Will this take long, dahling?' asked Lola, who was dressed in tight slacks, a cashmere sweater and a pink scarf tied around her hair. Her eyes were obscured by a pair of dark glasses, and she was casually sitting on the boot of her car smoking a small Sobranie cigarette.

'As long as it must,' I said, 'and I'm sorry for the inconvenience.'

'Do your best, dear,' she intoned patronisingly, 'but if I'm not dead in mysterious circumstances by teatime, someone is going to have some serious explaining to do.'

I turned my attention to the wreckage. Spontaneous break-ups were uncommon but not unheard of, and it was JAID's job to try to find the cause so other books wouldn't suffer the same fate. Losing a cast of a thousand was not just a personal tragedy, but expensive. When a book-club edition of *War and Peace* disintegrated without warning a few months ago as it passed over Human Drama, everyone within the debris field was picking brass buttons and lengthy digressions out of their hair for a week. The JAID investigator assigned to the case painstakingly reconstructed the book only to find that a batch of verbs had been packed incorrectly at the aft expansion joint, and had overheated. Punctuation lock had no effect, and in a last desperate attempt to bring the book under control, the engineers initiated Emergency Volume Separation. A good idea, but undertaken too quickly. The smaller and lighter Epilogues could not alter course in time and collided with Volume Four, which in turn collided with Volume Three, and so forth. Of the twenty-six thousand characters involved in the disaster, only five survived. Verb quality control and emergency procedures were dramatically improved after this, and nothing like it had happened since.

'It seems to be a bed-sitting room of some variety,' murmured Sprockett as he peered inside the large lump of scrap, 'probably ten pounds a week – furnished, naturally.'

'Naturally.'

'Are we looking for anything in particular?'

'An International Standard Book Number,' I said, 'an ISBN. We need to know what the book is and where it came from before we can start trying to figure out what went wrong. It's sometimes harder than it seems. The wreckage is often badly mangled, widely scattered – and there are a lot of books out there.'

We stepped into the bed-sitting room, which had landed upside down, with all of the contents strewn around inside. It was well described, so was either a popular book given depth and colour by Reader Feedback, or pre-Feedback altogether. The room hadn't been painted for a while, the carpets were threadbare and the furniture had seen better days. It might seem trivial, but it was these sorts of clues that allowed us to pinpoint which book it was from.

'Potboiler?' I suggested.

'It's from HumDram if it is,' replied Sprockett as he picked up a torn *Abbey Road* album, 'post 1969, at any rate.'

We searched for half an hour among the debris but found no sign of an ISBN.

'This book could be any one of thousands,' said Sprockett.

'*Millions.*'

With nothing more to see here, we stepped back outside the bed-sitting room, and I laid a map of the BookWorld on the bonnet of Lola's car and marked in where the section had been found. This done, I called in Pickford Removals, and within twenty minutes the bed-sitting room had been loaded on to the back of a flatbed for onward delivery to the double garage at the back of my house. This was ostensibly to allow the books in which they had landed to carry on unhindered. Not that a ton of tattered paragraph would necessarily be a problem. The entire cast of *A Tale of Two Cities* had steadfastly ignored a runaway pink gorilla that had evaded capture for eighty-seven years, but as far as we know had not been spotted by readers once.

'I'm sorry to have troubled you,' I said to Lola, who stubbed out her cigarette and climbed into her car. She stamped on the accelerator and the Delahaye shot across the car park, drove straight through the wooden barrier behind her and landed on top of the Mairzy Doats sandwich bar ten storeys below with a crunch.

'Come on,' I said to Sprockett, 'work to be done.'

The debris field extended across four genres, and we spent the next three hours listening to residents who claimed that falling book-junk had 'completely ruined their entrance', and on one rare occasion, actually had. There was a reasonable quantity of wreckage, but nothing quite as large as the bed-sitting room. A yellow-painted back axle, the remains of at least nine tigers, a few playing cards, some lengths of silk, a hatstand, sections of a box-girder bridge, nine apples, parts of a raccoon and a quantity of slate. There was a lot of unrecognisable scrap, too, much of it desyntaxed sentences that made no sense at all.

We found only one piece of human remains – a thumb – but it may not have been a thumb at all but simply reformed graphemes.

'Graphemes?' asked Sprockett when I mentioned it.

'Everything in the BookWorld is constructed of them,' I explained, 'letters and punctuation: the building blocks of the textual world.'

'So why might that thumb not actually be a thumb?'

'Because once broken down below the "word" unit, a grapheme might come from anywhere. The same "S" can serve equally well in a sword, a sausage, a ship, a sailor or even the sun. It doesn't help that under extreme pressure and heat, graphemes often separate out and then fuse back together into something else entirely. At Jurisfiction basic training we'd been shown how a "sheet of card", once heated up white hot and then struck with a blacksmith's hammer, could be made into "cod feathers" and then back again.'

'Ah,' said Sprockett, 'I see.'

'Because of this anything under a few words long found at an accident site can be disregarded as evidence – it might once have been something else entirely.'

Oddly enough, Graphusion and Graphission, while occurring naturally in the Text Sea, were hard to do synthetically in the Book-World, but simplicity itself in the Outland. The long and short of it was that victims of extreme trauma in the BookWorld were rarely found. A sprinkling of graphemes were soon absorbed into the fabric of the book it fell upon, and left no trace.

Once Sprockett and I had logged all that we'd found and dispatched it via Pickford's to my double garage, I called Mrs Malaprop to check all was well. It was, generally speaking. Pickwick was suspicious that there might be goblins around after all and Carmine was spending her time rehearsing with the various members of the cast. Whitby Jett had called to say that now Carmine was there, he would be taking me out to Bar Humbug for a drink and nibbles at nine – and no arguments.

I'd known him for nearly two years, and I think I'd just come to the end of a very long trail of excuses and reasons why I couldn't go out on a date. I sighed. There was still one. Perhaps the *only* one I'd ever had. I told Mrs Malaprop I would be home in half an hour, thought for a moment and then turned to Sprockett.

'Can I shut you down for a while?'

'Madam, that is a *most* improper suggestion.'

'I'm about to do something illegal, and since you are incapable of lying, I don't want you in a position where you have to divide your loyalties between your duties as a butler and your duties to the truth.'

'Most thoughtful, ma'am. Conflicting loyalties do little but strip teeth off my cogs. Shall I shut down immediately?'

'Not yet.'

We hailed a cab at the corner of Heller and Vonnegut. The cabby had issues with clockwork people – 'all that infernal ticking' – but since Sprockett was legally speaking nothing more nor less than a carriage clock, he was consigned to the boot.

'I don't mind being treated as baggage,' he said agreeably, 'in fact, I prefer it. Promise you'll restart me?'

'I promise.'

And after he had settled back against the spare wheel in the boot, I pressed the Emergency Spring Release button located under his inspection cover. There was a loud whirring noise and Sprockett went limp.

I shut the boot, settled into the cab and closed the door.

'Where to?'

'Poetry.'

7

The Lady of Shalott

'... Here in the BookWorld the protagonists and antag-
onists, gatekeepers, shape-shifters, heroes, villains, bit-parts,
knaves, comedians and goblins were united in that they
possessed a clearly defined motive for what they were
doing: Entertainment and Enlightenment. As far as any of
us could see, no such luxury existed in the unpredictable world
of the readers. The Outland was extraordinarily well named ...'

Bradshaw's BookWorld Companion

The taxi was the usual yellow-and-check variety, and could either
run on wheels in the conventional manner or fly using advanced
Technobabble™ vectored gravitational inversion thrusters. This had
been demanded by the Sci-Fi fraternity, who had been whingeing
on about hover-cars and jet-packs for decades, and needed appeasing
before they went and did something stupid, like allow someone to
make a movie based on the title of the book known as *I, Robot*.

The driver was an elderly woman with white hair who grumbled about how she had just given a fare to three Triffids, and how
they hadn't bothered to tip, and left soil in the footwells, and were
horribly drunk on paraquat.

'Poetry?' she repeated. 'No worries, pet. High Road or Low
Road?'

She meant either up high, dodging among the planetoid-sized
books that were constantly moving across the sky, or down low on
the ground, within the streets and byways. Taking the High Road
was a skilful endeavour that meant either slipstreaming behind a
particularly large book, or latching on to a novel going in roughly

73

the same direction and being carried to one's destination in a series of piggyback rides. It was faster if things went well, but more dangerous and prone to delays.

'Low Road,' I said, since the traffic between Poetry and Fiction was limited, and one could orbit for hours over the coast, waiting for a novel heading in the right direction.

'Jolly good,' she said, clicking the *fare on board* sign. 'Cash, account, goats, chickens, salt, pebbles, ants or barter?'

'Barter. I'll swap you two hours of my butler.'

'Can he mix cocktails?'

'He can do a Tahiti Tingle – with umbrella.'

'Deal.'

We took the Dickens expressway through HumDram, avoided the afternoon jam at the Brontë–Austen interchange and took a short cut through Shrive Plaza to rejoin the expressway at Picoult Junction, and from there to the Carnegie Underpass, part of the network of tunnels that connected the various islands that made up the observable BookWorld.

'How are you enjoying the new BookWorld?' I asked, by way of conversation.

'Too many baobabs and not enough smells,' she said, 'but otherwise enjoyable.'

After a few minutes with the cabby telling me in a cheerful voice how she'd had Bagheera in the back of her cab once, we emerged blinking at the tunnel exit and the island of Poetry, where we were waved through by a border guard who was too busy checking the paperwork on a consignment of iambic pentameters to worry much about us.

We made our way slowly down Keats Avenue until we came to Tennyson Boulevard, and I ordered her to stop outside Locksley Hall, and to wait for me around the corner. I got out, waited until she had gone, then walked past *The Lotus-Eaters* and *The Charge of the Light Brigade* to a small gate entwined with brambles, and from there into a glorious English summer's day. I walked up the river, past long fields of barley and rye that seemed to clothe the wold and touch the sky, then through the field where a road ran by, which led to many-towered Camelot. I walked along the river, turned a corner and found the island in the river. I looked around as aspens quivered and a breeze and a shiver ran up and down my spine; I really wasn't meant to be here and could get into serious trouble if I was discovered. I took a deep breath, crossed a small bridge and found myself facing a square grey building with towers at each corner. I didn't knock as I knew the Lady of Shalott quite well, and entered unbidden to walk the two flights of stairs to the tower room.

'Hello!' said the Lady, pausing from the tapestry upon which she was engaged. 'I didn't expect to see you again so soon.'

The Lady of Shalott was of an indeterminate age and might once have been plain before the rigours of artistic interpretation got working on her. This was the annoying side of the Feedback Loops; irrespective of how she had once looked or even *wanted* to look, she was now a pre-Raphaelite beauty with long flaxen tresses, flowing white gowns and a silver forehead band. She wasn't the only one to be physically morphed by Reader Expectation. Miss Havisham was now elderly whether she liked it or not, and Sherlock Holmes wore a deerstalker and smoked a ridiculously large pipe. The problem wasn't just confined to the classics. Harry Potter was seriously pissed off that he'd have to spend the rest of his life looking like Daniel Radcliffe.

'Good afternoon, My Lady,' I said, curtseying, 'I would like to conduct more research.'

'Such adherence to duty is much to be admired,' replied the Lady. 'How are your readings going?'

'Over a thousand,' I returned, lying spectacularly. If I didn't pretend to be popular, she'd never have granted me access.

'That's wonderful news. Make good use of the time. I could get into a lot of trouble for this.'

Satisfied, she left her tapestry and summoned me to the window that faced towards Camelot. The Lady of Shalott took great care not to look out of the window, but instead gently stroked a mirror that was held in a large bronze hanger, and angled it towards the window, as if to see the view outside. But this mirror wasn't like other mirrors; the surface grew misty, turned to the colour of slate, then displayed an image quite unlike the reflection one might expect.

'Usual place?' she asked.

'Usual place.'

The image coalesced into a suburban street in the Old Town of Swindon, and the Lady of Shalott touched me on the shoulder.

'I'll leave you to it,' she told me, and quietly returned to her tapestry, which seemed to depict David Hasselhoff in various episodes from *Baywatch*, Series 2.

I stared into the mirror. The image flickered occasionally, and was mildly desaturated in colour, but was otherwise clear and sharp.

'Left forty-five degrees.'

The mirror shifted to look up the suburban road to the house where Thursday and Landen lived. But this wasn't a book some-where, or a memory. This was the RealWorld, the Outland. The Lady of Shalott uniquely possessed a window into reality and could see whatever she wanted, whenever she wanted to. Great lives, great events – even *Baywatch*. The images she saw were woven into a tapestry and she couldn't look outside her window on pain of death. It was all a bit weird, but that's Tennyson for you.

The view was live, and aside from the fact that it was mute, was almost as good as being there.

'Move forward six yards.'

The viewpoint moved forward to a front door that was very familiar to me. I had a similar front door in my own book but my

76

version didn't have peeling paint or the random fine crackle that natural weathering brings. I sensed my heart beat faster.

'Go inside.'

The viewpoint drifted through the door, where the hall was less familiar. Thursday and Landen's real house was only ever described briefly to the ghost writer who wrote my series, so the interior was different. I jumped as someone moved past the mirror. It was a young girl aged no more than twelve, and she looked very serious for her years. This would have been Thursday and Landen's daughter Tuesday, as brilliant as Uncle Mycroft, but in the 'confusing petulant' state of pubescence. Nothing was right and everything wrong. If it wasn't problems over the revectoring of electro-gravitational field theory, it was her brother, Friday, who she regarded as a total loser and layabout.

'Advance two yards.'

The viewpoint moved forward to the hall table. I could see that Thursday was not in as her bag, keys, mobile phone and battered leather jacket were absent. It didn't suggest she was missing as the red-haired gentleman had suggested; only that she wasn't at home right now.

'Advance six yards, rotate left twenty.'

The viewpoint moved into the kitchen, where a man was sitting at the table, attempting to help Tuesday with her GSD uniScripture homework. He was greying at the temples and had a kindly face that was *very* familiar. This was Landen Parke-Laine, Thursday's husband. I blinked as my eyes moistened. They were talking, and he laughed. I couldn't hear him, but imagined as best I could how he might have sounded. Sort of like . . . *music*.

'One-twenty degrees to the right, pull out a yard.'

The mirror did as I asked so I could see the family scene. I didn't have this. None of this. No husband, no children. Despite the real Thursday's wishes that Landen should be included in the series after I took over, he wasn't – and neither were any of the children. Thursday was overridden by a senator named Jobsworth over at the Council of Genres. So they reverted to the previous plan and had Landen continue to die in a house fire in the first chapter of *The Eyre Affair*, a clumsy attempt to give purpose to the written Thursday's fictious crime-fighting. The plot device may have been clunky, but the loss had been exceptionally well written; I felt it every minute of every day. Being fictional is a double-edged sword. You get to savour the really good times over and over, but the same is true of the bad. For every defeat of the Goliath Corporation, there is the loss of Miss Havisham, and for every moment in Mycroft's company there is that day in the Crimea. The delight at returning Jane Eyre to her book and thwarting Acheron is forever tempered by the inevitable loss of Landen, again and again – for ever.

So I stood there, staring at what should have been mine. I wanted to be with the children I should have been allowed to have, and spend my life expending time and energy in the glorious hope that I would one day become parentally redundant. In my bleaker moments Pickwick and Mrs Malaprop attempted to console me by explaining I only had loss to give relevance to what drove my character through the narrative, but it was meagre consolation. I should have had a written Landen and written children to keep me company.

I watched Landen for several more minutes. Every movement, every nuance. I watched how he spoke to Tuesday with humour and infinite patience. I watched how he scratched his ear, how he laughed, how he smiled.

Friday joined them. My would-be son was a fine fellow – handsome like his father. Perhaps a bit rudderless at that age, but thought and function would eventually arrive in the fullness of time. I wanted to give him some guidance, but he had his mother for that. The real me. The real *her*. Besides, the mirror saw only in one direction. They had no idea that I was there, no idea that I felt as I did. I watched for a few more minutes until Landen got up and walked to the sink, poured himself a glass of water, and stared out of the window.

'Pull out into the garden three yards, right ninety degrees.'

My viewpoint drifted through the kitchen wall and after a brief glimpse of central-heating pipes and a bored-looking mouse, I was now outside looking at Landen, who was just the other side of the window. Although he couldn't see me, we were staring into each other's eyes.

'Whitby has asked me out to the Bar Humbug,' I whispered, 'I wanted you to know that I'm going.'

Landen couldn't hear me, but I knew I had to tell him. It was by way of apology. I blinked away tears, but then frowned. Landen was blinking away tears, too. *Something had happened.* Thursday wasn't here, but for how long? An argument? Had she *died* in the Outland? I looked at the children, who were busy with homework. They seemed unconcerned. Whatever it was, it was a burden shouldered by Landen alone.

'When did you last see Thursday?' I whispered.

Landen took a deep breath, wiped his eyes and returned to the children. I put out my hand to touch the mirror, but it simply rippled, like water in a pool.

'Left thirty degrees, three yards forward.'

The mirror complied and I found myself close enough to the pinboard above the telephone to read the notes. I peered among the receipts, pictures and old theatre tickets before finding what I was looking for. A telephone message in Thursday's hand telling Landen that his sister wanted to talk to him. But that wasn't important. It was dated seven days ago. If Thursday *was* missing, it had been for a week at most.

'Did you see what you wanted?'

I jumped. The Lady of Shalott had returned, and was standing just behind me.

'I think so,' I replied hastily. 'It was the – ah – state of her pinboard I was looking at. You know what they say: "a view into a woman's ephemera is a window to her soul".'

'Do they say that?' asked the Lady of Shalott doubtfully.

'Frequently.'

I made ready to leave. The visits to Shalott were as frequent as I could make them without arousing suspicion, and the views they offered all too fleeting. I wanted to know where Thursday was, sure, but I had to see Landen and the kids, too. *Had* to.

I thanked her, and she walked me to the door. But this wasn't a favour, and she and I both knew it. I wasn't allowed to be in Poetry without just cause, and I certainly wasn't allowed to sneak-peek the Outland. She handed me a wooden box.

'You will look after them, won't you?'

'Of course,' I replied, and placed the box in my shoulder bag. I walked outside the castle and returned to where the taxi was waiting to take me home. I was no more the wiser as to where Thursday was. I took a deep breath. It had been, as always, *difficult*. I loved and hated seeing him all at the same time. But it helped when it came to finally going on a date with Whitby. It lessened the sense of betrayal.

8

The Shield

'... The evidence for the existence of Dark Reading Matter remains obscure, at best.** Supposedly the vast amount of unread material either forgotten or deleted, the DRM is also said to be home to the Unread: zombie-like husks of former characters, their humanity sucked from their heads by continued unreadliness. It is generally agreed that these stories belong to meta-myth – stories within stories, and used by drill-sergeants at Character College to frighten recruits into compliance ...'

Bradshaw's BookWorld Companion

The queue to get out of Poetry was long, as always. The smuggling of Metaphor out of the genre was a serious problem, and one which made the border guards extremely vigilant. The increased scarcity of raw Metaphor in Fiction had driven prices sky high, and people would take unbelievably foolish risks to smuggle it across. I'd heard stories of Metaphor being hidden in baggage, swallowed, even dressed up to look like ordinary objects whose *meanings* were then disguised to cloak the Metaphor. The problem then was trying to explain why you had a 'Brooding Thunderstorm' or 'Broad sunlit uplands' in your luggage.

'Can we take the High Road?' I asked.

She turned around to look at me. Taking the High Road out of Poetry meant only one thing – that I wanted to avoid any entanglements with the border guards.

'My friend Jake was carrying a mule without realising it last week,' said the cabby in a meaningful tone. 'The mule had two kilos of raw Metonym on him – hidden in the saddlebags.'

Metonym wasn't as dangerous as smuggling raw Metaphor, but

the underworld would try anything to turn a buck, and had set up labs to enrich variable forms of Metaphor into the real McCoy. Extracting the *like* from simile was the easiest method, but the resulting Metaphor was as weak as wet paper. Synecdoche was used in much the same way; the best minds in Jurisfiction were constantly trying to outwit them, and raided Met-labs on an almost daily basis.

'Did he get to keep his cab?' I asked. 'Your friend Jake, I mean.'

'His entire car was reduced to text with the Metonym still in it.'

'Reduced to text?' I echoed. 'Sounds like a hammer to break a nut.'

'Poeticals are like that,' said the cabby with a disrespectful snort, 'prone to fits of violent passion. I think it's all that absinthe. The point is this: I can get you out of Poetry, but it will cost.'

'I'll lend you my butler for an afternoon.'

'One afternoon and a garden party.'

'A garden party.'

'Done.'

The cabby flipped the vectored thrust nozzles and in an instant we were climbing almost vertically upwards. It took less than a minute to reach the low-lying book traffic, and within a few seconds we had latched on to an academic paper moving from Physics to Biology. We stayed there for a few minutes and then detached, hovered for a moment and then reattached to the keel of an oil tanker that was part of a Bermuda Triangle book on its way to Fiction. We were under the massive rudder at the back, with one of the vast propellers looming over us.

'We'll ride this baby all the way into Fiction,' said the cabby as she took out some knitting, 'about twenty minutes. We could fly the whole way, but we'd probably be picked up by the Book Traffic Controllers and get busted.'

'Don't look now, but I think we just have.'

The flashing red lights of a Jurispoetry squad car close by had alerted me to the fact that the cabby wasn't quite as good as I thought she was. We could have detached there and then and dropped the mile towards the Text Sea before levelling out and making a run for the coast, but it was a risky undertaking. Cutting and running meant only one thing: guilty.

'Oh, craps,' said the cabby, dropping a knitting stitch in surprise, 'I hope you've got some friends in high places.'

'Hello,' I said to the officer, who was now standing outside the car. He was dressed in a baggy white shirt and smelled strongly of rhyming couplets. He stared at me with the supercilious look of someone who knows they have the upper hand, and was certainly going to milk it.

'Oh, to sneak across the border, when it's plain you should not oughta?'

I had to think quickly. Unlike the Poetry government officials who conversed in rhyme royal, this was a lowly traffic cop who spoke only the gutter doggerel of the streets. He was using a soft-rhyming AA, so probably not that bright. I hit him with some AABCCB.

'*Au contraire*, my friend, we did not intend, to break any poetical code. We were waved through, by others of your crew, and simply took the upper road.'

But he didn't go for it.

'I can see your little plan, but your stanzas barely scan. You, madam, I must nab, get your butt from out the cab.'

I climbed out and succumbed to a search. He soon found the box the Lady of Shalott had given me.

'Well, lookee here, what have we got? Is this Metaphor or is it not?'

'Not one but other, I must confess, the situation's now a mess.'

He opened the box and stared. It wasn't Metaphor, but contraband nonetheless.

'You're in big trouble smuggling this loot. What else you got? Let's pop the boot.'

We did, and there was Sprockett. The officer stared at him for a moment.

'I'm sure you can explain away, why a dead butler's in your boot today?'

'He's a *clockwork* butler, Duplex-5, and even paused he's still alive.'

The officer had seen enough, and while his partner interviewed the cabby, who made a far better pretence at innocence than I, he brought out a charge sheet to take down some details.

'Name?'

'Thursday Next.'

The officer looked at me, then at my New Agey clothes, then at Sprockett.

'Now which one could that be? The heroine or the one who likes to hug a tree?'

In for a penny, in for a pound. I had to hope that this guard could be fooled as easily as the Elvis back in Conspiracy.

'I am she, the Thursday proper. Those that cross me come a cropper.'

'That seems likely, but before I yield, let me check your Juris-fiction shield.'

I passed it across. The officer took one look at it, put away his charge sheet and told his partner that they were leaving. He smiled and handed me back my badge.

'It's an honour I'll be reckoned. Sorry to have kept you for even a second.'

I signed my name in his autograph book and with growing confusion climbed back into the cab as the Jurispoetry car detached from the hull and fell away from the tanker, leaving us to continue our trip unmolested.

'You're Thursday Next?' said the cabby, her attitude suddenly changed. 'This ride is for free, kiddo. But listen: the next time you're in the RealWorld, can you find out why there have to be over a hundred different brands of soap? I'd really like to know.'

'Okay,' I muttered, 'no problem.'

The remainder of the journey was unremarkable, except for one thing: I spent the entire journey staring at the Jurisfiction shield which had allowed me not once but twice to squeak out of trouble. It wasn't my shield at all. It was Thursday's. The *real* Thursday's. *Someone had slipped it in my pocket that morning.* And the more I thought about the morning's events, the more I realised that I may have become involved – quite against my will – in a matter of some considerable consequence.

9

Home

———

'Rumour has it that undiscovered genres were hidden among the thick vegetation and impenetrable canopy in the far north of the island. Primitive, anarchic, strange, and untouched by narrative convention, they were occasionally discovered and inducted into the known BookWorld, where they started off fresh and exciting before ultimately becoming Mimicked, Overused, Tired and then Passé. BookWorld naturalists argued strongly that some genres should remain hidden in order to keep the BookWorld from homogenising, but their voices went unheeded . . .'

Bradshaw's BookWorld Companion, 3rd Edition

'I had the most curious dream,' mused Sprockett as soon as I had rewound him fully, 'in which I was a full-hunter silent repeater. There was also this gramophone – you know, one of those wind-up varieties – and she was running overspeed and playing "Temptation Rag". And then there was this monkey hitting cymbals together and I—'

He checked himself.

'I'm frightfully sorry, ma'am. My protocol gearing can become a bit gummy during deactivation. You are not offended by my drivel?'

'Not in the least. In fact, I didn't know machines *could* dream.'

'I dream often,' replied the butler thoughtfully, 'mostly about being a toaster.'

'Dualit or Morphy Richards?'

He seemed mildly insulted that I should have to ask.

'A Dualit four-slot, *naturally*. But perhaps,' he added, his eyebrow pointer clicking from 'Puzzled' to 'Indignant', 'I only *believe* I dream. Sometimes I think it is merely a construct to enable me to better understand humans.'

'Listen, I should warn you about Pickwick,' I said as we walked up the garden path.

'What is a Pickwick?'

'It's a dodo.'

'I thought they were extinct?'

'They may yet become so. She's trouble, so be careful.'

'Thank you, ma'am. I shall.'

I pushed open the front door and was met by the sound of laughter. Carmine was sitting around the table with Bowden Cable and Acheron Hades, two of the other co-stars from the series. They were all sharing a joke, or at least they were until I walked in, when everyone fell silent.

'Hello, Thursday,' said Bowden, who I'd never really got along with, despite his counterpart in the RealWorld being one of Thursday's best friends, 'we were just telling Carmine the best way to play Thursday.'

'The best way is the way I play her,' I said in a firm yet friendly manner, 'dignified.'

'Of course,' said Bowden. 'Who's your friend?'

'Sprockett,' I replied, 'my butler.'

'I didn't know you needed a butler,' said Bowden.

'Everyone needs a butler. He was going to be stoned, so I took him with me.'

'What do cog-based life-forms get stoned with?' asked Bowden in an impertinent manner. 'Vegetable oil?'

'Actually, sir,' intoned Sprockett, 'it's sewing machine lubricant for a mild tipple. Many feel that the exuberant effects of Three-in-One are worth pursuing, although I have never partaken myself. For those that have hit rock bottom where life has become nothing more than a semi-conscious slide from one partial winding to the next, it's WD-40.'

'Oh,' said Bowden, who had been put firmly in his place by Sprockett's forthrightness, 'I see.'

'Hmm,' said Acheron, peering at Sprockett's data-plate with great interest, 'are you the Duplex-6?'

'Five, sir. The Six's release has been delayed. A series of mainspring failures have put beta-testing back several months, and now I hear the Six has pressure compensation issues on the primary ethical escapement module.'

'What does that mean?'

'I have to admit I'm not entirely sure, sir. The main problem with clockwork sentience is that we can *never* understand the level of our own complexity – for to do so would require an even *greater* level of complexity. At present, we can deal with day-to-day maintenance issues, but all we can ever know for sure is that we function. We tick, therefore we are.'

Pickwick asked me how I thought we could afford such an extravagance, but the real disapproval came from Mrs Malaprop.

'Coo dafter noon, Mr Sprockett,' she said coldly, 'I hope you will be fully aquatinted with the *specific* roles of mousecreeper and butler?'

'Indeed, Mrs Malaprop,' replied Sprockett, bowing low, 'and I don't require much space – I can easily fit in the cupboard under the stairs.'

'You will knot,' replied Mrs Malaprop with great indignation, 'I am resizing there. You may have the earring cupboard.'

'Then with your permission I shall go and repack,' announced Sprockett.

'You mean you're leaving?' I asked.

'Repack my knee bearings,' he explained, 'with grease. Knees, despite much design work, continue to be the Duplex-5's Achilles heel.'

And leaving us all to muse upon his odd choice of words, he departed.

'At least *try* to be nice to him,' I said to Mrs Malaprop when he had gone, 'and I want you to order some oils of varying grades to make him feel welcome – and make sure all the clocks are kept wound. Cog-based life-forms take great offence at stopped clocks.'

'As madam washes,' replied Mrs Malaprop, which was her way of telling me to get stuffed.

'If you don't need us, we're going to go and rehearse Acheron's death scene on the roof of Thornfield Hall,' said Carmine.

'You'll need to unlock Bertha,' I replied, handing her the key, 'and don't forget to put the bite mask on her.'

I watched them go with an odd feeling that I couldn't describe. Despite myself being the protagonist, most of the characters were already here when I took over, and few of them were happy with my interpretation of Thursday, despite it being the one that Thursday herself had approved. They had all preferred the sex-and-violence Thursday who had turned a blind eye to the many scams they had had cooking. Because of this, I hadn't really got on with any of them. In fact, the out-of-book relationship with the rest of the cast could best be described as 'barely cordial'. Carmine seemed to get on with them a lot better. I shouldn't have minded, but I did.

'She's going to be trouble, that one,' said Pickwick, who was doing the crossword while perched on the dresser.

'All she has to be is a good Thursday,' I murmured, 'everything else is immaterial. Mrs Malaprop?'

'Yes, madam?'

'Did you put anything in my pocket this morning? For a practical joke or anything?'

'A brat tickle *joke*, madam?' she enquired in a shocked tone. 'Malaprops always avoid potentially Hummus situations.'

'I didn't think so. I'll be in my study. Will you have Sprockett bring in some tea?'

'Very good, madam.'

'Pickwick? I need the paper.'

'You'll have to wait,' she said without looking up, 'I'm doing the crossword.'

I didn't have time for this, so simply took the paper, ripped off the crossword section and handed it back to her. I ignored her expression of outrage and walked into my study and shut the door.

I moved quietly to the French windows and stepped out into the garden to release the Lost Positives that the Lady of Shalott had given me. She had a soft spot for the orphaned prefix-less words, and thought they had more chance to thrive in Fiction than in Poetry. I let the *defatigable* scamps out of their box. They were *kempt* and *shevelled* but their behaviour was *peccable* if not mildly *gruntled*. They started acting in a *petuous* manner and ran around in circles in a very *toward* manner.

I then returned to my study and spent twenty minutes staring at Thursday's shield. The only way it could have got into my pocket was from the red-haired gentleman sitting next to me on the tram. And if that was the case, he had been in contact with Thursday quite recently – or at least, some time in the past week. It didn't prove she was missing in the BookWorld any more than it proved she was missing in the RealWorld. I had only a husband's tears and the word of a murderer.

'Your tea and shortbread, ma'am,' said Sprockett, placing the tray upon my desk. 'A very comfortable house you have. I must confess that in a weak moment and quite against your advice, I lent that odd-looking bird twenty pounds for her kidney operation.'

I sighed. 'I warned you about Pickwick. She doesn't need a kidney operation, and her mother isn't in "dire straits", no matter what she says.'

'Ah,' replied Sprockett, 'do you think I might be able to get my money back?'

'Not without a lot of squawking. Is Mrs Malaprop causing you any trouble, by the way?'

'No, ma'am. We agreed to arm-wrestle for seniority in the house, and even though she attempted to cheat, I believe that we are all square now.'

'I was given this by someone on a tram,' I said, passing the real Thursday's shield across to Sprockett.

His eyebrow pointed to 'Puzzled', then 'Thinking', then 'Worried'.

'That would explain the ease with which I escaped the stoning in Conspiracy.'

'And later, getting out of Poetry.'

'I don't recall that.'

'You were dreaming about toasters. Can you call the Jurisfiction front desk and ask for Thursday Next? Tell them it's me and I need to speak to her.'

Sprockett stood in the corner to make the call. A request like this would be better coming from my butler.

'They tell me that she is "on assignment" at present,' replied Sprockett after talking quietly to himself for a few seconds.

'Tell them it's the written Thursday and I'll call again.'

I wondered quite how she could be on assignment without her shield, and idly turned over the newspaper. I stopped. The banner headline read: *Famed Jurisfiction Agent to Lead Peace Talks*. Thursday was due to table the talks on Friday, less than a week away. All of a sudden her 'absent' status took on a more menacing angle. If she was missing now, things could get very bad indeed.

For the past three years Racy Novel and its leader Speedy Muffler had been causing trouble far in excess of his size, readership or importance. Sandwiched precariously between Women's Fiction and Outdated Religious Dogma with Erotica to the far north and Comedy to the south, the large yet proudly anarchic genre had been troublesome ever since it was declared a member of the 'Axis of Unreadable' along with Misery Memoirs and Celebrity Bio. Muffler, stung by the comparison to voyeuristic drivel or the meaningless non-adventures of celebrities, decided to expand his relevance within Fiction by attempting to push out his borders. The CofG responded to his aggression by transferring *Lady Chatterley's Lover* out of Racy Novel and into Human Drama, then moving *The History of Tom Jones* to Erotica. Sanctions soon followed which prevented anyone from supplying Racy Novel with good dialogue, plot or characterisation. This did nothing to appease Speedy Muffler, and he claimed the sanctions were preventing him developing as a genre – quite against BookWorld law and the Character's Charter. The trouble was, Muffler and Racy Novel couldn't be ignored since they were one of the major exporters of Metaphor. When Muffler claimed to possess a 'Dirty Bomb' capable of hurling scenes of a gratuitously sexual nature far into Women's Fiction, the BookWorld finally took notice, and the peace talks were set. Thursday Next would be the chief negotiator, and she had good form. When Scandinavian Detectives threatened to cede from Crime, it was she who brought them back.

'You seem perturbed,' remarked Sprockett. 'Is anything the matter?'

'I have reason to believe that the real Thursday Next might be missing,' I replied guardedly, 'and that's not good for all sorts of reasons.'

'Has she gone missing before?' asked Sprockett.

'Many times.'

'Then it's probably one of those . . . again.'

I hoped he was right, but even if he wasn't, I wasn't quite sure what could be done about it. I was an under-read A8-Class character with no power, and less influence. Besides, Jurisfiction were doubt-less on to it. Commander Bradshaw, the head of Jurisfiction, was one of Thursday's closest friends.

There was a knock on the door and Mrs Malaprop came in.

'Miss Next? There awesome gentlemen to see you.'

'Who are they?'

'They didn't give their Gnomes.'

The visitors didn't wait and strode in. They weren't the sort of people I wanted to see, but their presence might well reinforce my theories about Thursday. They were the Men in Plaid.

Several things seemed to happen at once. Sprockett's eyebrow quivered at Mrs Malaprop, who got his meaning and knocked over an ornamental vase which fell to the floor with a crash. The Men in Plaid turned to see what was going on, and at that very moment Sprockett grabbed Thursday's shield from the desk and threw it hard into the ceiling, where it stuck, embedded in the plasterboard. By the time the Men in Plaid looked back towards us, Sprockett was tidying my papers on the desk.

'Good afternoon, gentlemen,' I said in a friendly tone, 'what can I do for you?'

Like trousers, pear pips, twins and bookends, MiPs always came in pairs. They were without emotion, and were designed to do what they were told to do, and nothing else.

'So,' said the Man in Plaid, 'you are Thursday Next A8 V–67987–FP?'

'Yes.'

'Date of composure?'

'Third of June 2006. What is this about?'

'Routine, Miss Next,' said the second MiP. 'We are looking for some property stolen from a leading Jurisfiction agent, and we thought you might be able to help us. I won't mince my words. We think you have it.'

94

I resisted the temptation to look up. The shield was in plain sight, embedded in the ceiling.

'Do you want me to try to guess what you're after, or are you going to tell me?'

The MiP exchanged glances.

'It has come to our attention,' said the taller of the two, 'that someone's been waving Thursday Next's Jurisfiction shield around. They used it to get out of Poetry an hour ago. Were you in Poetry today, Miss Next?'

I wasn't meant to be there, so the answer had to be no.

'No.'

They stared at me.

'The officers involved told us that someone of your description had a robotic butler in the boot of a taxi. Do you still deny this?'

I looked at Sprockett, who stared impassively ahead.

'There're probably *hundreds* of robotic manservants in Fiction,' I replied, 'and all of them are technically luggage. But since automata are incapable of misstatements, why don't you ask him yourself?'

They did, and Sprockett could answer without lying that he had absolutely no knowledge of the trip at all.

'Perhaps it was Thursday herself,' I suggested. 'Have you asked her?'

There was, perhaps, a subtle change in the Plaid's demeanour. But if she *was* missing as I supposed, they weren't going to let on.

'How about Conspiracy?' asked the smaller Woman in Plaid. 'We have a report from Elvis561 that someone looking a lot like Thursday and holding her Jurisfiction shield rescued a mechanical man from stoning.'

'That was definitely me,' I said, 'I was on JAID business.'

They both stared at me. It was highly uncomfortable.

'Then you *did* have her shield?'

'I used my JAID shield. Here.'

I passed it across and they stared at it. It was nothing like a Jurisfiction shield.

'The Elvis must have been mistaken,' I continued. 'There is a certain degree of inbuilt hyperbole to the genre that might generate outrageous claims, wouldn't you agree?'

I stared at them intently as I tried to read their demeanour but their emotionless construction made them impossible to penetrate. They probably didn't do well in singles bars, but would doubtless do well in poker tournaments.

'Very well,' said the first Man in Plaid, 'we will leave you for now. One more thing: a call to Thursday Next at Jurisfiction was traced to this book not ten minutes ago. Was there a reason for this?'

'I have a new understudy,' I explained. 'I thought Thursday might like to give her a few tips on how to play her. If you see her, will you pass my message along?'

'We're not messengers,' said the second Plaid, and they left without another word.

There was a moment of silence after they had left. I had just lied to the Men in Plaid, which was illegal, and even if they thought I was telling the truth, being on their radar was probably not conducive to good health. But one thing that did cross my mind was this: if Thursday was missing, the Men in Plaid had been ordered to find her, and they didn't yet know of the connection between myself and the red-haired gentleman.

But I didn't have time to muse on it any further, as I heard the Read Alarm go off. Somewhere in the Outland a reader had picked up one of my books. Luckily for us, things can happen instantaneously in the BookWorld, so I dashed through to the kitchen to find Carmine already dressed and ready to go. I half thought of taking over, but I had to let her give it a whirl sooner or later.

'It's barely teatime in the Outland,' I said, glancing at the clock, 'someone must be taking a break. Are you ready?'

Carmine nodded.

I turned to Mrs Malaprop, who was monitoring the progress of all the readings on a circular screen that plotted in word-for-word detail which readers were where, and in what book.

'It's Slope oak,' she said, '*Lost in a Good Book*, page 122, SpecOps Twilight Homes. I'll contract Granny Next.'

She flipped a switch on the intercom and her voice echoed around the series on the intercom.

'*Hear this, hear this. Would Granny Next pro-seed toe-wads TN2, P122.*'

'An easy scene,' I said, turning to Carmine. 'How's your ping-pong?'

'Not bad.'

'It doesn't matter. Granny Next will crush you anyway.'

'Who's "Slope oak"?'

'She means "slowpoke", it's the name we give to a reader who has been working their way through the series at a snail's pace. When he falters – which he often does – you should try to alter your dialogue for simplicity. You'll feel his read-rate increase when you do, and we aim only to help. The reader is everything, yes?'

She looked up at me and bit her lip nervously.

'The reader is everything,' she repeated, 'but you'll step in if there are more than twenty concurrent reads, yes?'

Being read simultaneously was often described as: 'like trying to visit everywhere in Paris at the same time during rush hour'. The simile was lost on me, but I made a point of never wanting to visit Paris, real or imaginary.

'Don't worry,' I told her, 'you'll be fine. We've got at least four hours before the other readers come on stream. Take a deep breath and repeat the First Person's credo: "Pace, Atmosphere, Plot, Prose, Character".'

'Pace, Atmosphere, Plot, Prose, Character.'

'Good. Give them hell.'

And she gave me a wan smile and headed off towards the SpecOps Twilight Homes, which were cemented in just between Thornfield Hall and the interior Skyrail set. I watched her go with an odd feeling. I liked the time off, but I liked being Thursday, too – even if it was to an audience of only one.

'Here,' I said, passing the Snooze access codes to Mrs Malaprop, 'keep a close eye on her.'

'This is a last resort, yes?' asked Mrs Malaprop, who licked kittens more than anyone else I knew.

'Last resort. Call me and I'll come running.'

I walked out of the kitchen. There was work to be done.

10

Epizeuxis

'**Maps of the BookWorld are constantly updated as the genres snake back and forth in response to Outland trends and fads.** The borders move so rapidly, in fact, that any notion of a fully updated map is considered laughable, and most maps are these days published with *average* borders that reflect recent reading trends . . .'

Bradshaw's BookWorld Companion, 3rd Edition

Despite the unwanted attentions of the Men in Plaid, the warnings from the red-haired gentleman and the worrying possibility of Thursday being missing, I spent a busy and anxious afternoon going through the heap of bookjunk in the garage. I was, to be honest, torn. Part of me wanted nothing better than to agree with Red Herring's assessment that this was an 'unrepeatable' accident, and part of me was suspicious. The closer I examined the bookjunk, the worse it looked. It appeared that something, while not *exactly* rotten in the state of the BookWorld, was far from fresh.

At a little after five and with a rising sense of foreboding, I called Sprockett into my study to compare notes.

'So what do you have?' I asked, letting him air his discoveries first.

He led me across to where the *Atlas of the BookWorld* lay open on my desk. He indicated the page that depicted the south-eastern part of the island, and showed me where he had plotted the crashed book's debris trail by a series of black crosses. Most sections of text would have been pulverised into graphemes and simply absorbed, which explains why we rarely find anything when short stories or limericks come to grief – just a hollow concussion in the distance.

Almost all of the debris had been strewn across the Aviation genre, with the notable exception of the bed-sitting room already discovered inside Conspiracy, and a Triumph motorcycle within Thriller (spy) that narrowly missed George Smiley as it travelled through an early draft of *Tinker, Tailor, Soldier, Hatmaker*. The book seemed to have disintegrated somewhere above Deighton and then strewn objects in a roughly straight line north, in the direction of the Great Library and the Ungenred Zone.

'What would tigers and a macaroon be doing in an Aviation novel?' asked Mrs Malaprop, who was cleaning with a feather duster, but actually wanted to be part of the investigation.

'They might be scrambled graphemes and not actually in the book at all. Best ignored.'

'There doesn't seem to be any curve to the debris trail at all,' added Pickwick, who had entered unseen and jumped on to the table to look more closely. I wouldn't have minded so much if she hadn't upset the inkwell, and then stood clumsily in the ink.

'You're right,' I said. 'Mind your feet. And that means either a rapid break-up or the book – whatever it was – was not from the Aviation genre.'

'Look here,' said Pickwick as she pointed with one of her claws, 'if we extend the debris field line backwards we come out of Aviation, across Military, and end up right here in Adventure – somewhere around *King Solomon's Mines*.'

'Which might explain the tigers.'

'But not the macaroon.'

'Or the box-girder bridges – or the Triumph Bonneville motorcycle.'

'I didn't say it *was* Haggard,' said Pickwick, 'only that it came from Adventure.'

Incredibly, Pickwick was actually being helpful. Probably because she'd taken Sprockett for some cash, and had already had her nap but was not yet ready for her afternoon snack, she was in an unusually good temper.

'I have an idea,' said Sprockett. 'How about unscrambling the letters of the items we found, thus finding tantalising clues as to what the book might have been about?'

'To an outside observer that would seem entirely logical,' I replied, 'but for one thing: anagram-related clues were outlawed six years ago by the NCU.'

'NCU?'

'Narrative Clunker Unit. Villains haven't been allowed to be albinos for years, identical twins as plot devices are banned, and double negatives are a complete no-no. Forget anagrams.'

'Isn't there a block box data recorder in every book?' asked Mrs Malaprop. 'We could analyse the tea lemon tree.'

'Usually,' I replied, 'but engineering contracts have to be spread around the BookWorld and the construction of Book Data Recorders was subcontracted to James McGuffin and Co. of the Suspense genre, so they have a tendency to go missing until dramatically being found right at the end of an investigation. It's undoubtedly suspenseful, but a little useless. Want to see what I found?'

We walked out through the French windows and through the garden to my double garage, which was another example of the inverted physics of the BookWorld. The more you filled the garage, the emptier it appeared. But it could never be *entirely* empty, as that would require an infinite amount of stuff – or in the case of a double garage, *twice* an infinite amount of stuff.

All the sections of crashed book were laid out on the concrete floor, ostensibly to try to find a reason for the accident, or even to figure out a rough plot of the mystery book. We had a few page numbers, but nothing attached to any dialogue. It was a mess.

I walked past the yellow-painted back axle, pushed aside a fridge-freezer and beckoned them to one particular piece of wreckage.

'What do you make of this?' I asked.

We were standing over the bent Triumph motorcycle, and I told them to be quiet. There was a whisper in the air, and if you leaned close to the damaged motorcycle, you could hear it:

> The works that built the cycle worked;
> The cycle's labour laboured on.
> And workers sought and workers bought
> the managers out and managed 'owt
> until the cycle's cycle cycled round.
> But markets moved and markets shifted,
> to Eastern trade that Eastern made.
> Loans were pleaded loans were needed,
> the workers' workers worked their last.
> But ruin didn't do as ruin does;
> for Triumph's collapse led to Triumph's triumph.

'I don't get it,' said Pickwick, who had always favoured Harley-Davidson.

'It's a poem that charts the fall and rise of the Triumph Motorcycle Company in the late seventies and early eighties,' I said. 'It's seeped out of the descriptive flux of the motorcycle – a glowing after-ember of the accident.'

'That's not unusual,' replied Pickwick. 'Poetry and prose are different facets of the same basic element. When prose breaks down it often spontaneously rhymes. Poetry is prose in another form, and prose is simply poetry waiting to happen.'

'Epizeuxis,' murmured Sprockett, 'a rhetorical device that repeats the same word in the same sentence for increased dramatic effect. This book was almost certainly destroyed by a Rhetorical Worm.'

I had come to the same conclusion myself. The Worm would attempt to restructure sentences, and when that failed it would take words from other sentences, leaving dangerous holes in the narrative. Once there were no more complete words to be taken, the worm would start to harvest letters to make up the shortfall, weakening the structure until the entire book disintegrated. In Real-World terms, it would be like instantaneously removing every rivet from an aircraft while in flight.

'The problem is,' I said slowly, 'that Rhetorical Worms don't occur naturally. They're used in the demolition business to tear apart sections of scrapped book. It's cheaper and safer than chains, hooks and crowbars. A well-placed Worm can burrow into prose, dissolve away tired exposition and leave description and dialogue untouched. Either the book was carrying unlicensed Worms that were accidentally activated, or it was—'

'*Sabotage!*' hissed Mrs Malaprop, and I felt myself suddenly go quite cold. Such a device would require a level of sophistication quite outside the realm of ordinary citizens. There were stories of the Council of Genre's Men in Plaid using rhetorical devices to cause injury or death, but it was mostly conjecture – drummed up by Conspiracy, no doubt.

'Okay,' I said, 'we have the *possibility* of skulduggery – but it's not the only explanation. Epizeuxis is often used as a rhetorical device.'

'But so blatantly and in a poem to describe the failure of a motorcycle manufacturing cooperative?' exclaimed Pickwick. 'What kind of nut would try something like that?'

'We still need to find out what the book was called,' I said as we walked back into the house. 'We need an ISBN. Did we check the thumb we found for fingerprints?'

'Not a single one.'

'That's annoying. Those severed hands we found a few weeks ago had fingerprints all over them.'

'What about DNA evidence?' asked Sprockett.

'DNA fingerprinting is still under a blanket ban,' I explained. 'Forensic Procedural are allowed to use it, but you know how tight the Crime genre can be.'

Sadly, this was true. The Guild of Detectives had argued that although DNA fingerprinting had a use in the RealWorld, such annoyingly precise and utterly non-cerebral detection methods really had no place in Fiction. And because the Crime lobby represented such a huge part of Fiction, the Council of Genres had reluctantly agreed. Mind you, detection rates hadn't suffered as a result, so everyone was happy.

I looked up at the Read-O-Meter. There were twelve simultaneous readings going on, and Carmine hadn't hit the panic button, so she was doing fine. I had a look at the clock and then went upstairs to have a bath and change. Despite all that was going on, what with sabotaged books, Worms and missing Jurisfiction agents, I still had a date with Whitby Jett. I tried a call to Jurisfiction myself and was told that Thursday Next was still unavailable. I dried, then tried several dresses on but didn't like any of them. I had just dismissed the sixth and was rummaging in the bureau for a yellow top I remember buying last time I was in Chicklit, when I came across a photograph. It was one I had wanted to throw away, but had instead pushed to the back of a drawer. It was a backstory snap of me and Landen, taken when we were in the Crimea, before Landen lost a leg, and I lost a brother. Happy days. I stared at it for a long time, then rang for Sprockett.

'Ma'am?'

'Is Whitby downstairs?'

'Yes, ma'am. He's waiting in the kitchen with a bunch of flowers the size of the Amazonian basin.'

'Would you send him my apologies and ask him to leave? Politely, of course.'

'Ma'am?'

'I need to keep an eye on Carmine. It's her first day and I need to stand by in case of mishaps.'

'Miss Carmine is doing very well, by all accounts, ma'am, and Mr Jett seems happily effusive over the prospect of an evening with you. I believe his conduct has all the hallmarks of . . . love, ma'am.'

'Sprockett,' I said, 'just do this for me, would you? Tell him I'm busy and I'll meet him for lunch tomorrow.'

'Very good, ma'am. Where shall I say you will be meeting him?'

'I'll call him.'

I came downstairs twenty minutes later to find the flowers on the hall table. I walked into the book and found Carmine about to play the croquet match in *Well of Lost Plots*. I told her my date was cancelled, and that I'd take over from her. I think she was secretly relieved.

'Don't forget there's a party tonight at *Castle of Skeddan Jiarg*,' I told her. 'The Queen said to drop in any time.'

'I think I might just do that,' she said with a smile. 'I could get hyphenated, let my hair down and chat up a goblin or something.'

I didn't like the sound of this.

'I don't mean to sound judgemental. Actually, come to think of it,' I said, changing my mind, 'I *do* mean to sound judgemental. You mustn't bring goblins home. Quite apart from the whole hygiene and theft issue, Pickwick can be a real prude. She'll be plocking on about it for months and, quite frankly, I could do without her endless complaints.'

She winked.

'I will be *most* discreet. Why don't you join me when you're done? I know goblins aren't everyone's cup of tea, but what they lack in physical beauty they make up for in endurance.'

I told her I didn't really feel like going to a party or dancing all night, and she gave me a hug before skipping off.

Reading-wise, it wasn't such a bad evening. The PhD student gave up pretty soon to watch *Deal or No Deal*, a popular woodworking programme in the Outland, and the new readers were for the most part forgiving, with only a few of them requiring extra attention to get them over some of the more wayward plot points. As for the rereads, they pretty much looked after themselves, and added a useful amount of feedback, too – the curtains had never looked brighter, and Pickwick positively shone.

But most of all, they kept my mind off Landen – and Whitby.

I I

Plot Thickens

'... **Minor narrative changes were often ignored, but major variations were stamped on without mercy.** Perpetrators would be rounded up and banished to a copy of *Bunty* or *Sparky* until suitably contrite. Repeat offenders were suspended, and after three strikes you were erased – usually without warning. Some thought it worth the risk. After all, being unread was arguably no different from erasure. Some put it this way: better to be dead than unread . . .'

Bradshaw's BookWorld Companion, 7th Edition

I was up and about while everyone else in the book was still sleepily inactive. There had been no readings at all since 2.00 a.m., and I wanted to be in costume and ready on the off-chance that anyone read a few pages before breakfast. It paid to keep at a state of readiness, just in case. There had been trouble inside *Captain Corelli's Mandolin*, when a sudden reinterest in the book caught everyone napping – the first hundred pages or so have yet to fully recover.

I walked about the settings of the series, checking to make sure everything was set and ready to go. My tour wasn't just a technical housekeeping exercise, either – it was about a sense of pride. Despite the lack of readers and a certain 'dissatisfaction' from certain members of the cast that I might improve the readability by spicing up the prose with a bit more sex and violence, I still wanted to keep the books going as well as I could – and to Thursday's approval, which was more important than the author's.

Once I had made sure everything was to my satisfaction, I called Whitby to apologise for standing him up. He took it better than I had expected, but I could sense he was annoyed. I told him I would *definitely* be free for lunch, suggested the expensive and needlessly spacious Elbow Rooms, then pretended that Pickwick had broken something so I could end the conversation.

I took a deep breath, cursed myself for being so stupid, took a pager with me and walked down the road to Stubbs, the outrageously expensive coffee shop on the corner.

'Could I not have a coffee?' I said, meaning I wanted an empty cup. Stubbs had become so expensive that no one could afford the coffee, but since the ambience in the café was so good and the establishment so fashionable, it was always full.

'What would you not like?' asked Paul, who wore black gowns and a wig owing to a syntaxtual head-cold that made him unable to differentiate himself between a *barista* and a *barrister*.

'Better not give me a latte,' I replied, 'and better not make it a large one.'

'How did the date with Whitby go?'

'So-so.'

Paul raised an eyebrow, made no comment and handed me an empty cup. I went to a booth at the back of the store and sat down. I came here most mornings, and usually read the paper over my non-coffee. I scanned the headlines of *The Word*, but if Thursday was missing, they didn't know about it. The lead story was about how Oversized Books had gained a victory at the Council of Genres. Constantly irked by snide comments about taking more than their allotted shelf-space, they had sought to have their own genre, and succeeded. A representative for Oversized Books had praised 'common sense' and said they looked forward to 'moving to their own island as soon as one big enough was made available'.

There was more about Racy Novel with Speedy Muffler claiming that troop movements near his borders were 'an act of aggression'. In rebuttal, Senator Jobsworth of the Council of Genres reiterated that there would be no troop movements ahead of the peace talks on Friday.

'If Thursday is missing,' I said to myself, 'there won't be any peace talks.'

'Mumbling to yourself?'

I looked up. It was Acheron Hades, the designated evildoer and antagonist from *The Eyre Affair*. Inside the book he was a homicidal maniac who would surgically remove people's faces for fun, but outside the book he collected stamps and wrote really bad poetry.

'Peace talks,' I said, showing him the paper.

'I'm not going to hold my breath,' he remarked. 'Speedy Muffler is the master of brinksmanship. Any deal on the table will unravel the following morning – military intervention is the only thing that will stop him.'

Acheron's attitude was not untypical. There were few who didn't think an all-out genre war wasn't pretty much inevitable between Women's Fiction and Racy Novel. The more absorbing question was: 'will it be broadcast live?' and then: 'will it involve me or damage my own genre?'

'Dogma will almost certainly be dragged into the fray,' I said gloomily.

'And Comedy to the south,' added Acheron, 'and they won't like it. I don't think they were joking when they said they would defend their land to the last giggle.'

The door opened and the King and Queen walked in. They looked a little the worse for wear. I nodded a greeting and they ordered a cappuccino each, which sent Paul into something of a panic – I don't think he'd ever made one before.

'By the way,' said Acheron, 'I think Carmy is the best under-study yet.'

'Carmy?'

'Carmine. *Great* interpretation. Are you going to keep her?'

'I've . . . not decided yet.'

'Just so you know I approve,' he said, 'she can vanquish me any day of the week.' He stared into his empty cup for a moment. 'Can I talk to you about something?'

'Is it about your poetry?'

'It's about Bertha Rochester.'

'Biting again?'

Acheron showed me his hand, which had nasty tooth-marks on it.

'Painful,' I agreed. 'I told you to keep the bite mask on until the last moment. But you do throw her to her death. She's allowed to struggle a *bit*.'

'That's another thing,' he said as he pulled a pained expression, 'does she have to look at me in that accusatory way when I chuck her off the roof? It makes me feel all funny inside.'

Unlike Acheron, who differed wildly from his in-book persona, Bertha really *was* bonkers. She had come to us after a gruelling forty-six-year stint as Anne Catherick in *The Woman in White*, and was now quite beyond any form of rehabilitation. In a cruel and ironic twist, Grace Poole kept our version of Bertha Rochester locked up securely in the attic. It was safer for everyone that way.

'I'll have a word,' I said, then asked after a pause: 'So . . . why do you think Carmine is so good?'

'Her interpretation is respectful, but with an edginess that is both sympathetic and noir.'

'And you think that's better than my interpretation?'

'Not better,' replied Acheron diplomatically, 'different. And there's nothing wrong with *that*,' he added cautiously, finding a piece of invisible fluff on his jacket. 'Carmine just plays her in a way that is, well, how shall I put it?'

'More readable?'

'She's an A4 – you're an A8. You'd *expect* her to exhibit a bit more depth.'

'Thanks for that.'

'Don't sweat it. Carmine can't handle quantity, and when and if she can, she'll be off to the bright lights of HumDram/Highbrow. Your job is assured. Besides,' he added in a lighter tone, 'if it *did* come to a vote, I'd go with you.'

'I'm grateful for that at the very least,' I replied despondently. 'So you prefer the real Thursday Next to a more marketable one?'

'Well, yes – and the free time does afford me the luxury of composing poetry – a *most* absorbing pastime.'

It wasn't what I really wanted to hear, and after chatting for a few more minutes he left. I finished the paper and wandered back to the book. I had a brief chat with the series propmaster on the way. He was the technician responsible for all the interactive objects in the series – items that could be handled or manipulated in some way.

'We've managed to repair your car,' he said, 'but go easy on it during the car chase. If you could just pull up sharply rather than slewing sideways, I'd really appreciate it.'

We were working to a budget these days. The remaking of the BookWorld had sneakily reorganised its budgetary systems. Instead of the 'Single Book Payment' we now earned a 'Reader Stipend' for every reading, with a labyrinthine system of bonuses and extra payments for targets. It wasn't universally liked. Any book that fell below the hundred readers a week level could find itself hit by a double whammy: not enough funds to maintain the fabric of the novel, yet not enough Feedback Loop to hope the readers would do it for you.

I got back to the house at mid-morning to find Pickwick had already laid the table for lunch. She often picked up fads and trends in the BookWorld and just recently had caught the 'reality bug' and insisted we sat for every meal, even though there was nothing to eat, and we didn't need to. She also insisted that we play parlour games together in the evenings. This would have been fine if she didn't have to win at everything, and watching a dodo cheat badly at Ker-plunk was not a happy spectacle.

I found Carmine in the kitchen looking a little green about the gills and with an ice pack on her head. Pickwick was sitting on the sideboard attempting to unravel a completed Sudoku and glaring at her.

'Problems?' I asked.

'N-n-n-none at all,' groaned Carmine, 'I j-j-just think I hit the hyphens a little t-t-too hard last n-n-night.'

She groaned, closed her eyes and pressed the ice pack more firmly to her head.

'If you're hyphenated while working you'll be in serious trouble,' I said in my most scolding voice, 'and as your mentor, so will I.'

'Yeah, yeah,' murmured Carmine, eyes firmly closed, 'I'll be fine. B-b-but can you p-p-p-please get the b-b-birdbrain over there to shut up?'

'I'm sorry,' said Pickwick haughtily, 'but was the drunken tart addressing me?'

'Why, is there *another* b-b-birdbrain present?'

'Okay, okay,' I said, 'calm down, you two. What's the problem?'

'That b-birdbrain insists on staring at m-me and sighing.'

'Is this true?'

Pickwick ruffled her feathers in an aggrieved manner.

'She brought a goblin home, and they're nothing but trouble. What's more, I think she is *entirely* unsuitable for the important job of being Thursday. We all like a hyphen from time to time, but consorting with pointy-eared homunculi is *totally out of order!*'

She squawked the last bit, and Carmine rolled her eyes.

'I didn't b-bring a g-goblin home.'

'He followed you home. It amounts to the same thing.'

'You're j-just sour because you're not g-g-getting any,' sneered Carmine, 'and anyway, Horace is n-n-not like other g-g-goblins.'

'Hang on,' I said, 'so you *did* bring a goblin home?'

'He g-g-got locked out of his b-b-book. What was I meant to d-d-do?'

I threw up my arms.

'Carmine!'

'D-don't you be so j-judgemental,' she replied indignantly, 'look at yourself. F-f-five books in one s-series, and each by a different g-g-ghost writer.'

'Your private life is your own,' I replied angrily, 'but goblins can't help themselves – or at least they *can* help themselves – to anything not nailed down.'

I ran upstairs to find my bedroom had been ransacked. Anything of even the slightest value had been stolen. Inviting a goblin to cross your threshold was a recipe for disaster, and certainly worse than doing the same with a vampire. With the latter all you got was a nasty bite, but the company, extraordinarily good sex and funny stories more than made up for it – apparently.

'That was dumb,' I said when I'd returned, 'he's taken almost everything.'

Carmine looked at me, then at Pickwick, then burst into tears and ran from the room.

'Goblins!' said Pickwick with a snort. 'They're just trouble with a capital G. By the way,' she added, now more cheery since she had been proved correct, 'Sprockett wanted to show you something. He's in your office.'

I walked through to my study, where Sprockett was indeed waiting for me. He wasn't alone. He had his foot on top of a struggling goblin, and a hessian sack full of stolen possessions was lying on the carpet.

'Your property, ma'am?' he asked. I nodded and he took the letter opener from the desk, held the goblin tightly by one ear and placed the opener to its throat. His eyebrow twitched. It was clearly a bluff. I decided to play along.

'No,' I said, 'you'll ruin the carpet. Do it outside.'

The goblin opened its eyes wide and stared at me in shocked amazement, then started to babble on about an 'influential uncle' who would 'do unpleasant things' if he 'went missing'.

'Just kidding,' I added, 'let him go.'

'Are you sure?' asked Sprockett. 'I can make it look like a shaving accident.'

'Yes, I'm sure. You,' I said, jabbing a finger at the goblin, 'are a disgrace. Place a single toe in my series again and I'll make you wish you'd never been written.'

Sprockett took his foot off the goblin and it ran to the window, paused on the sill for a moment, made an obscene gesture and then ran off. That was the trouble with being stuck in Fantasy – too many goblins, spells, ogres, wizards, elves and warlocks. I reckoned it frightened readers off.

'So,' I said, locking the window after him, 'what's the deal?'

'I was reappraising the condition of the wreckage from the debris field.'

He showed me the Triumph Bonneville's exhaust pipe. It had almost been folded in half by the impact. He pointed to a small patch on the chrome. There was a slight mottling about four inches long and an inch wide.

'A fault in the manufacturing?' I suggested.

'But it wasn't manufactured,' said Sprockett, 'it was *written*. It should be perfect – better than any real motorcycle.'

'You asked me in here to show me an imperfection on a Bonneville exhaust?'

'There's more. I found this orange inside the bedsit. Here.'

He tossed the orange across and I noticed that this *also* had a slight mottling on the side. He then showed me similar imperfections on a Polaroid camera, a toaster, a half-eaten sandwich and a plastic bath duck. Then, I got it.

'The mottling,' I said slowly, 'they are – *were* – ISBN numbers. Are you trying to tell me someone has *removed* all identification marks from this book?'

He didn't answer, which was answer enough. All doubts were off. *This wasn't an accident*. Someone had hacked into the novel's Source Code to delete the ISBNs in order to cover their tracks and ensure no one found out which book had been destroyed or why. The Epizeuxis Worm and now this. We didn't have a crashed book, we had a crime scene. But it wasn't *quite* that simple.

'Only Text Grand Central or the Council of Genres would have the power to scrub ISBNs and put together a rhetorical device,' I said, 'and while I'm not one to use coarse idioms, someone would have to be connected up the wazoo to pull this off. Have you attempted to find out what the ISBN actually was?'

Sprockett placed a series of photographs on the desk.

'I took the liberty of subjecting the marks to a complex series of photographic techniques that, while appearing to have the veneer of scientific reality, actually just sound good. Do you want the full two pages of dull exposition, or just the results?'

'Better just give me the results,' I said, looking at my watch. 'Whitby will be here any moment for a lunch date.'

'Might I enquire where you are going, ma'am?'

'We thought we'd try the Elbow Rooms.'

'A fine establishment. I meet up with the Hartzel chess-player every two weeks there to discuss Matters of the Cog. I'd avoid the lobster.'

'Food poisoning?'

'No, no, not on the menu – at the bar. *Very* opinionated and apt to lapse into unspeakably dull arthropod-related digressions. But see here.'

He handed me a photograph that was many images superimposed on top of one another. The revealed ISBN was indistinct, but legible. I jotted down the number in my notebook.

'Thank you, Sprockett. You're a star.'

'Madam is most kind.'

I fetched the unimaginatively titled *Cheshire Cat's Complete Guide to All Books Ever Written Everywhere* and looked up the ISBN. Our crashed book was from Self-Publishing and titled *The Murders on the Hareng Rouge*, by Adrian Dorset. I'd never heard of him. But it was Vanity, so I'd hardly be expected to. There was no other information. The ISBN database held only titles, authors, publisher's details, three-for-two offers, that kind of thing. I looked at the map we had pinned on the wall which charted the book's final journey. If you extended the line back through Adventure and past the Cliff of Notes it made landfall in Vanity. We'd never considered such a thing. It must have lifted off there and proceeded in an almost straight line to where the Council of Genres was located, but had come down over Conspiracy.

I sat down, leaned back in my chair and ran through the potential scenarios. It was possible *The Murders on the Hareng Rouge* was a potential world-beater on its way to being published. Jealousies ran deep in the BookWorld, and the possibility of someone in HumDram/Highbrow nobbling the potential competition was quite high. It had happened before; bad Vanity was universally disliked but tolerated in a condescending 'yes, well done, jolly good' kind of way, but good Vanity was reviled as the worst kind of upstart.

'Blast,' I said, as a more personal note added itself to the mix, 'it explains why I was asked to handle the investigation. No one expected me to find anything.'

Sprockett's eyebrow pointed to 'Bingo'.

'The thought had occurred to me, ma'am. In fact, the precise reason you were selected for this investigation given your lack of adequacy has been troubling me for some time.'

I thought about Acheron's comments regarding Carmine being more qualified than I.

'I so need that sort of comment right now.'

His eyebrow clicked from 'Bingo' to 'Apologetic'.

'Merely the facts as I see them, ma'am.'

I thought carefully. Part of me – the Thursday part – was outraged over the crime, but the rest of me was more realistic. There were some things that were simply not worth meddling with, and anyone willing to engineer the destruction of an entire book wouldn't think twice about eliminating me. There were few – if any – characters who couldn't be replaced.

'Have you told anyone about this?' I asked, and Sprockett shook his head.

'Keep it that way,' I murmured. 'I think all we've found is what Red Herring wanted me to find: an unprecedented event which is unrepeatable.'

'If asked for an opinion, ma'am,' said Sprockett in an unusually forceful turn of phrase, 'I should like to find out who asked Mr Herring to allocate you to this investigation.'

I stared at him. I should like to know too, but I couldn't think of a way to frame the question that wouldn't have me in the boot of a car heading towards the traditional place to dump bodies, in the New Jersey area of Crime.

'This was never meant to be reported,' I said, 'this was meant for looking the other way and carrying on with life as though nothing had happened. There was a good reason I was asked to do this, and I will not impugn my lack of competence by being irresponsibly accurate. I have a reputation to uphold.'

It was a hopelessly poor argument, and he and I both knew it. I drew a sheet of writing paper from my stationery drawer.

'Permission to speak openly?' he asked.

I took a deep breath.

'I don't want to hear what you have to say, but I should.'

'It's not what Thursday Next would have done.'

'No,' I replied, 'but then Thursday could deal with this sort of stuff. She *enjoyed* it. A woman has to know her limitations. If Herring had wanted this accident to be investigated properly, he would have given it to someone else. Maybe it's for the best. Maybe there really *are* wheels within wheels. Some stuff has to be left, for the good of all of us. We leave crime to the authorities, right?'

'That would certainly seem to be the safe and conventional option, ma'am.'

'Exactly,' I replied. 'Safe. Conventional. Besides, I have a series to look after, and dignity to be maintained for Thursday. If anything happened to me as likely as not Carmine would take over, and I'm not convinced she'd uphold the standards quite as I do, what with the goblins and the hyphenating and stuff.'

I looked away as I said it and began to rearrange the objects on my desk. I suddenly felt hot and a bit peculiar and didn't want to look Sprockett in the eye.

'As madam wishes.'

Sprockett bowed and withdrew, and I spent the next hour writing up a report for Herring. It wasn't easy. Try as I might I couldn't make the report last longer than forty words, and it deserved more than that. I managed at one point to write a hundred words, but after I'd taken out the bit about the Epizeuxis Worm and the scrubbed ISBNs, it was down to only thirty-seven again. I decided to ask Whitby his hypothetical opinion and finish the report after lunch.

I called the Jurisfiction offices again to see whether Thursday was available to talk.

'She's still missing,' I reported as I trotted into the kitchen. 'I might try to speak to her when I go over to deliver the report to Mr Herring this afternoon. Do you think I'm dressed okay for Whitby or should I . . .'

My voice had trailed off because something was wrong. Sprockett and Mrs Malaprop were looking at me in the sort of way I imagine disgruntled parents might.

'You tell her,' said Mrs Malaprop.

'It's Whitby,' said Sprockett.

I suddenly had a terrible thought. This being Fiction, long-unrequited romances often end in tragedy just before they finally begin, inevitably leading to a lifetime's conjecture over what might have happened, and all manner of tedious and ultimately over-written soul-searching. The scenario was almost as hideous as actually losing Whitby.

'He's dead?'

'No, ma'am, he's not dead. At least, he was still alive two minutes ago.'

'He was here? Why isn't he here now?'

Sprockett coughed politely.

'I am sorry to say, ma'am, that I had to send Mr Jett away.'

I stared at him, scarcely believing what I was hearing.

'Why would you do something like that?'

'I feel, ma'am, that he is *unsuitable*.'

'*What?*'

He showed me a newspaper clipping that was about two years old.

'I exhort you to read it, ma'am, no matter how difficult.'

So I did.

'It is the painful duty of this journalist,' went the article, 'to report an act of such base depravity that causes the worst excesses of Horror to pale into insignificance. Last Tuesday an unnamed man, for reasons known only to himself, set fire to a busload of nuns who were taking their orphaned puppies to a "How cute is your puppy?" competition. Unfortunately, the perpetrator of this base and heartless act is still at liberty, and . . .'

I stopped reading as a sense of confusion and disappointment welled up inside me. There was a picture accompanying the article, and even though the piece did not name Whitby, there was a photograph of a man who 'Jurisfiction wanted to question'. It was Jett, without a doubt – holding a two-gallon petrol can, and chuckling. I didn't really know what was worse – Whitby killing the busload of nuns or me having finally plucked up the courage to have lunch at the Elbow Rooms, only for the rug to be pulled from under my feet.

'Is this true?'

'I'm afraid so. I'm sorry, ma'am. Was I wrong to send him away?'

I sighed and stared at the report I was carrying.

'No, you were right.'

'Better call a cab. I'm going to tell Herring what he wants to hear. At least that way someone gets to be happy today. You can come too.'

It took twenty minutes to coax Carmine out of her bedroom. I assured her it wasn't so bad because Sprockett had caught the goblin and recovered the swag, so he wasn't *technically* a thief. I had to tell her that he wasn't *that* unhandsome – for a goblin – and that no,

I'm sure he wasn't just saying nice things to her so he could be invited across the threshold. I told her she was now on book duty as I would be out for a while and she replied: 'Yes, okay, fine' but wouldn't look at me, so I left her staring angrily at the patterned wallpaper in the front room.

12

Jurisfiction

'Budgetary overruns almost buried the Remaking before the planning stage, until relief came from an unexpected quarter. A spate of dodgy accounting practices in the Outland necessitated a new genre in Fiction: Creative Accountancy. Shunned by many as "not a proper genre at all", their skills at turning thin air into billion-dollar profits were suddenly of huge use, and the Remaking went ahead as planned. Enron may have been a pit of vipers in the Outland, but they quite literally saved the BookWorld . . .'

Bradshaw's BookWorld Companion, 16th Edition

I took the bus to LeGuin Central and then the first train to HumDram/Classics. As the train slowly steamed from the station I sat back and stared out of the window. I was mildly interested to learn that Heathcliff was on the same train, although we didn't see him – just a lot of screaming and fainting girls on the platform whenever we stopped. We halted briefly at Gaiman Junction before steaming on a wide arc to terminate at Shakespeare Terminus. There was a delay leaving the platform as security was being taken a little more seriously than usual. A group of heavily armed Men in Plaid were scrutinising everyone's ID.

'Do you think this is about the Racy Novel Peace Talks?' I asked a French Wilkins Micawber, who was there on an exchange trip.

'Mais oui. But I think zer CofG are being a lettle jittery 'bout Racy Novel,' he explained in a pointlessly overblown French accent. 'Zey think zat zere may be fizz columnists eager to cause – 'ow you say? *Mischief*. I'd not like to be without shirt and medallion while Barry White plays in zer background right now, I can tells you.'

'Reason for visit?' asked the Plaid.

'I have to report to Mr Lockheed regarding a crashed-book investigation.'

'Very well,' said the Plaid, 'and what's with the mechanical butler?'

'To lend tone to the proceedings.'

This was enough for the Man in Plaid, and with a gruff 'Welcome to the Classics, have an eloquent day' I was allowed to pass. On our way out of the station I noticed a small group of characters who had been pulled aside. Some of the women wore miniskirts, tube-tops and stilettos, and the men had shirts open to the navel. It seemed as though anyone even remotely resembling someone from Racy Novel was immediately under suspicion. They were protesting their innocence and complaining bitterly about the unfair character profiling, but to little avail.

We took a tram along Austen Boulevard and got out just outside the gates to *Sense and Sensibility*. This was a large compound, and a high wall topped with barbed wire surrounded the many settings that made up the book. On each corner were watchtowers, from which armed Plaid kept a constant lookout. Such tight security wasn't just to protect the Dashwoods – the residence of Norland Park within *Sense and Sensibility* was also the headquarters of Juris-fiction, Fiction's policing agency.

Waiting at the gates were a group of characters with day-passes, ready for the book tour. For some reason those in Sci-Fi had a thing about the Classics, so of the twenty or thirty characters waiting, at least two-thirds were aliens. Since most of them hailed from the poor end of the genre, they had a lot of tentacles and left sticky trails after themselves, which caused no end of cleaning up.

'No clockwork automata,' said one of the guards on duty, 'you should know better than that, Miss Next.'

I had to explain that I wasn't *that* Miss Next, and the guard peered more closely at me, grunted and then explained that a Duplex-4 had suffered a mainspring failure several months before and killed eight bystanders, so all cog-based life-forms below the Duplex-6 had been banned.

'The Six has been released?' asked Sprockett, who had a vested interest in the competition. To sentient machines, the primary cause of worry was obsolescence, closely followed by metal fatigue and inadequate servicing.

'It was launched just after the Remaking,' said the guard, 'but I've not seen one yet.'

'They must have rushed them into production,' murmured Sprockett. 'A risk, if they're still at the beta-test stage.'

I suggested to Sprockett that he nip into the local Stubbs and not have a coffee or two until I returned, to which he gratefully acquiesced.

After signing the visitors' book and a risk assessment that included 'erasure, swollen ankles and death by drowning', I was issued a visitor's pass and allowed to walk up the gravelled path towards the house. Since we were now actually *within* the back-story of *Sense and Sensibility*, the view upwards was not of the rest of the BookWorld – the curved inside of the sphere and books moving about – but of clouds and a clear blue sky. The trees gently rustled as though in a breeze, and the herbaceous borders were alive with a delicate symphony of colour. This was one of the better attributes of the Reader Feedback Loop. When readers imbue a book with their own interpretations the weather always comes first, then colours, symmetry, trees, architecture, fixtures and fittings and finally texture. Birdsong, however, is generally not something brought alive by the reader's imagination, so the birds still have to be provided. Since we were now in the unread zone of the novel, the birds were either off duty or populating another book elsewhere. There is a certain amount of economics within the BookWorld; Austen birds are the same as Brontë ones – listen carefully and you'll hear.

I stopped at the front door to Norland Park and gave my name to the footman, who looked as much like a frog as you can without actually being one. He gazed at me for a long time and opened his eyes so wide I thought for a moment they might fall out and readied myself with a pocket handkerchief in case they did. But they didn't fall out, and after another minute's thought he relaxed and said:

'You do look like her, don't you?'

I thought of telling him that he looked very much like a frog, but thought better of it.

'You're the first person not to confuse me with her for a while,' I remarked. 'How did you know?'

'The real Thursday always ignored me,' he replied, 'walked past without a word. But never in a bad way – she always did it respectful, like.'

'Do you get ignored a lot?'

'I do, and not just by ordinary citizens. I've been ignored by some of the greats, you know.' He then proceeded to list twenty or so major characters who hadn't acknowledged his existence on a regular basis. He had a particular fondness for David Copperfield, who he had escorted almost three hundred times 'without a glance in my direction'.

'That must be quite upsetting.'

'I'm a footman,' he explained, 'we're trained to be not-there-but-there. Being ignored is the yardstick of a footman's professional abilities. My father was sixty-seven years in the employ of the first Lord Spongg and wasn't acknowledged once. He went to his grave a fulfilled man. If you want to be ignored by the movers and shakers of the BookWorld,' concluded the frog-footman proudly, 'this is the place to do it.'

'You're very fortunate,' I said, humouring him. 'Some people don't get to be ignored at all.'

'Don't I know it,' he replied, licking the end of his pencil and consulting his clipboard. 'Now, reason for visit?'

'I'm to see Mr Lockheed at Accident Investigations.'

The frog-footman consulted his clipboard.

'Correct. This way.'

The entrance hall was large and empty except for a round mahogany table in the middle, upon which stood a vase of flowers. The way to Herring's office took us past the ballroom, from which Jurisfiction's agents were given their instructions and posted to all corners of the BookWorld to face adversaries so dangerous that it was truly astonishing that anyone ever survived. I had been in there a few times when I had been a trainee of the real Thursday, but had not visited since I failed my training day. I slowed my pace as we passed, for the door was open, and I could see Jurisfiction's elite talking and laughing. I recognised Emperor Zhark, and a large hedge-pig that could only be Mrs Tiggy-Winkle. The Red Queen was there too, and several others.

The frog-footman coughed his disapproval, and we made to move on. But at that moment a short man in late middle age and dressed as a big-game hunter stepped out of the open door. He was wearing a pith helmet and safari suit, and across his body was slung a Sam Browne belt and holster, with the outfit finished off with a pair of brown leather riding boots. Since Thursday's disappearance, he was probably the third-most important person in the BookWorld after Senator Jobsworth and Red Herring. His name was Commander Bradshaw, and his expert guidance at Jurisfiction had kept the agency at the top of its game for almost as long as anyone could remember

– his exploits ensured that he was hardly ever off the front page of *The Word*, and his much-updated *BookWorld Companion* was the definitive work on the BookWorld, both before and after the Remaking.

He was deep in conversation with a youngish agent. I felt out of place, so looked straight ahead and quickened my pace. But he noticed me and without pausing for a second took me firmly by the arm and steered me to an alcove.

'Thursday,' he hissed in an agitated manner, 'why are you dressed in those ridiculous clothes and where in heaven's name have you been?'

'I'm not her, sir. I'm the one who looks after her series. I'm actually A8 V-67987-FP.'

He frowned, then stared at me for a moment.

'You telling me you're the *written* one?'

I nodded and he burst into laughter.

'Well, strike me pink!' he said. 'You gave me a turn and no mistake. I was – ah – expecting Thursday to be here any moment,' he added, looking at his watch in an unsubtle manner. 'I suspect she has been delayed.'

His explanation didn't ring true at all. Thursday was *definitely* more missing than he would like me to know. We returned to where Bradshaw's companion was waiting for us. He was studiously ignoring the frog-footman, who, for his part, was accepting the snub with quiet dignity.

'I'd forgotten just how identical you looked,' he said. 'Are you keeping well?'

'I am, sir,' I managed to mumble. 'I trust you are well read?'

It was a stupid gaffe; Bradshaw's brand of jingoistic imperialist Fiction hadn't been read for a half-century. But he took no offence.

'Not read any more, and quite right too.' He laughed, then stared at me for a while before saying to his companion:

'You've met the other Thursday, the real one?'

'Sure have,' he replied, 'one helluva goddam fine operative.'

'Look alike, don't they? Apart from the clothes, of course.'

'Like two peas in a pod.'

Bradshaw thought for a moment.

'Has Thursday been down to see you recently?' he asked me with an air of feigned nonchalance.

'Not since the Remaking, sir,' I replied. 'May I ask a question?'

'Of course.'

'Am I to understand that Thursday Next is . . . *missing*?'

'She's currently on leave in the RealWorld,' he said in a dismissive manner, 'enjoying some time off with her family before the peace negotiations on Friday.'

'Are you sure about that? I saw—'

I checked myself. I could get into big trouble for sneak-peeking the RealWorld, and the Lady of Shalott could get into bigger trouble for letting me.

'What did you see?' asked Bradshaw.

'Nothing. I must have . . . dreamed it. I'm very sorry to have wasted your time, sir.'

He looked at me for a long time, trying to divine what, if anything, I knew. Finally, he said:

'You are keeping the Thursday Next series dignified, I trust?'

'Yes, sir – even at the expense of readability.'

'Being read isn't everything. Some of the best people are hardly read at all. Listen,' he said thoughtfully, staring at me with his intelligent blue eyes, 'would you do something for me?'

'Of course.'

He didn't get to finish because a man draped in the white linen robes of the most senior senatorial office had walked briskly through the front doors of Norland Park and into the entrance hall in which we stood.

'Oh, craps,' said Bradshaw under his breath. 'Just what we need: Jobsworth.'

If he was over here in person, it would be for a very good reason – probably to do with the Racy Novel Peace Talks.

I thought of dropping to one knee and averting my eyes as the frog-footman had done, but for some reason I didn't. The Thursday part of me, I suppose. Jobsworth was not alone. As well as the usual phalanx of staff, hangers-on and deputies, there was Barnes, his executive assistant, Colonel Barksdale, the head of the Avoiding War Department, and Mr Herring, who was busy reading a report and hadn't yet seen me.

'Good morning, Bradshaw,' said Jobsworth. Bradshaw wished the Senator good morning, then the same to Mr Herring and Colonel Barksdale. Barnes was too far down the pecking order to be greeted, as were all the other members of Jobsworth's staff. The Senator made to speak, then saw me. His eyes opened wide.

'Great Panjandrum!' he said. 'Thursday?'

Bradshaw looked at me, then at the Senator. I opened my mouth to speak but Bradshaw held up a hand. In such company it was *strictly* speak-when-spoken-to. Protocol in the BookWorld was like grammatical rules – rigidly structured, arcane, and fiercely defended by librarians wielding wooden rulers with painful accuracy.

'No, Senator, it's the *written* version.'

'Truthfully?' asked Jobsworth. 'She looks an awful lot like her.'

'If she *was* the real one, do you think she would be here accompanied by that, that . . . what's your name?'

The frog-footman looked startled at being spoken to.

'Wesley,' he said in a quiet voice.

'Right,' said Bradshaw, not really listening, 'being shown around by Frog Guy? If this *were* the one, she'd be in the office discussing the peace talks and the Metaphor crisis.'

'I'll vouch that she's the written one,' said Herring, who had just looked up. 'Are you here on JAID business, Next?'

'I am, sir.'

'Then you can take your findings direct to Lockheed.'

It seemed a good moment to leave, so I bobbed politely and began to withdraw.

'Wait,' said the Senator. 'Bradshaw, why were you speaking to her if she's just the copy?'

For a fleeting moment, Bradshaw looked uncomfortable.

'I was asking her if . . . she could ask Lorina Peabody to head up the Talking Animal Division of Jurisfiction.'

'Who the hell's Lorina Peabody?'

'She's a dodo,' I said.

Jobsworth stared at Bradshaw suspiciously, and then at me.

'Introduce us,' he said after a pause.

'Very well,' said Bradshaw with a sigh. 'Senior Senator Giles Jobsworth, Head of Fiction and emissary to the Great Panjandrum, the written Thursday Next.'

'Hello,' he said, shaking me by the hand, and giving me the smile of someone who was considering how best one could be exploited.

'Honoured, Mr Senator, sir,' I replied dutifully.

Jobsworth was perhaps sixty or sixty-five, greying at the temples, and had the look of someone weighed heavily by responsibility. He stepped forward and put a finger under my chin. I should have been more overawed in his presence, but I wasn't. In fact, I had every reason to dislike him. When the Senior Senator had been merely a Senator, he had blocked my series from having Landen in it. He had said having no Landen was 'as the author intended', but that didn't really help, to be honest.

'It looks *exactly* like her,' he breathed.

'Like two goddam peas in a pod,' agreed Bradshaw's companion.

'I'm mirrored with her, Mr Senator,' I explained. 'The books were built using H-29 biographical architecture before they were moved to Fiction, so my looks are directly linked to hers. I age at the same rate, and even grow the same scars in sympath—'

'Fascinating. Does it have skills and an intellect to match, Commander Bradshaw?'

'It does not – nor any dress sense. What's your interest in an A8 copy of Thursday Next, Mr Senior Senator?'

'The interests of the Council are not necessarily the interests of Jurisfiction, Bradshaw.'

They stared at one another for several seconds. I expect this happened quite a lot. Jurisfiction was a policing agency, working under the Council, who were wholly political. I can't imagine they *ever* got on.

'Sir?' said Barnes, gently coaxing the Senator to stick to his schedule. 'You have a meeting.'

'Very well,' said the Head of Fiction, and strode off into the Jurisfiction offices with Herring, Barksdale and his entourage. Bradshaw stared at me for a moment, then told me I was excused. I needed no further bidding, and curtsied politely before hurrying off with the frog-footman.

'Well, thanks for that,' said the frog-footman sarcastically, 'you just ruined my six-year "being ignored by Commander Bradshaw" record.'

'He didn't remember your name,' I said, trying to be helpful, 'and was horribly insensitive when he called you "Frog Guy".'

'Well, okay,' said the frog-footman, 'that does take the sting out a little bit. But tell me,' he said, staring at me with his large protruding eyes and broad mouth, 'why did he call me Frog Guy?'

'I was up for Jurisfiction once,' I said, quickly changing the subject, 'but it didn't work out.'

'Me too,' replied the footman sadly; his mind didn't seem to pause on any one subject for long. 'I didn't make it past the "what is your name" question. You?'

'Training day. Froze when the going got tough. Nearly got my mentor killed.'

'To fail spectacularly is a loser's paradise,' said the frog-footman wistfully. 'This way.'

14

Stamped and Filed

'. . . Distilling Metaphor out of raw euphemism was wasteful and expensive, and the euphemism-producing genres on the island were always squeezing the market. Besides, the by-product of Metaphor using the Cracked Euphemism Process liberates Irony238 and dangerous quantities of alliteration, which are endowed with downright dangerous disposal difficulties . . .'

Bradshaw's BookWorld Companion, 9th Edition

We walked down the seemingly endless corridors, every door placarded with the name of the department contained within. One was labelled 'Old Jokes' and another 'Noun to Verb Conversion Unit'. Just past the offices of the Synonym Squad and the Danvers Union headquarters was a small office simply labelled 'JAID'.

'Right, well,' I said, 'I'll see myself out when I'm done.'

'I'm afraid not,' replied the frog-footman, 'I am instructed to escort you both in *and* out.'

So while the frog-footman sat on a chair in the corridor, I knocked on the door.

'Mr Herring told me you would be stopping by,' said Lockheed as I entered. 'Do come in, have a seat. Tea?'

'No, thank you.'

I looked around. The office was roomy, had a large window and was panelled in light pine. The pictures that decorated the walls all depicted a book disaster of some sort, mostly with Lockheed featured prominently in the foreground, grinning broadly. There was little clutter, and the single filing cabinet probably contained nothing but a kettle and some biscuits. Jurisfiction had finally managed to commit itself to a paperless office – all files were committed to the prodigious memory of Captain Phantastic, just down the hall.

'Impressive office, eh?' said Lockheed. 'We even have a window – with a view. Come and have a look.'

I walked over to the window and looked out. All I could see was a brick wall barely six feet away.

'Very nice,' I murmured.

'If you lean right out with someone hanging on to your shirt-tails you can almost see the sky but not quite. Would you like to try?'

'No thanks.'

'So,' said Lockheed, sitting down on his swivel chair and offering me a seat, 'something to report to Mr Herring about the accident?'

I swallowed hard.

'It was simply that,' I said, an odd leaden feeling dropping down inside me, 'an accident.'

Lockheed breathed a visible sigh of relief.

'Mr Herring will be delighted. When he hears bad news he usually likes to hit someone about the head with an iron bar, and I'm often the closest. Are you *sure* there is nothing to report?'

I wondered for a moment whether to report the Epizeuxis Worm, scrubbed ISBNs and the Vanity roots of *The Murders on the Hareng Rouge*. Not necessarily because it was the right thing to do, but simply to watch the eye-popping effect it might have on Lockheed.

'Nothing, sir.'

'Unprecedented and unrepeatable?'

'Exactly so.'

I felt the curious leaden feeling again. I didn't know what it was; I patted my chest and cleared my throat.

'Little cog, big machine,' said Lockheed as he filled out a form for me to sign. 'We are here to facilitate, not to pontificate. If we can sew this whole incident shut, the sooner we can get on with our lives and maintain our unimpeachable one hundred per cent dealt-with rate. Wheels within wheels, Thursday.'

'Wheels within wheels, sir.'

'Did you find out what the book was, by the way?'

'Not a clue,' I lied. 'I didn't find a single ISBN so I thought "Why bother?" and decided to simply give up.'

I didn't know why I was suddenly being sarcastic. It may have been something to do with the odd leaden feeling inside. Lockheed, however, missed the sarcasm completely. Most D3s did.

'Splendid!' he said. 'I can see you and Commander Herring will be getting on very well. You can expect a few more incidents heading your way with this kind of flagrant level of inspired lack of interest. Sign here . . . and *here*.'

He handed the form over and I paused, then signed on the dotted line. This isn't what Thursday would have done, but then I wasn't Thursday.

'Excellent,' he said, rising from his seat, 'I'll take this along to Captain Phantastic for memorising.'

'Why don't I take it?' I suggested. The odd leaden feeling in me had released a sense of *purpose*, but to what end I was not sure. 'You can stay here and have some tea and biscuits or something.'

I nodded my head in the direction of the filing cabinet.

'Goodness me, that is so *very* kind,' replied Lockheed, condemning the lost souls in the unknown book to eternal anonymity with a ridiculously large rubber stamp before handing the form to me. 'Fourth door on the left.'

'Right you are.'

I opened the door, thanked him again and found the frogfootman waiting for me in the corridor. I told him I had some filing to do and he led me past the doors marked 'Piano Division', 'Italics' and 'Pebbles (Miscellaneous)' before we got to a door marked:

'Records'. The frog-footman told me he'd wait for me there, and I stepped inside.

The room was small and shabby and had a half-dozen people waiting to be seen, so I sat on a chair to wait my turn.

'Thursday Next,' I said to the gloomy-looking individual sitting next to me, who was reading a paper and seemed to have a toad actually *growing* out of the top of his head. The pink skin of his balding pate seemed to merge with the browny-green of the toad. 'The copy,' I added, before he asked. But the man ignored me. The toad growing out of his head, however, was more polite.

'Ah,' said the toad, 'a good copy?'

'I do okay.'

'Humph,' said the toad, before adding: 'Tell me, do I look stupid with a human growing out of my bottom?'

'Not at all,' I replied politely. 'In fact, I think it's rather fetching.'

'Do you really?' said the toad with a smile.

'Who are you talking to?' asked the man, looking up from his paper.

'The toad.'

The man looked around.

'What toad?'

'What did the man just say?' asked the toad.

'I like your books,' said the woman on the other side of me. 'When are we going to see some more?'

'Five is all you'll get,' I said, happy to get away from the man-toad. 'What are you seeing Captain Phantastic for?'

'I'm head of the Metaphor Allocation Committee,' she explained. 'Once we move to the Metaphor Credit Trading System, those books with an excess of Metaphor will be able to trade it on the floor of the Narrative Device Exchange. Naturally, more complex figurative devices such as Hypothetical Futures and Analogy & Simile

Trust Funds will have to be regulated; we can't have Hyperbole ending up as overvalued as it was – the bottom dropped out of the Litotes market which, as anyone will tell you, was most undesirable.'

'*Most* undesirable,' I remarked, having not understood a word, 'and how will Captain Phantastic help with all this?'

She shrugged.

'I just want to run the idea past him. There might be a historical precedent that could suggest Collateralised Metaphor Obligations might be a bad idea. Even so,' she added, 'we might do it anyway – just for kicks and giggles. Excuse me.'

While we had been talking Captain Phantastic had been dealing with each enquiry at lightning speed. This was not surprising as the Records Office did not rely on anything as mundane as magnetic storage, paper filing or even a linked alien super-mind. It had in its possession instead a single elephant with a prodigiously large memory. It was efficient, simple, and required only buns, hay and peanuts to operate.

When it was my turn I walked nervously into his office.

'Hello,' said the elephant in a nasally-trumpety-blocked-nose sort of voice. I noticed he was dressed in an unusual pinstripe three-piece suit, unusual in that not only did it have a fob-watch the size of a saucepan in the waistcoat pocket, but had the pinstripes running horizontally.

'So, how can I help?'

'Jurisfiction Accident Investigation Department,' I said, holding up my shield. I paused as a sudden thought struck me. Not about elephants, or even of a toad with a man growing out of its bottom, nor of the volatile Metaphor market. I suddenly thought about *lying*. Of subterfuge. It was wrong but in a *right* kind of way, because I had finally figured out what the leaden feeling was. It was a deficiency of Right Thing To Do – and I needed to remedy the shortfall, and fast.

'We're investigating a crashed book out in Aviation,' I said, tearing up the accident report behind my back, 'and we need some background information on *The Murders on the Hareng Rouge* by Adrian Dorset.'

'Of course,' trumpeted the elephant, 'take a seat, Miss—?'

'Next. *Thursday* Next. But I'm not—'

'It's all right,' he said, 'I know. I know everything. More even than the Cheshire Cat. And that's saying something. I'm Captain Phantastic, by the way, but you can call me "The Captain". You and I haven't met but the real Thursday and I go back a ways – even partnered together during the whole sorry issue surrounding *The Cat in the Hat III – Revenge of the Things*. Did you hear about it?'

'I'm sorry, I didn't.'

'No matter.'

And he sniffed me delicately for a moment with his trunk.

'Do you have a chicken living in your house?'

'A dodo.'

'Would that be Lorina?'

'We call her Pickwick these days, but yes.'

'Tell her that Captain Phantastic is still waiting for that date she promised.'

I wasn't aware that Pickwick dated elephants – or anyone, come to that.

'Did she promise you recently?'

'Eighty-six years, three months and two days ago. Would you like me to relate the conversation? I can do it word for word.'

'No thanks. I'll give her the message.'

The Captain leaned back on his chair and closed his eyes.

'Now, *The Murders on the Hareng Rouge*. I try to read most books, but for obvious reasons those in Vanity I delegate. So many books, so little time. Listen, you don't have a bun on you, do you? Raisins or otherwise, I'm not fussy.'

'I'm afraid not.'

'Shame. Okay, well, there's not much to tell, really. *The Murders on the Hareng Rouge* was a junker on its way to be scrapped.'

I wasn't expecting this.

'I'm sorry?'

'It was a stinker. One of the very worst books ever written. Self-published by one Adrian H. Dorset, who, as far as we know, has not written anything else. He printed two copies and comb-bound them in his local print shop. Semi-autobiographical, it was the story of a man coming to terms with the death of his wife, and how he then immersed himself in work to try to take revenge on the person he thought responsible. Flat, trite and uninspiring, the author burned it as a form of catharsis. By rigid convention, the version here in the BookWorld had to be scrapped before sundown. Did it hurt anyone?'

'Only the people in it.'

'It should have been empty,' said the elephant. 'Scrapped books always have the occupants reallocated before the book is torn apart.'

'We found the remains of *someone*.'

'How much?'

'A thumb.'

The elephant shrugged. 'A hitchhiker, perhaps?' concluded Phantastic. 'Or reformed graphemes?'

'We thought the same.'

'In any event, that's all I have.'

'You're sure it was a junker?' I asked, trying to figure out why anyone would risk almost certain erasure by deleting the ISBNs and then using demolition-grade Epizeuxis to destroy an unreadable book from Vanity that was destined to be scrapped anyway.

'Completely sure.'

I thanked Captain Phantastic for his time, promised to bring some buns next time, and walked out of his office, deep in thought.

'You were in there a while,' said the frog-footman as he escorted me from the building.

'The Captain likes to talk,' I said. '"Hannibal said this, me and Dumbo did that, Horton's my best friend, I was Celeste's first choice, she took Babar on the rebound" – you know what it's like.'

'After Madame Bovary,' said the frog-footman, rolling his eyes, 'the Captain is the worst name-dropper I've ever been ignored by.'

I went and found Sprockett in the local Stubbs. He had got chatting to a Mystical Meg Fortune-Telling Automaton and discovered that they were distantly related.

'I've got you a fortune-card, ma'am,' said Sprockett. 'Archie was a great-great-uncle to us both, and Meg's father-in-law is Gort.'

'Nice chap?'

'So long as you don't get him annoyed.'

I looked at the small card he had given me. It read: 'Avoid eating oysters if there is no pay cheque in the month', which is one of those generic pieces of wisdom that Mechanical Mystics often hand out, along with 'Every chapter a new beginning' and 'What has a clause at the end of the pause?'

Sprockett hailed a cab and we were soon trundling off in the direction of Fantasy.

'Did all go as planned, ma'am?' he asked as we made our way back out of the genre on the Dickens Freeway.

I paused. It was better if Sprockett didn't know the investigation was covertly still running. Better for me, and better for him. Despite being a cog-based life-form, he could still suffer at the hands of inquisitors, and needed deniability. If I was going to go down, I'd go down on my own.

In ten minutes I had told him everything. He nodded sagely, his gears whirring as he took it all in. Once I was done he suggested that we didn't tell anyone as Carmine might tell the goblin and Pickwick was apt to blurt things out randomly to strangers. Mrs Malaprop we didn't have to worry about – no one would be able to understand her. Besides, she probably already knew.

'The less people that know the better.'

'Fewer. The *fewer* people that know the better.'

'That's what I meant.'

'That's what *who* meant?'

'Wait – who's speaking now?'

'I don't know.'

'You *must* know.'

'Damn. It must be me – you wouldn't say "Damn", would you?'

'I might.'

We both sat there for an empty moment, waiting for either a speech marker or a descriptive line. It was one of those things that happened every now and again in the BookWorld – akin to an empty, pregnant silence in the middle of an Outland dinner party.

'So,' said Sprockett once we had sorted ourselves out, 'what's the plan?'

'I don't know our next move,' I said, 'but until I do, we do nothing – which is excellent cover for what we should be doing – nothing.'

'An inspired plan,' said Sprockett.

The taxi slowed down and stopped as the traffic ground to a halt. The cabby made some enquiries and found that a truckload of *their* had collided with a trailer containing *there* going in the opposite direction, and had spread there contents across the road.

'Their will be a few hiccups after that,' said the cabby, and I agreed. Homophone mishaps often seeped out into the RealWorld and infected the Outlanders, causing theire to be all manner of confusions.

'I know a short cut through Comedy,' said the cabby, who was, purely as an irrelevant aside, an anteater named Ralph. 'It shouldn't be too onerous – the risibility is currently at thirty yards and the mirth-rate down to 1.9.'

'What about puns?'

'Always about, but they're not funny, so the chance of unbridled hysteria is low.'

Trips through Comedy were usually avoided as the giggling could be painful and sometimes fatal, but the comedy in Comedy had been muted of late. I told him to go ahead and we pulled out of the traffic and drove off in the opposite direction.

'What kind of man sets fire to a busload of nuns?' I asked, Whitby still annoyingly on my mind.

'I cannot answer that, ma'am, but I suspect one who is neither kind, nor considerate.'

There was a pause.

'May I ask a question as regards the subject of empathy, something I am at a loss to understand?'

'Of course.'

'Since I have neither set a nun or puppy on fire nor gleefully pushed an old lady downstairs, does that make me kind and compassionate?'

'Not really,' I replied, 'it makes you normal, and respectful of accepted social rules.'

'But not compassionate?'

'To be compassionate you have to demonstrate it in some sort of act that shows you care for someone.'

'Care for someone? Care as in how a butler cares for someone?'

'More than that.'

'I'm not sure I can envisage any greater care than that which a butler can offer.'

And he sat and buzzed to himself in such deep thought that I had to give him two extra winds, much to the cabby's sniffy disapproval.

We entered Comedy a few miles farther on by way of the

Thurber Freeway, then took a funny turn at Bad Joke and bumped along a back road of compacted mother-in-law one-liners. We passed the Knock–Knock quarry, where we were held up for a few minutes while they did some blasting, then continued on past Limericks, Amusing Anecdotes and Talking-Horse Gags to the empty wilderness known as the Burlesque Depression. The huge influx of stand-up comedians in the RealWorld had overjoked the stocks of natural glee, and the stony comedic landscape was now almost barren. As an emergency measure, unfunny comedy sneakily branded 'alternative' was now flooding the RealWorld until the natural stock of jokes had replenished itself. The lack of comedy in Comedy was no laughing matter.

Almost from nowhere a car shot past us at speed and, as it did so, swerved violently. The cabby attempted to avoid a collision and spun the wheel hard to the left. He over-corrected, slewed sideways and hit the fence at the side of the road. There was a crunch as splintered wood flew everywhere, the windscreen crazed and the taxi thumped down the short embankment, ran across some rough ground and came to rest against a tree with a clatter and a hiss.

'Are you okay?' I asked. Sprockett nodded, even though I could see he had a crack in his porcelain face. The cabby looked a bit shocked and was about to open his door when I placed a hand on his shoulder.

'Wait. Don't anyone move . . . I think we've driven into a mimefield.'

15

The Mimefield

'Books moving from Non-Fiction to Fiction was uncommon, but it did happen. The most recent immigrant was *I Got Beaten Every Day for Eight Years by My Drunken Father* from Misery Memoirs, when it was discovered the author had made most of it up. By all accounts *Eight Years* had to leave in disgrace, tail between bruised legs, but I think the cast was secretly delighted. There is nowhere more depressing than Misery Memoirs, and the few visitors it has are usually characters-in-training who have a tricky scene to do in Human Drama and need some inspiration . . .'

Bradshaw's BookWorld Companion, 10th Edition

Sprockett and the cabby looked outside. Surrounding the car were five hundred or so mimes, all dressed uniformly in tight black slacks, a stripy top, white face paint and a large hat with a flower stuck in the top. They were miming in the most terrifying fashion, their hideous faces contorted with exaggerated expressions, their bodies moving in a frighteningly sinuous movement that denied written description. The cabby panicked and started the engine. It burst into life and he popped the car into reverse.

'Hold it,' I said looking out of the rear window, 'you can't go backwards – there's a mime stuck inside a pretend glass cube just behind you. Wait – he's out. No, hang on, there's another, bigger pretend glass cube outside the smaller one.'

The cabby started to sob.

'Calm down,' I said, 'panic is the mind-killer. We can get out of this alive if we keep our heads straight. Turn the engine off.'

We looked outside as the mimes, now curious, moved closer. I almost cried out as one looked in the car while he was doing a routine with a balloon that was heavy, then light, then immovable.

'What are they doing?' asked the cabby, his voice tremulous with rising fear. 'I don't understand.'

Comedy was one of those genres that, while appearing quite jolly, was actually highly dangerous. In order to generate new jokes, the custodians of the genre had tried to use non-written and non-verbal comedy as a growing medium. Mimes had no real home in a written or spoken canon, but some of their movements and actions could cross-fertilise with others that did. Slapstick was used for the same effect, as was a well-timed look, a comedy pause and silly expressions, voices and walks.

'Don't move,' said Sprockett. 'Mimes don't generally attack unless they are threatened.'

'How do you threaten a mime?'

'By sighing during a performance, looking away, rolling your eyes – that sort of thing. Mimes hate being ignored or having their performance interrupted. In that respect, they're almost as touchy as poets.'

We did as I suggested and looked on as the mimes continued their strange movements, and we laughed and applauded at the right moment. Some of the mimes appeared to hardly move at all and adopt poses like statues, and others seemed to be walking against the wind. There was also a lot of going in and out of doors that weren't there, canoeing and pretending to walk up and down stairs. It was all *very* mystifying. Mind you, I was worried about just how long we could laugh and applaud. Every moment we paused, they became dangerously aggressive once more.

After another five minutes of this odd posturing, the cabby couldn't take it any more. He flung open his door and made a run for it. We watched with growing horror as the unfortunate taxi driver was suddenly copied in his every movement and expression.

Two mimes walked close behind him while another engaged in some curiously expressive banter. Within half a minute it was all over, and the cabby's bloodied clothes were all that remained upon the ground.

I looked at Sprockett, whose eyebrow flicked up to 'Doubtful', which meant he was out of ideas. Now that they had been blooded, the mood of the mimes seemed to have changed. A minute ago their features had been ridiculously smiley, but now they wore doleful expressions of overblown sadness. They also seemed to be approaching the car. Once they got in, it would be all over. Or at least, it would for me.

'Lean forward.'

'Might I enquire as to why, ma'am?'

'I'm going to press your emergency spring release,' I said. 'You'll be nothing to them but an inert box of cogs – they'll not touch you. Someone will chance across you in a few months and you can be rewound. You can tell them what happened.'

He looked at me and buzzed quietly in thought.

'Would that be a compassionate act on your behalf, ma'am?'

'I suppose so. Only one of us need die.'

Sprockett thought about this for a moment.

'I'm sorry, ma'am, but I may have to politely decline your offer. A butler never leaves his position and is loyal until death.'

I made a grab for the access panel on the back of his left shoulder but he caught my hand with surprising speed.

'In this matter, ma'am,' he said firmly, 'my cogs are made up.'

I agreed and Sprockett let go of my arm as several mimes improvised a trampoline routine on the back bumper.

'Okay,' I said as a sudden thought struck me, 'here's the plan: I need you to act like a robot.'

'How do I do that?'

'You tell me. *You're* the robot, after all.'

'Don't anyone move . . . I think we've driven into a mimefield.'

'Agreed. But the whole point of the Duplex series is that we *act* human in order to function more seamlessly with our masters. "More human than the dumbest human" is the Duplex Corporation's motto. I don't know the first thing about actually *being* a robot.'

'You're going to have to give it your best shot.'

Sprockett raised his eyebrow as a shower of broken glass erupted from the rear window. The mimes had become markedly more aggressive when we didn't laugh or applaud hard enough during a not-very-amusing routine where they pretended to sculpt a statue out of clay.

'Very well,' said Sprockett. He opened the car door and stepped out. His gait was sporadic and clumsy, and at the end of each movement, there seemed to be a slight 'spring' to his actions that gave the impression of increased mass. The effect upon the mimes was instantaneous, and dramatic. They all took a step back and gazed in wide-eyed astonishment as Sprockett lumbered from the car with me close behind. A few of them dropped to their knees and others fell into paroxysms of exaggerated crying.

'What do I do?' whispered Sprockett. 'I can't keep this up for long.'

'Head back towards the road.'

So he did, and I followed him. The mimes stayed with us, their grief and sadness changing to anger and surprise. Sprockett continued, his limbs flailing in short staccato movements. It wasn't working. The mimes closed in and, just when their white gloves were upon us, they suddenly paused and exhibited the sort of mock surprise you can feign by opening your mouth wide and placing both hands on your cheeks. The reason for this was soon apparent. One of their number had started to *copy* Sprockett in a series of similar robotic moves. Uncertain at first, the moves soon gained fluidity until his gestures exactly matched Sprockett's. Within a few seconds the 'robot' idea had spread among them like a virus, and the field was full of five hundred or so mimes, all acting like robots. As soon as they were all distracted in this fashion I yelled 'Run' and we sprinted back to the road.

'Well,' said Sprockett, stretching the barbed quip-wire back across the hole in the fence to keep the five hundred or so mimes from escaping, 'I think that was a close-run thing, ma'am. Might I congratulate you on your quick thinking?'

'Let's just say it was a team effort.'

He bowed politely, and I sat on a rock by the side of the road to regain my composure. I looked around. The dusty track was empty in both directions, and aside from the books drifting silently overhead and the now robotic mimes, the only signs of life were corralled Jokes of Questionable Taste sitting silently in fenced-off areas a little way distant.

'Did you get a good look at that car that passed us?' I asked.

'Yes, ma'am. I believe it was a 1949 Buick Roadmaster.'

'Men in Plaid?'

'So it would appear. Their capacity for causing us harm and annoyance seems not to be abating.'

I saw it more simply: *they had just tried to kill us.* The only question that remained was: 'Why?' and more worryingly: 'How much longer before they succeed?'

Just then a rattly pick-up stopped opposite us. The bearded driver was staring at us with an amused twinkle in his eye. He was a Funnster, one of a hardy breed of crusty old men and women who spent their days trapping gags and taking them to market.

'Have an accident?' he asked.

It was the height of bad manners in Comedy to decline a feed-line when offered, so I had to think quickly.

'No thanks,' I replied, 'we've already had one.'

The Funnster laughed, took off his hat and mopped the sweat from his brow. He looked for a while at the mimes, who had evolved their new 'robot' idea into robots going downstairs, robots canoeing, robots getting stuck inside glass cubes and robots walking against the wind.

'Looks like you may have started something,' said the Funnster with a chuckle, climbing out of the cab and rummaging for a net and a baseball bat in the flatbed. 'Wait here.'

A few moments later we were bowling down the road towards the local railway station, sitting in the back of the flatbed. On one side of us there was a mime who was miming a robot being trapped inside a net while *actually* being trapped inside a net, and on the other side of us a mature Austrian gentleman with a beard, a small hat and the look of someone who was trying to figure out what we were thinking, and why we were thinking it. After considering us for a moment he leaned forward and said:

'How many Sigmund Freuds does it take to change a light bulb?'

'I don't know,' I said. 'How many?'

'Penis,' said the Freud, then quickly corrected himself. 'I mean father. No, wait! One. One Sigmund Freud. All it takes. Yes. *Verflucht und zugenäht!*' He added gloomily, '*Wenn ich nur beim Aalsezieren geblieben wäre!*'

16

Commander Bradshaw

'**Perils for the unwary #231: The Literalism.** Usually a result of substandard wiring in the Synonym distribution box or a ripple in the contextual flux, the Literalism can appear randomly, without warning. Example: one of the loan sharks inside *Get Shorty* turned out to be a three-ton Great White with "Hertz Shark Rental" stamped on the side, and it was all the cast could do to keep a straight face and carry on as though nothing had happened. Peril rating: Medium-high. Action: Walk away.'

Bradshaw's BookWorld Companion, 5th Edition

We were dropped off at Cooper Central, thanked the Funnster and said farewell to Freud, who had become all wobbly and tearful. We bought some tickets and then gave them to the fez-wearing inspector, who hailed us with the customary 'Just like that' before directing us to our carriage. Within a few minutes the train was steaming out of the station and towards Fantasy.

We weren't the only people in the compartment eager to get out of Comedy. A small man who wore the off-duty fatigues of a foot soldier enlisted in the Clown Army was looking about nervously and sweating. You could tell he was off duty because he wasn't wearing his bright red nose and his long shoes were carefully strapped to his kitbag.

'What's your unit?' I asked.

'6th Clown,' he said nervously, 'Supply and Gigglistics. We deploy next week to Bawdy Romp, the buffer zone between Comedy and Racy Novel. Purely as a precaution, you understand. I'm on leave and certainly not stealing military equipment, no ma'am.'

And he stared at his feet, leaving Sprockett and me to wonder what he *was* stealing, and whether it was hazardous. The Clown Army's supply division was notoriously porous, and sneeze and itching powder often found its way into the wrong hands, such as Blyton separatists – always an angry mob.

'I hope your deployment goes well.'

'Thank you,' said the clown, and stared out of the window.

We sat in silence for a while.

'Ma'am?' asked Sprockett, who had been buzzing quietly to himself in the corner.

'Yes?'

'Why do you think we were attacked?'

'Because of what we know.'

'But who knows what we know? Others have to *know* that we know. Just *us* knowing it isn't enough – unless we attacked ourselves, which isn't likely.'

I thought carefully. There were at least half a dozen people who might have had an idea that the investigation wasn't totally open and shut, all the way from Captain Phantastic to Pickwick/Lorina. But it was also possible we were being silenced for some other reason entirely, an accident or even a textual glitch, such as happens from time to time in the BookWorld.

'The attempt on our life *might* have been a lexicographical Literalism,' I said. 'After all, comedians often "kill" their audiences or "die" on stage, and the phrases "you'll be the death of me" and "it was so funny I could have died" might all have colluded to cause us harm.'

I was fooling myself. Although Buick Roadmasters *did* exist independently of the Men in Plaid, it seemed too suspicious to ignore. Besides, running people off the road was something that occurred in Crime, where it would be unusual to drive five miles without it happening at least twice. It was much more unlikely in Comedy. Or at least, not without a punchline. But then again, maybe my 'no thanks, I've already had one' *was* the punchline. Comedy was never straightforward. When all the good jokes had left, only the dubiously amusing stuff remained. Was the mimefield funny or not? To us, I think not. But it might have been funny to *someone*.

I stared out of the window, thinking about my current predicament. I had a junker on its way to the scrapyard from Vanity that someone had destroyed, then tried to cover their tracks in case of discovery. The accident had been handed to the least skilled accident investigator for a quick and easy resolution, and I had almost been murdered by the Men in Plaid. I had compounded my difficulties by lying to Lockheed and gaining intelligence from Captain Phantastic under false pretences, and I had not only failed to deliver a legal accident report, but had destroyed it. If I were found out I would be confined to my series and as likely as not lose Carmine and possibly Sprockett as well.

It was a good moment to pack it all in, accept the level of my own incompetence and start concentrating on what should be my primary goal: increasing readership of the Thursday Next series. Thursday, after all, could look after herself – she had done so on numerous occasions. If I shared my plans with Sprockett, I reasoned, it would be an affirmation of my resolve, and harder to go back on.

'Sprockett?'

He started out of 'stand-by mode' with a buzz.

'A cocktail, ma'am?'

'No, thank you. It's just that I've decided to . . .'

I sighed and rubbed my temples.

'Decided to what, ma'am?'

'Nothing.'

And I slumped down into my seat, cursing the Thursday in me.

The train slowed to a halt at the border between Fantasy and Comedy and the off-duty clown started fidgeting.

'Identification, please.'

One of the border guards was standing at the doorway, and we all rummaged for our identification papers.

'I'll deal with this,' said a familiar voice, and Commander Bradshaw appeared in the corridor. He flashed his own ID at the border guard, who saluted smartly and moved on. Sprockett and I both stood up politely, as did the clown, who didn't want to be left out.

'Please,' said Bradshaw, 'sit down.'

'What's this, a joke?' he asked, indicating the clown once we had all sat and Sprockett had offered Bradshaw a cocktail.

'A lance corporal in the 6th Clown,' I said, 'Supply and Gigglistics.'

'Oh yes?' said Bradshaw with a smile. 'And what would you be smuggling across the border?'

The clown sighed resignedly and opened his kitbag to reveal boxes of Military Grade Custard Pies. He wasn't a very good smuggler. Few were.

'It's shankers for you, my lad,' said Bradshaw sternly. 'CPs are banned in every genre outside Comedy. I'd turn you in but I'm busy. If you can dispose of them all before we get to Gaiman Junction, I'll overlook it.'

'How would I do that?'

'Do you have a spoon in your kitbag?'

So while the off-duty clown began to eat his way through four dozen custard pies, Bradshaw explained what he was there for.

'*Please* don't ask Lorina to contact me,' he said, 'that was just for Jobsworth to hear.'

'I figured.'

'Is she still a colossal pain in the butt, by the way?'

'Getting worse, if anything.'

Bradshaw looked at Sprockett, who took the cue and shimmered from the compartment with the clown, who was already on his ninth custard pie and groaning quietly to himself. Sprockett returned momentarily with the Chicago Fizz he had mixed for Bradshaw, then departed again.

Bradshaw leaned forward, looked to left and right and whispered:

'Are you her? The real one, I mean?'

'No.'

He stared at me for a while.

'Are you sure? You're not doing some sort of deep-cover double bluff or something?'

'Yes, quite sure. I think I know who I am.'

'Prove it.'

'I can't. You'll have to take my word for it. Believe me, I wish I was.'

Bradshaw seemed satisfied with this, and stared at me for quite some time. He wasn't here on a social visit.

'What can I do for you, sir?'

'The thing is,' he began, taking a sip from his Chicago Fizz, 'that we're in a bit of a pickle here in the BookWorld what with Speedy Muffler and the whole Racy Novel debacle. Add to that the dwindling Metaphor issue, the eBook accelerators using a disproportionate amount of Text Grand Central's throughput capacity, and all the other day-to-day whatnot we have to handle, and I'm sure you'll appreciate that we need the real Thursday now more than ever. Do we agree?'

'We do.'

He sighed and ran his fingers through his hair.

'She was due to go as the Jurisfiction delegate to the Racy Novel Peace Talks on Friday. I'll have to send Emperor Zhark instead, and his negotiating skills are more along the lines of: "Annihilate first, ask questions later", but without the "ask questions later" part.'

'She may turn up.'

He shook his head.

'I knew she was going undercover, but she said she'd check in without fail. She didn't. That's not like her. She might be stuck in a book somewhere, lost in a book somewhere – even held against her will. The possibilities are endless.'

'If she was lost, wouldn't she have a Textmarker™ homing beacon on her?'

'True – but textual sieve coverage is patchy even on Fiction, and absent entirely across at least two-thirds of the BookWorld. We've sent unmanned probes into the most impenetrable tomes at Antiquarian and dispatched agents into almost every genre there is – nothing. The BookWorld is a big place. We've even considered that she might be in the DRM.'

I raised an eyebrow. If they were considering this, they really were desperate. The DRM was the Dark Reading Matter – the unseeable part of the BookWorld.

'It's been almost two weeks,' continued Bradshaw, 'and I fear the worst might have happened.'

'Dead?'

'Worse – retired back to the RealWorld.'

He stopped and stared at me. It wasn't just Thursday's absence from Jurisfiction that he was worried about; he had lost a good friend, too. Thursday trusted Commander Bradshaw implicitly. I thought I should do likewise.

'I sneak-peeked the Outland yesterday,' I said. 'I realise it was wrong. But it seemed to me that Landen was missing her too.'

Bradshaw raised an eyebrow.

'Truthfully?'

'Yes, sir.'

He took a sip of the cocktail, set it down and strode about the compartment for some minutes.

'Look here,' he said, 'desperate situations call for desperate measures. I want you to talk to Landen and see if you can find anything out. Perhaps find her in time for the peace talks.'

'Talk to Landen? How can I do that?'

'By travelling to the RealWorld.'

My heart nearly missed a beat.

'You're joking.'

'No joke, Miss Next. In fact, I'll tell you a joke so you'll know the difference. How many Sigmund Freuds does it take to change a light bulb?'

'I've heard it.'

'You have? Blast. In any event, you look *exactly* like Thursday – the best cover in the world. And what could possibly go wrong?'

There was actually quite a lot, but before I could itemise the first sixteen, Bradshaw had moved on.

'Splendid. All transfictional travel has been strictly banned this past eighteen months so you'll be doing this covertly. If anyone finds out, I'll deny everything. Most of all, you can't tell anyone from the Council of Genres. If Jobsworth or Red Herring finds I've been breaking the transfictional travel embargo, they'll want to send their own representative. And I can't have that. Do you understand?'

'Yes, but—'

'Then that's all agreed,' said Bradshaw, handing me a signed authority. 'This will give you access to Norland Park to see Professor Plum on the pretext of adding eBook accelerators to your series. He'll know why you're there. I'll also contact my deep-cover agents to offer you every assistance in the Outland. Any questions?'

I had several hundred, but didn't know where to start. Bradshaw took my silence to mean I didn't have any, and shook me by the hand.

'Good to have you on board. Twelve hours in the RealWorld isn't long, but enough to at least get an idea of what's happened to her. I could send you out for longer, but Thursday has many enemies in the RealWorld, and they'll be on to you pretty quick.

If you die out there you die for real, and I'm not having that on my conscience. Shall we say tomorrow morning? Oh, and officially speaking, I was never here.'

'You were never here.'

'Good show. Appreciate a girl who knows they weren't somewhere. Oh, and thank your man for the Chicago Fizz, will you – but next time, a little less gherkin. Cheerio.'

And without another word he opened the outside door, a motorcycle drew alongside the train, Bradshaw hopped on to the pillion and was gone.

'Might I enquire of madam what that was all about?' asked Sprockett, who returned with a very ill-looking clown.

'A little too much gherkin in the Chicago Fizz.'

'He came all the way over here just to tell you that?'

'No – I'm going to the RealWorld to look for Thursday so we can get her to the peace talks on Friday.'

'In that case,' said Sprockett, 'I'd better lay out your things. Will madam be staying long?'

'Twelve hours.'

'I'll pack you a toothbrush, a scrunchie and some clean socks.'

'I'd be grateful.'

I spent the rest of the journey fretting about my trip to reality. It was only a twelve-hour trip – barely a flash in and out – but that wasn't important. What *was* important was that I would meet Landen in person, and although the notion of that filled me with a tingly sensation of anticipation, his rejection of me when he found out I wasn't his wife would be – well, not pleasant for him and me. I almost thought of not going. Bradshaw couldn't exactly punish me for not doing something he hadn't told me to do. But then there was the possibility that I might help to find Thursday, and that filled me with the same sense of purpose I had felt when I had lied to Lockheed and Captain Phantastic.

I sighed inwardly. Life was easier when I was just a character in a book, going from Preface to Acknowledgements without a care in the world.

Within another twenty minutes the train steamed into Gaiman Junction and we took the bus home.

'You're back,' said Pickwick, who liked to open any conversation by pointing out the obvious.

'Yes indeed,' I replied, 'what's the news?'

'My water dish is empty.'

'That's because you just trod in it.'

Pickwick looked at her foot.

'I have a wet foot . . . and my water dish is empty.'

'Anything else?'

'I saw Carmine with that goblin again. Sitting in the *niche d'amour* at the bottom of the garden, they were.'

'As long as she doesn't invite him over the threshold again, I'm not bothered.'

'You should be. Goblins. *Nasty*. Full of diseases.'

'That's Carmine's lookout. I told you: I'm not bothered.'

Actually, I was. I had tried to give Carmine a dressing-down for her poor choice in men but she just stared at me and retorted that, yes, Horace *might* be a thief, but at least he hadn't set fire to a busload of nuns.

'Any news of Whitby?' I asked.

'Being questioned in custardy,' replied Mrs Malaprop, who had walked in with a clipboard full of reports that all needed my signature. 'His pasta is catching up with him. How were things at Jurisfiction?'

I didn't tell them what had happened as it was safer that way.

'Captain Phantastic said you owed him a date,' I said to Pickwick.

'The Captain?' she said with a fond smile. 'I'm amazed he remembers – it was a long time ago. We were both young and foolish, and I'd do anything for a dare. Ah, Frederic – so many cats, so little recipes.'

'*Few* recipes.'

'What?'

'So many cats, so *few* recipes,' I said, pleased that I had figured out who had been talking earlier.

Pickwick looked at me disdainfully, muttered 'Amateur' and marched out.

'The investigation is still on,' I said to Mrs Malaprop as soon as Pickwick had gone, 'but keep it under your hat, will you?'

'Squirtainly, ma'am. I found this note pinned to the newel post.'

> *Gone to find Horace, back in half an hour.*
> *PS: I don't care what Pickwick thinks.*

'Horace?'

'The goblin.'

I wasn't particularly annoyed with Carmine for chasing after the goblin – as long as he wasn't invited back in again – but I *was* very annoyed that she had gone AWOL. It meant that for the past ten minutes, there was no one here to play Thursday. If word had got out there might have been a panic from the other characters, and it was against at least nine regulations that I could think of.

'Do we report her as absinthe without leaf?' asked Mrs Malaprop.

I scrunched up the note. Reporting her as missing would get Jurisfiction involved, and Carmine would probably be shipped off to spend the next decade in *Roger Red-Hat*.

'No,' I said, 'but let me know the moment she gets back so I can give her a rocket.'

Sprockett knocked and entered, his eyebrow pointing firmly at the 'Worried' mark.

'Excuse me, ma'am, but the Men in Plaid are back.'

'So soon? You'd better admit th—'

'Thursday Next?' said the first of the MiPs as he walked in the door.

'Yes?'

'You're coming with us,' said the second.

'I can't leave the series,' I said, 'my understudy is on her lunch.'

'That's not what the board says,' observed the first, pointing at Carmine's status on the indicator board, which was now blinking an orange 'at readiness' light, despite the fact that she was out looking for Horace. 'Is she AWOL?'

'No,' I lied.

'Then she's in?'

'Yes,' I lied again.

'Then you can come with us.'

I looked at Mrs Malaprop and Sprockett. They knew what needed to be done – find Carmine at the earliest opportunity.

The Man in Plaid who seemed to be in charge jerked a thumb in the direction of the front door and we walked outside. Predictably it was a Buick Roadmaster, but that wasn't the end of the story. The left-hand mudguard was dented and streaked with yellow paint – the sort of yellow paint that taxis are painted in. This was the car that forced us off the road and into the mimefield.

'Am I in some sort of trouble?'

'You are if you don't come with us.'

17

The Council of Genres

———

'The Council of Genres is the administrative body that look after all aspects of BookWorld regulation. From policy decisions in the main debating chamber to the day-to-day running of ordinary BookWorld affairs, supply of plot devices and even the word supply coming in from the Text Sea. They control the Book Inspectorate, which governs which books are to be published and which to be demolished, and also manage Text Grand Central and Jurisfiction.'

Bradshaw's BookWorld Companion, 11th Edition

I sat between the Men in Plaid in the back, which was uncomfortable as they seemed to have a plethora of weapons beneath their suits, all of which poked me painfully in the ribs.

'So,' I said brightly, doing what I hoped Thursday would do – show no fear. 'How long have you been in plaid?'

'It's not plaid. It's tartan.'

'Right,' said the second one, 'tartan.'

And despite more questions of a similiar nature, they declined to talk further. I hoped to goodness Mrs Malaprop and Sprockett managed to hunt Carmine down in time for the early evening readers.

We drove past Political Thriller on the Ludlum Freeway and made our way towards the towering heights of the Great Library, and I guessed where we were headed. On the twenty-sixth floor would be the Council of Genres and Senator Jobsworth, the man from whom the Men in Plaid ultimately drew their authority, and like Bradshaw, he must have figured out a way in which a Thursday Next lookalike could be exploited.

The security was even tighter here, and the Roadmaster slowed to negotiate the concrete roadblocks and high anti-bookjump mesh. We were waved through with only a cursory glance and drove slowly across a narrow bridge and into the Ungenred Zone. This was an area of independent narrative-free space where the governing body of the BookWorld could exist free from influence and bias. Or that was the theory, at least. I'd been a few times to the Council of Genres, but only with the real Thursday. Ordinary citizens didn't come here unless strictly on business. If we wanted to pretend we had influence we could take any grievances to our Genre Representative and they would intercede on our behalf – or so the theory went.

'Where are you taking me?' I asked.

'Senator Jobsworth is gracing you with an interview.'

'That high, huh?'

Having the Great Library and the Ungenred Zone on Fiction Island was not without problems. Theoretically speaking, if it was located here then it must be potentially readable by the RealWorld population, something which the CofG were not happy about. If it became common knowledge that there was a text-based realm on the other side of the printed page, hacking into the BookWorld would be a far bigger problem than it was already. The Outlander corporation known as Goliath had been attempting to find a way in for decades, but aside from their transfictional tour bus quaintly named 'The Austen Rover' and the occasional Bookhacker, the independent existence of the BookWorld remained secret.

Even so, Council officials were taking no chances and the entire Ungenred Zone was rendered invisible to potential Bookhackers by the simple expedient of not being written about. At least, not directly. The adventures in my own series hinted at a BookWorld but it was heavily fictionalised, since the ghost writer had no collaboration from Thursday when writing them. There was only the vaguest reference to the Great Library, and nothing about Jurisfiction or the Council of Genres. Despite this, some of the more talented readers in the Outland had managed to hack into the zone by exploiting a hole in the defences that allowed one to 'read between the lines'. To counter this, the CofG had all the borders covered in Soporific paint the shade of young lettuces, which worked a treat. Every attempted incursion into the Ungenred Zone was met by drowsiness followed by an almost instantaneous torpor on the part of the potential hacker. It had exactly the same effect as the emergency 'Snooze' button, except that no kittens were ever hurt or injured.

The Roadmaster drove up to the BookWorld's main port, where the Metaphoric River joined the Text Sea by a series of locks, weirs, traps and sluices. The port was large, and several hundred scrawl-trawlers rode gently in the swell, grammasites wheeling above the mast-tops, hoping to dart down and snatch a dropped article.

On the dockside was the day's catch. Most scrawlers simply netted the words that basked upon the surface for a quick and easy sale to the wordsmiths, while others deep-trawled for binary clause systems, whereby a verb and a noun had clumped together in a symbiotic relationship to form a proto-sentence. But even these hardened scrawlers were in awe of those who hunted fully formed sentences. These weather-beaten text-seadogs would sail far across the Text Sea in search of an entire paragraph, descriptive zinger or even an original comedy monologue – the elusive *Moby Shtick* that legends speak of.

Facing the docks and beyond the coils of ropes, nets, harpoons and infinitive-splitters were several rows of single-storey workshops where the words and letters were crocheted, knitted, sewn, glued, riveted or nailed together into sentences, depending on the softness of the prose for which they were destined. The completed sentences were either rough-sorted into bundles and sold direct to the Well of Lost Plots or woven into 'standard paragraphs' on power looms, the nouns, verbs and adjectives left loose so the end-user could make their own choices.

The Buick pulled to a stop outside the main entrance of the Great Library and we climbed out. The Library was housed in a towering Gothic skyscraper that stood as a reminder of the Book-World before it was remade. Back then the area below the Great Library was simply unexplored jungle. All of that was swept away in the nine minutes of the Remaking. The BookWorld may be slow when it comes to changing fashions and storytelling conventions, but it can rebuild itself in a flash if required.

I paused for a moment. It was impossible not to be impressed by the Great Library, and this in a world noted for its superlative structures, settings and depth. Just by way of example, the landscape inside *Lord of the Rings* was *so* stunning and *so* stupendous that it could be absorbed as a form of nourishment. The huge tourism opportunities within the trilogy had been long understood and exploited, and even though the battles were exciting and fun to watch, most people went only for the valleys, rivers, waterfalls, crags, trees and moss.

I stepped into the lobby of the Library, and paid my respects to those names on the Boojumorial – a marble tablet that commemorated Jurisfiction agents from both the Real and BookWorlds who lost their lives in the protection of the written word. They may have been carbon or text based, but here they were equal; no preference was given to the real over the imaginary. My companions, however, owing to either indifference or long acquaintance with the Honoured Erased, paid it no heed at all. We walked towards the circular void that ran through the building, and I looked up. Twenty-six floors above us, the glazed roof was just visible. Twenty-six floors of every book that had ever been written, and here logged faithfully in alphabetical order for mostly serial continuity purposes.

It wasn't necessary to have the Library any more, but it paid to have a back-up in case something went wrong. And something always *did* go wrong. Although infuriating, it was unavoidable. With all the drama to hand, it was inevitable that the BookWorld would spontaneously erupt into intrigue which would then set off a chain reaction of unexpected consequences. If the BookWorld were itself a book, it would be self-writing.

I looked down. Below me were the twenty-six basements that made up the Well of Lost Plots – the place where all books are built. As I looked I could see flashes of light as inspiration fired off in small bursts of energy. A really good idea could burn brightly for many months, and give nearby books-in-progress much-needed warmth.

We entered the lift, and I felt myself grow increasingly apprehensive as the ancient device slowly clanked its way to the top. The Senator's summons may have been related to Bradshaw's recent request, our chance meeting in Norland Park, or something else entirely – I had no idea. The lift doors opened and the CofG opened out in front of us, a seething mass of offices, desks, meeting rooms and people scurrying back and forth in a ceaseless quest to keep the BookWorld running as efficiently as possible. The chamber was bigger in here than it appeared from the outside, but nothing was particularly linear or even logical within the BookWorld; the fabric of imagination is elastic, and that was reflected within the Council of Genres.

I passed the big viewing windows, where I had stood with the real Thursday when she was my mentor, and peered out at a Book-World that appeared deceptively orderly. Because I was quite high and the island dished to fit snugly on the inside face of the sphere, I could clearly see every part of it, from the volcanoes in the far north all the way down to Vanity Island off the southern tip. I could even see my own series as a dark smudge in the distance.

I was escorted away from the viewing windows and walked past the public gallery above the debating chamber. There was a session in progress, and although conducted in **Courier Bold**, the antiquated yet universal language of the BookWorld, I could make out that it was a discussion about the possibility of Text Sea levels rising owing to the advent of eBooks. I'd heard about this issue. The argument went that because eBooks were composed almost entirely of electrons and barely any ink and paper at all, the scrawltrawlers' work would be cut by 90 per cent overnight, and there would be possible inundation of the low-lying areas of the BookWorld – essentially Maritime and Disaster. This argument was countered by another delegate, who maintained that eBooks were the way of the future, and since the power of a book is undiminished irrespective of the carrier medium, no such panic was necessary. Still another delegate suggested that the advent of eBooks might actually *increase* the demand for new material and thus cause a shortage of words – something which the BookWorld must be prepared for by the construction of more scrawltrawlers and the training up of extra scrawlermen. All three were experts, and all three had conflicting views. I was reminded of Clarke's Second Law of Egodynamics: 'For every expert, there is an equal and opposite expert'.

'Come on,' said one of the Plaids, 'we're not bleeding tour guides.'

We walked down a corridor, past more security, then arrived at an opulent antechamber with expansive views across the Book-World.

'Miss Next?' said a friendly clerk holding a clipboard. 'The Senator will see you now.'

18

Senator Jobsworth

'**Dark Reading Matter: The hypothetical last resting place of books never published, ideas never penned and poems held only in the heart by poets who died without passing them on.** Theoretical Bibliologists have proved that the Background Story Radiation was appreciably more than the apparent quantity of STORY in the BookWorld. No one had any idea where it might be, or how you could reach it. DRM's existence remained theoretical, at best.'

Bradshaw's BookWorld Companion, 4th Edition

The Senator was seated behind his desk as I was ushered into his office. Several men and women dressed in the uniform of almost every military conflict there was were in attendance, as well as a couple of high-ranking generals, Colonel Barksdale and Mr Herring.

'Would you excuse us?' said the Senator, and everyone except Red Herring and Colonel Barksdale filed out, looking at me suspiciously as they did so. I stood in front of Jobsworth's desk while he finished what he was doing. I didn't know which book he had come from, but wagging tongues suggested he was an illegal immigrant from Quackery, a sub-genre within Lies & Self-Delusion, just off the north coast. I don't think anyone ever raised it with him, or if they did, no answer was forthcoming. It didn't really much matter since Jobsworth had been the overall leader of the Council of Genres for as long as it had been in existence, and his unassailable position looked set to continue for long into the future. He had the ear, apparently, of the Great Panjandrum himself, who could fix almost everything when he had a mind to.

'They say she's dead, you know,' said Jobsworth, striding to the large window in his office which looked out over the BookWorld, the islands of the various categories of books patches of verdant green against the dark slatey-grey of the Text Sea. 'Killed in the Outland, killed in the BookWorld – who knows. What do you think?'

'I have no opinion on the matter, sir. I just play her in the series.'

'You must have *some* idea?'

I looked across at the chief-of-staff, who was gazing at me intently. 'No.'

Jobsworth stared at me for a long time, then grunted and looked outside his office again. But this time he wasn't looking at the larger BookWorld, but the island of Fiction below him. Crime was just to the north, but the areas I knew best – Adventure, Fantasy and Sci-Fi – were situated in the south-east, out of sight. It was Herring who spoke next.

'Ever been up-country?'

'I've been to Crime.'

'Farther. Towards Racy Novel.'

'No.'

'So there is a good chance they haven't seen you up there? Or even know about you?'

I suddenly had a very unpleasant feeling, and turned back to Jobsworth.

'What is it you want me to do, Senator?'

'A small favour. I wouldn't ask you if it wasn't important. And if you do this for us, I'm sure it will stand in your favour if you reapply to join Jurisfiction.'

I was right. If that was the carrot, I could be in for some serious stick.

'It's nothing too onerous,' added Colonel Barksdale, who had so many campaign medals on his chest that he was probably bullet-proof, 'it simply requires you to take Thursday's place at the peace talks on Friday.'

I was momentarily lost for words. I should have tried to extricate myself, but I had paused too long.

'Splendid,' said Jobsworth, and crossed to a scale model of the island which was built on a large oak table. 'Let me give you some background.'

'Would you excuse me?' said Herring. 'I have to revise the upcoming Linguistic Hygiene Bill if we're to have any chance of rejecting it.'

'Thank you, Red.'

Herring wished me good day, thanked me for my selfless adherence to duty and walked from the room. Jobsworth beckoned me closer to the large model of the island, where the topography was perfectly realised in miniature, along with the individual genres with their borders, railway networks, major rivers and capital novels. He swept his hand in the direction of the northern genres.

'You've heard about Speedy Muffler's threats to the peace talks on Friday?'

I said that I had.

'Speedy Muffler claims to have developed a dirty bomb,' announced Jobsworth with a grimace. 'A loosely bound collection of badly described scenes of a sexual nature. The detonation of such a bomb could cause untold damage, flinging wholly gratuitous sex scenes as far as *Mrs Dalloway*.'

'But has he really?' I asked, since the possession of the bomb was only conjecture, much like Comedy's claim to be experimenting with a fifty-megaton-yield Malaprop device.

'Do you know,' said Jobsworth, 'it doesn't matter. Feminist and Dogma are taking the threat seriously and are massing armies on the border ready to take pre-emptive action ahead of the peace talks. And we can't have that.'

'Invasion?' I said. 'What would Feminist and Dogma do with Racy Novel?'

'They'll simply push the rogue genre up north towards Porn and DeSade. *Fanny Hill*, *The Story of O* and *The Adventures of Tom Jones* will be annexed back into Classics, and the territory shared between them. Comedy will still insist upon the buffer zone of Bedroom Farce, and since Comedy is regarded with a certain sense of reluctant admiration by Romance and Dogma, they'll not want to go any farther.'

He took a deep breath.

'But we can't risk that kind of disruption. The genres might take months to rebuild to current strength, and the prose will suffer terribly. With the advent of eBooks in the Outland, this is not a good time to have a cross-genre war. The battle between Sci-Fi and Horror all those years ago has left its mark; their reputation as serious literature has still to recover completely – and the civil war inside Fantasy has left the reading public with an entirely unwarranted dismal view of the genre. I can't have Romance and Female Crime marginalised in the same way – it's 43.9 per cent of our readership.'

'I'm not sure what I can do,' I said. 'I'm not much good at negotiating. I tend to want everyone to simply hug and make up.'

'I'm not asking you to *do* anything, you little fool. We're putting it about that you – the *real* Thursday – have irritable vowel syndrome and can't speak, so Emperor Zhark will be doing the talking. You'll just sit there and nod and look serious. Muffler might be a troublemaker, but even he will knuckle under if he thinks Thursday Next might be annoyed if he shouts too loudly. How about it?'

He was asking too much. No, it was more than that – it was *insane*, even by Council of Genre standards. If Muffler found out I wasn't her, things might get even worse, and I wasn't going to have a cross-genre war on my conscience.

'I may have to politely decline,' I said.

He stared at me for a moment, then opened a buff file on his desk.

'Hmm,' he said, 'looks like we have a lot of illegal narrative flexations in your series, doesn't it?'

'I'm playing Thursday as Thursday wants me to.'

'We only have your word for that. There is also a possible charge of your understudy consorting with undesirables, and most seriously: you harbouring an illegal alien from Vanity.'

He meant Sprockett.

'We call it Self-Publishing these days.'

'Immaterial. We'll be taking the Metaphoric River route up-country via paddle steamer. I'll have a car pick you up on Friday morning at seven. Are we agreed?'

I took a deep breath.

'Yes, sir.'

'Excellent!'

He pressed a button on his desk.

'Miss Next, you must also understand that in matters of Book-World politics like this, it is essential you do not speak to anyone, *especially* that busybody Bradshaw. Jurisfiction have a twisted vision of the good work we do at the Council, and I don't want him to get the wrong idea. Do you understand?'

If there was any lingering doubt that the CofG and Jurisfiction distrusted each other, it was dispelled. Neither wanted the other to know what they were asking me to do. The clerk came back in and I was escorted from the building by the same two Men in Plaid who had brought me there.

In a very short time I was deposited back at my front door, and the Roadmaster pulled silently away. Sprockett was waiting for me in the hall, his single eyebrow pointer clicking alternately between 'Quizzical' and 'Uncomfortable'.

But he knew what to do.

'Can I interest ma'am in a Ludlow Scorcher?'

I told him a cocktail would go down very well so long as he went easy on the parsley, and related what had just happened with Jobsworth. I decided not to mention the threats he had made regarding Sprockett and Carmine, but *did* mention the fact that I would be going up-country on Friday – and also the dent and streak of yellow paint on the Men in Plaid's Buick Roadmaster.

'The fact they haven't tried to kill us again tends to indicate they believe that we have abandoned the investigation,' said Sprockett, handing me the cocktail. 'Are you sure it was *our* yellow paint on the side of their Roadmaster?'

'What else is painted yellow in the BookWorld?'

As soon as I said it I suddenly remembered something. I stood up and quickly walked to the double garage at the bottom of the garden, Sprockett close behind.

'Ma'am?' he said as I swung open the double doors and started to poke among the bookjunk for what I was looking for. I found it easily enough; the back axle that had once been painted yellow. There was no sign of an ISBN, scrubbed or otherwise.

'It wasn't from *The Murders on the Hareng Rouge*,' I said excitedly, 'it's from a TransGenreTaxi. There was a cab attached to *Murders* when it went down, piggybacking from one part of the BookWorld to another. The sabotage might not have been aimed at the book at all – *it might have been aimed at whoever was in the cab!*'

'Or both,' said Sprockett, annoyingly muddying the waters.

'Or both,' I agreed.

'Where *is* the rest of the cab?' asked Sprockett.

'Who knows? Either vaporised or embedded somewhere in the unread backwaters of Thriller. Here's the deal: you're going to call the TransGenreTaxi offices and find out about any missing cabs, and

I'm going to find out more about *The Murders on the Hareng Rouge* and Adrian Dorset.'

'But where, ma'am? If Captain Phantastic doesn't know, it's unknowable.'

'In the RealWorld, Sprockett. Cheers.'

I tried the Scorcher. It wasn't too bad. A bit loamy for my taste but otherwise good.

I went upstairs and packed a small holdall. A few clothes and some spare underwear – I'd heard all the scare stories – then worried about whether to take my pistol or not, but eventually did. After that I dithered over taking ammunition, and decided to, but only one cartridge and of the armour-piercing variety. I argued to myself that I would be too scared to use it, so wouldn't. I gave Carmine some last-minute instructions in case of emergencies, ignored her protestations about 'having to face more readers than she was happy with' and then ordered a cab.

'If I have to press the Snooze button,' said Mrs Malaprop as I waited, 'it's on your conch-seance not mine.'

'Agreed.'

'Where to?' asked the cabby when he pulled up ten minutes later.

'Norland Park,' I said, '*Sense and Sensibility*. Any route you like.'

But at that moment someone else got in the cab by way of the opposite door. He was wearing a large floppy hat which partially obscured his features.

'Sorry,' I said, 'cab taken.'

The other passenger lifted the brim of the hat so I could see his face. It was Whitby.

'It's okay,' I said to the cabby, and we moved off.

'Holy cow!' I said, turning to Whitby. 'You've got a nerve. When were you going to tell me about setting fire to that busload of nuns? Two years I spent building myself up to a date, and then I find that you're a homicidal maniac.'

'*Lots* of people are homicidal maniacs,' he replied. 'Throw a stick into Crime and you'll hit six of them.'

'But we're not in Crime, are we?'

He stared at me for a moment.

'I've done lots of good in my life, Thursday – helped people to narrative independence, coached generics through entrance exams, was EZ-Read's "Employee of the Month" three months running, and I even helped little old ladies across the road – some when they actually wanted to go. Do I get credit for that? No. All you want to think about is the nuns.'

'*Orphaned* nuns,' I reminded him.

'Actually, it was the puppies who were orphaned,' he said petulantly. 'Let's stick to the facts here.'

'Does it matter?'

'Not really. But I don't think that one teensy-teensy incident with a small busload of nuns and puppies should taint a man's life.'

'I think it does, Whitby. You might have told me.'

'I couldn't.'

'Why?'

He sighed.

'You remember Dermot McGruber? EZ-Read's rep over in HumDram?'

'Yes.'

'He wanted to impress a girl. But he'd done some seriously bad shit when he was a character in Crime.'

'The nuns?'

'Right. With a backstory like that hanging around his neck and guilt consuming his every moment, he couldn't even *begin* to get a date. So I said I'd look after his backstory for the weekend so he could ask her out, guilt free and with an easy heart.'

'That was generous of you.'

He shrugged.

'He helped me out once when I over-ordered some EZ-Read PlotHoleFiller. I owed him. A weekend of overpowering guilt seemed easy enough. I could keep myself to myself, get totally hyphenated and no one need ever know.'

'Let me guess,' I said, 'he's legged it.'

Whitby nodded as the cabby changed down a gear and moved on to the Dickens Freeway.

'I don't know where Dermot's gone. In fact, I think he might have been planning this for a while. I feel such an idiot – and what's more, I think he put Jurisfiction on to me. You won't tell them, will you?'

'Not yet, but I will. You can't set fire to people – nuns or other-wise – and expect to get away with it.'

'I know,' he said sadly, 'it weighs heavily on my conscience. The yapping, oh, the *yapping*.'

I sat in silence for a moment. The thing about a backstory is that once you've taken it on, it's true and real, irrespective of who owned it before you. You could move it on, of course, but it was understandably tricky. Who wants a busload of burning nuns and puppies on their conscience?

'So what do you want?' I asked.

'I just wanted to see you,' he said simply, 'and hear your voice.'

'Well, now you have,' I replied, a bit more harshly than perhaps I should have. 'Maybe we should say goodbye.'

'I'm living over in Hemingway if you need anything,' he said, not wanting to give up on the slimmest chance a date wasn't still possible, '127, *To Have and Have Not*. If you need anything, just whistle. You can drop me on this corner, driver.'

The cabby pulled up and Whitby got out. He told me to take care and then hurried off around a street corner. The taxi moved on and I slumped back into my seat as we turned on to Austen Boulevard. I thought of turning him in, then of not turning him in. It was a tricky call but, luckily, the least of my worries.

I wasn't feeling that good about the trip, to be honest. A nervy, sickly feeling was festering in the pit of my stomach – and not just from the difficulty of making the move across, nor what I might find there or the truth about *The Murders on the Hareng Rouge*. Notwithstanding the recent developments with Whitby, I was most worried about meeting Landen. He was the man I was written to love and never meet. And I was going to meet him.

19
Juristech, Inc.

———

'**The Juristech museum is open Monday to Friday, half-days Wednesdays.** A whole range of technologies both past and present are on display, including an impressive array of Book-World weaponry, grammasite traps, word dams, eject-o-hats, textmarkers, grapheme-splitters and Noun to Verb alchemic technologies. On Tuesdays there is a technical demonstration of the Textual Sieve (not to be missed).'
Bradshaw's BookWorld Companion, 3rd Edition

I turned up at the front gate of *Sense and Sensibility* and showed the guards the authority given to me by Bradshaw. They rang through and spoke briefly to Juristech before I was once more issued with a docket and ushered in. At the front door I met the frog-footman, who was surprised to see me again so soon.

'You again?' he said, staring at the docket. 'What do you want with Juristech?'

Fortified by the mission entrusted to me by Bradshaw, I was no longer so frightened of him.

'None of your business,' I replied, and his face lit up. This was more how he liked it.

'Labs or office?'

'Labs.'

He guided me through the long corridors of Norland Park, down several flights of steps and in an elevator or two before we stopped outside an inconspicuous door with two milk bottles outside.

'The Juristech labs,' announced the frog-footman. 'My instructions are to wait for you.'

'It'll be a long wait. Pick me up in twelve hours. Here,' I said, handing him a Rubik's Cube, 'see if you can figure this out.'

The frog-footman stared at the cube curiously. All six faces were quite naturally the same colour, and all was orderly and neat.

'You have to try to make it random,' I said, 'by twisting the faces.'

The frog-footman twisted the faces in a fairly haphazard manner, but try as he might, every face remained the same colour. For a BookWorld puzzle, it was a classic. The lack of randomness within the orderly structure of the BookWorld tended not to permit disorder. As far as I knew, no one had yet managed to scramble a Rubik's, but I thought it might pass the time for him.

'Thank you,' replied the frog-footman, and sat cross-legged on the floor, twisting the cube this way and that as he tried to scramble the faces.

I knocked on the door, and it was soon answered by a small man in a brown boiler-suit that was liberally covered in oil stains, food and science merit badges.

'Good Lord!' he said when he saw me. 'Thursday? Come inside quick.'

Once safely away from the prying ears of the frog-footman I explained who I was – or more importantly, who I wasn't – and showed Professor Plum the authority from Bradshaw.

'Did he give you a codeword?'

'What?'

'A codeword.'

'The Commander didn't say anything about a codeword.'

'Correct. There is no codeword – but only Bradshaw would know that. Follow me.'

The basement was twice the size of a cathedral and quite full to capacity of machinery. An army of technicians scurried around looking purposeful while lights blinked on and off as arcs of electricity discharged into the air at regular intervals.

'That's mostly for effect,' explained Plum as we moved among the machines. 'It's sometimes important to have a machine's form and function in equilibrium. Who wants an Italiciser that can be carried around in the pocket? Much better to have a large device that flashes lights randomly and occasionally goes "bzzz".'

I agreed, even if I'd never *seen* an Italiciser, much less *used* one. 'All this technology,' I mused. 'Is there any limit to what you can do?'

'If there is we haven't found it,' replied Plum. 'We can figure out most technologies, and those that we can't are subcontracted to Technobabble™ Industries, who can usually cobble something together. The good thing about being in the BookWorld is that we aren't hobbled by anything as awkward as physical laws. The Real-World must be an arse to do science in, but given how difficult it is I suppose breakthroughs are of greater value. In here, for example, perpetual-motion machines are quite feasible.'

'What's stopping us using them?'

'Finding a way to make them *stop*. Once we've figured that out, we'll have perpetual engines in every minicab and bus in the Book-World.'

He paused while I stared at a machine that could transform dark humour to sarcasm and then back again with no loss of narrative mass.

'As you know,' continued Plum, 'the Council of Genres permits us to suspend the rules of physics in order that we can develop the somewhat unique technologies that the BookWorld requires. See this?'

We had stopped next to a large machine that seemed to be nothing but a riveted tube about a yard thick running the entire length of the workshop. It appeared through one wall and then vanished out the other. If I didn't know any better I would have thought it a throughput pipe or footnoterphone conduit.

'This is just a small part of the Large Metaphor Collider.'

'What does that do?'

Professor Plum stopped for a moment at the control panel.

'You know we've got a serious Metaphor deficit at present?'

I nodded. The problem was well documented. Most of Fiction's rhetorical power, dramatic irony and pathos was brought by the mighty Metaphoric River that snaked about the island. But the huge influx of novels in the past century had exacted a burden on the waterway as the much-needed Metaphor was abstracted on a massive scale, and these days it was no longer considered possible that the river could supply all of Fiction's requirements, and hence the trade in raw Metaphor and Juristech's attempts to synthesise it.

'This collider,' continued Professor Plum, 'will take depleted Metaphor – simile, in effect – and accelerate it in a circular trackway over eighteen miles long to a velocity approaching ninety-five per cent of Absurd, at which point it will be collided with Indisputable Fact. There is a brief flash of energy as the two opposing modes of communication are fused together and then explode in a burst of high-energy sub-comprehension particles. We then record the event as traces on a sheet of Basildon Bond writing paper.'

'The flimsy blue variety?'

'*Exactly*. In this manner we not only hope to figure out the individual building blocks of STORY in order to have a better understanding of how it all works, but also use it as a way of extracting usable quantities of Metaphor from even the most prosaic, tired or clumsily constructed simile.'

'Does it work?'

'I was just about to test it. You can help, if you want.'

I said I would be delighted, and Plum pointed me in the direction of a lidded crucible that was steaming gently to itself.

'You'll find some tongs and gloves over there – I need that simile in the accelerator chamber.'

186

The crucible was not steaming from heat, but from cold. Liquid nitrogen was keeping the raw simile in an inactive state. So much so that I couldn't tell what it was, as the meaning and allusion were all contracted and frozen into one lump. I put on the gloves and, using the wooden pincers, placed the simile in the acceleration chamber.

'Excellent,' said Plum, who closed the door and then spun a wheel on the front to effect a secure lock. He then pressed a button and there was a low humming noise which gradually increased in pitch as the simile started to move around the accelerator. There was a dial marked 'Absurd Velocity', and the needle began to rise as the simile zipped round at ever increasing speeds.

'The Council of Genres are very keen to have this up and running as soon as possible,' he said, staring at the dials carefully. 'Synthesising Metaphor is the Holy Grail of the BookWorld, if you don't count finding the Holy Grail, which confusingly is *also* the Holy Grail of the BookWorld.'

The Large Metaphor Collider had by now wound itself up to a whine so high pitched that I couldn't hear it, and all the equipment on the desk was vibrating. As the needle nudged up to .95 Absurd, Plum took a deep breath and pressed the Red Button, which instantaneously brought Indisputable Fact into the path of the absurdly fast simile.

It was difficult to describe what happened next. The machine changed from being something akin to an engine with a throttle stuck wide open to a Brave New Dawn. I saw the Clouds Open, and the Rain Stop. The Lark Ascended and I saw St John on the island of Patmos, and a New Heaven and a New Earth. I saw . . . but in another second those feelings had vanished, and all we were left with was the collider, humming down to speed.

'What was that?' I asked.

'A sudden flash of pure Metaphor,' replied Plum excitedly. 'This kind of event usually liberates about 120 PicoMets.'

'Is that safe?'

'Don't worry,' he said with a smile, 'the background Metaphor level is about 50 PicoMets, and a fatal dose up around the 40 MilliMet mark. You'd have to do something daft to read that, although there have been accidents. A few years ago a colleague of mine was experimenting with a few grams of dead Metaphor when it went critical. He was bathed in almost 100 MilliMets, and started barking on about "Prometheus, stealing fire from the gods" before he exploded into a ball of fire and ascended into the night sky, where he could be seen for many weeks, a salutary lesson on the dangers of playing with Metaphor. Wrecked the laboratory, too. Let me see.'

Professor Plum pulled the single sheet of Basildon Bond from the annihilation chamber and looked at it, brows knitted. The paper had recorded the sub-word particles. Some were dotted, others coloured, and some hatched. There was even a legend at the bottom explaining what each one meant. Fiction has no time for lengthy and potentially confusing data analysis, so experimentation is always followed by easily interpretable and generally unequivocal results.

'That's Alliteration,' said Plum, tracing the various paths with his finger, 'Anaphora, Epistrophe, Epizeuxis, Analepsis, Hyperbole and Polyptoton.'

In all, he could list twenty-nine sub-meaning particles, but of pure Metaphor there was no evidence at all.

'You felt it, though, didn't you?'

I answered that I had. A feeling of a new dawn, and old things being swept away.

Plum stared at the paper for a long time. So long, in fact, that I thought he might have gone to sleep standing up and might need catching when he fell over.

'Well,' he said at last, 'back to the drawing board.'

'But we felt something, didn't we?' I said.

'Without proof, we've got nothing,' he said in a resigned voice.

'Perhaps Metaphor has no mass. If so, I'm very surprised – although it might explain why Dark Reading Matter is undetectable. It could be mostly Metaphorical. Come on. Let's get you real.'

The Professor led me to the back of the workshop, past the entrance to a scrubbing device for de-clichéing otherwise healthy idioms, and down a corridor to a door obscured by several discarded packing cases and a stack of unread copies of the almost fatally dull *Juristech Review*.

'We haven't used the Jumper for over eighteen months,' he explained, struggling with the padlock, which had grown rusty with age, 'not since the imaginatively titled "RealWorld Travel Ban" banned all travel to the RealWorld.'

'Why the ban?'

'I didn't ask and neither should you. If anyone at the CofG gets wind of this, you and me are nothing but Text.'

I didn't like the sound of this.

'But Bradshaw—'

'Bradshaw is a good man,' interrupted Plum, 'but in matters like this, he'd deny he even knew you. And me. And himself, if it came to it. I agree with him. To maintain the integrity of Jurisfiction, I would accept being reduced to a bucket of graphemes. And so should you.'

He left me thinking about this and pulled open the door. He paused, the interior of the lab a dark hole.

'You can leave now if you want to.'

'No, I'm okay,' I said, even though I wasn't. 'Let's just get on with it, yes?'

He turned the dark off and the blackness faded down to reveal a large room that was musty and hung with cobwebs. Occasionally there was a low rumble, and dust trickled from the ceiling.

'The Carnegie Underpass,' explained Plum. 'It runs directly over-head.'

In the middle of the room was a large machine that looked like a collection of sieves, each lined up one in front of the other. The sieves began with one that might have been designed to make chips so long as you could hurl a potato at it fast enough, and the rest were of rapidly decreasing mesh, until the penultimate one was no more than a fine wire gauze. The last of all was a thin sheet of silver that shimmered in the microscopic currents of air that moved around the workshop. Beyond this was the wide end of a copper funnel with the sharp end finishing in a point no bigger than a pin – and beyond this, a small drop of blue something-or-other within a localised gravitational field that kept it suspended in the air. Around the room were an array of computers covered with more dials, levers, switches and meters than I had ever seen before.

'What exactly is it?' I asked, not unnaturally, and with a certain degree of trepidation.

'It's the Large Textual Sieve Array,' he explained. 'Although the construction and methodology of Textual Sieves remain generally unexplained, they can be used for a number of functions. Cross-triangulation searches, the "locking" of text within books – and more controversially, for making fictional people real, even if for only a short period.'

'How long?'

'I can send you out for forty-eight hours, but Bradshaw insisted you went for only twelve. As soon as that time is up you'll spontaneously return. We'll send you in at midday, and you'll be out at midnight – pumpkin hour. If you want to stay longer you'll have to Blue Fairy, but then you're there for good and have to suffer the worst rigours of being real – growing old, death and daytime television.'

The twelve-hour pumpkin option suited me fine and I told him so. I'd heard many stories about the RealWorld, and although it sounded an interesting place to visit, you'd not want to live there.

'So how does it work?'

'Simplicity itself. You see this howitzer?'

He pointed at a large-calibre cannon that was pointed directly at the sieves. It was mounted on a small carriage and was gaily decorated with red stars and had 'The Flying Zambinis' painted on the side.

'You are placed in this cannon and then fired into the array at .346 Absurd speed. The mesh of the first sieve is quite broad, to break down your base description into individual words. The next breaks the words down into letters, and then the letters are divided further into sub-calligraphic particles until you hit the silver sheet, which has holes in it one tenth the size of a polyptoton. After that,' he concluded as he tapped the large funnel, 'your descriptive dust is compressed in the Pittmaniser to a concentrated pellet of ultra-dense prose, where the several thousand words of your description take up less space than one millionth of a full stop. Put it another way – if all Fiction were compressed to the same degree, it would take up the space of an averagely sized rabbit.'

'I like comparative factoids like that.'

'Me too. This tiny speck of you is then injected at speed into a drop of AntiBook where your essence is rebuilt into something closely resembling human. By controlling the Sieve Array I can drop you wherever you want in the RealWorld.'

'Does it hurt?'

'Quite a lot, actually,' he admitted, 'but only fleetingly. You'll barely have enough time to scream before it will be over. The return is not so dramatic. You'll simply find yourself in our arrivals suite, which is just behind that door.'

'Do you have any advice?'

'I've never been there myself,' confessed Plum, 'but they say if you can handle the first ten minutes you're good for the whole twelve hours. If you can't hack it, then just find a quiet wardrobe in which to hide until the free-return brings you back.'

I found his comments disconcerting.

'What is there one might not be able to handle?'

Professor Plum made a clicky noise with his tongue.

'It's highly disorderly,' he explained, 'not like here. There is no easily definable plot and you can run yourself ragged wondering what the significance of a chance encounter can be. You'll also find that for the most part there is no shorthand to the narrative, so everything happens in a long and painfully drawn-out sequence. Apparently, the talk can be confusing – in general, most people just say the first thing that comes into their head.'

'Is it as bad as they say it is?'

'I've heard it's worse. Here in the BookWorld we say what needs to be said for the story to proceed. Out there? Well, you can discount at least eighty per cent of chat as just meaningless drivel.'

'I never thought the percentage was *that* high.'

'In some individuals it can be as high as ninety-two per cent. The people to listen to are the ones who don't say very much.'

'Oh.'

'There are fun things too,' said Plum, sensing my disappointment. 'You'll get used to it in the end, but if you go out there accepting that seventy-five per cent of talk is utter twaddle and eighty-five per cent of people's lives are spent prannying around, you won't go far wrong. But above all, don't be annoyed or distracted when random things happen to absolutely no purpose.'

'There's always a purpose,' I said, amused by the notion of utter pointlessness, 'even if you don't understand what it is until much later.'

'That's the big difference between here and there,' said Plum. 'When things happen after a randomly pointless event, all that follows is simply unintended consequences, and not a coherent narrative thrust that propels the story forward.'

I rolled the idea of 'unintended consequences' around in my head.

'Nope,' I said finally, 'you've got me on that one.'

'It confuses me too,' admitted Plum, 'but that's the RealWorld for you. A brutal and beautiful place, run for the most part on passion, fads, incentives and mathematics. A *lot* of mathematics.'

'That's it?' I asked, astonished by the brevity with which Plum could sum up the world that had, after all, made us.

'Pretty much,' he replied glumly, 'and some very good cuisine. And the smells. You'll like those, I assure you. And real sex – not like the oddly described stuff we have to make do with in here.'

'I assure you I'm not going to the RealWorld for the sex.'

'When tourism was permitted, many visitors used it for little else. Anything that is impossible to describe adequately in the Book-World was much sought after, and coincidentally, usually beginning with C: Cooking, Copulation, Caravaggio, Coastlines and Chocolate. Will you do me a favour and bring some back? I adore chocolate. As much as you can carry, in fact. And none of that Lindt or Suchard muck – Cadbury's the thing.'

I promised him I would, and he opened the hatch at the back of the cannon.

'Good luck,' he said. 'Don't worry if it seems a bit odd to begin with. You're made in the image of the Flesh-and-bloods, so there's nothing you can't figure out as long as you keep your wits about you. It helps if you crouch tight, like a hedgehog. It's why Mrs Tiggy-Winkle was so good at moving across.'

I crawled inside and crunched myself up into the fetal position. Plum instructed me to hold my breath when he reached the count of two: it helped to have a breath in one when you arrived, as breathing out can give a good indication of how breathing actually works. I thanked him for the advice and he closed the hatch. I looked along the barrel of the cannon to the muzzle, and beyond that the series of textual sieves that would chop me into the smallest component parts imaginable. I admit it, I was nervous. I waited for about a minute in the gloom, then when nothing had happened, I called out.

'Sorry!' came Plum's voice. 'I'm just winding her up to speed. If I don't get you to *exactly* .346 Absurd speed, all you'll be is a tattered mass of text caught in the sieves. If I fire you too fast, you'll be embedded in the back of the laboratory.'

'What would happen then?'

'Paper over you, I suppose.'

I wasn't particularly reassured by this, but waited patiently for another half-minute until I heard a faint whine that grew in pitch as Plum counted down from ten. When he got to five the whine had grown so loud I could hardly hear him, so I guessed when two would be and took a deep breath. I was just thinking that perhaps this wasn't such a great idea after all and I should really be getting back to my series and staying there for a sensible period of time – such as forever – when there was a noise like a thousand metallic frogs all croaking at the same time, and my body was suddenly skewered by a thousand hot needles. Before I could cry out the pain passed, and after a low hum and a sensation of treacle, Klein blue and Wagner all mixed together but not very well, there was a brilliant flash of light.

20

Alive!

'**The "Alive" simulator at the BookWorld conference is one of those devices that all characters should try at least once.** The experience of being real has two purposes: first, to assist characters in their quest for a greater understanding of people, and second, to discourage characters from ever attempting to escape to the RealWorld. Most customers last ten minutes before hitting the panic button and being led shaken from the simulator.'

Bradshaw's BookWorld Companion, 8th Edition

I heard a gurgling sound and a heavy thumping and felt something odd in my nose that generated backstory memories that I hadn't had for a while – something about going for walks in the park when I was small. It was dark, too, and I felt a pain in my chest. I didn't know what it was until, with a sound like a tornado, a hot gush of foul air erupted from within me and blew out of my mouth. Before I could recover from this shock, I spontaneously did the opposite and drew in an equally fast gush of air that cooled my teeth and tasted of pine needles.

'It's called breathing,' came a voice close at hand. 'It's very simple, and everyone does it. Just relax and go with the flow.'

'I used to "take a breath" and "exhale uneasily" at home,' I managed to say, 'but this is quite different.'

'Those were merely descriptive terms intended to suggest a mood,' came the voice again. 'Here you are doing it to stay alive. Can you hear a thumping and a gushing noise, and a few rumbles, grunts, squeaks and growls?'

'Yes?'

'It's your body. The thumping is your heart. It's all new to you so will fit oddly, like a new pair of shoes, but you'll get used to it. Feel your wrist.'

I did so and was surprised to note that my skin was warm, soft and ever so slightly tacky. It was also thumping. It was my pulse, and I was sweating. Not for any descriptive reasons, but because I was *alive*. After a few minutes of doing nothing but breathing, I spoke again.

'What's that random sensation of memories I keep on getting?'

'It's smells. They have a way of firing off recollections. No one knows why.'

I didn't understand, and moved rapidly on.

'Why can't I see anything?'

'You need to open your eyes.'

So I did. I sat and blinked for some minutes. The view was quite astonishing, not only in terms of range, but *detail*. I had been used to seeing only what was relevant within a scene. Back home, anything extra would have been unnecessary, and was a pasty shade of magnolia with the texture of uncooked dough. Here, there was *everything*, in all directions, in full colour and in full detail. Several books' worth of description was just sitting there, with no one to revel in its glorious detail except me. The trees swayed ever so gently in the breeze, and the clouds moved slowly across the heavens. It was summer, and the flower beds had erupted in a sumptuous palette of colour, while on the air were delicate tastes of cooking and garbage and rain and earth. I could hear stuff, too, not one thing at a time, but all things at all times. The delicate symphony of sounds that reached my ears were so heaped upon one another that it was difficult to separate anything out at all, and I sat there, quite numbed by the overload of sensations.

'How do they filter it out?' I asked.

'Humans filter well,' said the voice. 'In fact, they can filter out almost anything. Sound, vision, smells, love, anger, passion, reason. Everything except hunger and thirst, cold and hot. No need to hurry. Take your time.'

I sat there for an hour, attempting to make sense of the world, and did reasonably well, all things considered. In that time I managed to figure out I was sitting on a park bench in a small and well-kept park hemmed in by red-brick houses on every side. There was a children's play area, a pond, a flower bed and two trees, both silver birch. A main road was to one side, and on a building opposite were two hoardings. One was advertising the Goliath Corporation's supposed good work on behalf of the community, and another 'Daphne Farquitt Day' on Friday, which began with a celebration of her works and ended with a Farquitt Readathon. It was a name I recognised, of course. The popularity of the romance author dictated that she had a genre all of her own.

'It's beautiful!' I said at last. 'I could stay here and watch the clouds for the whole twelve hours alone!'

'Many do,' came the voice again.

I looked around. Aside from an impertinent squirrel foraging on the grass, I was entirely alone.

'Who are you?' I asked. 'And why can't I see you?'

'Bradshaw asked me to keep an eye on you,' came the voice. 'The name's Square – Agent Square. If you want to know why you can't see me it's because I'm from Flatland and only bounded in two dimensions. At the moment I'm presenting my edge to you. Since I have no thickness, I am effectively invisible. Watch.'

A line a half-inch thick and two foot long appeared in the air quite near me. The line separated and opened out into a thin rectangle, which broadened until it was a square, hanging in the air.

'How do you do?' I said.

'Oh, can't complain,' said Square. 'A spot of trapezoidism in this chill weather, but heigh-ho. I worked with the real Thursday several times; do you really look like her?'

'You can't see, then?'

'Since I am only two-dimensional,' said Agent Square, 'I can only see the world as a series of infinitely thin slices, like a ham. May I approach and have a look?'

Square moved closer, and out of curiosity I put my hand inside the area bounded by his vertices, and a soft bluish light gave me four rings around my fingers.

'Four discs is all I can see,' said Square. 'Viewing one dimension up is always a bit confusing. Mind you, for you people bounded in three dimensions, it's no different.'

'I don't understand.'

'Time,' said Square, 'is your next dimension, so to anyone in the RealWorld it appears as your third spatial dimension does to me – a thin slice in plain view but with the abstract notions of "forward" and "beyond" unseeable. May I?'

Square approached me and then tilted to form a narrow rectangle and then again became a line, vanished and then reappeared. It was as though he were tilting in front of me in order to allow his two-dimensional frame of reference to scan my features. Once satisfied, Square withdrew.

'Spooky!' he said. 'You *do* look just like her. What's the mission?'

'To find Thursday.'

'Nothing hard, then.'

I made to stand up, but everything felt funny, so I sat down again.

'Why does my face feel all draggy?' I asked. 'The underneath of my arms, too, and my boobs – everything feels all, well, *weighted down.*'

'That'll be gravity,' said Square with a sigh.

'We have gravity in the BookWorld,' I said. 'It's not like this.'

'No, we just talk as though gravity existed. There's a huge difference. In the BookWorld gravity is simply useful. Here it is the
effect of mass upon space-time. It would be manageable if it were
constant, but it isn't. Acceleration forces can give one a localised
gravitational effect that is quite disconcerting; if you're only here
for twelve hours, I'd stay well clear of trains, elevators, aeroplanes
and cars. Very odd, I'm told, although I don't notice it myself. By
the way, do you have a timer on your watch? You're only here for
twelve hours, remember.'

I looked at my watch, which only had hands, and a face.

'No.'

'You'll get used to that, too. If this were the BookWorld, you'd
have one of those watches that counts down from twelve hours to
add some suspense. Believe me, the plot in this world takes a bit
of getting used to. I've not done anything for Bradshaw for six
months. That's nothing in the BookWorld; barely half a dozen words.
Out here, it really *is* six months. Hell's teeth! The boredom. There's
a limit to how much reality TV one can watch, although it's become
a lot easier for me since they brought in flat screens. Now, what
do you want to do first?'

'Walking would be a good start.'

Agent Square was a good teacher, and within the space of twenty
minutes I had mastered the concept of mass and the ticklish practical considerations of coping with momentum. Though easy to
someone who had been doing it for years, being able to lean back
when negotiating a sharp stop to avoid falling over was an acquired
skill.

'Bipedal movement is the skill of controlled falling,' said Square.
'If it wasn't so commonplace it would seem miraculous – like much
out here, to be truthful.'

I found the 'walking straight' part fairly easy to master, but learning
to conserve momentum while doing a right-hander at speed was

a lot harder, and I was flailing my arms for balance until Square patiently taught me how angular velocity, centripetal forces and shoe/ground friction coefficients all worked together.

'Outlanders must be very good at maths,' I said, struggling with the vast quantity of complex equations necessary to recover after a stumble.

'So good they do it without thinking,' he said. 'Wait until you see someone riding a unicycle – it's maths to die for.'

The physical walking I soon got the hang of, but the rapidly moving pavement beneath me I found disconcerting – not to mention the highly constricting pull and drag of my clothes. Square told me to keep my eyes on the horizon and not look down, and after ten or so laps around the small park, I was ready to venture out farther.

We walked out of the park and down the street, and I stared at the intricate detail with which the RealWorld was imbued. The stains, the corrosion, the reflections – none of it could be adequately explained or described, and I became fascinated by every detail.

'What's that?'

'A spider.'

'And that?'

'A dog turd.'

'So *that's* what they look like. Who's that person over there?'

'Which one?' asked Square, tilting his body so his infinitely thin frame of reference sliced in the direction I was pointing.

'I don't see anything.'

But there *was* something there – a wispy human-like form through which I could see the wall and hedge beyond. I had met Marley's Ghost once when he was doing one of those tedious 'Grammasite Awareness' talks, and it was like him – transparent. I'd queued up for autographs afterwards but when I'd asked him for a personalisation his agent told me to sod off. He wouldn't sign memorabilia, either.

'What did you expect?' Marley's Ghost had said when I protested. 'Albert Schweitzer?'

'Ghosts?' said Square when I explained what I could see. 'Perhaps. There is much unexplained in the world. It behoves one to be wary at all times. Just when you think you've got the hang of it, along comes string theory, collateralised debt obligations or Björk's new album, and bam! You're as confused as you were when you first started.'

We arrived at the Clary-Lamarr travelport soon after. As in Fiction, this was the main transportation hub in Swindon where the Skyrail and mainline bullet services met. From here you could travel off to the west and Bristol and the steamer ports, or east to London and the Gravitube. This was the business district, and the impressively high glassy towers disgorged a constant stream of people, all working together to make Swindon the powerhouse it was, deservedly titled 'The Jewel of the M4'. My Swindon was pretty similar, even if it lagged behind by eight years, the time that had elapsed since my series was written.

'What's that?' I asked, pointing towards a steel latticework tower that was being built on a hill to the south of the city. It was only half-built, but looked large enough to dwarf the skyscrapers when complete.

'It's part of the Anti-Smote Strategic Defence Shield that will one day protect a sinful citizenry from God's wrath – a series of force-fields supported by steel pylons. Not even the most powerful smiting by the angriest or most vengeful God will make it through – it is claimed.'

'That sounds pretty daft.'

'That's the whole point,' he said, 'it's *meant* to be daft. The Commonsense Party's unswervingly sensible management of the country has left the nation with a woefully high stupidity surplus that needs to be safely discharged. It's hoped that the extraordinarily pointless and ridiculously expensive Defence Shield will be enough to deplete the stupidity in time to more sensibly deal with a bigger problem that's coming up.'

'What could be a bigger problem than God's wrath upon his creations and a cleansing fire falling from the heavens?'

'I'm not sure. Something to do with polar bears.'

I sighed.

'It's been a while since I had any concept of current affairs,' I said. 'All of this was barely thought of when I was penned.'

'I keep abreast of things,' said Square. 'It's the closest thing to Story they have out here. Makes me feel less homesick. You've been here an hour and you can walk pretty well, so you're doing okay. The next thing you need to learn is *interaction*, and how humans all manage to live together without descending into chaos. The best places for appreciating this are crowds.'

'Crowds?'

'Right. Humans are more or less identical except for a few peculiar habits generally delineated by geographic circumstances and historical precedent. But essentially, they're all identical and reading from the same rulebook. To get along you have to appreciate the rules, but also know that other people know the rules – and that *they* know that *you* know the rules. Get it?'

'No.'

'You will. Observe the crowds for a moment.'

I watched as the thousand or so individuals milled around the Skyrail port, all of them heading in one of six directions, and moving on their own yet as one. Astonishingly, *without* bumping into one another and falling over. It was a most remarkable sight. The only people not doing the 'avoidance ballet' were the wispy Marley-like ones, who flitted around unobserved.

'I'm still seeing the transparent humans.'

'How insubstantial are they?'

'Pretty smoky. And they all look so *sad*.'

This was true. They all wandered about looking very dejected, as if the world were pressing heavily on their shoulders. I had tried to catch the eye of one or two, but they had stead-fastly ignored me, and, it seemed, everyone else. I knew about 'ghosts' but always thought they were a fictional construct, like some of the odder facets of Japanese culture. But Square was uninterested in my transparent people, and wanted to carry on with my education.

'If you can manage crowd work you can handle almost anything,' said Square. 'You know about flocks of starlings and shoals of fish, how they all seem to move at the same time?'

I told him that I had heard of this, but not witnessed it.

'Humans are exactly the same when they get into crowds. By using subtle sensory cues and working to a set of basic rules, you can enter a crowd all heading in different directions and come out the other side without touching anyone or causing an accident.'

'How?' I said, looking suspiciously at the swirling mass of humanity.

'Think of it as a subtle dance, where you have to avoid touching anyone. You have to jog and dodge your way around, but also have to know when people are going to dodge and jink round *you*. Give it a whirl.'

I stepped into the crowd and almost immediately a woman stopped dead in front of me.

'Sorry,' I said, and walked on. I could sense I was disrupting the smooth liquidity of the crowd, and by the noises people were making, it wasn't appreciated. I got to the other side of the street without bumping into anyone, but only just.

'Not so easy, is it?' said Square, and I had to admit he was right. I had thought being in the RealWorld would be easy, or at least a

203

lot like home, but it wasn't. Nothing here was assumed; everything had to be actually *done*, and witnessed. Weirder still, once something *was* done it had gone, and the knowledge of it faded almost immediately into memory. Once or twice I found myself attempting to move backwards or forwards in time before realising that was not how it worked. If I wanted to be five minutes in the future, I had to laboriously *run* the five minutes in real time, and if I wanted to go back, I couldn't. It was how I imagined the narrator in *À la recherche du temps perdu* spent most of his life – trapped in a noisy, brightly coloured cage barely two or three seconds wide.

After twenty minutes I could walk through the crowd without too much difficulty, but once or twice found myself in the situation where the person I was trying to avoid met me head on, and I moved left, and they did, so I moved right and they did too, and so on, up to five times, which elicited nothing more than a chuckle from my dancing partner.

'The old "back and forth" happens a lot when real and fictional people meet,' said Square when I had returned to where he was waiting for me. 'If the Outlanders had any idea we were among them, it would be the surest way to tell. That and a certain confusion when it comes to everyday tasks. If you see someone unable to boil a kettle, open a sash window or comprehend that they have an appalling haircut, it probably means they're fictional.'

'Hmm,' I said. 'Why is that woman in the annoyingly flamboyant clothes staring at me?'

'Probably because she recognises you.'

'Don't I have to know who she is before she can recognise me?'

'It doesn't work that way.'

'Thursday?' said the woman, bounding up to me with a huge grin and a clatter of beads. 'Is that really you? Where have you been hiding these past few months?'

I recognised her from the vague approximation that had made

it through to my series. It was Cordelia Flakk, ex-SpecOps publicity guru, and now – well, I had no idea what she did.

'Hello, Cordelia.'

'How are Landen and the kids?'

'Apparently, they're very well.'

'Did you hear about Hermione? Went to the slammer for trying to fiddle her taxes and then tried to escape. She was caught between the wire with two sabre-toothed tigers. They didn't know what had happened to her until a bangle and parts of her synthetic kidney turned up in one of the sabre's . . . well, I don't want the story to get too gruesome.'

'Too late.'

'You old wag, you! Will you be coming to Penelope's for the Daphne Farquitt reading party Friday afternoon? She wants us all to come round to her place for the readathon, and she's dying to show off her new man.' She leaned closer. 'A *Neanderthal*, you know. Frightfully polite, of course, but likes to sleep in the garden shed. She has a few stories about matters south, I should warrant – a few glasses and she'll spill the beans, if you know what I mean.'

The woman laughed.

'Goodness, is that the time? How I prattle so!' She suddenly lowered her voice. 'By the way, are you still dealing in cheese?'

'Not really—'

'A pound of Limburger would set us straight. Just a taster, then – anything, in fact; I mean it's not like we're asking for any X-14. Oh. Sorry, is that still a sore point? Why not bring a taster of cheese to Penelope's do on Friday? We can enhance it with some pineapple chunks. Cheese and Farquitt! Naughty us! Ta-ra!'

And she tossed her head and moved off.

'Did you understand any of that?' asked Square.

'About one word in eight.'

'That many?'

I stood there, stunned by the fact that I had no idea what Thursday actually *did* in the RealWorld, nor what had happened and what hadn't. The recent exchange told me that she *had* been involved in the illegal cheese market, and we had walked past the abandoned Special Operations Division headquarters earlier, so I knew that at least some of her SpecOps adventures had been real. But what else had happened in her life I had no idea. If anyone asked me anything specific, I was going to have to wing it, or simply grin stupidly. Best of all, stay well away from anyone who might know me.

'Was that meeting at all relevant?' I asked Square. 'In the grand scheme of things, I mean?'

'Probably not,' replied Square, 'just a chance meeting that means nothing. If this were a book, Cordelia wouldn't have survived the first draft.'

I spent the next two hours walking around, trying to figure out how the world worked. It was confusing and tiring, and it seemed that much energy was expended for very little outcome. I had my first real pee, which was pretty bizarre, then ate some chocolate, which was hugely enjoyable. Mostly, I listened in to conversations and was dismayed to note that Professor Plum had been correct. A lot of what was said was superficially very banal. Less of a sense of communication, and more to do with being comfortable and secure among members of one's own species – the modern equivalent of being huddled together in the dark.

'There seems to be a tremendous fear of being alone,' I said once we had stopped for a break in the graveyard of the Blessed Lady of the Lobster.

'My theory is that it's all misdirection.'

'From what?'

'The depressing certainty that, one day, all of us will die.'

'Speak for yourself. What's your story, Square?'

'I used to work in Flatland but was fired after "artistic differences" with Circle. After that I was recruited by Bradshaw for deep-cover operations in the Outland. I was out here on assignment when the RealWorld travel ban took place so I took Blue Fairy, became real and volunteered to stay.'

He sighed deeply, in a thin, two-dimensional sort of way. 'Blue Fairy' was the term used to describe the only way in which fictional people could become real, and unsurprisingly, the Blue Fairy from *Pinocchio* was the only person who could do it. She used to do it for free if you asked nicely and had a chit from the CofG, but now she is not permitted to conduct any realisations at all, and is paid handsomely by the Council for the honour of doing nothing. Good work if you can get it.

'When do you get to go home?' I asked.

'I don't get to return home. The only good thing about this place is that it's fantastically roomy. Are you ready?'

I said I was, and we walked the three blocks to Landen and Thursday's house, situated in a quiet part of the Old Town. I asked Square to keep a low profile, took a deep breath, walked up the garden path and stared at the front door, heart beating furiously. This time, for real.

21

Landen Parke-Laine

'**The manufacture of robots, automatons and assorted mechanical people is undertaken by the Duplex Corporation, situated on the border of SF and Fantasy.** Most automata are energy-cell-powered these days, but the factory still produces a "Classic" line of clockwork men to satisfy clients who require something more retro. Despite problems with emotion, adverse wear and the continuous windings, the Duplex range of robots (currently in its sixth incarnation) remains popular. Tours of the factory by arrangement.'

Bradshaw's BookWorld Companion, 6th Edition

I knocked twice. There was the sound of noises from within, and the door opened. It was Landen, and we stared at one another for a few seconds.

'Hello,' I said.

'Hello,' said Landen.

'Hello,' I said again.

'Are you her?' he asked.

'No, not really.'

'Then you'd better come in.'

He moved aside and I stepped into the hallway that was similar to mine, but only in layout. Thursday's real house was more real, more worn, more lived in. The banisters were chipped, the newel post was draped with discarded clothes and a tidemark of children's fingermarks ran along the wall and up the staircase. Pictures hung askew, and there was a small cobweb around the lampshade. Landen led me through to the kitchen, which was a big extension at the back of the house, partly consuming the garden and with a large glazed roof above the junk-strewn kitchen table. It was packed with the chaotic assortment of the minutiae of life being lived – not the sanitised shorthand we get in the BookWorld, even with the Reader Feedback Loop set to 'Max'. Life seemed to be a lot messier than people wanted Fiction to be. Feedback reflected hopes, not realities. I looked around carefully, and sat in the seat that he had indicated.

'Tea?' he asked.

'Do I drink it?'

'Gallons of it, usually.'

'At a single sitting?'

'No, generally one cup at a time.'

'Then I'd love some, thank you.'

He went to put the kettle on.

'You look a lot like Thursday,' he said.

'I'm often mistaken for her,' I replied, feeling less nervous around familiar questions. 'In fact, I'm surprised you needed so little convincing I wasn't the real Thursday.'

'I don't know that for certain,' he replied. 'Not yet, anyway. I'd like you to be her, naturally, but there have been others who looked a lot like her. Not quite as much as you do, but pretty similar. Goliath are keen to know what Thursday gets up to when she's not at home, and have sent one or two to try to trick me into giving information. The first was just a voice on the phone, then one who could only be seen from a distance. The last one almost took me in, but up close she didn't pass muster. Her texture was all wrong, the smell was different, the smile lopsided and ears too high. I don't know why they keep sending them, to be honest – nor where they end up. After I booted the last one out of the door, someone from Goliath's Synthetic Human Division came round demanding to know what I'd done with it. Then, after I asked about the legality of such a device, they denied there had been any, or even that he was from the Synthetic Human Division. He then asked to read the gas meter.'

'So how can they lose two synthetic Thursdays?'

'They lost three. There was *another*, that I hadn't even seen. They said it was the best yet. They dropped it off two weeks ago near Clary-Lamarr, and hadn't heard anything since. Are you that one?'

'No.'

'Are you sure?'

'Yes,' I replied, vaguely indignant. 'I'm not a Goliath robot.'

'Not a robot – a *Synthetic*. Human in everything but name.'

I took a deep breath. I had to lay my cards on the table.

'She's missing, isn't she?'

There was a flicker of consternation on Landen's face.

'Not at all. Her absences are quite long, admittedly, but we're always in constant communication.'

'From the BookWorld?'

He laughed.

'That old chestnut! It was never *proved* she could move across at will. I think you've perhaps spent a little too much time listening to deranged theories.'

It sounded like a cover story to keep the real nature of the Book-World secret. I didn't expect him to tell me anything. He didn't know who or what I was, after all. But he had to know.

'I'm the *written* her,' I told him. 'She may have spoken to you about me. I was the tree-hugging version in *The Great Samuel Pepys Fiasco*, who then took over from evil Thursday, who was deleted with *Pepys*. I run books one to five, now – less along the lines of the old Thursday, but more how the real Thursday wanted them to be. Less sex and violence. It explains why we're out of print.'

But if I thought he would be surprised or shocked, I was mistaken.

I guess when you're married to Thursday, the nature of weird becomes somewhat relative. Landen smiled.

'That's a novel approach. Mind you, there's nothing you've told me that I couldn't find out by rereading *First among Sequels*. Goliath have access to that book, too, so if you *were* one of the synthetic Thursdays, I'd expect you to come up with something like that.'

'Commander Bradshaw of Jurisfiction sent me.'

He stared at me. The relevance wasn't lost on him. Jurisfiction and Bradshaw were never mentioned in the books.

'I'm not yet convinced,' he said, giving nothing away, 'but let's suppose Thursday *is* missing – you want my help to find her?'

'If she's missing, then you and I can help each other. I'll be going home in less than twelve hours. Any information learned out here might be helpful.'

He took a deep breath.

'She's been gone four weeks, that much is common knowledge. Everyone wants to find her. It's a national obsession. *The Mole*, *The Toad*, Goliath, SO-5, the police, the Cheese Squad, the government, the NSA – and now you claim the BookWorld, too.'

'Do you have any idea where she is?'

He poured the boiling water into the teapot.

'No. And the thing is,' he added, looking at the clock, 'that we need to resolve this one way or another pretty soon.'

'Because of the police and the NSA and whatnot?'

Landen laughed.

'No, not *them*. The kids. Friday won't get away from his shift at B&Q until six, but Tuesday will be home in two hours, and although my mind has been rendered as supple as custard when it comes to things Thursday, the kids are still at an impressionable age – besides, I don't think the doors in the house will take much more slamming.'

And he smiled again, but it was sadder, and more uncertain.

'I understand.'

'Do you? *Can* you?'

'I think so.'

'Hmm,' he said, thinking carefully. 'Does anyone else know you're here?'

'Cordelia Flakk's the only one we need to worry about.'

'That's bad,' he murmured, 'Flakk's the worst gossip in the city. I've a feeling you've less than forty minutes before the press start to knock at the door, two hours before the police arrive with an arrest warrant, and three hours before President van de Poste demands you hand over the plans.'

'What plans?'

'The *secret* plans.'

'I don't have any secret plans.'

'I'd keep that to yourself.'

He poured out the tea and placed it in front of me. He was standing close to me and I felt myself shiver in his proximity. I wanted to take him in my arms and hug him tightly and breathe in great lungfuls of Landen with my face buried in his collar. I'd dreamed of the moment for years. Instead, I did nothing and cursed my restraint.

'Does Thursday know the president?'

'He often seeks her counsel. Thursday?'

'Yes?'

'How like her are you?'

I rolled up my sleeve to reveal a long scar on my forearm.

'I don't know how I got that one.'

'That was Tiger.'

'Was Tiger a tiger?'

'No, Tiger was a leopard. Your mother's. Only Mrs Next would name a leopard Tiger. May I?'

213

'Please do.'

He looked at my scalp, where there was another scar, just above my hairline.

'That was Norman Johnson at the close of the 1989 Superhoop,' I said, '*Something Rotten*, page 285.'

He went and sat at the other end of the table, and stared at me for a while.

'You even smell like her,' he said, 'and rub your forehead when you're thinking in the same way. I have a lot of respect for Goliath, but they never got Synthetics this good.'

'So you believe I'm the written one?'

'There's another possible explanation.'

'Who would I be if not Goliath or the written one?'

He looked at me for a long time, a look of concern on his face. I understood what he was trying to say.

'You think I might *be* Thursday, but suffering some sort of weird delusion?'

'Stranger things have happened.'

'I've spent my entire life in books,' I explained, 'I'm really only five years old. I can remember popping out of the Character Press as plain old D-8 V-67987, and my first day at St Tabularasa's. I did well so was streamed into the First Person fast-track programme. I can tell you about Sprockett and Carmine and how Pickwick doesn't approve of her bringing goblins home and likes to bore us stupid by quoting Latin mottos, and the new book that arrived in the neighbourhood. And there's Bradshaw, and the Metaphor shortage, and Jobsworth wanting me to go up-country to help deal with Speedy Muffler in the peace talks on Friday. That's me. I'm *not* Thursday. I'm nothing like her. Show me a frightening situation, and I'll run a mile. Square will vouch for me.'

And I called his name, but there was no answer.

'Right,' I said, wondering where he had gone, 'that makes me look stupid.'

We both fell silent and Landen stared at me for a long time. I saw his eyes moisten, and mine spontaneously did the same.

'I so want to be her,' I sniffed as my eyes blurred with tears, 'but I'm not.'

Before I knew it I had discovered what crying actually means when you do it for real. He gave me his handkerchief and hugged me, and I responded by wrapping my arms around his neck tight. It felt *wonderful*. Natural – like two parts of a jigsaw. When I had calmed down, he gently took my hands from around him and held them in his, staring into my eyes.

'Here's the thing,' he said at last, 'if you're *not* the real Thursday, we must come clean to the kids and explain that you're not. I can't have them being disappointed again. But if you *are* the real Thursday, you must stay so we can look after you. It's possible that you just *think* you're not Thursday. All that stuff about the BookWorld – it could be Aornis up to her tricks again.'

'Aornis, sister of Acheron?'

He raised an eyebrow.

'How many children do Thursday and I have?' he asked.

'Two.'

'That's in your favour as the written Thursday. Aornis gave the *real* Thursday a mindworm so she thought she had a third child – another daughter – and Thursday was always worrying about her. We helped her by pretending there was and occasionally, in lucid moments, she would realise what was going on. Then she'd forget and was worrying about her missing daughter again.'

I tried to imagine what it might be like having a child who was a figment but could not. If Aornis was anything like the written Acheron, she was pretty unpleasant. Still, I was kind of glad I didn't know about the extra daughter. I had an idea.

215

'I'm only here until midnight,' I told him. 'If you see me vanish in front of your eyes will you believe I'm from the Book-World?'

'Yes,' he said, 'I'll believe you. But if you don't vanish, will you believe that you *might* be Thursday but, well, nuts?'

'I could be the missing Goliath *synthetic* Thursday,' I said, 'with a well-researched cover story.'

Landen smiled.

'Being married to you has never been boring.'

I was pondering over the consequences of being either mad or synthetic when Thursday's mother arrived.

'Thursday!' she squealed, having let herself in. 'You naughty girl! Where have you been?'

The real version of my mother was quite different from the written one. The real one was a lot older – at least seventy, by my guess – but didn't seem to have lost any of her youthful vigour. She was a little grey, a little hunched, and a little odd.

'Here for long?' she asked.

'Only until midnight,' I managed to mutter.

'Shame!' she said, then turned to Landen. 'Is this one of the Synthetics?'

'The jury's still out.'

Mrs Next walked up close and peered at me through her spectacles, as one might regard a stubborn stain on the carpet.

'It's very lifelike. Does she have the scars?'

Landen nodded.

'I know how to check,' she said, and cut me a slice of Battenberg cake.

'Here,' she said, and handed it over. 'Your favourite.'

I took a large bite, and even though it had some yellow coating on the outside that was almost indescribably nasty, I smiled politely, and tried to eat it as quickly as I could.

'Very nice,' I managed to say.

'Hmm,' said Mrs Next, 'that doesn't sound like her at all. Thursday *hates* marzipan.'

'Is that what it is?' I said, running to the sink to spit it out. I knew I didn't like it, I just didn't know what it was. I had thought Marzipan was a boy band.

'Hmm,' said my mother, 'this doesn't really help. Hating it *does* make her Thursday, but pretending to like it to spare my feelings definitely does *not* make her Thursday.'

'It's a tricky one,' agreed Landen.

They stared at me for a long time as they tried to figure out what to do, and how best to tell whether I was the real one or the written one. Nothing I could say would convince them either way, and the only way to truly know – if I vanished at pumpkin hour – was a bit pointless, since by then I would no longer be around for them to answer any questions I might have, which was a bit like devising a 100 per cent destructive test for counterfeit tenners.

The doorbell rang.

'That will be the first of your fan club,' said Landen and went off to answer it.

'So,' said Mrs Next, 'loopy, fictional or synthetic. Which would you prefer?'

'Loopy, I guess,' I said sadly.

'Me too. But the shitstorm that will be unleashed when she gets back is not something I'd like anyone to face. President van de Poste won't be able to make his anti-smote shield without you and the secret plans, and as a key witness in the Stiltonista cheese-smuggling trial, you'll need round-the-clock protection. And that's before we get into the fun Goliath have in store for you.'

'She made a few enemies, right?'

'Only a few thousand. Start causing trouble among the criminal fraternity and no end of unfair retribution starts coming your way.

217

Would you excuse me? I am in need of the facilities. The bad plumbing needs to meet the bad plumbing, so to speak.'

And she tottered off in the direction of the downstairs loo.

I sat there for a moment unsure of what to think or do. I called out to Square but to no avail, then heard a noise. I looked up and noticed that the broom cupboard door was ajar. Looking at me through the crack were two bright eyes. The door opened a little farther and a small girl aged about eight stepped out. She was like the spirits I had seen around the place – that is to say, mildly transparent; I could see the bottle of Brasso on the shelf directly behind her.

'You're the last person I want to see,' I said as my heart fell.

'That's not a very nice thing to say,' said the girl.

'Let me guess,' I said, 'you're the mindworm.'

'I prefer Jenny,' said Jenny indignantly. 'Who are you?'

'If I can see you, I guess I'm the real Thursday – just insane. Still, at least this way I don't have to worry about Carmine and the goblin any more.'

'You're not insane,' said Jenny, 'and you're not Thursday either.'

'I could be making you up,' I remarked, 'and making up your denial, too.'

She shook her head.

'Creating figments like me takes a serious amount of effort, and you're not that good.'

'Thanks. Insulted by someone else's delusion.'

'Jenny.'

'Jenny, then. So how can I see you?'

'You're not just seeing *me*, are you?'

'No,' I said, 'there are others. Lots of them.'

'Then you see what I mean. What does Landen think you are?'

I shrugged.

'The real Thursday mad, I think.'

'Don't upset him,' said Jenny, 'Thursday wouldn't like it.'

'Thursday could be dead.'

'I know for a fact that she isn't.'

'How?'

But at that moment Landen came pacing down the corridor, and Jenny jumped back into the broom cupboard.

'That was your old buddy Lydia Startright, wanting to get an exclusive before the network vans turned up. I told her you weren't here and I had no idea where you were.'

'Did she believe you?'

'She's an excellent journalist – of course not.'

We sat in silence for some moments. I didn't think I would tell him I'd just seen Jenny, but the seeds of doubt had been sown. I *could* be the real Thursday. And even though the ramifications of being someone suffering bizarre delusions were *not* good news, the possibility that I would be with the man I loved was some consolation.

'Ask me some questions,' I said finally. 'I want to convince myself I'm not her.'

'What's my middle name?' he asked.

'Is it . . . Whitby?'

'Not even close. Where was our first date?'

'At the Alhambra. The Richard III thing.'

'No, that was later. Where did I lose my leg?'

'You've lost a leg?'

Mrs Next came back into the room.

'You never told me you'd bought a gold-plated toilet.'

Landen frowned.

'We don't have a gold-plated toilet.'

'Oh dear,' said Mrs Next, 'I think I've just peed in your tuba.'

She then muttered something about 'the shocking price of dodo feed' and went out without saying goodbye to either of us.

'Daft as a brush,' said Landen, 'and just a teeny-weeny bit repulsive.'

'Plock.'

I turned. A dodo stood at the open door. It was nothing like the Pickwick/Lorina back home. This dodo was *old*. Her beak was worn and scaly, she had no feathers and her left foot had a tremor. She was dressed in an all-over body-warmer made of fleecy material, and was staring at me curiously.

'Pickwick?'

'Plock?' said the dodo, cocking her head on one side. She walked unsteadily up to me, and looked very closely at me for a long time.

'Plock plock,' she said, and rubbed her beak affectionately on my trouser leg before walking over to her water dish.

'Pickwick thinks you're real.'

'Pickwick has a brain the size of a petit-pois.'

'True.'

The doorbell went again.

'That will be the Toad News Network.'

As soon as he had gone, the broom cupboard door opened again.

'Has he gone?' asked Jenny.

I nodded.

'Right, then. I'll show you what I mean about Thursday not being dead. Come with me.'

22

Jenny

___

'Places to eat #15: *The Bar Humbug*. 68, Christmas Carol.
Very cheap food served in an authentically austere and utterly
miserable Dickensian atmosphere. Waifs wait at tables, and portions
are notoriously small. People with silly names particularly welcome,
and those of archaic job title (beadle, proctor, sexton, etc.) can
eat for free.'

Bradshaw's BookWorld Companion, 5th Edition

Jenny opened the back door and checked to make sure the coast
was clear.

'Why do you do that?' I asked. 'Check that no one's coming?
Only I can see you, right?'

Jenny looked at me and raised an eyebrow.

'When you're illusory like me,' she said, with great clarity, 'it pays
to keep an eye out for imaginary foes.'

She checked again and beckoned me out. I followed her down
to the end of the garden and opened the door that led into the
garages behind. I knew my car would be kept here, but Thursday's
figment had no time to waste, and hurriedly led me down the rear
access road until we came back out on to the same street. Landen
had been correct. Parked outside the house was a large Toad News
Network van, complete with transmitter dish ready for bouncing a
live feed to a handy airship.

'Landen will be surprised to find me not there.'

'Nothing could surprise Landen. This way.'

'Miss Next?' asked a man who had just got out of a car opposite. 'May I have a word?'

I looked around but Jenny seemed to have vanished.

'I suppose so.'

'I just heard about your return. I'm a *huge* fan of your work. Adrian Vole of the Wapcaplit and Vole advertising agency. We understand you travel in Fiction, and were wondering if you wanted to do a bit of product placement around the written world.'

'I hardly think that's appropriate, do you?' I said, adding quickly: 'Even if there is a BookWorld, which is by no means proven.'

'Thirty grand to plug the Toast Marketing Board in the Thursday Next series. You can introduce it how you want.'

'I've never even *heard* of the Toast Marketing Board.'

'You wouldn't. It's new. What do you say?'

'What do you think I'm going to say?'

'Yes,' said Vole unhappily, 'we thought you'd tell us to stick it in our ear. Here's a cheque. If you cash it, we know you're on board.'

I took the cheque and moved on. Oddly enough, as soon as Vole turned away, Jenny was back.

'What's going on?' asked Square, who had suddenly reappeared. 'It's not like the BookWorld where I can be five or six places at once.'

'Landen thinks I might actually *be* Thursday,' I said, 'and if I can see Jenny, then he might be right.'

'Who's Jenny? I don't see anyone.'

'She's one of the wraiths I've been seeing. And if I am Thursday, then I'm simply imagining you.'

'Who are you talking to?' asked the figment Jenny, which seemed a bit impertinent, given her less-than-definite existence.

'Agent Square,' I said, 'in Jurisfiction deep cover.'

'Who are you talking to?' asked Square.

I sighed. This was getting more and more complex, but in a way, I was heartened that they couldn't see or hear one another. If they were *both* in my head, they should be able to converse – unless I was more insane than I thought possible.

'I'll tell you about it later,' I said, as we crossed another road, walked through the graveyard of the Blessed Lady of the Lobster, took a right down the hill and then an immediate left, where we found a small apartment block. Jenny led us into the lobby and we paused while she consulted the names on the postboxes.

'Fifth floor.'

We took the stairs as neither I nor Square wanted to go in the elevator, and arrived at the upstairs corridor, from where four apartments could be accessed. As I walked along the corridor one of the doors opened and a nurse walked out, glanced at me and moved off towards the elevators. As the door closed on the apartment, I could see that other medics were in attendance, clustered around a bed.

'You brought me here to see a guy dying?'

'Sort of,' replied Jenny, 'but not him in there – him out here.'

She pointed. At the far end of the corridor were five more of the wraith-like figures I had seen earlier. They all stood around looking solemn, trying to comfort one of their number, who flickered in and out like a badly tuned TV set. They all spoke in a low growl that I couldn't really understand, and as I walked closer I noticed that they were dressed rather oddly.

'You brought me here to see some spooks?'

'They're not spooks,' said Jenny, 'they're like me and you, Thursday – made up. Figments, inventions. Created in the white-hot heat of a child's imagination, they linger on even when redundancy renders them invisible from their creators. Sometimes people catch a glimpse of them, but for the most part, they're invisible. You can see them because you're fictional. So can I. You, them, me – we're all one and the same. A living fiction that needs no book.'

I looked closer at the figures. They were partially dressed as clowns, had bold, large features, and spoke in a simple dialect of basic verbs and a limited number of nouns.

'They're . . . imaginary childhood friends, aren't they?'

Jenny smiled.

'Bravo, Thursday – a chip off the old block. They follow their creators about, an echo of a vibrant childhood imagination.'

She indicated the one who was flickering.

'Pookles here is about to leave – they can have no independent existence without their creator.'

As we watched, the flickering imaginary friend started shaking hands with the others, hugging them and thanking them, then, with a final bright burst, it vanished. Almost immediately we heard a cry of grief from the bedroom behind us, and one by one the ethereal figures took their leave, walking through us and along the corridor, leaning on each other for support, and shaking their heads sadly.

'So where does Thursday come into all of this?'

'This is how I know she's still alive. *I'm still here.* Unlike you, who are the figment of a ghost writer and now carved into a textual matrix, a part of Thursday is all I am. If she were dead, I wouldn't be around to be thought of. I'm bound to her, like a dog on a leash.'

'Right,' I said, 'I get that. But it doesn't tell us where she is. Any ideas? The Dark Reading Matter, for instance?'

'That was one of her interests, certainly, but the whole Racy Novel stuff had taken over her life. The last time we spoke she said something about Lyell being boring.'

'Lyell? Boring?'

'Yes. I don't know who Lyell was, or why he should be boring, but boring he was – and Thursday didn't like it. Not one little bit.'

Jenny shook her head and took me by the hand.

'I miss her, Thursday. It's lonely not being directly imagined on a day-to-day basis.'

We walked back towards Landen's house.

'I'm confused,' said Square, 'what, precisely, is going on?'

'I'm not really sure. I feel like I'm following in Thursday's foot-steps, only several hundred yards behind and . . . hello, that's odd.'

I looked around. Jenny, who had been with us just a second ago, was nowhere to be seen. I twisted this way and that to see where she had gone, and as I was doing so, a black van screeched to a halt in front of me. Within a few moments the sliding door had opened, I had been bundled inside in a less-than-polite manner, and had a sack put over my head. With another screech of tyres the van set off and, to make matters worse, I was then immediately sat upon by someone who smelled strongly of Gorgonzola.

23

The Stiltonista

'The most cost-effective way to tour the BookWorld is by bus. A "BookWorld Rover" is the preferred method, giving you unlimited travel for a month. Delays might be expected at the borders between islands, but for the discerning tourist eager to see the BookWorld at a leisurely pace, the Rover ticket is ideal. Next page: Working your passage on a scrawltrawler. Not for the faint-hearted.'

Bradshaw's BookWorld Companion, 5th Edition

Any attempt to describe the journey would have been futile, as the varying degrees of gravitational flux that I encountered were unpleasantly distracting. Suffice to say that all the lurches, bumps, swerves and twists made me feel quite peculiar, and I wondered how anyone could undertake journeys on a regular basis, and not only become ambivalent to the horrors, but actually enjoy it. The journey thankfully ended after not too long, and once the van came to a stop and I was rather impolitely hauled from the back and placed on a chair, the sack was pulled from my head.

I was in a deserted warehouse. There were puddles of water on the floor, and holes in the ceiling – which probably accounted for the puddles on the floor. The windows were broken, and green streaks of algae had formed on the walls. In several places brambles had started to grow, and the odd pile of rubble and twisted metal sat in a heap. I wasn't alone. Aside from the four men who had brought me in the van, there was a Rolls-Royce motor car and three other men. Two of them seemed to be body-guards, and the third was undoubtedly the leader. He was dressed

227

in a well-tailored mohair suit that clung impossibly to his bony frame. His features were drawn and sunken – he looked like a skull that someone had thrown some skin at.

'I am Keitel Potblack,' he said in the tone of someone who felt I should know who he was, and not fail to be impressed, 'head of the Wiltshire Stiltonista. Your failure to remain properly dead is becoming something of an inconvenience.'

I laughed at the ridiculousness of the situation. This guy dealt in cheese, and he was acting as though he were a Bond villain.

'You're kidding, right?'

'I don't kid,' said Mr Potblack.

'Oh,' I said, 'right.'

I looked at him, then at the men standing next to him, one of whom was carrying a spade.

'Going gardening?'

They exchanged glances, as though this was the sort of comment they expected.

'It's up to you. Now, are you the real Thursday or just another copy?'

'I'm not her,' I said, 'so if you can take me home I'd be really grateful.'

'If you're not her,' said Potblack, 'I have no further need for you.'

'Good. If you could tell your driver to go easy a bit on the way back, that would be—'

'Mr Blue? Would you do the honours?'

The man with the spade walked towards me, and all of a sudden I realised that if he was digging anything over today, it would be me.

'You want to talk?' I said, the ease with which I stayed calm surprising even me. 'So let's talk.'

'So you are Thursday?'

'Yes,' I replied, which was no lie – I was *a* Thursday.

The man with the spade walked back to his position to the left of his boss. I noticed as he did so that one edge of the spade had been sharpened.

'Okay,' said Potblack, who seemed annoyed that I wasn't more frightened than I was. Perhaps if I had known who he was, I would have been. But this was Thursday's life, not mine.

'In the past,' began Potblack in a slow, deliberate speech, 'we may have had an "understanding" over who deals what cheese where. Perhaps you think I was being too harsh when I started dealing in really strong cheeses, but I am a businessman. The stronger the cheese, the more people will pay. Business is good, and we want to keep it that way. If the government lift the cheese ban as threatened, then it could be very bad business for all of us. The last thing we want is legal cheese.'

I vaguely knew what he was talking about, but not the details. Last thing I'd heard was that cheese in the Outland was subject to a swingeingly large amount of duty, but it seemed that the government, in an attempt to control the burgeoning illegal cheese market, had tried cheese prohibition. From Potblack's jewellery, car and ability to supply, the ban didn't seem to be working.

'So what do you want me to do?' I asked. 'It's not like I have the ear of the president, now, is it . . . ?'

The Stiltonista looked at his henchman with the spade, who picked it up again. I was wrong, I *did* have the ear of the president – Landen said so earlier.

'. . . any more. I don't have his ear *any more*. But I'm sure I could give him a call and advise him to keep prohibition in place.'

Potblack stared at me and narrowed his eyes.

'You're being uncharacteristically compliant.'

'. . . but characteristically *realistic*,' I said cheerfully. 'You're the one with the sharpened spade.'

229

'Hmm,' said the Stiltonista, 'very well. But I want to offer an incentive to make sure that once released you don't "forget" your part of the bargain.'

'Bargain?' I echoed. 'You mean I get something from this?'

'You do. You get to keep your life, your husband gets to keep his, and your children get to keep their fingers.'

The man with the spade tapped it on the ground as if to emphasise the point, and the steel rang out with a threatening *ting-ting-ting-ting*. I stared at the Stiltonista for a moment, and when I spoke I tried to convey as much menace as I could – surprisingly easy, for I *was* angry – and it wasn't the sort of anger I get when I fluff my lines or my father misses a cue and comes in late. It wasn't even the sort of anger I felt when Horace the goblin nicked all my stuff or Carmine went AWOL. This was *Real* anger. The sort of 'don't-shit-with-me' stuff that mothers feel when you threaten their children.

'Dear oh dear,' I said, sadly shaking my head, 'and we were getting on so well. I said I'd help you out, and you respond by threatening my kids. That's not only insulting, it's impolite. There's a new deal: you let me go right now and promise never to even *look* at my husband or children, and I will let you live to see tomorrow's dawn.'

The Stiltonista bit his lip ever so subtly. It was clear that I had a reputation, and it moved in front of me like a bulldozer. Despite the fact that I was outnumbered six to one, Potblack obviously considered that at the very least I should not be underrated. Thursday, it seemed, was a formidable foe – and highly dangerous if you got on the wrong side of her.

'You're not in any position to be doing deals.'

'I don't want anyone to think me unfair,' I said, 'I'll give you until the count of three. One.'

There was the sound of safety catches being released from the men behind me. They were quite obviously armed, and from the sound of it, heavily.

'I'm sorry we couldn't do any sort of deal, Miss Next,' said Potblack with renewed confidence. 'Perhaps you would like to reconsider. My men will finish you before you get to three, and you'll end up with all the others – six feet under the Savernake forest, a feast for the worms. I apologise if I have been impolite, but as you understand, a lot rides on a lifted prohibition, and I speak not only for myself but for many cheese suppliers up and down the country. We can make this work to the best advantage of all of us, I'm sure – and even perhaps offer up some sort of compensatory payment.'

'Two.'

'You really don't understand, do you?' said the Stiltonista in a voice that now carried an echo of uncertainty. 'It doesn't have to end like this for you.'

I didn't have a plan of action, but that didn't seem to be a problem for the plan of action had *me*, and before I knew what had happened I had the barrel of my pistol pressed hard against the Stiltonista's throat, and the man with the spade was flat on his back unconscious. The goon next to me had managed to get his hand to the butt of his automatic, but no farther. The rest were just blinking stupidly. Oddly, I didn't feel nervous in the least. It felt as if I was someone else. As if someone else was *inside* me.

'You see what happens when you're impolite,' I said, 'and don't struggle. This is an armour-piercer. Once it's gone through only Exxon will be able to retrieve it – or you.'

He stopped struggling.

'Tell them to drop their weapons.'

He did, and they did.

'Right,' I said, unsure what to do next, 'this is the plan . . .'

If there was a plan, I never found out what it was, for a voice rang out from one corner of the warehouse.

'*Armed police!* You are surrounded. Do *exactly* as we tell you. Carefully and slowly put your hands behind your head.'

The Stiltonista's goons did as the voice asked, and seemed to know the drill, as they also lay flat on their faces without being asked.

'And you, Next.'

I placed my pistol carefully on the floor, kicked it away and then obediently placed my hands on the back of my head and lay on the ground quite close to where Potblack now lay.

'I'll get you for this if it's the last thing I do, Next.'

He said it without looking at me, his voice a low growl.

'Really?' I replied evenly. 'Try to get me or my family and I'll happily ensure that it is.'

He grumbled and faced the other way.

I heard the patter of feet and within a few seconds I felt my arms being pulled behind me and bound with a plastic tie. They weren't rough, though – they were almost gentle.

'Got a weapon here,' said a voice, quickly followed by: 'Got several weapons here.'

'Thursday, Thursday,' came the voice that had been behind the bullhorn. It was deep and earthy and was exactly how I expected Spike to sound. He was one of Thursday's SpecOps pals – someone who had been only too happy to feature in the series. It was the only recognition he'd ever got.

'Spike?'

'Hello, old friend,' he said, 'what have you got for us?'

'Keitel Potblack, head of the Swindon Stiltonista,' I said, 'threatened to kill me, wanted to bribe me to block the repeal of prohibition, and is also guilty of putting three of Goliath's synthetic Thursdays under the Savernake forest.'

'You've nothing to connect me with the Stiltonistas,' said Mr

Potblack. 'I happened to be here perusing a potential property development when I was set upon by this madwoman.'

'We've got a bootful of Gorgonzola here,' said one of the armed officers, 'at least fifty kilos.'

'For personal use,' said Potblack in an unconvincing sort of voice.

'And your armed associates?'

'I employed them as decorators this morning. I am shocked, *shocked*, to discover they are armed.'

Spike helped me to my feet and walked me across to the front of the Rolls-Royce.

'It's good to see you again, Thursday. The Cheese Squad will have a field day with this lot. How in heaven's name did you nail Potblack of all people? We've been after him for years.'

'Let's just say I have a magnetic personality.'

Spike laughed.

'Still the same. Tell me, do you want to do some moonlighting? The undead are about to be culled again, and there aren't many with a Class IV Zombie hunter's licence about – or at least, none that don't drool a lot and mumble.'

I thought carefully.

'If I'm around tomorrow, I'm totally up for it.'

It was quite fun being Thursday. I had a sudden thought.

'Spike, if you weren't here to arrest Potblack, what were you here for?'

'We've been trailing you for the past hour, Thursday.'

'Why?'

'Because if we know you're here, so will *they*.'

'*They* being . . . ?'

'Who else? Goliath.'

'I can handle them.'

'I don't think so,' said Spike. 'You've been gone a month, right?'

'In a manner of speaking.'

'Three weeks ago SpecOps announced they'd been privatised. The Goliath Corporation now run not only SpecOps, but the police as well. Almost the first thing Goliath did was charge you with crimes against humanity, murder, theft, illegal possession of a firearm, the discharge of a weapon in a public place, murder, impersonating a SpecOps officer, cheese smuggling, assorted motoring offences and murder. It's quite a list. They must *really* hate you to dream up so many spurious charges.'

'I think the feeling's pretty much mutual. Does that mean I'm under arrest?'

'We tried to arrest you but you escaped.'

He smiled and removed the plastic cuffs with a flick-knife.

'Now go before Flanker gets here.'

It was too late. A group of blue-suited individuals had arrived, brandishing Goliath IDs and a lot of attitude. The leader of the group I recognised from the description I had in the series – Commander Flanker, once head of SO-1, the police that police the police, and now presumably answering to Goliath.

'Thank you, Officer Stoker,' said Flanker, 'for securing our prisoner.'

'You can have her once we're done,' said Spike, pulling himself up to his full height – he was well over six foot six. 'Miss Next is charged with the illegal possession of a firearm and I need to process her.'

'The charge of crimes against humanity has precedence, Stoker.'

'Your bullshit charge is bigger than my bullshit charge?'

'We could argue this all night, but the outcome remains the same. She is coming with me to be interrogated at Goliathopolis.'

'Over my dead body,' said Spike.

'I'm sure that can be arranged.'

They growled at one another, but there was little, it seemed, Spike could do. Within a half-hour I was in the back of a large automobile being driven to the Clary-Lamarr travelport to be put on a private bullet train to Goliathopolis.

I took a deep breath. Being Thursday was exciting and was certainly distracting. I'd hardly thought about Whitby at all.

24

Goliath

———

'**Perils for the unwary #16: Big Martin.** A large cat-like beast who is never seen but always leaves a trail of damage and mayhem in its wake. A Big Martin event can always be avoided owing to the ample warning given by a series of cats that gradually increase in size. The universal "Rule of Three" should be adopted: simply put, the third Big Martin warning should be considered the last, and it is time to leave.'

Bradshaw's BookWorld Companion, 2nd Edition

'Well,' said Flanker as we sat in the plush interior of the bullet train, 'we'll be at Goliathopolis in an hour, and your debrief can begin.'

'Mr Flanker, sir,' said one of the accompanying heavies, a small man with a rounded face and a crew cut like a tennis ball, 'have you checked she's not one of ours?'

'Good point,' said Flanker. 'Would you be so kind?'

The two heavies needed no extra encouragement, and while one held me down the other clasped my upper eyelid and peered underneath. It wasn't painful but it *was* undignified, and the agent looking at my eye had been eating an onion sandwich not long before, and his breath was pretty unpleasant.

'She's not one of our Thursdays,' said the agent, and they released me.

'I'm delighted to hear it,' I said – and I was. There were now only two possibilities regarding who I was: me, or Thursday. 'Potblack killed them all,' I added, 'and had them buried in the Savernake.'

'I don't know what you're talking about,' replied Flanker airily. 'Goliath no longer conduct experiments into Synthetics. It's against the law. Oh,' he added, 'I forgot. We *are* the law. Shall I come straight to the point? We've been contracted to complete Phase One of the Anti-Smote Defence Shield by the end of the year, and the penalties are severe for non-compliance. We're not in the business of paying severe penalties, so tell us where the secret plans are and we can release you and drop all the charges.'

It felt like covering for a character in a book without being told what the book was about, who was in it, or even what your character had been doing up until then. I'd done it twice in the Book-World, so had some experience in these matters. But at least I was beginning to understand what was going on.

'The plans are in a safe place,' I replied, assuming they were, 'but if you think you can simply ask questions and I'll simply answer them, you've got another think coming.'

'Oh, this is just the preamble,' said Flanker in an unpleasant tone, 'so I can tell the board that I did ask you, and you refused. We can cut the information out of you, but it's a very messy business. Now, where are the plans?'

'As I said: somewhere safe.'

Flanker was quiet for a moment.

'Do you have any idea how much trouble you have caused Goliath?'

'I'm hoping it's a lot.'

'You'd be right. Just getting you off the streets is a small triumph, but we have other plans. The Goliath Advanced Weapons Division have been wanting to get hold of you for a long time.'

'I won't help you make any weapons, Flanker.'

'It's simpler than that, Thursday. Since you have been so devastatingly destructive to us over the years, we have decided that *you* would make the ideal weapon. We can make excellent visual copies, but none of them have the unique skills that make you the dangerous person you are. Now we have you and that precious brain of yours,

238

with a couple of modifications in your moral compass, our Thursday MKV will be the ultimate killing machine. Of course, the host rarely survives the procedure, but we can replace you with another copy. I'm sure Landen won't notice. In fact, with a couple of modifications, we can improve you for him – make the new Thursday more . . . compliant to his wishes.'

'What makes you think that I'm not already? If he was only a quarter of the man he is, he'd still be ten times more of a man than you.'

Flanker ignored me and the bullet train moved off. We were soon zipping through the countryside, humming along thirty feet above the induction rail. When another bullet train passed in the opposite direction we gently moved to the left of the induction wave and the train opposite shot past us in a blur.

I stared at Flanker, who was sitting there grinning at me. If he could have started to laugh maniacally, he would have. But the thing was, this didn't sound like the Flanker in my books. Pain in the arse he might have been, but Goliath lackey he most certainly wasn't. His life was SpecOps, and although a strict rules man, that was all he was. I had an idea.

'When did they replace you, Flanker?'

'What do you mean?'

'This isn't you. Shit you might have been, evil-toady-Goliath-lackey-shit you most definitely weren't. Ever had a look at your own eyelid? Just to make sure?'

He laughed uneasily but then excused himself and went to the bathroom. When he came back, he looked somewhat pale and sat down in silence.

'When was I replaced?' he asked one of the heavies. I'd not really given them much thought, but now I looked at them they also seemed to be vaguely familiar, as though they had been described to me long ago. There were plenty of Goliath personalities in my book, but the litigious multinational had always insisted no actual names could be used, nor realistic descriptions – they went farther by denying anything in the *Thursday Next* books ever took place, something that Thursday told me was anything but the truth.

'This morning,' said one of the heavies in a matter-of-fact tone, 'and you're for retirement this evening. You're what we call a day-player.'

Flanker put on a good face of being unperturbed and picked up the phone that connected him to the central command for the bullet-train. Before he could speak the other heavy leaned forward and placed his finger on the 'off hook' button.

'Even if I am only a day-player,' said Flanker, 'I still outrank you.'

'You're not the ranking officer here,' said the other heavy, 'you're just the friendly face of Goliath – and I say that without any sense of irony.'

Flanker looked at me, then at the heavies, then out of the window. He said nothing for perhaps thirty seconds, but I knew he was going to make a move. The trouble was, so did the heavies. Flanker reached for his gun but no sooner had he grasped the butt than he suddenly stopped, his eyes rolled upwards into his head and he collapsed without a noise. It was as though he'd been switched off. The Goliath heavy showed me a small remote with a single button on it.

'Useful little gadget,' he said. 'All of our enemies should have one. Boris? Get rid of him and then fetch Miss Next a cup of tea.'

The synthetic Flanker was unceremoniously dragged from the compartment by Boris, and the first heavy moved into Flanker's old place.

'An excellent move,' he said with the air of authority, 'to pit one of your foes against another. Worthy of the real Thursday. Now, where is she?'

'I'm her,' I said, suddenly realising that while this whole Goliath adventure was kind of amusing, it wasn't helping me find out where Thursday had actually gone. The sum total of my knowledge was that she had been gone a month, was not dead, and had said that Lyell was boring. Goliath didn't have her, so I was wasting my time here. I needed to get back to Swindon.

'Are you a day-player as well?' I asked.

'No,' said the man, 'I'm real. I check every morning. I know better than most that Goliath can't be trusted. Now, where are you from and where's Thursday?'

'I'm her. You don't need to look any farther.'

'You're not her,' he said, 'because you don't recognise me. It surprised me at first, which was why I had to make sure you weren't one of ours gone rogue. They do that sometimes. Despite our best attempts to create Synthetics with little or no emotions, empathy tends to invade the mind like a virus. It's most troublesome. Flanker would have killed you this morning if I'd told him to, and by the afternoon he dies trying to protect you. It's just too bad. Now, where's Thursday?'

Finally, I figured it out. The one person at Goliath who had more reason to hate me than any other.

'You're Jack Schitt, aren't you?'

He stared at me for a moment, and smiled.

'By all that's great and greedy,' he said, staring at me in wonder, 'what a coup. You're the written one, aren't you?'

'No.'

But he knew I was lying. Unwittingly, I had revealed everything. Jack Schitt wasn't his real name; *it was his name in the series*. I didn't know what his real name was, but he would certainly have known his fictional counterpart. He pulled the phone off the hook and punched a few buttons.

'It's me. Listen carefully: it's not Thursday, it's the *written* Thursday. Yes, I'm positive. She could melt back any second so we need to get her Blue Fairyed the second we're on Goliath soil. I don't care what it takes. If she's not real by teatime, heads will roll. And no, I'm not talking figuratively.'

He hung up the phone and stared at me with a soft triumphal grin.

'When are you due back?'

I stared back at him, a feeling of genuine fear starting to fill me. My actions so far had been based on the certainty that I would return. The idea of staying here for ever was not in the game plan.

'What happened to the Austen Rover, Next?'

'The what?'

'The Austen Rover. Our experimental transfictional tour bus. The real Thursday travelled with it on its inaugural flight and never returned. Where is it?'

'I don't know what you're talking about, and besides, the Blue Fairy is fictional and lives inside *Pinocchio*. She doesn't do any actualising these days. The Council of Genres forbade it.'

'Better and better,' he said, waving away the second heavy, who had returned with my tea, and closing the compartment door, 'so you *are* from the BookWorld. And I was bluffing; we don't have a Blue Fairy. But we have the next best thing: *Green* Fairy.'

'I've never heard of the Green Fairy.'

'It's a concoction of our own. It's not so much a fairy – more like a magnetic containment facility designed to keep fictional characters from crossing back. I understand that the first few hours can be *excruciatingly* painful, and it gets worse from there. You'll talk – they always do. How do you suppose we managed to get the inside information necessary to even begin research into the Book Project? Perhaps we can't make you real, but we can keep you here indefinitely – or at least, until such time as you can't bear it any longer and agree to help us. Make it easy for yourself, Thursday: where is the Austen Rover?'

'I have no idea.'

'You'll tell us eventually. A few hours of Green Fairy will loosen your tongue.'

'Goliath wouldn't last twenty minutes inside Fiction,' I said, but I wasn't convinced. If this 'Jack Schitt' was even half as devious as the written one, we were in big trouble. Thursday had devoted a great deal of time and effort to ensure that the Goliath Corporation didn't get into Fiction, either to dump toxic waste, use the people within it as unpaid labour – or even just to find another market to dominate and exploit.

I said nothing, which probably was all he wanted to know. It was the worst luck that he had been the one to figure me out. The real Thursday had once imprisoned the so-called Jack Schitt within Poe's *The Raven*, so here was a man with some experience of being in the BookWorld.

'So what's your name?' I asked. 'If not Jack Schitt?'

'It was a ridiculous name, not to mention insulting,' he snorted. 'I'm Dorset. Adrian Dorset.'

25

An Intervention

———

'**Places to eat #28:** *The Inn Uendo,* 3578 **Comedy Boulevard.**
Made famous as the meeting place of the Toilet Humour Appre-
ciation Society, most of whose motions are passed while seated
at the bar. The Double Entendre bar and grill is also highly
recommended, and if you require satiating, the friendly waiting
staff will be able to offer relief at the table.'

Bradshaw's BookWorld Companion, 5th Edition

'Adrian Dorset?' I said. 'Are you sure?'

'No, I'm not sure at all.'

'What's your name, then?'

'You're not as smart as her, are you? Of *course* it's Dorset. I think
I know my own name.'

'The Adrian Dorset who wrote *The Murders on the Hareng Rouge?*'

He looked surprised for a moment.

'The worthless scribblings of a man who was fooling himself
that he could write. It was following the death of Anne, but I don't
expect you'd know anything about that, would you?'

I shook my head.

'Anne was my wife,' he said, 'head of the Book Project. She was
on board the Austen Rover's inaugural journey. Thursday told me
what had happened to her, and what she had done before she died.
I don't blame Thursday. Not any more. Revenge is for losers, cash
is the winning currency. I burned the book a month ago. I didn't
need it any more. I'm over her.'

He looked down at his feet and I suddenly felt sorry for him.

'I'm sorry for your loss.'

'Thank you.'

He said very little for the rest of the journey, and I watched out of the window as the English countryside zipped beneath us at breathtaking speed; we had nothing as fast as this in the BookWorld – not even in SF, where they were a lot more conservative than they made out. As we approached Liverpool and the Tarbuck International Travelport, the traffic became more intense as other bullet gondolas joined the induction rail and clumped around for a while before moving off in separate directions. At all times the small, bullet-shaped craft, each no bigger than a bus, kept well spaced from one another, moving apart and together as congestion dictated.

The intercom buzzed and Dorset picked it up, looked at me, then said: 'Security override seventeen' before listening for a while and then saying: '*Bastards*. Very well.'

'Problems?'

'Nothing to worry your sweet fictional head about.'

We glided to a halt on Platform 24 at Tarbuck International. The doors hissed open but we didn't move, and a few minutes later a small, meek-looking man arrived. He was wearing a dark suit and a bowler hat, and was carrying a small briefcase. When he spoke his voice was thin and reedy, and his nose was red from a recent cold.

'Good afternoon, Mr Meakle,' said my captor, without getting up.

'Good afternoon,' said Meakle, who looked strikingly similar to a bit-part early on in my series. 'You will release Miss Next to the custody of a federal marshal.'

He indicated several marshals who were all standing on the platform outside the bullet.

'I'm afraid not, old chap,' said Dorset or Schitt or whoever he was. 'Miss Next is under arrest for crimes against humanity, which effectively trumps anything you might have in store for her.'

'You're right *and* wrong,' said Mr Meakle. 'She is under arrest, but *house* arrest, and will remain there until the government decides the best course of action. National heroes are not treated as common prisoners, Mr Dorset.'

'I have the authority of the police and SpecOps,' replied Dorset cooly, 'an authority given to us under mandate from the Minister of Justice.'

The bureaucrat opened his case and took out a sheet of paper.

'I repeat, Miss Next is to be taken into custody by a federal marshal. Here is an executive order signed personally by President Redmond van de Poste. Need I say more?'

Dorset took the document and studied it minutely. I could tell from his expression that all was very much in order. He handed it back, looked at me and told me the game was 'far from over'.

I was taken across the concourse to where Meakle had his own private bullet with the presidential seal painted on it, and within a few moments we were skimming back south across the countryside.

'Thank you.'

Mr Meakle seemed distracted, as though this was just one of many jobs he had to do in a single day. It looked, in fact, as though he worked from the bullet.

'My pleasure,' said Mr Meakle. 'Where can we drop you?'

I asked for Swindon, and he relayed the instructions through the phone.

'I know I speak for the President when we say how good it is to see you back,' he added. 'NSA officials and SO-5 will be briefed to protect you from Goliath. Can I schedule a meeting with the President any time soon? We are eager to receive the secret plans as soon as we can, and hope that the security arrangements meet with your satisfaction.'

I told him I'd meet with them tomorrow. Meakle nodded solemnly, and returned to his work.

I sat back in my seat and ran the events of the afternoon through my head. I had just got to the bit where Spike had rescued me from the Stiltonista when I started to feel very peculiar. I began to have odd thoughts, then couldn't figure out why I'd thought them. The world started to soften around the edges and I could feel myself begin to lose consciousness. I thought for a moment I might be dying, as I could feel my conscious mind start to close down. Before I knew it I had closed my eyes and an overwhelming darkness stole over me. I might indeed have died, but I hadn't, and I slept quite soundly until Mr Meakle woke me when we arrived back at Clary-Lamarr.

26

Family

'**Places to visit in the BookWorld #7:** *Poetry Island.* Although at first glance a wild and powerful place, by turns beautiful, wayward, passionate and thought-provoking, any visit longer than a few hours will start to have an *exaggerating* effect on the senses. Upbeat poems will tend to have you laughing uncontrollably, while sombre poems will have you questioning your own worth in a most hideously self-obsessed manner. Early explorers of Poetry spent weeks acclimatising in Walter de la Mare and Longfellow before daring to explore the Romantics . . .'

Bradshaw's BookWorld Companion, 12th Edition

'Where did you get to?' asked Landen as soon as I tapped on the back door to be let in. 'I was thinking you'd gone missing again.'

'I brought down the Stiltonista, was arrested for crimes against humanity, found out where the other Thursdays are buried, was almost kidnapped by Goliath and was then rescued by the Attorney-General.'

'Is that all?'

'No. I found out what ghosts are. They're childhood memories. Oh, and the President wants to see me tomorrow to discuss the Anti-Smote Strategic Defence Shield – I think it's what the whole "secret plans" deal is all about.'

'Are you sure you're not Thursday?'

'Positive. Hey, listen: Jack Schitt's real name is Adrian Dorset. How weird is that?'

'Not weird at all. You and I have known for years. Jack Schitt is a daft pseudonym – not to mention actionable.'

'Perhaps so – but he wrote *The Murders on the Hareng Rouge*, the book I was asking you about.'

'And the significance of this is . . . ?'

'I don't know, but the RealWorld's kind of wild with all this strange stuff going on, although it's a good job this isn't Fiction – it wouldn't really make any sense at all.'

I was becoming quite animated by now – randomness has an intoxicating effect on the preordained.

'By the way,' I added, 'do you want thirty grand?'

Landen raised an eyebrow in surprise.

'You earned thirty thousand pounds this afternoon . . . *as well*?'

'From a Vole.'

'What the . . . No, I don't want to know. But yes, we could do with the cash so long as it's not illegally earned.'

'Here you go,' I said, handing him the crumpled cheque.

I'd have to make good on my side of the bargain, but I felt sure I could drop some Toast Marketing Board references into the series without much problem.

'Oh, and if you see anyone who looks like NSA or SpecOps watching the house, don't be alarmed. The President is protecting us – I don't think Goliath are too keen on me right now.'

'Were they ever?'

'Not really. But I know what they're up to and it's particularly unpleasant. In fact, I shouldn't really hang around. I'll only make things dangerous for you.'

'Until we prove you're not my wife,' he said, 'you're staying.'

It seemed like a generous sentiment, so I accepted gracefully.

'Listen,' he said, 'just in case I'm wrong and you really *are* written, you should know something.'

'Yes?'

'You know I said I didn't know where she was?'

I nodded.

'That's not *strictly* true. I didn't know whether I could trust you. You see, when Thursday went to the BookWorld she *always* came and went via her office at Acme Carpets. Bowden is the manager over there, and when she went missing I asked him to go and look for her.'

'She wasn't in her office?'

'No – *and the door was locked from the inside.*'

He let this information sink in. She had gone to the BookWorld four weeks ago – and not returned.

'So,' he said, 'if you're *not* her, it's where you need to be looking. If you *are* her, it's where you need to go to find out what has happened to you.'

I stared at him and bit my lip. Thursday was definitely some-where in the BookWorld. Lost, alone, perhaps hurt – who knows? But at least I had somewhere to start. My mission, such as it was, was at least a partial success.

'Well then,' said Landen, clapping his hands together, 'you'd better meet Tuesday.'

So I sat down at the kitchen table, and felt all goosebumpy and hot. I'd felt less nervous facing down Potblack, but this was different. Landen and the children were everything that I'd ever wanted. Potblack was just a jumped-up cheesemonger.

Tuesday wandered shyly into the room and stared at me intently.

'Hello,' I said, 'I'm not your mother.'

'You look like her. Dad says that you might be Mum but you don't know it.'

'That's possible too,' I said, 'and I'd like to be.'

'Could she be?' Tuesday asked Landen.

'It's possible, but we won't know until later.'

'Oh well,' said Tuesday, sitting next to me at the kitchen table, 'do you want to see what I'm working on?'

'Sure.'

So she opened her exercise book and showed me a sketch of an idea she'd had.

'This is a sundial that works in the overcast – or even indoors. This is a method of sending power wirelessly using music, and what do you make of this?'

She showed me several pages of complex mathematical notation.

'Looks important.'

'It's an algorithm that can predict the movement of cats with ninety-seven per cent accuracy,' she explained with a smile. 'I'm presenting it to Nuffield College the day after tomorrow. Do you want to come?'

Over the next few minutes she explained her work, which was far ranging in its originality and depth. The real Thursday's inventor uncle Mycroft was dead now, but his intellect had crossed to Tuesday. If she was working out the complex mathematics required to accurately predict random events at age twelve, her work when adult would be awe-inspiring. She spoke to me of her latest work: a plausible method to crack one of the most intractable problems in modern physics – that of attempting to instil a sense of urgency into teenagers. After that, she explained how she was designing daylight fireworks which would sparkle darkness in the light, and then finally the possibility of using beamed electron fields as a kind of impermeable barrier with such diverse applications as going underwater without the need for an aqualung or to protect one from rockfalls or even for use as an umbrella. 'Especially useful,' remarked Tuesday, 'for an electron-field umbrella wouldn't catch in anyone's eye and never needs shaking.'

After Tuesday had gone off to fetch a photograph album I turned to Landen.

'She's the secret plans, isn't she?'

He looked at me but said nothing, which I took to mean she

was. Tuesday's intellect would be the driving force behind the government's Anti-Smote Strategic Defence Shield.

'I guess we're just about to find out if you're the Goliath Thursday,' said Landen. 'If you are, you'll be contacting them straight away.'

I wouldn't, of course.

'How long do you think before they figure it out?'

'I don't know,' replied Landen, scraping the carrots he had been chopping into a saucepan, 'but know this: I'll die to protect her.'

'Me too.'

Landen smiled.

'Are you sure you're not her?'

'I'm sure.'

Tuesday came back with the photograph album and I joined her as she leafed through the family holidays of which I had no knowledge. I stared at the Thursday in the pictures and tried to figure her out. She never looked totally relaxed – not as much as Landen and the kids, anyway – but clearly loved them all, even if she seemed to be looking around her, as though on the lookout for anyone wishing to do them or her harm. There were very few pictures in which she was smiling. She took life seriously, but her family kept her anchored, and probably as sane as she could ever hope to be. Tuesday took my hand and held it tightly without really thinking and as we chatted it crossed my mind that I could *become* Thursday, if the real one never showed up. I could go Blue Fairy, and all this would be mine. For a fleeting moment it seemed like a good, worthy and attainable idea, but reality quickly returned. I was fooling myself. The longer I listened to Tuesday, the more I realised just how much she needed her mother. Not any mother, but *her* mother. I would never be anything more than a pale reflection.

'Landen,' I said when Tuesday had gone off to watch *Bonzo the Wonder Hound* Series 12, 'I shouldn't have come.'

'Nonsense.'

'No, really. It was a huge mistake. I can't be her, no matter how much I want to.'

'You sell yourself short – I'm more convinced by the second. The way you sat with Tuesday.'

'Yes?'

'That's how Thursday used to do it. Proud, loving – but not understanding a single word she said.'

'Land, I'm not her. I've got no idea what's going on, I didn't recognise Adrian Dorset, I didn't know that you'd lost a leg and, and, and . . . I can't see Jenny. I should just go and hide in a large cupboard somewhere until I'm whisked back into Fiction.'

He stared at me for a moment.

'I never said her name was Jenny.'

'*Damn.*'

He took a step closer and held my hand.

'You saw her?'

I nodded my head.

'Jenny mentioned Thursday saying "Lyell was boring". Does that make any sense to you?'

'Thursday didn't discuss her BookWorld work with me. She pretended it was a secret, and I pretended I didn't know about it. Same as the SpecOps work. But I don't know anyone called Lyell, and she *hated* boring people. Except me.'

'You're not boring.'

'I am, but I'm okay with it. I'm the anchor. The shoulder.'

'And you're all right with the support role?'

He laughed.

'Of course! It's my *function*. Besides, I love her. More than anything on the planet – with the possible exception of Tuesday and Friday. And I'm actually quite fond of Jenny, too, even though she doesn't exist.'

'You're a good man.'

He smiled.

'No, I'm an average man . . . with a truly extraordinary wife.'

I rubbed my temples with the frustration of it all. I so wanted to be her, and have all this, Landen, the kids. There was a dull throb in my head, and I felt hot and prickly. It was a lot easier being fictional – always assuming that I was, of course.

'That's another reason I should leave,' I said in a harsher tone than I might have wished. 'This morning I knew who I was and what I was doing. Now? I've got no idea.'

And I started to sob.

'Hey, hey,' he said, resting a hand on mine, 'don't cry. There's four hours to go before you vanish or not, and I'm not sure I can wait that long. I'm pretty confident you're her. You called me "Land", you saw Jenny, you're a bit odd, you love the kids. But there's one simple way I'll be able to tell.'

'And what's that?'

'Kiss me.'

I felt myself shiver with anticipation and my heart – my real heart, that is, not the descriptive one – suddenly thumped faster. I placed my hand on his cheek, which was warm to the touch, and leaned forward. I felt his breath on my face and our lips were just about to touch when suddenly I once more felt the hot needles and Klein-Blue Wagnerian treacle, and I was back in the arrivals lounge at Juristech. As Plum had promised, there was a glass of water and some biscuits waiting for me. I picked up the water glass and threw it at the wall.

27

Back Early

'. . . Plot 9 (Human Drama) revolved around a protagonist returning to a dying parent to seek reconciliation for past strife, and then finding new meaning to their lives. If you lived anywhere but HumDram, "doing a plot 9" was considered a serious insult, the Outlander equivalent of being told "to go screw yourself" . . .'

Bradshaw's BookWorld Companion, 3rd Edition

I found Professor Plum working on his Large Metaphor Collider. As soon as he saw me he pressed a couple of buttons on his mobile-footnoterphone, said a few words and smiled at me.

'Oh!' he said in some surprise. 'You're back.'

'What happened? I wasn't meant to come back for another four hours!'

'Transfictional travel isn't an exact science,' he replied with a shrug. 'Sometimes you'll pop back early for no adequately explained reason.'

'Can you send me back out there? I was right in the middle of something important.'

'If Bradshaw allows it, I'll be more than happy to.'

'Please?'

'There are safety issues,' he explained. 'The more you stay out there, the shorter time you can spend there. Bradshaw used to travel across quite often, but these days he can barely stay out for ten minutes before popping back.'

I thought about the excitement I had felt just as I was about to kiss Landen, and the potential chain of events that might have occurred from there on in.

'I *really* need to get back, Professor. Lives – um – depend on it.'

'Whose lives?'

Commander Bradshaw had appeared in the laboratory. But he didn't walk in, he had bookjumped in. I hadn't seen that for a while; it was considered very common, and was actively discouraged. The Ungenred Zone and Racy Novel, to name but two, even had anti-jump sieves set up on their borders – large sails of a fine mesh that snagged the punctuation in one's description, and brought one down to earth with a thump.

'I'm very busy,' he said, glancing at his watch, 'walk with me.'

So I walked with Bradshaw out of the labs, past the frog-footman, who followed at a discreet distance, and up the stairs.

'So,' said Bradshaw. 'How did you get on?'

'Not very well. *Lots* happened, but I've got no way of knowing which of the facts were significant and which weren't.'

'The RealWorld is like that. It's possible nothing was significant or everything. It scares the bejeezus out of me, I can tell you – and I don't scare easily. Anything about Thursday's whereabouts?'

I told him about the locked room at Acme.

'Hmm,' he said, '*definitely* in here somewhere. I'll ask Professor Plum to attempt another Textual Sieve Triangulation.'

He thought for a moment.

'How were Landen and the kids?'

'As well as might be expected. Permission to speak honestly, sir?'

'I welcome nothing else.'

'Is it possible that Thursday is alive and well but just suffering some bizarre mental aberration?'

He stared at me.

'You think you might be Thursday?'

I shrugged.

'Landen seems to think so. I saw Jenny and I could do things – fight, think on my feet and disarm a man in under a second. Things I never knew I could do.'

He smiled and patted my arm.

'It's not uncommon to have feelings of elevated status after visiting the RealWorld. It'll soon pass.'

'But *could* I tell if I was real? Could anyone tell?'

'There are lots of signs,' said Bradshaw, 'but here's the easiest: what am I doing now?'

'I don't know.'

'How about now?'

'As far as I can tell, you're not doing anything at all.'

Bradshaw took his finger off my nose and smiled.

'I suppressed my action line. The real Thursday could have seen what I was doing; you had to rely on the description. You're fictional, my dear, through and through.'

'But I could be just *thinking* you did that – the same as I *thought* I saw Jenny, and all my backstory about being the written Thursday. I could be . . . delusional.'

'And part of this delusion is you *thinking* you might be delusional? And me here right now talking to you?'

'I suppose so.'

'Pull yourself together, girl,' he snapped, 'and don't be such a bloody fool. If you *were* Thursday you'd be saving the BookWorld, not blundering around the Outland like a petulant bull in a china shop. This is Fiction, not Psychology.'

'I'm sorry, sir.'

'That's okay. Now, is there anything else to report?'

I told him about Jenny, the comment about Lyell, and how Goliath had developed a Green Fairy and wanted to know where the Austen Rover had ended up.

'Goliath are an ongoing thorn,' said Bradshaw grimly, 'but we're dealing with the problem. Anything else?'

I thought for a moment. If I couldn't trust Bradshaw, I couldn't trust anyone.

'This morning Jobsworth and Red Herring asked me to pretend to be Thursday and go to the peace talks on Friday.'

'We thought they might.'

'Should I go?'

'It would be my advice that you shouldn't. Don't be insulted by this, but civilians are ill equipped to deal with anything beyond that which is normally expected of them. The BookWorld is fraught with dangers, and your time is best served bringing as many readers as you can to your series, and then keeping them.'

'Can I go back to the RealWorld?'

'No.'

'I have unfinished business. I did go on a somewhat risky mission for you – I could have ended up erased or dead – or both.'

'You have the gratitude of the Head of Jurisfiction,' he said, 'that should be enough. He's not your husband, Thursday. He's Thursday's. Go back to your book and just forget about everything that's happened. You're not her, and never can be. Understand?'

'Yes, sir.'

'Excellent. Appreciate a girl who knows when to call it a day. Frog guy will see you out. Good day.'

And so saying, he turned on his heel and walked into the ballroom. The door closed behind him, leaving me confused, drained and missing Landen. I thought of going to find Whitby to cry on his shoulder, but then I remembered about the nuns.

'Damn,' I said, to no one in particular.

The frog-footman saw me to the front door, then handed me the Rubik's Cube I had lent him.

'Here,' he said, 'it's got me flummoxed, I can tell you.'

Despite working on the puzzle during my absence, the cube had remained resolutely unsolved – all six sides were still the same, unbroken colours.

28

Home Again

'. . . **There are multiple BookWorlds, all coexisting in parallel planes, and each unique to their own language.** Naturally, varying tastes around the Outland make for varying popularity of genres, so no two BookWorlds are ever the same. Generally, they keep themselves to themselves, except for the annual BookWorld conference where the equivalent characters get together to discuss translation issues. It invariably ends in arguments and recrimination.'

Bradshaw's BookWorld Companion, 2nd Edition

I climbed out of the Porsche, slammed the door and leaned against the stone wall. We'd just done the 'bad time' section within *The Eyre Affair*, which was always tiring and a bit spacey. Despite our best endeavours, our sole reader had simply given up and left us dangling less than a page before the end of that chapter – the Outlander equivalent of letting someone reach the punchline before announcing you'd heard the joke before.

Bowden climbed out to join me. I got on better with him than I did with the character who played my father, but that wasn't saying much: like saying sparrows got on better with cats than robins did. Bowden had a thing going with the previous written Thursday, and when he tried to hit on me at the Christmas party, I'd tipped an entire quiche in his lap. Our relationship on- and off-book had been strained ever since.

'That was just plain *embarrassing*,' said Bowden, 'you were barely even trying.'

I'd taken over from Carmine the second I got home, so I couldn't blame her. I should have let her just carry on – she was doing fine, after all, but, well, I needed the distraction.

'So we had a bit of wastage,' I said, 'it happens.'

Reader 'wastage' was something one had to get used to, but never did. Most of the time it was simply that our book wasn't 'the reader's thing,' which was borne with a philosophical shrug. We'd lost six readers at one hit once when my brother Joffy went AWOL and missed out an entire chapter. It had never been more tempting to hit the Snooze button. Mind you, in the annals of Reader Wastage, our six readers were peanuts. *Stig of the Dump* once lost seven hundred readers in the early seventies when Stig was kidnapped by *Homo erectus* fundamentalists, eager to push a pro-megalith agenda. Unusually, terms were agreed with the kidnappers and a new megalith section was inserted into the book. It messed slightly with the whole dream/reality issue, but never dented the popularity of the novel. On that occasion the Snooze button *was* pressed, which accounts for the lack of a sequel. Kitten death – even *written* kitten death – carries a lot of stigma. Barney eventually handed over the reins to a replacement and works these days at Text Grand Central; Stig is now much in demand as an after-dinner non-speaker.

'So what's up?' asked Bowden. 'I've seen more dynamic performances in *Mystery on the Island*.'

I shrugged.

'Things aren't going that well for me at the moment.'

'Man trouble?'

'Of a sort.'

'Do you want some advice?'

'Thank you, Bowden, I would.'

'Get your arse into gear and act like a mature character. You're making us the laughing stock of Speculative Fantasy. Our readership is in free-fall. Want to go the way of *Raphael's Walrus*?'

It wasn't the sort of advice I was expecting.

'So you'd prefer the old Thursday, would you?' I replied indignantly. 'With the gratuitous sex and violence?'

'At least it got us read.'

'Yes,' I replied, 'but by who? We want the *quality* readers – not the prurient ones who—'

'You're a terrible snob, you know that?'

'I am not.'

'You should value *all* readers. If you want to breathe the rarefied atmosphere of "quality readership" then why don't you sod off to HumDram and do a Plot 9?'

'Because,' I said, 'I'm trying to do what the real Thursday wants.'

'And where is she?' he asked with a sneer. 'Not been down this way for months. You keep banging on about the greater glory of your illustrious namesake, but if she *really* cared for us, she'd drop in from time to time.'

I fell silent. There was some truth in this. It had been six months since she'd visited, and only then because she wanted to borrow Mrs Malaprop to put up some shelves.

'Listen,' said Bowden, 'you're nice enough in a scatty kind of way, but if you try to add any new scenarios you'll just make trouble for us. If you're going to change anything, revert to the previous Thursday. It's within the remit for "character interpretation". And since she was once that way, there's a precedent. More readers, and no risk. Who the hell are the Toast Marketing Board anyway?'

'It's a *secret* plan,' I remarked defensively, 'to improve readership. You're going to have to trust me. And while I'm in charge, we'll do it my way, thank you very much. I may even decide,' I added daringly, 'to add some more about the BookWorld in the stories. It would make it more realistic, and readers might find it amusing.'

It was a bold statement. The CofG went to great expense to ensure readers didn't find out about the inner workings of the

BookWorld. I left Bowden looking shocked and opened a door in the Yorkshire Dales setting, then took a short cut through the SpecOps building to find myself back home. Carmine and Sprockett were waiting in the kitchen and sensed something was wrong.

'I met Mr and Mrs Goblin,' said Carmine, 'and they seem very—'

'– I'm really not that bothered, Carmine. You're taking over for a while. I've added something about the Toast Marketing Board. It'll require line changes on these pages here and an extra scene.'

I handed her the new pages and she looked at me with a quizzical expression. Making up new scenes was utterly forbidden, and we both knew it.

'I'll take responsibility. Now get on with it or I'll have Mrs Malaprop stand in for me – she'd kill for some First Person time in her logbook.'

Carmine said no more and hurried from the room.

'I'm hungry,' said Pickwick, waddling in from the living room.

'You know where the cupboard is.'

'*What* did you say?'

'I said you know where the cupboard is.'

Pickwick opened her eyes wide in shock. She wasn't used to being talked to that way.

'Don't use that tone of voice with me, Miss Next!'

'Or else what?'

Pickwick waddled up and pecked me as hard as she could on the knee. It wasn't remotely painful, as a dodo's beak is quite blunt. If she'd been a woodpecker I might have had more reason to complain. I held her beak shut with my finger and thumb and then leaned down so close that she went cross-eyed trying to look up at me.

'Look here,' I said, 'try to peck me again and I'll lock you in the toolshed overnight. Understand?'

Pickwick nodded her beak and I let go, and she very quietly

sidled from the room. There was a mechanical cough from behind me. It was Sprockett, and his eyebrow pointer was indicating 'Puzzled'.

'How did the trip to the RealWorld go?' he asked.

'Not great.'

'So I observe, ma'am.'

I sat down at the kitchen table and ran my fingers through my hair.

'Perhaps if ma'am would like to change out of your work costume? I could run a bath – perhaps a long soak might help.'

I looked down at the clothes I was wearing. It was classic Thursday: Levi's, boots and a shirt, faded leather jacket and shoulder holster. I felt more at home in these now than I felt in my cheesecloth skirt and tie-dye top. In fact, I would be happy never to see a sandal again, much less wear one.

'You know,' I said as Sprockett brought me a cup of tea, 'I thought it was odd in the BookWorld. Out in the RealWorld it's positively *insane.*'

'How was Landen?'

'Dangerously perfect.'

I told him all that had happened. Of Jack Schitt being Adrian Dorset, of Goliath, the Toast Marketing Board and the contention from Jenny that Thursday couldn't be dead. I also told him my suspicions that I might actually be her, despite what Bradshaw had said and much evidence to the contrary.

'And then I lost a reader and got pissed off with Bowden, Carmine and Pickwick,' I added.

'Any clues as to Miss Next's whereabouts?' asked Sprockett as he attempted to keep me on the task in hand.

'Only that Lyell is boring. How many Lyells are there in the BookWorld?'

Sprockett buzzed for a moment.

'Seven thousand, give or take. None of them particularly boring – that's a trait generally attached to Geralds, Brians and Horaces – or at least, here in the BookWorld it is.'

'Interviewing every Lyell would take too long. Friday and the peace talks are not getting any farther away.'

'Did you speak to the Jack Schitt here in the series?'

'First thing when I got back.'

'And—?'

'He knew nothing about Adrian Dorset or *Murders*. Didn't even know that Jack wasn't his real name.'

'But it's a bit of a stretch, isn't it?' said Sprockett, his eyebrow pointer returning to 'Puzzled'. 'I mean, it can't be a coincidence. Jack Schitt's book being the accident book?'

'In the Outland there *are* coincidences. It's only in the Book-World they're considered relevant. What about you? Come up with anything?'

'I went and spoke to TransGenreTaxis. To see if they were missing anyone.'

'And?'

'They wouldn't give me any information. I think it was a mixture of corporate policy, laziness and overt coggism.'

'Really?' I replied. 'We'll see about that.'

I went next door to the study, fetched a chair and pulled Thursday's shield from where it was still embedded in the ceiling. I turned the shiny badge over in my hand. It was encased in a soft leather wallet, and was well worn with use. It could get me almost anywhere in the BookWorld, no questions asked.

'Why would the red-haired gentleman have given this to me?'

'Maybe he was asked to,' said Sprockett. 'Thursday has many friends, but there is only one person she knows she can truly trust.'

'And who's that?'

'Herself.'

'That's what the red-haired man told me,' I said, suddenly real-ising that recent events may have had some greater purpose behind them. 'Something happened. Thursday must have left instructions for him to get out of his story, find me and ask me to help.'

'Why didn't he say so directly?' asked Sprockett, not unreason-ably.

'This is Fiction,' I explained. 'The exigency of drama requires events to be clouded in ambiguity.'

I placed Thursday's badge in my pocket.

'Is using the shield wise?' asked Sprockett. 'The last time you used it the Men in Plaid were on to us within the hour.'

'It opens doors. And what's more, I don't care if the Men in Plaid do arrive. We'll do as Thursday would do.'

'And what would that be, ma'am?'

I opened the bureau drawer, took out my second-best pistol and emptied all the ammunition I had into my jacket pocket.

'We kick some butt, Sprockett.'

'Very good, ma'am.'

29

TransGenreTaxis

'The TransGenreTaxi service had been going for almost as long as the BookWorld had been self-aware, and had adapted to the Remaking with barely a murmur. TGTs are clean, the drivers have an encyclopedic knowledge of the BookWorld that would put a librarian to shame, and can be relied upon to bend the rules when required – for a fee. Traditionally, they rarely have change for a twenty.'

Bradshaw's BookWorld Companion, 2nd Edition

The TransGenreTaxi head office was housed over in Non-Fiction within the pages of the less-than-thrilling *World Taxi Review*, published bi-monthly. But travelling all the way to Non-Fiction would take a needlessly long time and alert the Men in Plaid before we'd even got as far as Zoology. Luckily for us, there was a regional office located within *The First Men in the Moon*, over in Sci-Fi/Classic. It was rumoured that the propulsion system used by the taxis was based upon a modified Cavorite design, but this was pooh-poohed by SF purists as 'unworkable'. Mind you, so was the 'inside of a sphere BookWorld', but that seemed to work fine, too.

The dispatch clerk was a small, deeply harassed individual, who had the look of someone who had unwisely conditioned his hair and then slept on it wet.

'No refunds!' he said as soon as we entered.

'I'm not after a refund.'

'You wouldn't get one if you were. What can I do for you?'

'We're looking for a missing taxi. Took a fare from Vanity early yesterday morning.'

The dispatch clerk was unfazed.

'I'm afraid to say that company policy is quite strict on this matter, madam. You'll need a Jurisfiction warrant—'

'– How's this?' I asked, slapping Thursday's shield on the counter.

The dispatch clerk stared at the badge, then at me. He thought for a moment and picked up a clipboard from under the counter, then started to flick through the attached pages. There were a lot of them.

'You're fortunate we still have them,' he said. 'We file with Captain Phantastic in an hour.'

He searched through them, chatting as he did so.

'We lose a couple of taxis every day to erasure, wastage, accidental reabsorption or simply being used in books. For obvious reasons we're keen to hide the actual number of accidents for fear of frightening people from our cabs.'

'Most thoughtful of you.'

'You're in luck,' he said, staring at his notes. 'The only taxi missing that morning was Car 1517. Its last known fare was a pick-up from Sargasso Plaza, opposite the entrance to Fanfiction.'

'On Vanity Island?'

'Right. The driver departed Sargasso Plaza bound for the Ungenred Zone at 8.23. And that was the last we heard.'

'You didn't think about reporting it?'

'We usually wait a week. Besides, search parties are expensive.'

'Do we have a passenger name?'

'Tuesday Laste.'

Sprockett and I looked at one another. We seemed finally to be getting somewhere.

'And the name of the driver?'

'Gatsby.'

'The Great Gatsby drives taxis in his spare time?'

'No, his younger and less handsome or less intelligent brother – the Mediocre Gatsby. He lives in Parody Valley over in Vanity. Here's his address.'

We thanked him and left the office.

'*Tuesday Laste*?' repeated Sprockett as we hailed a cab.

'Almost certainly Thursday.'

Sprockett's eyebrow pointer switched from 'Puzzled' to 'Bingo', paused for a moment and then switched to 'Worried'.

'Problems?' I asked as we climbed into the cab.

'In the shape of a Buick,' replied Sprockett, indicating a Road-master that had just pulled up outside the TransGenreTaxi office. It was the Men in Plaid, and they were following the same trail as us. I leaned forward.

'Vanity Island,' I said to the driver, 'and step on it.'

Vanity wasn't a place conventionally published people liked to visit as it was a bizarre mixture of the best and worst prose, where descriptive passages of exceptional beauty rubbed shoulders with dialogue so spectacularly poor it could make one's ears bleed. We skimmed low across the narrow straits that separated Vanity from the mainland, and circled the craggy island, past sprawling shanty towns of abandoned novellas, half-described castles and ragged descriptions of variable quality, before coming to land in a small square just outside Parody Valley.

'You can wait for us,' I said to the cabby, who gave me a sarcastic 'yeah, right' and left almost immediately, which made me regret I'd paid up front and tipped him.

We took a left turn into Cold Comfort Boulevard and made our way past unpublished pastiches and parodies of famous novels that were only on Vanity at all owing to them being just within the law. If they had used the same character names as the parodied novel, they were removed to the copyright-tolerance haven of Fanfiction. This was situated on a smaller island close by, and joined to Vanity by a narrow stone arched bridge a half-mile long, guarded by a game show host.

'How long before the Men in Plaid follow us here?' asked Sprockett.

'Five or ten minutes,' I replied, and we quickened our pace.

Given that parodies — even unpublished ones — have a shelf-life governed by the currency of the novel that is being parodied, the small sub-genre was dominated by that year's favourite: uneven 'D. J. Growling' rip-offs. We walked on, and once past the still-popular Tolkien pastiches we were in the unread Parody hinterland, based on books either out of print themselves, or so far off the Zeitgeist Radar that they had little or no meaning. We took a left turn by *When Nine Bells Toll, Hello My Lovely* and *I, Robert* before finding the book we were looking for: an outrageously unfunny Fitzgerald parody entitled *The Diamond as Big as the South Mimms Travelodge*.

Mediocre's apartment was above a set of garages. There was a brand-new taxi parked in an empty bay beneath, and we carefully climbed the rickety stairs. I knocked on the screen door and after a few moments a woman of slovenly demeanour appeared on the threshold gnawing a chicken drumstick. She had heavy eyeliner which had run, and looked as though she had just had a fight with a hairbrush — and lost.

'Yes?' she asked in a lazy manner. 'Can I help?'

I flashed Thursday's badge.

'Thursday Next,' I announced, 'and this is my butler, Sprockett. Your name is—?'

'Gatsby.'

This was unexpected.

'The Mediocre Gatsby?'

'No, the *Loser* Gatsby, the youngest of the three Gatsbys. I haven't seen Great for a while. How did it turn out with crazy Daisy? She looked like trouble to me.'

'Not . . . *terrific*, as I recall.'

'Did they let Mia Farrow play her in the movie?'

'I'm not sure. Is Mediocre here?'

'I've not seen the miserable fart for three days.' She sniffed, picking her nose. 'How did you know he was missing? I didn't call you.'

'May we come in?'

'I guess,' said Loser Gatsby with a shrug, and we walked into the apartment. Sprawled in the front room were half a dozen men and women who looked as though life had not been kind to them. One of the women had been crying recently, and two of the men still were.

'This is our "Siblings of More Famous BookWorld Personalities" self-help group,' explained Loser. 'That's Sharon Eyre, the younger and wholly disreputable sister of Jane; Roger Yossarian, the draft-dodger and coward; Brian Heep, who despite admonishments from his family continues to wash daily; Rupert Bond, still a virgin and can't keep a secret; Tracy Capulet, who has slept her way round Verona twice; and Nancy Potter, who is . . . well, let's just say she's a term that is subject to several international trademark agreements.'

'She's a Muggle?'

'Pretty much.'

They all nodded a greeting.

'We meet twice daily to try to iron out the feelings of low self-worth given our more famous family members. It's quite hard, I assure you, being a nobody when an elder sister or brother is iconic for all time. Tracy Capulet was telling us what it was like living in Verona.'

'It's "Juliet this, Juliet that" all day long,' said Tracy petulantly, 'Juliet's on the balcony, Juliet's shagging a Montague, Juliet's pretending to be dead – blah blah blah. I tell you, I'm totally sick of it.'

Sprockett moved to the window and peered out. The Men in Plaid would be here soon.

'This is a matter of some urgency,' I said. 'Does Mediocre have a room?'

Loser pointed to a door and before she could explain that it was locked, Sprockett had wrenched it off its hinges.

The room was grubby and the floor scattered with discarded pizza containers and empty hyphen cans. The TV was still on and was tuned to a shopping channel, and his record collection contained *Hooked on Classics* and the *Footloose* soundtrack. Mediocre lived up to his name.

'What do you make of this?' asked Sprockett, who had come across a large model of the Forth Rail Bridge. It had large spans that in reality would have thrust boldly across the Forth estuary, not just to connect two landmasses separated by a barrier that was also an arterial trade route, but to demonstrate man's technological prowess in the face of natural obstacles.

'It's not a bridge,' I whispered, 'it's *Metaphor*.'

We started opening boxes and found three more bridges, two rivers and a distant mountain range, swathed in mist with a road leading to unknown valleys beyond. The Loser Gatsby was at the door, mouth open.

'Tell me,' I said, 'where did your brother get all this?'

'I don't know.'

'Truthfully?'

'I'm a loser,' she said. 'If I'd known about this little lot I would have sold it all, gone on a bender and had a dolphin tattooed on my left boob.'

Her logic was impeccable. I questioned her further, but she knew nothing.

'In two minutes the Men in Plaid will be coming through that door,' I told her. 'Believe me, you don't want to be here when they do.'

I didn't need to say it twice, and she and the rest of the loser literary siblings made a hasty exit down the stairs.

'So,' said Sprockett, staring at all the Metaphor. 'Stolen?'

'Not if Mediocre was as his name suggests,' I replied. 'How much do you think this is all worth?'

'Twenty grand,' said Sprockett. 'People will pay good money to get hold of raw Metaphor. There's enough here to keep a man comfortable for a long time.'

'Or even enrol at Character College,' I said, holding up a prospectus from St Tabularasa's. 'Looks like Mediocre was trying to better himself and shed his epithet. A cabby couldn't earn this much in a decade of Octobers,' I added. 'I reckon we're looking at a bribe.'

'To do what?'

'I don't know. Either Mediocre was bribed to do something pretty dreadful, or whoever offered the bribe had Metaphor to spare.'

I picked up Mediocre's account book. It outlined all the journeys he had done, and which needed to be billed. The last day was not there, of course, but the previous day *was*.

'Well, well,' I said, 'looks like Thursday went on a trip to Biography the day before she vanished. And that's not all,' I added. 'Every single fare Mediocre accepted was picked up from the same place – Sargasso Plaza, just outside the entrance to Fanfiction. Coincidence?'

'We have company,' murmured Sprockett, who had been standing at the window.

I joined him and noted that a 1949 Buick Roadmaster had pulled up outside the building. Two Men in Plaid got out and looked around.

'Time we weren't here.'

We crossed to the other side of the room and let ourselves out of the French windows, which opened on to a veranda. From there we climbed down on to the roof of a garden shed, then let ourselves out into an alley beyond. We walked back around the house and watched as the Plaid went into the building.

'What now, ma'am?'

I handed him a set of keys I'd found in Mediocre's room and nodded towards the brand-new taxi parked outside.

'Can you drive one of those?'

'If it has wheels I can drive it, ma'am. Are we heading for Biography?'

'We are.'

'And what will we do when we get there?'

'Find out if Lyell is as boring as Thursday said he was.'

30

High Orbit

'... Sooner or later a resident of the BookWorld will start to question what is *beyond* the internal sphere that we call home. Stated simply, what would happen if one burrowed directly downwards? In pursuit of an answer, noted explorer Arne Saknussemm undertook a mission to find out, and entered a disused Metaphor mine to see if a way through could be found. As this edition went to press, he has not yet returned ...'

Bradshaw's BookWorld Companion, 3rd Edition

Sprockett reversed the cab out of the garage, engaged the Technobabble™ Swivelmatic vectored ion plasma drive and powered vertically upwards from Parody Valley and Vanity. I was pressed back into my seat by the acceleration and the ascent angle, and might have been frightened had my mind not been wrestling with what we had discovered so far – or even with what we had still yet to find out.

Within a few minutes we were hanging in the heavens a couple of thousand feet from the surface, right at the cruising altitude of local books that were being moved around Fiction. Below us the islands that made up the Fiction archipelago were laid out in precise detail.

'Would it be impertinent to point out that visiting another island in the BookWorld without transit papers is strictly forbidden?'

'What does Thursday Next care for transit papers?'

'I would politely point out that you're not her, ma'am.'

'I might as well be. I have a shield and look like her. Who can say I'm not?'

'Who indeed, ma'am.'

I looked behind us and out to sea. Biography was situated beyond Artistic Criticism and it was unlikely that any books would be going that way at this lower level. I wound down the window, poked my head out and looked up. Several miles above us I could see the high-level books criss-crossing the sky, their journey made less arduous by travelling at the precise altitude where the force of gravity from below cancels the force of gravity from above – the *Gravopause*. At that height you could usually find someone going your way – so long as you could get up there. The Technobabble™ drive on the cab would get us to local traffic height, but after that we were on our own.

We had to wait a nail-biting two and three-quarter minutes, every second worrying that the Plaid would spot us.

'Buckle up, ma'am,' said Sprockett, 'looks like an author's been discovered.'

As we watched, an entire section of Vanity Island seemed to fall away. A book had been accepted into the mainstream and was rising from the flanks of Mount Sleeper, trailing the debris of a ramshackle group of shameless Zadie Smith rip-offs which had been unwisely built on top of it.

The settings – mostly of a winter scene in London, it appeared – rotated slowly about its axis as it rose vertically to meet us, and just as it transitioned into forward flight, Sprockett stepped on the throttle and accelerated to meet the book, which loomed as large as eight cathedrals in the windscreen. As soon as we were close enough Sprockett slewed the vehicle to a stop on the side of a dream sequence – a picnic the family had once taken on a grassy hill in spring, where a silver pond alive with bulrushes lay within the dappled glade of beech trees.

'Congratulations on the publication,' I said to a small boy who was playing with a tin train, and he waved shyly in return. We weren't there for long. Piggybacking around the BookWorld was a dark art that needed calm nerves and good timing; within a few minutes Sprockett lifted off again and made the short hop to a historical novel that was moving up to join the High Stream in order to make its way to History for fact-checking. They looked less friendly in this book, so Sprockett simply fired one of the vehicle's two grapnels into the soft intertextual matrix to which the book's settings were bolted, and we began the tow into the high orbit dangling on the end of a slender length of steel cable.

'Okay,' I said as we moved steadily upwards, the cab's altimeter winding around like a top, 'how's this for a scenario? Thursday is investigating something that requires her to stay out of sight. She hides out in Vanity, somewhere near Sargasso Plaza. The Mediocre Gatsby always hangs out there, waiting for fares. He takes her to Biography, and the following day picks her up to go to the Council of Genres. He piggybacks *The Murders on the Hareng Rouge*, which is heading – ISBN already scrubbed – towards the Ungenred Zone to be scrapped. Somewhere above Aviation the Rhetorical device is activated. The book explodes into a zillion fragments within a fraction of a second, taking with it Thursday, Mediocre and the TransGenreTaxi. It's just another book coming to grief which would be swiftly investigated, and then as swiftly dismissed as an accident.'

'Barmouth Blaster?' asked Sprockett, offering me a cocktail.

'Thank you.'

'So we were right – it wasn't an attack on the book at all,' murmured Sprockett, adding the ice and lemon to the cocktail shaker along with half a can of Red Bull, a Strepsil and two onions, 'it was a hit on the taxi – with Thursday Next inside. Which means that Mediocre must have been bribed to piggyback that particular book—'

'—but knew nothing of the reason. He was tricked into attending his own execution, as well as Thursday's.'

We sat in silence for some minutes as we were towed ever upwards, thinking about what we had just uncovered. In the Real-World such a convoluted method of murder would be faintly ridiculous, but in the BookWorld, all murders happened this way.

'Your Barmouth Blaster, ma'am.'

'Thank you.'

'Ma'am?'

'Yes?'

'Why was Ms Next murdered?'

There were at least seventy-two people who had tried to kill her over the years, and narrowing it down was going to be tricky. I decided to head for the most obvious.

'Without Thursday the Racy Novel peace talks might well fail. Who would benefit most from a genre war in the north of the island?'

'Men in Plaid,' said Sprockett.

'Hardly likely,' I replied. 'They're simply mopping up for someone else – or simply want to find Thursday – or are just being wicked for the hell of it.'

'You misunderstand me, madam,' he said politely. 'I mean Men in Plaid – *behind us*!'

I turned and looked out of the cab's rear window. Sprockett was right. Far below was not one Buick Roadmaster, but three. They would also have TechnoBabble™ Scramjamcious Gravitational Flux Throb-O-Tron Torque Converter drive systems, and knowing the Men in Plaid, considerably more advanced than ours, and twice as nonsensical.

'How far to the Gravopause?' I asked.

'We're almost there.'

Despite the Gravopause's usefulness for getting about, one had to be careful. If you had the misfortune to move *above* this altitude and had insufficient thrust to escape, you could be caught in the dead centre of the sphere for ever. There was a small moon in the gravitational dead spot made from accreted book traffic that had accidentally fallen in and been unable to escape. From the dizzy heights we had now reached, I could actually see the moon above us, seemingly no bigger than a pea.

Within a half minute more we had reached the Gravopause, and Sprockett cast off the towline and we drifted onwards, safely in orbit. All that was required now was to coast along until we were above Biography, and then dip the cab into a downward trajectory and let gravity take over.

'Ma'am, would you wind me up?' said Sprockett. 'I can see fun and games ahead and I wouldn't want to risk spring depletion at an inopportune moment.'

I leaned forward and wound him until his indicator was just below the red line. I felt his bronze outer casing flex with the increased tension.

'The Men in Plaid are gaining,' I said, looking behind us.

The three Roadmasters were in V formation about a half-mile away and had just reached the Gravopause. At the rate they were going they would be upon us in under five minutes.

'I'm going to head for that cluster of book traffic,' announced Sprockett, opening the throttle and accelerating towards a loose gaggle of several hundred books that appeared to be all heading in the same direction. As we drew closer I could see that they were mostly Non-Fiction, and of considerable size. It was the renegade Oversized Book section, on their way to their new home.

They grew dramatically in size as we approached, and as we passed between *John Deere Tractors* and *Clarice Cliff Tableware*, they towered over us like skyscrapers.

'Hold tight,' said Sprockett, and he pulled the cab hard over and darted behind *Lighthouses of Maine*.

'They're still behind us,' I barked, peering out of the rear wind-shield as the Boon Island Lightstation flashed past on our left-hand side, foghorn blaring, 'or at least, one is.'

'They only attack one at a time,' replied Sprockett, his eyebrow flicking past 'Indignant' to 'Peeved', 'and in that respect they're very like baddies in seventies martial arts movies. Hold tight.'

Sprockett skimmed past *Best of National Geographic* so close I could taste the hot dust of the Serengeti, and then pulled up sharply in front of *Chronicle of Britain*. I felt myself pressed hard into my seat. My vision grew grey, then faded out entirely. My arms and head felt intolerably heavy, and a second later I was unconscious as Sprockett – his body designed to tolerate up to 17.6 G – pulled the cab into an almost vertical climb. I came around again as soon as he reached the top of the book, and he immediately plunged the cab into a near-vertical dive.

'Still behind us?'

They were. I could see the emotionless features of the Plaids as they edged closer. Sprockett corkscrewed around *Knitting Toy Animals for Pleasure and Profit* as the passenger in the Roadmaster leaned out of the window and fired a shot which flew wide to blow a ragged hole in *Knitting Toy Animals* as we sped on, and a blue knitted giraffe named Natalie began a long slow fall to the Text Sea, sixteen miles below.

'These Men in Plaid are made of stern stuff,' said Sprockett, his eyebrow pointer clicking from 'Peeved' to 'Puzzled' to 'Indignant', then almost to 'Severely Peeved' before settling on 'Peeved' again. 'Hold tight.'

The Oversized Books were now moving in a more random fashion as they tried to avoid us, and Sprockett dived to get more speed, then pulled up and headed towards where *What Do People Do All Day?* and *ABC With Dewin the Dog* were about to collide, cover to cover. There was barely a ten foot gap either side as we

'The passenger in the Roadmaster fired a shot which blew a ragged hole in *Knitting Toy Animals*, and a blue giraffe named Natalie began a long slow fall to the Text Sea, sixteen miles below.'

flew between then, and the gap narrowed as we moved on. I barely had a chance to wave a cheery 'hello' to a worried looking Lowly Worm as the covers closed together a split-second before we shot out the other side. The Roadmaster was less fortunate and there was a tremendous detonation as the car was crushed between the two books, the worried shouts of Scarry's folk mixing with Dewin the Dog's furious barking.

'Do you see the others ma'am?' asked Sprockett as we swerved hard to miss the greatest Oversized Book of all time but the abrupt sideways movement cause a ventral compressor stall on the Technobabble™ drive, and we went spiralling downwards out of control until Sprockett achieved an emergency relight.

'On the left!' I yelled as the second Roadmaster swept past, a shot from an Eraserhead removing half the rear bumper and a wing. Sprockett jinked hard, spiralled up for a second, then shot past *Cooking for Fusspots* and *Helmut Newton Nudes*.

'Rewind me again, ma'am, if you please,' said Sprockett, hauling sideways on the wheel to avoid the *Times Atlas*. The exertions on his frame had depleted his spring at a furious rate – I'd have to remain conscious if only to rewind him.

'Watch out!'

It was too late. We had taken a hard left at *Titanic Revisited* and were met by a group of Oversized Books that had bunched together tightly for self-protection. There was no time to avoid them, and all we could see was a sabre jet fragmenting in front of us as we loomed ever closer to *Lichtenstein*. But just when I thought we were dead for sure, Sprockett pulled the wheel hard over and we entered *The Works of Thomas Gainsborough* through a small thermal exhaust port near the preface.

I stared wide eyed as Sprockett drove the cab through the paintings of Gainsborough at over a hundred miles per hour. We shot through early landscapes, dodged past *Cornard Wood*, burst into portraiture at *John Plampin*, then twisted and turned past a dozen or so well-dressed dignitaries, who for their part looked as startled and horrified as we did. We went between the knees of Mr Byam and at one point nearly knocked the hat off Mrs Siddons. But still the Roadmaster stuck to us like glue, not able to fire at us with the constant movement, but awaiting the opportunity with a certain calm detachment. We doubled back around the *Blue Boy* as Sprockett searched for the exit.

'Can you see a way out, ma'am?'

'There!' I said, having heard a lowing in the distance. 'Behind the third cow from the left in *The Watering Place*.'

We passed *The Harvest Wagon* for a second time as Sprockett lowered the nose and accelerated across the painted landscape, the Roadmaster still close behind. We turned sharp left as the Duchess of Devonshire loomed up in front of us, and there was a thump as we hit something. The Roadmaster behind us misjudged the turning and struck the Duchess on the shins, the resulting explosion scattering metal fragments that struck the back of the cab with a metallic rattle.

In another second we were clear, none the worse for our rapid traverse aside from a brace of partridge that had jammed in the wipers and cracked the screen.

'What did they hit?' asked Sprockett.

'The Duchess of Devonshire – took off both legs.'

'She'll be a half-portrait from now on. Whoops.'

The third Roadmaster had appeared in front of us and another Eraserhead had taken the taxi light off the roof and blasted a hole into *Classic Bedford Single-Deckers*, releasing several Plaxton-bodied coaches to tumble out into the void.

'We're causing too much damage,' I said, catching sight of the now chaotic movement of the Oversized Books, some of them on fire, others locked in collision and one, *Detroit's Muscle Cars*, falling to earth in a slow death spiral, the huge forces breaking apart the book and spilling 1972 Dodge Chargers across the BookWorld. 'We need to leave the Oversized Book section.'

'Logically, it places us in grave danger, ma'am.'

'But we are endangering *others*, Sprockett.'

'I place our chances of survival in open orbit at less than 1.7 per cent, ma'am.'

'Nevertheless,' I said, 'we are causing more destruction and death than we are worth.'

His eyebrow pointer clicked to 'Puzzled'.

'I do not understand.'

'It's the right thing to do, Sprockett. Not for us, but for *them*.'

'Is this *compassion*, ma'am? The following of the correct course irrespective of the outcome?'

The Duplex-5s were never great at this sort of stuff.

'You should always place others before yourself.'

'Even if it means certain destruction?'

'Yes, Sprockett, that's *exactly* what it means.'

He buzzed to himself for a moment in deep thought.

'Thank you for explaining it to me, ma'am,' he replied, 'I think I understand now.'

He peeled away from the Oversized Books and headed off into clear air. The last Buick Roadmaster was not far behind, and with no books to take cover behind, the end didn't seem far off. I pulled out my pistol and attempted to load it, but all the cartridges had spilled out of my pockets and into the footwell, and with Sprockett's constant bobbing and weaving, they were proving almost impossible to pick up.

But just then, the car stopped moving about, and all was calm. I seized the opportunity and picked up an armour-piercing round, flicked it into my pistol and snapped it shut.

'Sprockett?'

He wasn't moving. I thought at first he might have run down or been hit, but then I noticed that his eyebrow pointer was stuck firmly on 'Thinking'. He had committed his entire mainspring to his thought processes, and had shut down all motor functions to enable him to think faster. When I looked at his spring tension indicator, I could see it visibly moving – Sprockett was thinking, and thinking *hard*.

The Buick Roadmaster gained ground until it was no more than ten yards away. The Man in Plaid in the passenger seat leaned out of the window, took careful aim, and fired.

The Eraserhead is one of a series of 'special function' cartridges that can be chambered within the large-calibre pistol common among BookWorld law-enforcers. A long history of implausibly survivable bullet wounds in Thriller and Crime had rendered characters in the BookWorld invulnerable to small-calibre weapons, so the Textual Disrupter was designed to instantly break the bonds that bind graphemes together. A well-placed Eraserhead can reduce anything in the BookWorld to nothing more than text: titanium, diamond, Mrs Malaprop's sponge cake – anything. The effective range of the pistol was limited to less than forty feet, but the shoulder-mounted rocket-propelled Eraserhead was effective up to a hundred yards, although highly inaccurate.

The Eraserhead struck the back of the cab and the entire boot section, spare wheel, bumper, jack and wheel-brace burst into a cloud of individual letters, leaving the back of the cab with only the rear part of the chassis and the back axle. One more shot and they would erase me, and half of the cab. Two more shots and we would be nothing but a few items of scrap letters, orbiting at the Gravopause until nudged up to the moon, or down to the Book-World.

I fired my own pistol in reply, but the armour-piercing round simply passed through the Roadmaster's windshield and left-side rear door pillar doing no lasting damage at all. I watched with detached fascination as the passenger reloaded, took aim, and fired.

The cab dodged sideways and the Eraserhead flew wide.

'Sprockett?'

'I was thinking, ma'am. I was *calculating*.'

I noticed then with a sense of horror that we were climbing. We were moving *above* the Gravopause.

'Sprockett,' I said nervously, 'if we get too high we'll be pulled into the gravitational dead spot. We'll *never* get out.'

'As I said, ma'am, I was calculating. Do as I instruct and there is an eighteen per cent probability that we will survive.'

'Those aren't good odds.'

'On the contrary, ma'am. Next to the 98.3 per cent possibility of being erased, they're staggeringly good.'

'They may not follow,' I said, looking around.

'They're Men in Plaid,' replied Sprockett, 'and painfully dogged. They'll follow.'

I watched the Roadmaster, and after pausing momentarily, they were soon following our slow fall towards the moon, and although not gaining, they were certainly keeping pace.

'Do you have any armour-piercing rounds left, ma'am?'

I said that I did.

'Have them to hand and only use them when I say.'

The long fall towards the moon was conducted at a greatly increased velocity. I peered over Sprockett's shoulder and noted the speedometer only went as fast as .5 Absurd. We exceeded that speed within half a minute and the glass on the instrument shattered. The moon went from the size of a pea to that of an orange and then a football, and as we moved ever closer I could see that the small moon was about a quarter of a mile in diameter and was indeed made of accreted junk – bits of books that had been nudged from the Gravopause and been lost. Pretty soon the moon was the biggest object in the sky, and just when we were less than five hundred feet from the surface, Sprockett rolled the cab inverted and pulled the vehicle into a tight orbit. I felt a lurch as we accelerated rapidly, had time to see several people on the surface waving at us desperately, then we were off and around and away again, flung out back towards the Gravopause in a slingshot manoeuvre.

'Now we will see if my calculations are correct,' murmured Sprockett, his eyebrow pointer clicking to 'Doubtful', then 'Apologetic', then back to 'Doubtful' again before settling on 'Worried'.

I looked around. The Roadmaster was gaining, perhaps as a result of their greater mass, but we were still out of range of their Eraserhead. We cannoned on, still at speeds in excess of Absurd, but all the while slowly decelerating. Sprockett had hoped we would be able to reach the Gravopause again, but if he had miscalculated and we fell short by even a few feet, we would inexorably fall back towards the moon, and end our days playing cribbage and I-Spy with the unfortunate souls who were already there.

'Fire at the Roadmaster, ma'am.'

'They're out of range.'

'It doesn't matter.'

So I did, and the shot missed by a mile, and Sprockett nodded and pointed towards a lone copy of *World Hotel Review* that was orbiting at the Gravopause and thereby offering us a convenient yardstick of where safety lay.

I could feel us slow down, and the needle on the shattered speedometer was now reading .25 Absurd and slowing by the second. *World Hotel Review* lay less than half a mile away, and it seemed doubtful that we would make it.

'Fire at them again.'

So I reloaded and did as he asked, and at his insistence, continued to fire.

'Is there a point to this?' I asked, after firing five times, and managing only to clip a wing mirror.

'If we can make them angry and act irrationally, there is every point to it, ma'am. The cab has no power remaining. I am relying on our momentum to reach the Gravopause.'

I realised then what his calculations had been for, although I failed to see what it had gained us aside from twenty extra minutes, and a never-before-seen view of the moon. The Men in Plaid would simply wait until we were once more within range, and then finish us off.

The Gravopause was barely one hundred yards distant when they fired again. We were now moving at less than a fast walking pace, and had drifted sideways. The last armour-piercer I'd fired had sent us in a gentle end-over-end spinning motion which, while not unpleasant, was certainly disconcerting.

The first Eraserhead took away the front left side of the car, and the second the back axle. I returned fire at Sprockett's request, and an odd sight we must have seemed, two helplessly drifting cars less than thirty feet apart, trading shots between one another.

'I hope this was part of your plan, Sprockett. That was my last round and I missed them again. I think my poor marksmanship has squandered our chances.'

'*Au contraire*, ma'am. Every shot you fire pushes us farther towards the Gravopause – and every shot they fire stops them from reaching it.'

I frowned and stared out of the window. The passenger in the Roadmaster pointed his weapon and fired it straight at us, but the disrupting power of the Eraserhead evaporated a few feet short of the battered cab in a sparkle of light. The Men in Plaid had acted irrationally, and as we drifted behind *World Hotel Review* and to safety, the Roadmaster hung in space for a moment, and then started to fall away in a slow trajectory that would eventually find them, a few weeks hence, adding permanently to the moon's mass.

I breathed a sigh of relief, rewound Sprockett, who had red-lined without me realising it, and sat back in my seat.

'Well done,' I said, 'you've just earned yourself an extra week's paid holiday.'

'I seek only to serve,' said Sprockett, his eyebrow clicking from 'Nervous' to 'Contented'.

He fired the last remaining grapnel into the back of *World Hotel Review*, sent out a distress signal and we were taken on board.

'The name's Thursday Next,' I said to the Duty Book Officer, a frightfully dapper individual who was also manager of the Hotel Ukrania in Moscow, a place that we soon learned 'offers a wide range of modern conveniences to suit both the business and leisure traveller'.

'I'd like to use your book-to-ground footnoterphone link,' I added, flashing Thursday's badge, 'and after that, I'll need to requisition a small family-run guest house in Ghent to take me all the way to Biography.'

'Certainly,' said the manager, eager to help what he thought was a Jurisfiction agent in distress. 'How about the Hotel Verhaegen? It provides elegant guest rooms in the heart of historical Ghent, and combines contemporary style in an authentic eighteenth-century residence.'

'It sounds perfect.'

'This way.'

As we made our way to the Belgium section of the book, we caught a glimpse of the Roadmaster, now a tiny speck in the distance.

31

Biography

'**Although Outlander authors kill, maim, disfigure and eviscerate BookPeople on a regular basis, no author has ever been held to account.** Lawyers are working on a test case to deal with serial offenders, but the mechanism for trans-fictional jurisdiction has yet to be finalised. When it is, some authors may have cause to regret their worst excesses.'

Bradshaw's BookWorld Companion, 16th Edition

The Hotel Verhaegen landed on the lawn outside one of the biographical tenements. I sat for some moments in silence in the lobby. For some odd reason my left leg wouldn't stop shaking, and when I tried to speak, it sounded as if I was hyphenated. I had been fine on the trip down, but as soon as I had started to think about the Men in Plaid who had tried so hard to kill us, I suddenly felt all hot and fearful. I thought for a moment it might have been a virus I'd picked up from the RealWorld until I realised I was in mild shock.

I rested for ten minutes, and after downing one of Sprockett's restoratives and writing 'very nice' in the guest book, I stepped from the Verhaegen, which lifted off behind us. The manager wasn't going to hang around – the pay and display fees in Biography were ridiculous.

'Sp-sprockett,' I said as we walked across the car park, 'where d-d-did you learn to d-drive like that?'

'My cousin Malcolm, ma'am.'

'He's a r-racing driver?'

'He's a racing *car*. Is madam all right?'

295

'Madam is surprised she didn't scream, vomit and then pass out. I owe you my life, Sprockett.'

'A good butler,' intoned Sprockett airily, 'should save their employer's life at least once a day, if not more.'

Luckily for us, the island of Biography had elected to maintain parts of the Great Library model during the Remaking, so while the geographic model gave it the appearance of a low-lying island mostly covered with well-kept gardens, exciting statuary and dignified pavilions of learning, the biographical subjects themselves lived in twenty-six large tower blocks, each designated by a single letter painted conveniently on the front.

The lobby of apartment block 'L' was roomy and bright, and connected to a games room where Humphrey Lyttelton was playing H. P. Lovecraft at ping-pong, and also a cafeteria, where we could see Abraham Lincoln and Martin Luther discussing the struggles of faith over conscience. In the lobby were eight different Lindsay Lohans, all arguing over which biographical study had been the least correct.

Even before I'd reached the front desk I knew we were in luck. The receptionist recognised me.

'Hello again, Miss Next,' he said cheerfully, 'how did the peace talks go?'

'They're not until Friday.'

'How silly of me. You can go straight up. I'll ring ahead to announce you.'

'Most kind,' I replied, still unsure who Thursday had seen. 'Remind me again which floor?'

'Fourth,' said the receptionist, and turned to the telephone switchboard.

We took the brass and cast-iron elevator, which was of the same design as the one in the Great Library – the two buildings shared similar BookWorld architecture. Even the paint was peeling in the same place.

'How long do you think before the Men in Plaid catch up with us?' asked Sprockett as the elevator moved upwards.

'I have no idea,' I replied, opening my pistol and chambering my last cartridge, a disrupter that was nicknamed 'The Cherry Fondue' as it was always the last one in the box, and extremely nasty, 'but the Hotel Verhaegen won't give them any clues – you filled in the register as "Mr and Mrs Dueffer", yes?'

'Y–es,' said Sprockett, his eyebrow pointer clicking to 'Apologetic'.

'Problems?'

'Indeed, ma'am. In an unthinking moment, I may have written "choice of oils open to improvement" in the comments section of the visitors' book.'

'We'll just have to hope they're not curious.'

I replaced the weapon in my shoulder holster and the lift doors opened on the fourth floor. We walked out and padded noiselessly down the corridor. We walked past Lysander, Lyons, Lyndsay, Lynch and Lynam before we got the Lyells.

'*Charles Lyell, Botanist*,' read Sprockett on the first door. 'Is botany boring?'

'I suspect that it isn't, given there is an entire island committed to little else.'

The next door was for *Sir James Lyell, Politician*.

'Boring, ma'am?' enquired Sprockett.

'Politicians' lives are never boring,' I assured him, and we moved to the next.

'*Sir Charles Lyell, Geologist*,' I read. 'Is geology more or less boring than politics or botany?'

Sprockett's pointer flicked to 'Bingo'.

'I believe, ma'am, that as regards boring, geology is less to do with *tediousness*, and more to do with . . . *drilling*.'

'Genius,' I remarked, mildly annoyed that I hadn't thought of it myself. Sir Charles Lyell was the father of modern geology. If Thursday had come to him, she was after the finest geological advice available in the BookWorld. I knocked on the door in a state of some excitement, and when I heard a shrill 'enter', we walked in.

The room was a large panelled study, the walls covered with bookcases, and a large walnut desk in the centre. It was not tidy; papers were strewn everywhere and a chair was overturned. The pictures were crooked and a plant pot on its side. The wall safe, usually hidden behind a picture of a rock, lay open, and empty.

A man of considerable presence was standing in the middle of the chaos. He had a high domed head, white sideburns and some-what small eyes that seemed to glisten slightly with inner thoughts of a distracting nature.

'Thursday?' he said when he saw me. 'I have to confess I am not pleased.'

'Oh?'

'Yes; you told me that my assignment with you would be of the utmost secrecy. Look at my study: ransacked!'

'Ah,' I said, looking around, 'I am most dreadfully sorry, Sir Charles. This was done after we came back from . . . ?'

'An afterlifetime's work *ruined*,' he said in a much-aggrieved tone. 'I am most displeased. Good Lord. Who is that mechanical man with the curiously emotive eyebrow?'

'My butler, Sir Charles. You have no objection?'

He stared at Sprockett curiously.

'When I was alive I pursued the advancement of scientific truth with all passion – I am afraid to say that I am at odds to explain Fiction, which often seems to have no basis in logic at all.'

'Some enjoy it precisely for that reason.'

'You may be right. Can he tidy?'

'We can both tidy, Sir Charles.'

And we started to pick up the papers.

'It is most unfortunate,' remarked Sir Charles, 'after we had done all that work together. *Most* unfortunate.'

I suddenly felt worried.

'Our work together?'

'The report!' he muttered. 'All the maps, notes, core samples, graphs, analysis – stolen!'

'Sir Charles,' I said, 'this might seem an odd request, but can you go over what was in the report?'

'Again?'

'Again.'

He blinked owlishly at me.

'Over tea, Miss Next. First we must . . . tidy.'

'Sir Charles,' I said in a more emphatic tone, 'you must tell me what was in the report, and *now*!'

He frowned at me.

'As you wish. All that Metaphor—'

He didn't have time to finish his sentence. With a tremendous crash, the door was pushed off its hinges and two Men in Plaid entered. From door to death was scarcely less than fifteen seconds, and much happened. Sprockett was between us and the MiPs and he valiantly made a lunge for the intruders. The first Plaid was quicker and in an instant had popped Sprockett's inspection panel and pressed his Emergency Spring Release. In an instant the butler fell lifeless. Before he had hit the floor the Plaid had advanced, knocked my pistol from my grasp and pushed me sideways. As I lay sprawling, the second Man in Plaid had picked up Sir Charles and thrown him bodily out of the window, while the first Plaid advanced on me, his expressionless eyes boring into mine like a pair of gimlets. We'd just killed six of their compatriots; I didn't think there was much room for negotiation.

I quickly scrambled across the floor and was grabbed by my foot. I wriggled out of my boot and it was this, I think, that saved us. The Man in Plaid was put off balance, and gave me the split second I needed to find my pistol. Without hesitation, I turned and fired. There was a 'whompa' noise and the air wobbled as the 'Cherry Fondue' hit home, and with an agonising scream of pain the Man in Plaid exploded into not graphemes but the infinitely more painful *words*, many of which embedded themselves into the woodwork like shards of glass. The blast caught the second Man in Plaid and cut him in two. He fell to the floor with a heavy thump, the lower half of him spilling cogs, springs and brass actuating rods on to the floor.

'You're robotic?' I said, moving closer. The Man in Plaid was moving his arms in a feeble manner and his eyes followed me as I approached. He was still functioning, but it was clear he was damaged well beyond economic repair. He looked as though he were out of warranty, too.

'You are impressive, Miss Next,' he managed to say, 'a worthy adversary.'

'Who sent you?'

'I don't answer questions. I ask them.'

I noticed I was shaking. I retrieved my boot, and walked to the broken window. Lying on the grass four storeys below was Sir Charles. The heavy impact had caused the binding matrix of his body to become fused to the ground, and he was beginning to merge with the lawn. I could see several people staring and pointing, first at me and then at the remains of Sir Charles. We didn't have long before someone called Jurisfaction. Lyell could be rewritten but these things take time and money, and Non-Fiction's budgets were tighter than ours.

Sprockett was lying flat on his face in an undignified manner, and I quickly rewound him. As soon as his gyros, thought cogs and speech diaphragm were up to speed, he sat up.

'I've had the most peculiar dream,' he told me, his eyebrow clicking through each emotion in turn and then back again, 'about being caught by my mother oiling a Mk2 Ford Capri in an "inappropriate" manner.'

'I didn't know you had a mother.'

'I don't – that's what was so peculiar.'

'See what you can get out of him,' I said, pointing to the damaged Man in Plaid. 'I'm going to have a look around.'

I didn't waste any time and hunted through the remains of Lyell's study to see what – if anything – had been left behind. The short answer was 'not much' until I went through the waste-paper basket and came across a pencil sketch of Racy Novel with WomFic to one side and Dogma on the other. A rough outline of the geology had been sketched in, and for the most part the strata were more or less identical beneath all the genres, except for a shaded patch the shape of a tailless salmon that seemed to be mostly beneath Racy Novel. I returned to where Sprockett had been talking with the badly damaged Plaid.

'He's a Duplex-6,' said Sprockett with a sense of deep respect. 'I was wondering how they managed to stay on our tail so easily during the Oversized Book section.'

'Who is he working for?'

'He won't tell us, but it's of no matter – the Duplex automaton's memories are recorded on punched tape. We can have it read.'

'So take out his tape and let's get out of here.'

In reply the Duplex-6 took a large brass key out of his jacket pocket and inserted it into the socket in the base of his neck. We could see he was almost run down, and before we could stop him, he had started to turn the key.

'Good Lord,' said Sprockett, 'the Duplex-6 has a self-wind capability.'

Sprockett tried to stop the damaged Man in Plaid from winding himself up, but the 6's superior strength was too much, and we watched with increased hopelessness as the Plaid's tension indicator neared the red line.

'We're leaving,' said Sprockett, and without waiting for a reply he took me by the hand and ran to the bathroom window and out to the fire escape at the back of the building.

We were two flights down when the Duplex-6's mainspring finally ruptured in an almighty outburst of stored mechanical energy. There was a loud *twuuung* noise and the shattered remains of the Man in Plaid erupted out of the windows of Lyell's apartment. We were showered with minute cogs, sprockets, spindles and dogs, chains, pushrods and actuators.

'A self-winding capability,' said Sprockett, who was obviously deeply impressed. 'I wonder if they would retrofit that feature for us Duplex-5s?'

32

Homecoming

'**Islands to visit in the BookWorld #124:** *Photography*. This beautifully expressive and lyrical island has been divided between Black-and-White and Colour for many years, and the two factions are almost constantly at war, an event that is itself documented by resident war photographers. The recording of the war recording is also recorded, with Martin Parr photographing the ears and neckties of those that are recording the people that are recording the people recording the events.'

Bradshaw's BookWorld Companion, 5th Edition

We dodged Jurisfiction officers for two hours and eventually negotiated a ride home aboard a copy of the recently discredited *President Formby War Diaries*, which was on a one-way trip to Historical Counterfactuals.

'May I be so bold,' said Sprockett, once we had landed and were on the train heading back towards Fantasy, and home, 'as to enquire about our next move?'

'Placating an angry Carmine, I should imagine – I've been away a lot these past few days. After that we'll have to recover anything Horace has stolen again, put up with petulant huffing and tutting from Pickwick – and my dopey father will be complaining about something, I shouldn't wonder.'

'I was referring to Racy Novel, ma'am. Should you call Commander Bradshaw again?'

I'd asked myself the same question on the way back from Biography. I had spoken to him briefly while on board the *World Hotel Review*. He had expressed surprise and alarm about the Men in

Plaid, and had also checked out Mediocre's address and reported back to us no sign of Metaphor – in bridges or otherwise. Unwisely, I had told him we were going on to Biography, and now I didn't know if I could trust him or not.

'He might have tipped off the Men in Plaid,' I said, after airing my thoughts, 'or he simply might be having his footnoterphone messages read in transit.'

It wasn't hard, apparently. All you needed to do was to sit in the footnoterphone ducts and read the messages as they flitted past.

'Even if he is on the level,' I added, 'it's not like we have any answers or evidence – just a geologist out to grass and a rough sketch of the strata beneath the northern part of Fiction.'

Sprockett nodded agreement.

'But,' I added, 'we know Thursday would have been working to avert war at the peace talks. If she *was* silenced, the attacks by the Men in Plaid would seem to implicate the Council of Genres, but the CofG want to avoid a war, not start one. It was Senator Jobsworth *himself* that wanted me to attend the peace talks tomorrow. The only person we know who seems to actually welcome war is Speedy Muffler himself.'

'Would he have access to Duplex-6 automatons that could be made to look like Men in Plaid?' asked Sprockett.

'Duplex will sell to anyone with the cash.'

'What about Red Herring, ma'am?'

'I'm not sure. Is Red Herring a red herring? Or is it the fact that we're meant to *think* Red Herring is a red herring that is actually the red herring?'

'Or perhaps the fact you're meant to think Red Herring *isn't* a red herring makes Red Herring a red herring after all.'

'We're talking serious meta-herrings here. Oh, craps, I'm lost again. Who's talking now?'

'It's you,' said Sprockett.

'Right.'

'Whatever is going on,' I said, 'it's big. *Really* big. If it's big enough to risk killing Thursday Next, destroying a book and subverting the Men in Plaid from their usual duties of frightening citizens to the more specific duty of frightening *individual* citizens, then there is no limit to what they might do. We need to keep our eyes open at all times.'

We took a cab from *LeGuin Central* and walked up to the house deep in thought. I had my hand on the butt of my pistol, just in case. I needn't have worried. Men in Plaid were never seen without their Buick Roadmaster, and the driveway was empty. I opened the front door and found a dozen members of the cast sitting around the kitchen table.

'Hello,' I said, somewhat surprised, 'have we got a cast meeting scheduled for this evening?'

'We have now,' replied Carmine.

My eyes flicked from face to face, and they seemed very serious. Most of the major players were there – my father, Bowden, Hades, Jack Schitt, Braxton, Rochester, Paige Turner, Joffy, Stig, Victor Analogy, my mother and even Bertha Rochester, although she had been put in a straitjacket, just in case she tried to bite anyone.

'What's going on?'

'You've been acting a bit irresponsibly recently,' said Carmine, 'running around the BookWorld, pretending to be her. You've been neglecting your duties. I've been covering for you far more than is written into my contract, and only yesterday you were shouting at us all.'

'I've had things on my mind,' I replied by way of excuse, '*important* things.'

'So *you* say. To the casual outside observer, you're simply getting delusions of adequacy. Play a strong character for too long and it tends to have an unhingeing effect.'

'And today,' said Bowden in an annoying *I told you so* sort of voice, 'you were threatening to tell the Outland all about the Book-World. There's a good reason why the real Thursday never put that part of the story in her books, you know.'

'I admit I might have gone too far on that point,' I conceded, but I could see they didn't believe me.

'None of us are happy,' said my father, 'and we feel you might be leading the series into disrepute. If the book gets punished for your transgressions, then we all have to suffer. Punish one, punish all. You know how it works.'

I did, all too well. To keep books in line, the entire cast is often disciplined for the misdeeds of one. It generated a certain degree of conformity within the cast – and a lot of ill-feeling.

'So what are you saying?' I asked.

My father nudged Bowden, who nudged Victor, who nudged Acheron Hades.

'We're saying,' said Hades slowly, 'that we might need to make some . . . *changes*.'

'Changes? What sort of changes?'

'Changes in leadership.'

'You want to have me fired? You can't do that.'

'In point of fact,' piped up Pickwick, 'we can. Article 218 of the Textual Code states: *If the nominated leader of a book acts in an unlawful or reckless manner that might affect the smooth operation of a book, they can be removed by a simple show of hands.*'

There was a deathly hush as they waited to see what I would say.

'The series is operating smoothly. It will be hard to prove reck-lessness on my behalf.'

'We don't need to,' replied Carmine, 'we need only prove unlaw-fulness.'

'And how would you do that?'

'The Toast Marketing Board subplot. *Totally* illegal. You wrote out the new pages in your own handwriting.'

'Listen,' I said, changing my tone to one of conciliation. 'We have an average weekly read-rate of 3.7 at present – remaindered, out of print and, technically speaking, unread. You need my leadership to try to turn this series around. If you want to negotiate, we can nego-tiate – everything's on the table. So let's talk. Who's for tea?'

They all stared at me in a stony-faced manner, and I suddenly felt that things were a lot worse than I'd thought. There had been grumblings before, but nothing like this.

'Well then,' I said, my temper rising, 'who's going to lead the book? Carmine?'

'I can handle it.'

'You can handle it *now*. What if the read-rate goes above forty? How screwed will you be then?'

'There is no need to be unkind,' said my father. 'With our support, she'll manage. At least she doesn't spend her days gallivanting around the BookWorld on arguably pointless quests for a namesake who doesn't even like you.'

That hurt.

'Well,' I replied in a sarcastic tone, 'how does consorting with a goblin fare on the "bringing the book into disrepute" stakes?'

'You can talk,' retorted Carmine, '*your* intended boyfriend set fire to a busload of nuns.'

'And puppies,' said Pickwick.

'*Orphaned* puppies,' added Rochester, dabbing his eyes with a handkerchief.

'Besides,' said Carmine, 'Horace and I have agreed to a trial separation.'

'I think we've all said quite enough,' announced Bowden in a haughty tone. 'All in favour of replacing Thursday with Carmine, raise a hand.'

They all raised a hand except Stig, who I know liked me, Bertha Rochester, who was in a straitjacket, and Pickwick.

'Thank you, Pickwick,' I said. 'Nice to know some friends haven't abandoned me.'

'Are we voting now?' asked Pickwick, waking with a start. 'I'm in.'

And she put a wing in the air.

'All right, you bunch of disloyal ingrates,' I said, taking the Snooze button access codes and key to the Core Containment from around my neck, 'have the job. Who cajoled you all when you thought you were rubbish? Who made sure we rehearsed all the way through the six weeks we were unread last winter?'

Victor looked at the ceiling and Pickwick stared at her foot. They all knew I had been holding things together for a while. The previous written Thursday had left the series in a terrible state. Everyone arguing with everyone else, and with a humour deficit that I had only just managed to plug.

'And a fat lot of good it did us,' replied Carmine angrily. 'We're the laughing stock of Speculative Fantasy.'

'We're still being read. Do you know what to do if there is a flameout on the eBook throughput intensifiers?'

Carmine's blank look told me she didn't.

'Or if the Metaphor depletes mid-scene? What about the irony injectors? How often should they be cleaned? Do you even *know* what an Adjectivore looks like or what happens if you get Robert Pestons behind the wainscotting?'

'Hey,' said Horace, who had been sitting unnoticed on top of the fridge, 'why don't you go do a Plot 9 on yourself? We can muddle through. With less than twenty active readers we've certainly got enough time.'

'*We?*' I demanded. 'Since when were you anything to do with this series?'

'Since Carmine asked me.'

'He has some very good ideas,' said Carmine. 'Even Pickwick thinks they're quite good. Isn't that so, Pickers?'

'Sort of,' said Pickwick, looking the other way huffily.

'We'd better get on,' said Hades in a pointed fashion, 'we've got some readings to attend to.'

'Right,' I said, lips pursed as I tried to control my temper, 'I'll let you get on with it.'

And without another word, I strode out of the house with as much dignity as I could muster. As soon as I was outside I sat on the garden wall, heart beating fast, and taking short gasps of air. I looked back at the series. It was a jagged collection of settings – the towers of Thornfield Hall set among the floodlights of the Swindon croquet field and the Penderyn Hotel. There were a few airships, too, but only 1/10th scale. It was all I'd ever known. It had seemed like *home*.

'You should look on the bright side, ma'am,' said Sprockett, handing me a Chicago Fizz he had conjured up, seemingly from nowhere.

'There *is* a bright side? No book, no home, no one to believe in me and no real idea what became of Thursday – or what the hell's going on. And in addition, I'd *really* like to punch Horace.'

'Punching goblins,' replied Sprockett soothingly, 'while offering short-term relief, has no long-term beneficial value.'

I sighed.

'You're right.'

'By referring to the "bright side", ma'am, I merely meant that the recent upset simply frees up your schedule for more pressing matters. You have larger fish to fry over the next couple of days.'

I stood up. Sprockett was right. To hell with the series – for the moment, at least.

'So where do you suggest we go now?'

'Vanity.'

33

The League of Cogmen

'... There are two languages peculiar to the BookWorld
of which a vague understanding will help the enthusiastic tourist: **Courier Bold** is the traditional language
of those in the support industries such as within the Well
of Lost Plots, and Lorem Ipsum is the gutter slang of
the underworld – useful to have a few phrases in case
you get into trouble in Horror or Noir.'

Bradshaw's BookWorld Companion, 1st Edition

Sprockett, I learned, lived in the Fantasy section of Vanity, not far
from Parody Valley. I was more at leisure to look about upon this,
my second visit, and I noticed that whereas in Fiction the landscape was well maintained, relatively open and with good infra-
structure, years of self-publishing in the same geographic area meant
that *Vanity* was untidy, chaotic and overcrowded.

The resident novels with their settings, props and characters now
occupied every spare corner of the island, and had accreted on top
of one another like alluvial deposits. Grand towers of imaginative
speculation had arisen from the bare rock, and the island was honey-
combed with passageways, tunnels and shafts in order to access the
scenes and settings now buried far below the surface. In some places
the books were so close that boundaries became blurred; a tiger
hunt in 1920s Bengal merged seamlessly with the TT races on the
Isle of Man; a space opera with the 1983 Tour de France. Space in
Vanity was limited.

'Don't let on you're published,' remarked Sprockett as we arrived
at his book, a badly worn tome cemented into a cliff face of similar

books, and supported on slender stilts that were anchored to the rock below. He needn't have – I knew the score. Vanity's beef with the rest of Fiction was long lived and not without some degree of justification.

I wiped my feet on the doormat as we entered, and noted that the novel was set mostly in the manor house that belonged to Professor Winterhope, Sprockett's creator, and was populated by a large and mildly eccentric family of mechanical men, none of whom looked as though they had been serviced for years.

'Welcome to the *League of Cogmen*,' said Mrs Winterhope once the professor had taken Sprockett off for an oil change and general service. 'Would you like some tea?'

I told her I would, and we walked into the front room, which was like my kitchen back home: a command centre and meeting place all in one. Mrs Winterhope introduced me to the cogmen, who had been wound sufficiently to converse, but were under strict orders not to move, in order not to wear themselves out – quite literally, as they had a limited stock of spare parts. Despite these obvious drawbacks, they still expressed the languorous attitude of the long unread. It didn't look as if they rehearsed much either, which was a lamentable lapse in professionalism, although I wasn't going to say so.

'We must thank you for rescuing Sprokky from that rabble in Conspiracy,' said Mrs Winterhope, putting an empty kettle on to a cold stove, 'and we were delighted to hear he was employed by Thursday Next – even if not the real one.'

'You're very kind.'

'Has our Sprockett been serving you well?'

'He has been beyond exemplary,' I told her, 'a gentleman's gentleman.'

'Excellent,' she replied. 'I can count on you to give good references?'

'I cannot see a scenario where I would let him go,' I said with a smile. 'He is utterly admirable in every respect.'

But Mrs Winterhope wasn't smiling.

'I understand,' she said slowly, 'that you have recently found yourself in diminished circumstances?'

This was true, of course. I had almost nothing except Sprockett and the clothes I was wearing.

'At present, yes, that is true,' I admitted somewhat sheepishly.

Mrs Winterhope poured the empty kettle into a teapot that I noted contained no tea.

'Sprockett is the most advanced automaton we possess,' she continued, 'and while not wishing to be indelicate in these matters, I cannot help thinking that his career may not be well served by someone who finds themselves – I'm sorry to be blunt – in a position of . . . *unreadiness*.'

She stared at me with a kind yet desperate expression and handed me an empty cup.

'Would you like no milk?'

'Yes, thank you,' I said, not wishing to embarrass them. Not a single reader in over seventeen years had graced their pages, so the Reader Stipend was unavailable to them, and they had, quite literally, nothing. The only possible avenue to a better life was through the one character who might conceivably find a placement in the world of wider readership. Four days ago I had been a potential help, now I was a millstone. I knew what I had to do.

'Yes,' I said to Mrs Winterhope, 'I understand.'

She nodded politely, and patted me on the arm.

'Will you stay with us tonight?' she asked. 'We have absolutely nothing, but we would be happy to share it with you.'

I told her I would be honoured to share in their nothing, then excused myself to go for a walk.

I left the novel and wandered down through the narrow streets to where the Tennyson Boardwalk ran alongside the beach. The walk was full of evening strollers and traders, mostly selling book-clearance salvage from those novels which had been recently scrapped. I stopped to lean on the decorative cast-iron railings, and absently watched the Text Sea lap against the foreshore, the jumbled collection of letters heaving and mixing in the swell. Every now and then a chance encounter would create a word and the constituent parts glowed with the joyous harmony of word construction. Farther down some kids were fishing these new words from the sea with hooked sticks. Three-letter constructions were thrown back to grow larger, but longer words were pulled ashore for possible sale. While I stood there watching they caught a *theodolite*, a *linoleum* and a *pumpkin*, although truth to tell the *pumpkin* was actually a *pump* and a *kin* that were 'tickled' together after being pulled from the Text Sea.

I couldn't help feeling a bit sorry for myself. I had no job, no book, no friends and no immediate prospects. The man I loved was real and wholly unavailable, the deputy man I loved was a mass murderer. More importantly, I was no nearer to discovering who had killed Thursday, nor what Sir Charles Lyell had unearthed about Racy Novel that was so potentially devastating that it was worth murdering him, Thursday and Mediocre for. The truth was this: I wasn't up to scratch. I had been trying too hard to be her, and I had failed.

I thought of Whitby, then of Landen, and what he had said about me actually *being* Thursday, and not knowing it. I wasn't in agreement with him over that one, and when I'd vanished in front of his eyes he would have known it too. I thought for a minute as I considered putting myself in Landen's shoes. He might try to get in touch with me – after all, we both wanted Thursday back. The question was this: if I wanted to contact someone in the Book-World, how would I go about it?

The Mediocre Gatsby had picked Thursday up in Sargasso Plaza, a stone's throw from where I was now, right on the south-east tip of Vanity. She was likely to have been hiding close by, somewhere she would have been off the Council of Genre's radar – somewhere even the Men in Plaid would fear to tread. And there it was, staring at me across the bay – Fanfiction. Where better to hide a Thursday than in a bunch of them? The small island was lit up by thousands of light bulbs strung from trees and lamp-posts. It was a busy place, that much I knew, and given that Vanity had been unfairly shunned by the rest of Fiction, the fact that Fanfiction was isolated still further gave one an idea of how poorly they were regarded.

I walked to the entrance of the narrow causeway and approached the two game-show hosts who were guarding the access. One was sitting on a high stool and dressed in a gold lamé suit, while the other was holding a hunting rifle.

'Hello, Thursday!' said the first host, beaming happily at me with a set of teeth so perfectly white that I had to blink in the glare. 'Back to win further prizes?'

It was Julian Sparkle of *Puzzlemania*. We had met a few years back when the real Thursday was attempting to train me up for Jurisfiction. He was what we called an *Anecdotal*, someone who lived in the oral tradition, ready to leap to the Outland when puzzles and brain-teasers were related – usually during boring car journeys, or in pubs. The last time we met I would almost certainly have been eaten by a tiger, if not for Thursday's brilliant intervention.

'I was actually thinking of visiting Fanfiction,' I replied.

'No problem,' said Julian in his sing-song voice. 'Anyone can go in – but no one can come out.'

As if to drive home the point, the second game-show host showed me the hunting rifle.

'Unless,' said Julian Sparkle, 'you want to play *Puzzlemania*?'

'What do I win?'

'A set of steak knives.'

'And if I lose?'

'We destroy you with a high-powered Eraserhead.'

'Fair enough,' I replied, 'I'm in.'

Sparkle smiled warmly, and I stepped to a mark on the floor which he indicated. As I did so, the lights seemed to dim, except for a bright spotlight on the two of us. There was a short blast of applause, seemingly from nowhere.

'So, Thursday Next, today we're going to play . . . "Escape across the Bridge".'

He indicated the long narrow causeway.

'It's very simple. We erase anyone we see walking towards us across the causeway. There is no way to go round the causeway, and you'll be dissolved in the Text Sea if you try to swim.'

'And?'

'That's it. We check the bridge every half-minute, and it takes four minutes to run across.'

As if to accentuate the point, the second host noticed someone trying to sneak across as we were talking. He shouldered the rifle and fired. The unfortunate escapee exploded in a chrysanthemum of text, which was quickly snapped up by the gulls.

'Ha-ha!' said the host, reloading the rifle. 'Bagged another Baggins.'

And he made a mark in his tally-book which contained several hundred other Baggins, three dozen Gandalfs, a plethora of Pratchett characters and sixty-seven Harry Potters.

'Right, then,' said Sparkle, 'off you toddle.'

'Don't you want the answer?'

He smiled in an oddly unpleasant way.

'You can figure it out for the return journey.'

I walked across the causeway with a curiously heavy heart as I had no idea how to get back, but once I arrived on the other side it seemed a party was in full swing. Everyone was chatting to everyone else, and the mildly depressed feeling I had felt over in Vanity seemed to vanish completely.

'What's the party about?' I asked a hobbit who had thrust a drink in my hand.

'Where *have* you been?' she said with a smile. 'Fanfiction isn't copying – it's a *celebration*. One long party, from the first capital letter to the last full stop!'

'I never thought of that.'

'Few do – especially the authors who should really accept the praise with better grace. They're a bunch of pompous fatheads, really – no slur intended. Nice clothes, by the way.'

'Thank you.'

And she wandered off.

'Thursday?'

I turned to find myself staring at, well, *myself*. I knew she wasn't me because she seemed somewhat narrow. In fact, now that I looked around, most people here were similar to real characters but of varying thickness. Some were barely flatter than normal, while others were so lacking in depth that they appeared only as an animated sheet of cardboard.

'Why is everyone so flat?' I asked.

'It's a natural consequence of being borrowed from somewhere else,' explained the Thursday, who was, I noted, less than half an inch thick but apparently normal in every other way. 'It doesn't make us any less real or lacking in quality. But being written by someone who might not *quite* understand the subconscious nuance of the character leaves us in varying degrees of flatness.'

This made sense. I'd never really thought about it before, but it explained why the Edward Rochester and indeed *all* the borrowed characters in my series were of varying degrees of depth. Some weren't that bad, but others – like Jane Eyre herself – were thin enough to be slipped under the door, and could sleep rolled up and inserted into a drainpipe.

'How's all that cloak-and-dagger stuff going?' asked Flat Thursday.

It seemed she thought I was the real one, and I wasn't going to deny it.

'It's going so-so,' I said. 'How much did I tell you?'

She laughed.

'You never tell us anything. Landen sent another message, by the way.'

'That's good,' I replied, attempting to hide my enthusiasm, 'lead on.'

Thursday turned, and as she did so she almost vanished as I saw her edge on.

'We all think Landen's totally Mr Dreamcake,' said Flat Thursday as we walked past a reinterpretation of Middle Earth that was every bit as good as the real one, only flatter, 'but he won't speak to anyone but the real one.'

We walked down Thursday Street and everything started to look vaguely familiar. The characters and settings were sort of similar, but the situations were not. The combinations were unusual, too, and although I had not personally supposed Thursday might battle the Daleks with Dr Who in a literary landscape, in here it was very much business as usual.

'He's in there,' said Thursday, and she ushered me into a large, square room with a stripped pine floor, a thin skirting board and empty walls painted in magnolia. In the middle of the room was Landen, and he smiled as I walked in. But it wasn't actually him; it was just a *feeling* of him.

'Hello, Landen.'

'Hello, Thursday. I needed to speak to you.'

'What about?'

'I'm sorry,' he said apologetically, 'my answers are limited.'

I stared at him for a moment. Flat Thursday had said this was *another* message, so he must be communicating on a one-way basis by writing a short story – possibly with he and his wife in conversation.

'Which Thursday do you want to talk to?' I asked.

'The written Thursday.'

So far so good.

'Do you *now* believe I'm from the BookWorld?'

'You vanished as I was about to kiss you. Thursday never did that. I'm sorry I doubted you.'

'Do you know what the real Thursday was doing with Sir Charles Lyell?'

'I'm sorry,' he said, 'my answers are limited.'

'Do you know who was trying to kill Thursday?'

'The Men in Plaid have tried to murder her on numerous occasions. At the last count she had killed six of them. She doesn't know who orders them to do it, or why.'

This was good news. Between Thursday and Sprockett and myself, we'd taken out fourteen Plaids.

'Where is she now? Do you know?'

'I'm sorry,' he said, 'my answers are limited.'

'Why did she ask the red-headed man to give me her badge?'

'She didn't – *I did.* As soon as she had been out of contact for over five days, I contacted Kiki.'

'Why did she ask *me* to help her?'

'She'd hoped you had evolved into something more closely resembling her. The only person she knew she could truly trust was . . . herself.'

This sounded encouraging.

'Can I trust Bradshaw?'

'I'm sorry,' he said, 'my answers are limited.'

'Is there anything else I should know?'

'She told me that in an emergency she would try to contact you. She said the circumstances of your confusion will be your path to enlightenment.'

'What did she mean by that?'

'I'm sorry,' he said, 'I have no more answers for you. I won't know if you even got these. Good luck, Thursday.'

He stopped talking, and just stood there blinking, awaiting any possible response from me.

'Listen,' I said, lowering my voice and looking around to make sure Flat Thursday wasn't listening, 'did you write in a kiss, just to make up for the one I missed earlier?'

'Good luck, Thursday,' he said again. 'I'm in a hurry, as I told your mother I'd help her with the Daphne Farquitt Readathon. Remember: *the circumstances of your confusion will be your path to enlightenment*. Four pounds of carrots, one medium cabbage, four-pack tin of beans, Moggilicious for Pickwick, pick up dry cleaning, toilet paper . . .'

I was confused until I realised that he had probably written the short story on the back of a shopping list. I watched and listened while he went through: 'tonic water, snacks and the latest Wayne Skunk album, *Lick the Toad*, before he stopped, smiled again and then just stood there blinking in a state of rest.

I walked back outside to where many Thursdays of varying thicknesses were waiting to be told a story and given a few tips. It felt as if I was doing a Thursday masterclass in a hall of mirrors, but I think they appreciated it. By the time I left two hours later, some of the thinner Thursdays were a little bit thicker.

'Might I enquire where madam has been?' asked Sprockett once I had returned to the League of Cogmen. 'Vanity can be a dangerous place for those published. Brigands, scoundrels, verb-artists and the unread lurk in the doorways, ready to steal the Essence of Read from the unwary.'

'I was in Fanfiction.'

Sprockett's eyebrow shot to 'Worried' in alarm.

'How did you get back across the causeway?'

'Quite easily. They shoot anyone trying to escape, and check the causeway every half-minute to make sure. You can't possibly run the distance in less than four minutes, so the answer seemed quite obvious.'

He diverted his mainspring to his thought cogs and whirred and clicked noisily for a full minute before giving up, and I had to tell him.

'That's quite clever.'

'Elementary, my dear Sprockett. Julian Sparkle was a bit annoyed. He said that he'd have to change the puzzle. I won these steak knifes. Perhaps Mrs Winterhope would like them?'

'I think she would be delighted. May I ask a question, ma'am?'

'Of course.'

'What are we going to do now?'

'I'm going to accept Senator Jobsworth's invitation to go to the peace talks tomorrow masquerading as the real Thursday Next. The paddle-steamer leaves at seven a.m. Everything that has happened is to do with Racy Novel and Speedy Muffler, and unless I start getting to the heart of the problem I'm not going to get anywhere. The Men in Plaid will think twice before doing anything while I'm in plain view, and Landen told me the way to find Thursday was: "The circumstances of your confusion will be your path to enlightenment". I don't understand that, but I *can* become more confused – going upriver with Jobsworth will *definitely* provide the extra confusion I need.'

Sprockett stared at me for a moment, and I could tell by the way his eyebrow was quivering between 'Thinking' and 'Worried' that he knew something was up.

'Don't you mean "we", ma'am?'

I pulled a letter from my pocket which I'd prepared while seated at a *You For Coffee?* franchise just off Sargasso Plaza.

'These are glowing references, Sprockett. They should allow you to find a position in Fiction without any problem. You have been a steadfast and loyal companion whom I am happy to have known as a friend. Thank you.'

I blinked as my eyes had started to mist, and Sprockett stared back at me with his blank porcelain features. His eyebrow pointed at all the possible emotions that were engraved on his forehead in turn. There was nothing for 'Sad', so it sprang backwards and forwards between 'Doubtful' and 'Worried'.

'I must protest, ma'am. I do not—'

'My mind is made up, Sprockett. I have nothing to offer. You have a bright future. It will please me greatly if you find onward employment that I can be proud of.'

Sprockett buzzed quietly to himself for a moment.

'This is compassion, isn't it?'

'Yes.'

'I can *recognise* it,' he said, 'but I am at odds to understand it. Shall we go indoors?'

We had boiled cabbage for dinner, which might have been improved had there been any cabbage to go in it. But the Winter-hopes were more than friendly, and after several rounds of bezique, which might have been more enjoyable had there been cards, Sprockett played the piano accordion without actually having a piano accordion, and the empty unread book didn't ring to the tune of the 'Beer Barrel Polka' until the small hours.

34
The Metaphoric Queen

'. . . Journeys up the Metaphoric River are hugely enjoyable and highly recommended. Since every genre is nourished by its heady waters, a paddle-steamer can take even the most walk-shy tourist to their chosen destination. As a bonus, there is traditionally at least one murder on board each trip – by paying a "consideration" to the head steward, they will ensure that it is not you.'

Bradshaw's BookWorld Companion, 1st Edition

The steamer was called *The Metaphoric Queen*, and when I arrived it was lying at the dockside just above the lock-gates that separated the river from the Text Sea. The *Queen* was a wooden superstructure on a steel hull, measured almost three hundred feet from stem to stern and was the very latest in luxury river travel. A covered walkway ran around the upper deck level, and behind the wheelhouse on the top deck was a single central stack that breathed out small puffs of smoke. As I approached I could see the crew making ready. They loaded and unloaded freight, polished the brasswork, checked the paddle for broken vanes and oiled the traction arm that turned the massive stern wheel.

The *Queen* had docked only an hour before, and the cargo was being offloaded when I arrived: crude Metaphor, sealed into twenty-gallon wooden casks and each stencilled 'Product of Racy Novel'. I watched as the casks were taken under guard and moved towards the Great Library, where they would be distilled into their component parts for onward trade.

'Welcome aboard!' said the captain as I walked up the gangplank.

'The Senator will be joining us shortly. The staterooms are through the first door on the left – tea will be served in ten minutes.'

I thanked him and moved aft to the rear deck, which afforded a good view of the docks and the river. The other passengers were already on board, and were exactly the sort of people one would expect to see on a journey of this type. There was a missionary, a businessman, a family of settlers eager to make a new home for themselves, two ladies of negotiable affection and, strangely enough, *several* odd foreigners who wore rumpled linen suits and looked a bit mad.

'I think someone made a mistake on the manifest,' came a voice close at hand.

I turned to find an adventurer standing next to me. He looked as though he had argued with a rake some time as a teenager and come off worse; three deep scars showed livid on his cheek and jaw. He was quite handsome in an understated sort of way with a plain shirt, grubby chinos and a revolver on his belt. He was wearing a battered trilby with a dark sweat-stain on the band, and didn't look as though he had shaved – or slept – for two days.

'A mistake on the manifest?'

'Three eccentric foreigners on a trip like this, rather than the mandatory one. Mind you, it could be worse. I was on a similar jaunt last year and instead of a single insultingly stereotypical Italian, all fast talking and gesticulating, we had six. Hell on earth, it was.'

As if in answer to this the three eccentric foreigners started to jostle one another in an infantile manner.

'It's Thursday Next, isn't it?'

I looked at him, trying to remember where I had seen him before. I stared for a little too long at the scars on his face and he touched the pink marks thoughtfully.

'I don't know how I got them,' he confessed, 'but they're supposed to make me look like I'm a man with an adventurous past.'

'Aren't you?'

324

'I'm really not sure. I was given the scars but no backstory to go with them. Perhaps it will be revealed to me later. It's an honour to meet you, I must say. My name's Foden. Drake Foden.'

We shook hands. I didn't want to deny I was her, given my reason for being here, so I decided to hit him with some pseudo-erudition I had picked up in HumDram.

'You're kind,' I replied, 'but last Thursday and next Thursday are still a week apart.'

'Deep,' he said with a smile. 'Where are you headed?'

'Upriver a way,' I said, giving little away, 'You?'

'Beyond Racy Novel,' he said, 'and into the Dismal Woods.'

'Hoping to find the source of the Metaphoric?'

'Is there one?'

He laughed. Most people these days agreed that the river couldn't actually have a source since it flowed in several directions at once. Instead of starting in one place and ending in another using the traditionally mundane 'downhill' plan, it would pretty much go as the mood took it. Indeed, the Metaphoric had been known to bunch up in Horror while Thriller suffered a drought, then, when all was considered lost, the river would suddenly break free and cause a flood throughout Comedy and HumDram. Not quite so devastating as one might imagine, for the Metaphoric brought with it the rhetorical nutrients necessary for good prose – the river was the lifeblood of Fiction, and nothing could exist without it.

The puzzle, therefore, was how the river replenished itself. It had long been known that the river flowed up into the Dismal Woods a tired and stagnant backwater and emerged reinvigorated and fizzing with a heady broth of creative alternatives four hundred miles to the west. Quite what mechanism existed to make this happen was a matter of some conjecture. Many adventurers had been lost trying to find out. Some said the secret was guarded by a Mysteriously

Vanished subplot that would devour all comers, while others maintained there existed a 'Fountain of Bestsellerdom' that could grant eternal life, and no one troubled to expend a further word in consequence.

'No,' said the adventurer, 'better men than me have been lost searching for the source of the Metaphoric. That's next year. This year I'm in training: I'm going to attempt to uncover the legendary Euphemasaurus graveyard.'

'Good luck,' I said, knowing full well that he would doubtless be dead in a week – the Euphemasaurus was a fearsome beast, and not conducive to being tracked. It would perhaps be a safer, easier and more productive quest to look for his own refrigerator.

'Who is that?' I asked as a man with his face obscured by a large pair of dark glasses hurried past and went below decks, followed by a porter carrying his suitcases.

'He's the mandatory MP-C12: Mysterious Passenger in Cabin Twelve. All sweaty journeys upriver have to carry the full complement of odd characters. It's a union thing.'

'Hence the foreigners?'

'Hence the foreigners. Mark my words, there'll be a mixed-race cook with a violent streak who only speaks Creole, a card-sharp and a man from the company.'

'Which company?'

'A company with commercial interests upriver. It doesn't really matter what.'

'You must have done this many times.'

'Actually it's my first. I only graduated from St Tabularasa's this morning.'

'Are you nervous?'

The adventurer smiled confidently.

'I'm running around inside screaming.'

I excused myself as Red Herring, Colonel Barksdale and Senator

Jobsworth had just arrived. They were accompanied by an entourage of perhaps a dozen staff, most of whom were simply faceless bureaucrats: D-class generics who did nothing but add background and tone to the general proceedings. Try to engage them in conversation and they would just blink stupidly and then stare at their feet.

'Good morning, Miss Next,' said Herring affably. 'A moment of your time, if you would?'

He was dressed in a light cotton suit and was overseeing the arrival of a riveted steel box that had been placed on the front deck by four burly river men, and was now being lashed in place.

'Gifts for Speedy Muffler?'

'Two dozen plot lines and some A-grade characterisation to show willing,' replied Herring, tipping the river men and checking the cords. 'Racy Novel doesn't have much of either, so it should go down well.'

I thought of saying that this was because of Council of Genre sanctions, but thought better of it.

'So,' he said, mopping his brow with a handkerchief, 'good to see you could make it.'

'All BookWorldians have a duty to avert war whenever it presents itself,' I said pointedly.

'Goes without saying. Your series is in good health, I trust?'

'Nothing a reissue in the Outland wouldn't fix.'

He steered me to the rail and lowered his voice.

'Have the Men in Plaid been bothering you?'

'Why do you ask, sir?'

'Speedy Muffler has . . . *friends* within government. Some people are sympathetic to his cause. They feel that he has been unfairly treated and may try to work against the peace.'

I didn't know who to trust on this boat so I decided to trust no one.

'I have seen a few Roadmasters following me over the past few days,' I replied cagily.

'Not that unusual,' said Herring. 'Fantasy is a hotbed of Imaginative Fundamentalism; if we didn't keep a Plaid presence on the streets to rein in Fantasy's worst excesses, we'd be in cross-genre anarchy before we knew it. We'd regulate it more than we do if it wasn't so damn readable.'

Herring was nothing if not conservative in his opinions, but that only reflected the dominant politics of Fiction. The opposition called for more deregulation and even the banning of genres themselves, dubbing them an 'affront to experimentation' and 'the measles of the BookWorld', while others called for greater formulaicism – if for nothing better than to appease publishers. A noise made me turn.

'Miss Next,' said Senator Jobsworth, 'I am most grateful for your attendance. Will you join me in the captain's cabin in twenty minutes?'

I told him I would, and he disappeared off towards his private rooms with his entourage. Red Herring looked at his watch nervously.

'Are we late leaving?' I asked.

'We're waiting for the official Jurisfiction delegate.'

We were kept waiting another ten minutes until a sleek spaceship that seemed to have been carved from a single block of obsidian approached from the south, circled twice, lowered its landing gear and, with a rolling blast from its swivelling thrusters, landed on the dockside. The entrance ramp lowered, and two imperial guards hurried down the ramp while one blue-skinned valet spread rose petals on the ground and two more played a brief alarum on trumpets. After a dramatic pause a tall figure swathed in a high-collared black cloak strode menacingly down the ramp. He had a pale complexion, high cheekbones and a small and very precise goatee.

This was His Merciless the Emperor Zhark, tyrannical ruler of a thousand star systems, and undisputed star of the 'Emperor Zhark' novels. He was also a senior Jurisfiction agent, and by all accounts, quite a sweetie – if you didn't count his habit of enslaving entire planets to be worked to death in his spice mines.

'Good morning, Your Mercilessness,' said Red Herring, stepping forward to greet him, 'no entourage today?'

'Hello, Herring, old chap. Where's my cabin? I've a splitting headache. I was up all night dealing with Star Corps – bloody nuisance they are. What am I doing here again?'

'You're the Jurisfiction delegate to the Racy Novel Peace Talks.'

'Who are we fighting?'

'No one, yet – that's why we call them "peace talks".'

'Couldn't we just lay waste to the entire region and put everyone to the sword? It would save a lot of boring chat and I can go back to bed.'

'I'm afraid not, Your Mercilessness.'

'Very well,' he said with a sigh, 'just don't expect me to bunk in with the cook again. He frightens me.'

'You have your own cabin this time, Emperor. We are already behind schedule. Steward?'

A steward stepped forward to take the Emperor's bag, which I noticed was made out of the skin of the uncle he had murdered to seize the Zharkian throne. Despite appearances, Zhark was a skilled negotiator; it was he and he alone who brought Forensic Procedural to the table and averted a potential fracturing of the Crime genre.

'Good Lord,' said Zhark when he saw me. 'Thursday?'

'The written one, Your Mercilessness,' I said, bowing low. 'We last met at the Paragon Tea Rooms.'

He stared at me for a moment. Sometimes he was slow on the uptake.

'You're the written one?'

'Yes, sir.'

He moved closer, looked to left and right and lowered his voice.

'Do you remember that waitress at the Paragon? The perky one who answered back a lot and was wholly disrespectful?'

'I think so.'

'You didn't get her number, did you?'

'I'm afraid not.'

'Never mind. Written Thursday, eh? Know where the real one is?'

'No, sir.'

'Bummer,' he said, and walked off towards his cabin.

35

We Go Upriver

'. . . **For those with adventure on their mind, a trip to observe the never-seen Euphemasaurus might be considered.** For a fee, the intrepid holidaymaker will be taken into the Dismal Woods in the far north of the island, where they will spend a pestilential four days being eaten alive by insects and bled white by leeches. Recovery is said to be three to six months, but the blurry pictures of "something in the distance" can be treasured for ever.'

Bradshaw's BookWorld Companion, 7th Edition

Within a few minutes the captain ordered the mooring ropes cast off, and with a blast of the whistle, a shudder from the deck and the venting of steam from the pistons, the stern wheel began to rotate and the boat pulled slowly away from the dock.

I watched the Great Library recede for a moment, and I suddenly realised that I was very much here on false pretences. I wasn't Thursday, and I was here on the coat-tails of a mystery that I had singularly failed to solve. This was frustrating because this being Fiction, most of the relevant facts would already have been demonstrated to me, but safely peppered with enough red herrings to ensure I couldn't see the true picture. Thursday would have spotted it all, and indeed, given her 'absent' status, had done so long ago. I still had no clear idea as to what was going on, but was fortified by the simple fact that I was here, and not cowering in a cupboard back home being bullied by Pickwick.

Luckily, my thoughts were interrupted by the adventurer, who asked me to meet him in the bar in an hour, and after that I went

331

to find my cabin – a cosy wood-lined cubbyhole with the sink bolted to the ceiling to save room. There was no electricity, but a single porthole gave ample light. I unpacked the small case I had brought with me and, after freshening up, I stepped outside, then stopped. I was next door to Cabin Twelve, where the Mysterious Passenger was staying. I heard raised voices from within.

'. . . *but I won't take your place at the talks,*' came the voice. I leaned closer but the conversation was muted and indistinct from then on, and I hurried off towards the captain's quarters, which were situated just behind the wheelhouse, two decks up.

The Senator was already there and had ensconced himself in a large and very worn wicker chair, from which spot he contemplated the river traffic that floated past as we made our way out of the Ungenred Zone and into Comedy. The captain and helmsman were also present, and they expertly steered a path past the many underwater obstructions, islands and sandbars. I decided to try to act as much like the real Thursday as I could.

'Do you expect a clear run up the river, Captain?' I asked.

The captain chuckled.

'It's always eventful, Miss Next. Someone will doubtless be murdered, there will be romantic intrigue, and after that we'll pass a deserted village with a lone survivor who will ramble incoherently about something that we don't understand but has relevance later on. Did you meet the adventurer? Youngish chap. Handsome.'

I said I had, and both he and the Senator laughed.

'What's the joke?'

'He's the fodder. There's always at least one on a trip like this. Someone for you to get attached to, probably sleep with but who then dies on the journey, saving your life. You won't tell him, will you? It'll ruin his day.'

'I'll try to keep it under my hat.'

'Do you have the route all planned, Captain?' asked Jobsworth, who was sipping on a pink gin handed to him by a steward dressed in starched whites.

'We'll stay on the Metaphoric until we've entered Comedy and moved past Sitcoms,' replied the captain, pointing to a map of the river, 'and after that we follow a tributary past Mother-in-Law Jokes and then to Edgy Rapids before cruising the flat plain of Bob Hope and Vaudeville. At the foothills of the Scatological Mountains we'll enter the sub-genre of Bedroom Farce and Bawdy Romp. Twenty minutes after that we stop at Middle Station, which marks the border into Racy Novel.'

'Emissaries from Speedy Muffler will meet us at *Fanny Hill*,' added Senator Jobsworth, 'and they will accompany us to Pornucopia, the capital.'

The conversation fell off after that, and after mustering some courage I spoke.

'Did you want to speak to me, Senator?' I asked.

'Yes,' he replied. 'I want you to understand that you are here simply as a face – nothing more. As already explained, we have been putting around the story that you have Irritable Vowel Syndrome, and are mute. You will not be party to talks, or preparations for talks. You will not express an opinion by gesticulating or written note unless we decide and are fully briefed. You'll be told where to appear, and when. Is that clear?'

'As a bell, sir.'

'Good. Off you toddle, then. Ah!' he added, much relieved. 'Come in, gentlemen.'

Red Herring, Colonel Barksdale and Zhark had just appeared at the doorway. I was no longer needed. I thought for a moment of voicing my concerns over what Thursday might have been up to, but I didn't know for certain what she had been up to, so I said nothing, bowed and withdrew politely from the wheelhouse.

I walked down the narrow companionway to the main deck, and found my way to the bar. I wasn't particularly bothered by the Senator's attitude; it was what I was expecting – a friendly welcome, then being put firmly in my place.

The bar was elegantly panelled in light wood with inlaid etched mirrors to give the illusion of greater space. The furniture was of leather, but had worn badly, and the horsehair stuffing was beginning to sprout at the seams. One of the mad-looking foreigners was asleep in an armchair, and at the bar was the adventurer. He looked more handsome than he had earlier, and his hat was placed on the bar next to him.

'Enjoying the trip?' I asked as I sat down.

'I thought it would be funnier steaming through Comedy.'

'It's less funny the closer you get.'

'Hm. Would you permit me to buy you a drink?'

'I buy my own drinks,' I told him, doing as Thursday would. It wasn't as if it was a drink, anyway. Alcohol doesn't do anything in the BookWorld, except act as narrative furniture in scenes like these. If you wanted to get off your head you'd hit the hyphens, but I needed my wits about me.

'A beer for me,' I said. 'Drake?'

'Scotch.'

The barman placed our drinks on the counter and I took a sip. The beer was a light amber-coloured liquid, but tasted like warm tea. This wasn't unusual since everything in the BookWorld tasted like warm tea – except warm tea itself, which tasted of dishwater. But since dishwater tasted of warm tea, warm tea actually might have tasted like warm tea after all.

'Are you part of the diplomatic mission?' asked Drake.

I told him that I was, and he grunted non-committally. Since the Senator said he was fodder and unlikely to last the next few hours, I thought it a safe bet to trust him.

'I overheard something odd outside the Mysterious Passenger's cabin.'

'That's entirely normal. You'll probably hear odd noises in the night, too, and if we've got time, someone will be found shot dead with a cryptic note close by.'

'Do you want to know what I overheard?'

'Not really. There'll be an impostor on the boat, too – and a shape-changer.'

'What, of the alien variety?' I asked, looking nervously about.

'No,' he replied, smiling at my naivety, 'someone who is not what they seem.'

'Isn't that the impostor?'

'There's a subtle difference,' mused Drake for a moment, staring at the ceiling, 'but I'm not sure *precisely* what it was. I was born yesterday, you know.'

'My name is Florent,' announced a new bar steward, who had just come on duty. 'Can I mix you a Tahiti Tingle?'

I frowned, then turned. It was Sprockett, dressed as a bar steward and sporting a ridiculous false moustache on his porcelain features. Since he didn't greet me I assumed he wanted to remain incognito, so I merely said I already had a drink and resumed my conversation with Drake.

'Are journeys upriver usually like this?' I asked.

'Apparently so. How do they think they're going to stop Speedy Muffler anyway?'

'By telling him that massed armies on the borders of WomFic and Dogma are waiting to invade if he so much as hiccups.'

'What makes you think Speedy Muffler is doing anything but rattling his sabre? The only people who have anything to gain by a war are the neighbouring genres, who get to divvy up the spoils.'

'I knew Speedy Muffler in the old days,' said one of the foreigners, who had joined us, 'long before the BookWorld was remade –

335

even before Herring and Barksdale and that idiot Jobsworth were about.'

'What do you know about Speedy Muffler?'

'That he wasn't always the leader of Racy Novel. He was once a minor character in Porn with delusions of grandeur. Muffler was up here in the days before Racy Novel, when the Frowned Upon genres were clustered in the north beyond Comedy. His name came to prominence when he quite suddenly started sending large quantities of Metaphor downriver. He wasn't licensed to do so, but because his supplies were consistent, the rules were relaxed. Pretty soon he was taking more and more territory for himself, but he kept on sending down the Metaphor, and the CofG kept on turning a blind eye until he publicly proclaimed the area as Racy Novel, which was when the CofG started to take notice.'

'By then it was too late,' added Drake. 'Speedy Muffler's power was established, his genre large enough to demand a chair at the Council of Genres.'

'I guess WomFic and Feminism were none too happy?'

'Not overawed, no. Especially when he used to turn up at high-level summits with his shirt open and declaring that feminists needed to "loosen up" and should groove with his love machine.'

'Is he still shipping Metaphor downriver?' I asked.

'Not as much as before,' said Drake, 'but still more than WomFic and Dogma. The area is rich in Metaphor, and whoever can send the most downriver is the wealthiest. Put simply: whoever controls the northern genres controls the Metaphor supply, and whoever controls the supply of Metaphor controls fiction. It's not by chance that WomFic and Crime have forty-three per cent of the Outland readership. If Squid Procedural had been positioned up here, everyone would be reading about Decapod Gumshoes, and loving it.'

'So why isn't Racy Novel read more than Women's? If he sends more Metaphor downriver, I mean?'

'Because of *sanctions*,' said Drake, looking at me oddly, 'imposed by WomFic and Dogma – and pretty much everyone else. Like it or not, Racy Novel isn't very highly thought of.'

'Is that fair?'

'You're asking a lot of *basic* questions,' said Drake. 'I thought Thursday Next would be well up on all this – especially if she's here for the peace talks.'

'I need to gauge local opinion,' I said quickly. 'This is Fiction, after all – interpretation trumps fact every time.'

'Oh,' said Drake, 'I see.'

I excused myself as Sprockett had just left the bar and I caught up with him farther down the steamer, just outside the store-room.

'Good morning, ma'am,' he whispered, 'how is it going?'

'What are you doing here?'

'I'm the bar steward.'

'I can see that.'

'I knew you couldn't *actually* let me go,' he said, 'I'm too good a butler for that. So I simply assumed you were being compassionate and thought this trip too dangerous for staff to accompany you. So I came anyway. What do you want me to do?'

I took a deep breath. It seemed as though butlers were like flat feet, dimples and troublesome aunts – you've got them for life.

'There's a Mysterious Passenger in Cabin Twelve. I want you to find out what he's doing here.'

'He doesn't *do* anything – he's simply the MP-C12. Have you figured out who the fodder is yet?'

'It's Drake.'

'Ooh. Will he be eaten by a crocodile? Or get a poison dart in the eye?'

'Just find out what you can about the Mysterious Passenger, would you? I overheard him say: "I won't take your place at the talks" and it might be significant.'

'Very good, ma'am. I'll make enquiries.'

36

Middle Station

———

'For those of you who have tired of the glitzy world of shopping and inappropriate boyfriends in Chicklit, a trip to Dubious Lifestyle Advice might be the next step. An hour in the hallowed halls of invented ills will leave you with at least ten problems you never knew you had, let alone existed.'

Bradshaw's BookWorld Companion, 7th Edition

It took us an hour to steam through Comedy, and while mostly light and airy and heard-it-beforeish, the atmosphere became more strained and intimidating as we chugged slowly through mother-in-law jokes and sexist banter. Despite being advised to stay out of sight, I elected to stay on deck and brazen out the worst abuses that came shouted unseen from the thick trees that covered the riverbank. The two ladies of negotiable affection had no difficulty with the comments, having heard much worse before, and simply issued their retorts with aplomb – delicately countering the more vulgar insinuations with amusing attacks on the male psyche, and various aspersions on their manhood or ability.

We came across the Middle Station at noon. The small trading town was right at the point where the Double Entendre River becomes the Innuendo, and although we had been travelling through the buffer genre of Bawdy Romp, replete with amusing sketches of people running in and out of each other's bedrooms in a retro-amusing manner, we were now very much within the influence of Racy Novel, and we all knew it. The first part of the journey had been a pleasing chug up the river; now we knew we were here for business, and a sense of brooding introspection had fallen upon the boat.

The arrival of the paddle-steamer at the Middle Station was welcomed not by sound, but by silence. The constant tramp-tramp-tramp of the engines, for three hours a constant background chorus, was almost deafeningly quiet when they stopped. I stood on the front deck as the steamer drifted towards the jetty. The Middle Station, usually a throbbing hub of activity, seemed deserted. Drake stood next to me, his hand on the butt of his revolver.

'I'm going ashore to check this out,' I said, 'and I think it would be better if you stayed here.'

'I disagree, Miss Next. It is *you* who will be staying here.'

There seemed no easy way to say this, so I came right out with it.

'Drake,' I said in a quiet voice, 'you're the fodder, due for a tragic yet potentially heroic end.'

He looked at me for a moment.

'It's very good of you to warn me, but that's not how I see it.'

'You think it's someone else?'

'I think the fodder is *you*, Thursday.'

'No, it's not.'

'What are you if you're not the fodder?'

'I'm the impostor.'

'You . . . could be the impostor *and* the fodder.'

'The unions would never allow it.'

'They might.'

'Look,' I said, 'we could argue this all day, but here's the thing: you only graduated this morning with a minimal backstory. I've been working the BookWorld for years – who's most likely to cop it in the next few hours?'

'You might just *think* you've been working the BookWorld for three years. It could be *your* backstory.'

'Okay,' I said, beginning to get angry, 'we'll both go out there and see who gets eaten by a crocodile or gets a poison dart in the eye. *Then* we'll know.'

'Deal.'

The rest of the peace delegation had joined us on deck and were staring silently towards the Middle Station. As we drew closer we could see that the houses had been recently burned, for wisps of smoke hung in the air with the faint smell of burnt custard. We waited for the steamer to drift towards the jetty until it touched with a faint bump. The crew made the steamer fast before jumping back on the boat, and we watched and waited as the vessel slowly swung around in the current. There was not a single sign of life anywhere on the station.

'Well,' said Colonel Barksdale after a few minutes, 'I've seen enough – doubtless skirmishers from Racy Novel causing trouble. Let's steam on deeper into the genre and start getting some face time with this lunatic.'

'We're not going anywhere until we get some coal,' said the captain.

I stepped off the steamer and on to the rickety old jetty, Drake at my side. We walked slowly into the town. Drake looked about anxiously, but not, I realised, because of the deserted Middle Station.

'You'll keep an eye out for crocodiles, won't you?'

'As long as you watch my back for poison darts.'

We came across the first body near the postbox on the corner. There was an ugly wound in the middle of his chest, and the small letters and words that made up his existence had been caught by the breeze and blown into the fishing nets that had been hung up to dry. We looked around and noticed more bodies and the detritus of conflict: discarded rubber chickens, feather dusters, strings of silk flags, spinning bow ties and custard-pie shrapnel that somehow seemed sadder and less funny than usual.

'Is this a garrison town?' I asked.

'No,' replied the adventurer.

'Then what's a lance-corporal of the 14th Motorised Clown doing up here?'

The corpse was indeed a member of Comedy's front-line troops. He had orange hair, a bulbous red nose and was dressed in camouflaged battledress, along with a pair of size 28 shoes. Not much good for marching, and a hangover from their days as an Alpine regiment.

Drake placed his hand on the clown's bright red nose.

'Still warm,' he said, 'probably been dead less than an hour. Any thoughts?'

'I don't know,' I said, picking up a nurse's hat from the ground. A little farther on a stethoscope was lying broken in the dust. 'But it wasn't just clowns who died here today.'

We walked farther on and came across a dozen or so other bodies. All clowns, all dead, and none meant to be here. Bawdy Romp was within Racy Novel's control and officially a demilitarised zone.

'This doesn't make sense,' said Drake. 'Comedy never had any beef with Racy Novel. Quite the reverse; they actually got on very well. Without Racy Novel, Comedy would be very poor indeed – especially for the stand-ups.'

'Let's not hang around. Where did the captain say the coal was?'

We walked farther into the station and saw more evidence of a pitched battle having taken place not long before. We found the remains of several burnt-out clown cars, and despite their being able to drive in either direction and having a device for shedding all the bodywork in order to lighten the vehicle for a speedy getaway, it hadn't done any good. There was evidence of atrocities, too. Medical staff had been killed. I noticed several pretty nurses and a handsome doctor lying in a doorway, and several crash carts were

342

strewn about. There were a few dead rustic serving wenches, too, a torn bodice and a couple of horses with ruggedly handsome and now very dead riders lying in the road amid scorched brickwork and smoking rubble. We came across more dead clowns; it seemed as though an entire company had been wiped out.

'Looks like someone was making sure Comedy couldn't come to Racy Novel's aid,' observed Drake.

'It makes me wonder why we're bothering with peace talks. Crocodile.'

'What?'

'Behind you.'

Drake jumped out of the way as the crocodile's jaws snapped shut.

'Thank you.'

'Now do you believe you might be the fodder?' I asked.

Drake thought for a moment.

'He could have been trying to eat his way through me to get to you.'

'Sure,' I said with a smile, 'and while we're on the subject: if I was the fodder, why didn't you warn me? I warned you.'

'Because I . . . didn't want to ruin your day?'

'How very generous of you.'

We found the coal heap amid a few more civilians – this time pretty secretaries who had died in the arms of their bosses. We filled a couple of wheelbarrows with coal before returning to the steamer. As soon as we were aboard the crew slipped the moorings, the captain ordered 'astern slow' and swung the bows into the limpid river. We took the left branch up the tributary known as the Innuendo, and pretty soon the steamer was at full speed once more. Despite misgivings, Jobsworth was adamant that the peace talks should go ahead.

'It seemed as though the entire 14th Clown Division had been wiped out.'

37
Revision

————

'Among all the genres on Fiction Island, Comedy is the only one which still demands compulsory military service and a bucket of water down the trousers for every citizen. Conscripts are trained in the clown martial art of Sla-Pstik, and do not graduate from military academy until they can kill silently with a frying pan and achieve fatal accuracy with a custard pie at forty yards. It's a bit like Sparta, only with jokes.'

Bradshaw's BookWorld Companion, 7th Edition

We convened in the bar soon afterwards and related everything we had seen at the Middle Station. Colonel Barksdale, Herring, Zhark and Senator Jobsworth listened carefully to all we had to say, but didn't seem to have any better idea of what was going on than we.

'There is no reason for the 14th Motorised Clown to be this far north,' declared Colonel Barksdale angrily. 'It is a flagrant breach of numerous peace agreements and specifically the 1996 Clown Army Proliferation Treaty.'

'Shouldn't you have known about it?' asked Emperor Zhark, who knew better than most the value of intelligence.

'The textual sieve network is patchy up here,' replied Barksdale in a sulky tone, 'we can't know everything. I can only think the 14th Clown must have been massing in the demilitarised zone as the potential allies of Racy Novel.'

'Then who killed them and all the civilians?' asked the adventurer, to which there didn't seem to be much of an answer. They all fell silent for a moment.

'When do we meet with the other delegates?' asked Jobsworth.

'In an hour,' replied Herring. 'Aunt Augusta of WomFic and Cardinal Fang of Outdated Religious Dogma are meeting us at *Fanny Hill*. Would you excuse me? We're out of footnoterphone range and I'm going to have to send a message to the Council via the short-wave colophone.'

Drake and I were dismissed as Jobsworth, Barksdale and Zhark had decided to discuss the finer points of the peace talks, something to which we could not be privy.

'I'm going to freshen up before we get there,' said Drake, 'and maybe rub on some crocodile repellant.'

I laughed, saw he was serious, turned the laugh into a cough and said: 'Good idea.'

We were now well within Racy Novel, and the rustling of bushes, groans and squeaks of delight echoed in from the riverbanks, where large privet hedges were grown to afford some sort of privacy for the residents. Every now and then a slip in the riverbank allowed us a brief glimpse of what went on, which was generally several scantily dressed people running around in a gleeful manner – usually in a bedroom somewhere, but occasionally in the outdoors, and once on the top deck of a London bus.

I made my way for'ard, where I was met by Sprockett, who beckoned me into a laundry cupboard.

'I took the opportunity to go through the Mysterious Passenger's belongings, ma'am.'

'And?'

'I came across some shoulder pads, knee pads, a chest protector and a gallon of fire retardant.'

'*What?*'

'Shoulder pads—'

'I heard. It just doesn't make any sense.'

'What doesn't?'

'All of it. From beginning to end. We reach *Fanny Hill* in half an hour and the peace talks begin as soon as we are escorted to Pornucopia. It's time to go over what we've found. I feel the answer is staring me in the face.'

'Shouldn't we gather all the suspects in the bar?' asked Sprockett, who was fast becoming infected by the *Metaphoric Queen*'s capacity for narrative formulaicism.

'No. And another thing—'

I was interrupted by a cry from outside, and the engine shifted to *slow ahead*. We stepped out of the laundry cupboard to see several crewmen run past, and we followed them to the upper rear deck, from where we could see across the top of the stern wheel. Behind us in midstream was a figure in one of the riverboat's four-man tenders. The man was rowing at a measured pace away from the boat, and given our forward speed, the distance between the two craft was rapidly increasing.

'Who is it?' asked Herring.

'It looks like the Mysterious Passenger from Cabin Twelve,' replied Drake, who had a small telescope, as befits an adventurer. 'He's even taken his luggage with him.'

'What's the meaning of this?' asked Jobsworth, who had just arrived.

Herring explained, and Jobsworth looked at us all in turn.

'Let me see.'

He looked through the telescope for a moment.

'He's taken his luggage with him.'

'That's what I said,' remarked Drake.

'Mr Herring,' said Jobsworth, 'what's going on here?'

'I've no idea, Mr Senator.'

'Advice?'

'Um – carry on?'

'Sounds good to me. Captain?'

347

'Sir?'

'Carry on.'

But the captain, long time a river man, knew more of the perils that can be found on the Metaphoric.

'We can't leave him out here, sir. The forests are full of Sirens eager to . . . well, how can I put it? He'll be captured and made to . . . Listen, he'll be killed.'

'Will it be quick?'

'No — it will be long and very drawn out. He might enjoy it to begin with, but he will eventually be discarded as a shrivelled husk of a man devoid of any clothes, humanity or moisture.'

But the Senator was made of sterner stuff.

'This mission is too important to delay, Captain. The Mysterious Passenger formerly of Cabin Twelve will have to remain exactly that. In every campaign there are casualties. Full ahead.'

'Yes, sir.'

And they all walked away. The engines ran up to full speed again and after a few more minutes the small boat was lost to view behind an overhanging tree on a bend in the river.

'I guess that's what Mysterious Passengers do,' said Drake with a shrug, 'be mysterious. Drink?'

'I'll see you down there,' I replied. 'I must admonish this bar steward for the lamentable lack of quality in his Tahiti Tingle.'

Drake nodded and moved off, and Sprockett and I sat on the curved bench on the upper rear deck to discuss recent events. From the Epizeuxis to the mimefield to the Men in Plaid to Sir Charles Lyell and the bed-sitting room.

'What had Thursday discovered that was so devastating to the peace process?' asked Sprockett.

'I don't know. I wish to Panjandrum I was more like her.'

I took the sketch I had found in Sir Charles's office out of my pocket. It was a map of Racy Novel with WomFic to one side and

Dogma on the other. There was a shaded patch the shape of a tail-less salmon that was mostly beneath Racy Novel.

As I stared at the picture I felt a sudden flush of new intelligence, as though a jigsaw had been thrown in the air and landed fully completed. Everything that had happened to me over the past few days had been inexorably pointing me in one direction. But up until now, I had been too slow or stupid to be able to sift the relevant facts from the herrings.

'By all the spellcheckers of isugfsf,' I said, pointing at Lyell's sketch. 'It's Metaphor. A trillion tons of the stuff waiting to be mined lying beneath our feet!'

'Yes?' said Sprockett, his eyebrow pointing at 'Doubtful'.

'That's what Lyell and Thursday had discovered,' I said excitedly. 'It's as Drake said: "Whoever controls the supply of Metaphor controls Fiction".'

'If so,' said Sprockett, carefully, 'Racy Novel would be sending more Metaphor downriver than anyone else. And they're not.'

I thought about this for a moment.

'Maybe Speedy Muffler isn't bad at all. Perhaps he's defending the Metaphor against greedy genres intent on mining it to exhaustion. Metaphor should be controlled – a glut in the market would make Fiction overtly highbrow, painfully ambiguous and potentially unreadable. The new star on the horizon would be the elephant in the room that might lead the BookWorld into a long winter's night.'

'That would be frightful,' replied Sprockett, recoiling in terror as the overmetaphorication hit him like a hammer, 'but how does that explain the 14th Clown's destruction? Or even who's responsible for all this?'

'I don't know,' I said, 'but Senator Jobsworth needs to hear about it.'

I jumped up and ran down the companionway to the captain's cabin, nearly colliding with Red Herring on the way.

'Sorry,' he said, 'I'm just going to find a doughnut – do you want one?'

'No thank you, sir.'

I found Senator Jobsworth discussing the talks with Emperor Zhark and Colonel Barksdale.

'Have you seen Herring?' asked Jobsworth. 'He should really be going through the final details with us.'

'He went to get a doughnut.'

'He did? Leave us now. We're very busy.'

'I have important information. I think I know why Thursday was assassinated.'

Jobsworth stared at me.

'Thursday's dead?'

'Well, no, because her imagination is still alive. It was an assassination attempt – in a crummy book written by Adrian Dorset.'

'Adrian Dorset?'

'Jack Schitt, if you must. It was the Epizeuxis that got her. And Mediocre.'

'Who's Mediocre?'

'Gatsby.'

'He's anything but mediocre, my girl.'

And both he and Zhark laughed in a patronising sort of way.

'Seriously,' I said hotly, 'Thursday was attacked and the reason—'

'Whatever it is I'm sure it's *fascinating*,' said Jobsworth, 'but it's going to have to wait. We enter the sub-genre Racy Classics in five minutes, and meet with the other delegates in forty-five. We have much work to do. If you really want to be helpful, make me a cup of tea or go and find Herring.'

'But—'

'GO!'

I mumbled an apology and backed out of the door, cursing my own weakness.

'That could have gone better,' said Sprockett. 'I'll try to find Herring for you.'

And with a mild buzz, he disappeared. I walked down to the lower deck feeling hot and frustrated. I didn't like to be talked to that way, but this could indeed wait. I'd leave it until Jobsworth had a quieter moment and then tell him – or perhaps speak to Speedy Muffler's people in private and see whether my suspicions were correct. Perhaps it was better *not* to talk to Jobsworth.

I went down to my cabin to wash my face but stopped at Cabin Twelve. The Mysterious Passenger's escape from the steamer still made no sense, so I pushed open the door and went in.

The bed was made up, as I might have suspected – we weren't due to return until tomorrow. I searched through the missing passenger's baggage and found none of the shoulder or knee pads that Sprockett had described, although the fire retardant was still there, unopened. There was a change of clothes, and nothing else. I was about to close the door when I suddenly realised – *the Mysterious Passenger had his luggage with him when we saw him rowing away.*

A flurry of unpleasant thoughts went through my head and I suddenly realised not only why the Mysterious Passenger would have knee pads, but who attacked the 14th Clown and what was going on in the Outland that made all this possible. This was a complex plot of considerable dimensions, and I was now certain who was behind it all. My first thought was to go and tell Jobsworth exactly what was happening, but I stopped as a far worse realisation dawned upon me. The plan would work only if everyone on board the *Metaphoric Queen* were to be assassinated.

I grabbed a fire axe and ran up the narrow companionway to the deck.

38

Answers

'Off the coast lies Vanity Island, and off Vanity lies Fan-fiction. Beyond Fanfiction is School Essays and beyond that Excuses for Not Doing School Essays. The latter is often the most eloquent, constructed as it is in the white-hot heat of panic, necessity, and the desire not to get a detention.'

Bradshaw's BookWorld Companion, 2nd Edition

One of Jobsworth's D3 minions had been given the task of keeping an eye on the riveted box that contained the valuable plot-line gifts for Speedy Muffler, and he noticed me only when I was halfway across the foredeck, my intention already clear to those present. He dropped his copy of *The Word* and took a pace towards me. I caught him on the solar plexus with the ball of my hand and he reeled over backwards. The foredeck would have been in plain view from the wheelhouse. The captain pulled on the steam whistle and a deafening blast echoed across Racy Novel, temporarily quenching the sounds of the enthusiastic moans that echoed across the water.

The whistle also drowned out the sound of the padlock being smashed off and I had the lid open and was looking at the contents when Zhark and Jobsworth arrived beside me. They stopped too, and stared inside the box.

'Those aren't plot lines,' said Jobsworth.

'No,' I replied, looking up the river to where I could just see *Lady Chatterley's Lover* appearing around the next bend, less than five hundred yards away, 'and you need to stop the boat before we get to Racy Classics.'

'Captain!' yelled Jobsworth, who knew how to act properly when evidence presented itself. The captain opened the wheelhouse window and leaned out, cupping a hand to his ear.

'Turn the *Queen* about and get us downstream. If we go up, I want to be taking only Racy Pulp with us!'

The captain needed no further bidding, and he ordered the helm hard over to turn mid-river.

I leaned closer and examined the contents of the box. It was a classy job. There was a single glass jar that contained, as far as I could see, a lot of foam. This was attached to a funnel and a time switch, and wrapped around all of this were a series of embarrassingly bad descriptions of sexual congress. Emperor Zhark moved closer and put on his glasses.

'By the seven-headed Zook of Zargon,' he breathed, 'it's full of anti-kern.'

'It's full of what?'

'Kerning is the adjustment of the white spaces between the letters,' he explained, 'in order to make the letters seem proportionally spaced. What this does is remove the white spaces entirely – within an instant, this entire boat and everyone in it will implode into nothing more than an oily puddle of ink floating on the river.'

I pointed to the poorly written descriptions of sexual congress wrapped around the device.

'With a few telltale descriptions of a sexual nature to point the finger towards Speedy Muffler.'

'So it would appear. *Blast!*'

Emperor Zhark had been examining the device carefully.

'What's up?'

'No blue wire. There's usually a choice of wires to cut and by long convention, it's always the blue one. Without that, there's no way we can know how to defuse it.'

I glanced at the timing device, which also by long convention was prominently featured – and had two and a half minutes to go.

'Can we throw it overboard?' asked Jobsworth.

'Not unless you want to see the entire Metaphoric River vanish in under a second.'

'We could abandon the steamer.'

'It'll be a tight fit in the one tender remaining – and those high privet hedges along the riverbank won't make for an easy escape.'

'I'll take it in a boat with me.'

It was Drake Foden, adventurer. 'I don't want any arguments,' he said, 'this is my function. I'm the fodder.'

'I told you he was,' said Barksdale, jabbing Jobsworth on the shoulder with his index finger.

There was no time to do anything else, and at a single word from the captain, the second tender was lowered over the side and the riveted box placed inside. Drake turned to me and took my hands in his.

'Goodbye, Thursday. I'm sorry we didn't get to sleep together and perhaps have a few jokes and get into a couple of scrapes and thus make this farewell more poignant and mournful, which it isn't.'

'Yes,' I replied, 'I'll always regret not knowing you at all or even liking you very much. Perhaps next time.'

'There won't be a next time.'

'I know that. Foden?'

'Yes?'

'You have something stuck in your teeth.'

'Here?'

'Other side.'

'Thanks.'

And without another word, Drake clambered aboard, cast off the mooring and began to row quickly away from the steamer.

'Hey,' I yelled across the water, 'aren't you glad it wasn't a poison dart in your—'

But I didn't get a chance to say any more. Drake, the tender and the iron box suddenly imploded with a sound like a cough going backwards, accompanied by a swift rush of air that sucked in to fill the void and made our ears pop. I'd never seen text destroyed so rapidly – even an Eraserhead takes half a second to work.

'Slow ahead,' ordered Jobsworth, 'and wire the delegation that we have been "unavoidably delayed".'

He turned to me.

'Just what in Wheatley's name is going on here, Next?'

My mind was still racing. There was the fate of the 14th Clown to think of, and the broader implications of regional stability, pretty nurses, handsome doctors and fire retardant.

'Time is of the essence. Mr Senator, I need you to do something without question.'

'And that is?'

'Shut down every single Feedback Loop north of *Three Men in a Boat*.'

'Are you mad?' he said. 'That's almost three hundred million books!'

'Mad? Perhaps. But if you don't do what I ask you'll have a genre war on your hands so devastating it will turn your blood to ice.'

'My blood is already ice, Miss Next.'

The Senator paused, then looked at Zhark, who nodded his agreement.

'Very well.'

Jobsworth instructed Barnes to get the message to Text Grand Central in any way he could – and to expedite Code Puce.

'And you,' said Jobsworth, pointing a finger at me, 'have some serious explaining to do.'

We convened in the bar almost immediately. Jobsworth was there with Herring, Barksdale, the captain and Emperor Zhark – as well as all of Jobsworth's D3s and Sprockett, who had divested himself of his bar steward disguise and was once more in full butler regalia.

'Where would you like me to start?' I asked.

'At the beginning,' said Jobsworth, 'and don't stop until you get to the end.'

I took a deep breath and showed them the map Lyell had drawn.

'We won't find out exactly *how* she knew until we find her, but the real Thursday Next became aware that there might exist a huge quantity of raw Metaphor under the northern genres. Such a state of affairs would throw the entire power balance of Fiction on its head, so she needed to make sure. She took leading geologist Sir Charles Lyell up-country to conduct some test drilling, and it seems she was right. Buried beneath Racy Novel are the largest reserves of untapped Metaphor the BookWorld has ever seen.'

I had everyone's attention by now – you could have heard a pin drop.

'It was potentially explosive news, and Thursday knew that she would be in severe danger if this got out – so she hid among the flatter Thursdays out in Fanfiction. Despite her precautions, her activities were being scrutinised without her knowledge, and Thursday – reliably touted as "the second-hardest person to kill in the BookWorld" – had to be got rid of. A cabby named The Mediocre Gatsby was bribed to hang around Fanfiction on the off-chance she would want picking up. A previously scrapped book called *The Murder on the Hareng Rouge* was being kept in Vanity and as soon as she was in the cab the book was dispatched to the Council of Genres. Mediocre piggybacked the book for the trip as instructed and a second later a Rhetorical Device was detonated, leaving the book, the cabby – and it was hoped Thursday herself – little more than textual confetti – a million graphemes littered all over Fiction.'

There was silence, so I carried on.

'That might have been the end of it. Most of the book was just small tattered remnants not dissimilar to the usual detritus that flutters occasionally from the heavens and is absorbed into the ground, except that for some reason Adrian Dorset described a bed-sitting room so well that it survived the sabotage intact and came to rest in Conspiracy, and JAID had to be alerted. This was tricky, because a diligent investigator might start to ask awkward questions, so they employed their most useless investigator to look into it. Me. And that's not a coincidence. Why would that be, Sprockett?'

'There are *no* coincidences in the BookWorld – so long as you don't count the last chapters in some of Charles Dickens's books.'

'Exactly. But we *do* find problems – the fact that someone scrubbed off the ISBNs to avoid discovery, and the Epizeuxis Device. And as we look, we find ourselves one step behind the Men in Plaid, who are silencing anyone who had anything to do with the attempted hit on Thursday Next.'

'Scrubbed ISBNs?' demanded Jobsworth. 'Rogue Men in Plaid? Dead geologists? Epizeuxis Devices? Who is responsible for this outrage?'

'One of us present here,' I said.

They all looked at one another.

'It was little things to begin with – things that didn't click until later. I learned from Adrian Dorset that he destroyed *The Murders on the Hareng Rouge* a month back, yet it was still floating around Vanity waiting to intercept Thursday. The rules state that it has to be scrapped immediately – on Red Herring's signature.'

They all looked at Herring, who had started to go pale.

'He controls the Book Transit Authority, and also the Men in Plaid. He's the second-in-command of the BookWorld, but he wanted more. He was after the top job, and what's more, control of the vast stores of Metaphor that are lying under Racy Novel. He knew that whoever controlled the Metaphor would control Fiction.'

'But how could he control Speedy Muffler and Racy Novel?' asked Zhark.

'That's the clever bit. He planned to invade – using an army mustered from one of the most powerful genres on the island.'

'Women's Fiction?' said Colonel Barksdale with a smirk. 'Not possible. They have neither the manpower nor the inclination.'

Emperor Zhark and Jobsworth nodded their heads vigorously; WomFic were wholly against any sort of warfare, and had agreed to sanctions only as a last resort.

'Not WomFic,' I said, 'a smaller sub-genre with enough shock troops to take on the 14th Clown and win. A genre that has for many years been the buffer zone between WomFic and Racy Novel. A genre that has successfully blended raciness and euphemism to create an empire that sells books by the billion – Daphne Farquitt. More readers than almost any other writer, and eighteen per cent of total global readership.'

'They don't have any troops,' scoffed Barksdale, 'you're mistaken.'

I chose my words carefully. Despite recent events, I'd be pushing my luck if I admitted I had been in the RealWorld.

'Today is Daphne Farquitt Day in the Outland. As we speak a massive readathon is in progress. At even conservative estimates there must be upwards of two hundred million readers making their way through Farquitt's 372 novels. There will be speed-reading events, trivia quizzes and read-ins. The power of the Feedback Loop will be astronomical – and easily enough to create an unstoppable army of ditzy romantic heroines and their lantern-jawed potential husbands/lovers.'

'The nurses, secretaries and medical equipment you saw at Middle Station?'

359

'*Exactly*,' I replied, 'not civilians at all – but the romantically involved honoured dead. The Farquitt army were working against Racy Novel by making a pre-emptive strike and eradicating any possible threat from Speedy Muffler's allies in Comedy. With the peace envoys all assassinated in an apparent Muffler attack, there would be no opposition to the total and complete invasion of Racy Novel by the Farquitt army, and with it, control of the vast stocks of Metaphor lying beneath our feet.'

There was silence in the room. They all looked stunned. Barksdale was the first to speak.

'That explanation,' he said in admiration, 'was of a complexity that would gather plaudits from even the most intractable of political thrillers. With all of us dead in an attack that could be blamed on Speedy Muffler, Red Herring would step into the top slot, direct his allies to annexe Racy Novel, secure the Metaphor and set himself up as supreme dictator of Fiction.'

'It's a brilliant scheme,' murmured Zhark in admiration, 'I'll *definitely* be using it on the Rambosians next week. The little devils. They love a good subjugation. Mr Senator?'

'A plan of titanic proportions. If he wasn't going to be erased for treason, I'd offer him a job.'

Red Herring was starting to shake when he heard this. He tried to speak but only a strangled squeak came out.

'Might I make an observation?' asked Sprockett.

'Go ahead,' replied Jobsworth, who was now in a generous mood.

'Mr Herring is here with us now – how could he seize power if he was assassinated along with the rest of us?'

Barksdale and Zhark's faces fell, and even Jobsworth's smile vanished. They looked at me.

'Simple,' I said, placing my hand on Herring's shoulder, 'this *isn't* Red Herring. Figuring that out was the key to the whole thing.'

'That's absurd,' remarked Jobsworth. 'We were discussing the minutiae of the peace talks on the way in. He can't be anything but.'

'I assure you,' said the faux-Herring, who had finally managed to find his voice, 'I'm *not* Red Herring.'

'He's right,' I said, 'this is Herring's stunt double, Fallon Hairbag. He took Herring's place when Red Herring made his escape in the boat's tender.'

'You're the Mysterious Passenger?' asked Zhark, and the Herring-that-wasn't nodded unhappily.

'Mr Herring promised me the pick of all the stunt work in the BookWorld if I did this for him. He said it was for a prank. That it would be funny.'

'I overheard Herring and his stunt double talking in the cabin – about "not doing the talks" – and then there was my butler's discovery of knee and elbow pads, as well as a gallon of fire retardant.'

'Whatever for?' asked Barksdale.

'Just in case I had to set myself on fire and leap out of a window waving my arms,' replied Fallon wistfully. 'It always pays to be prepared.'

'The switch was subtly done,' I said, 'but when I met the replaced Herring later on he was polite and asked me whether I wanted a doughnut – the real Herring would never have been so accommodating.'

'I've heard enough,' announced Senator Jobsworth, rising to his feet. 'Send word that the peace talks are postponed. I want an emergency meeting of everyone in the Debating Chamber this evening, a press conference at five and the WomFic and Farquitt senators in my office the minute we get back. Barnes?'

'Yes, sir?'

'Implement Emergency Snooze Protocol 7B on the whole Farquitt canon *immediately*. I want every Farquitt reader yawning and nodding off in under ten minutes. We need to not only close down their feedback – but send Daphne Farquitt a clear message that we will not be trifled with.'

'What about the kittens?' asked Zhark in a shocked tone.

'It's a feline compliant executive order,' replied Jobsworth grandly. 'No kittens will be harmed in the great Farquitt snoozeathon.'

While Barnes and the rest of the D3s scurried off to do Jobsworth's bidding, the Senator and the others put their heads together. I told Fallon to go and hide in his cabin until we got in, by which time he would doubtless be forgotten. He thanked me and gave me his card in case I needed someone to attempt to leap fourteen motor-cycles in a double-decker bus or something, and Sprockett and I went and sat on the foredeck to watch the riverbank drift slowly past. Despite keeping a careful eye out for Herring, we saw only the upturned tender he had escaped in, and figured that he was either making his escape to Farquitt, or had been eaten by a croc-odile who had mistaken him for fodder.

'Well,' said Sprockett, 'that denouement went very well. Your first?'

'Did it show?'

'Not at all.'

I was glad of this.

'I think Thursday might have been proud.'

'Yes,' agreed Sprockett, 'I think she might.'

39
Story-ending Options

'To finish off your Character Exchange Programme break, Thomas Cook (BookWorld) Limited are offering tourists the option to choose how they would like to end their holiday. The "Chase" or "Scooby-Doo" endings remain popular as do the "Death Scene" and "Reconciliation with sworn enemy". Traditionalists may be disappointed, though. The ever popular "Riding off into the sunset" option has recently had to be withdrawn owing to irreconcilable cliché issues . . .'

Bradshaw's BookWorld Companion, 15th Edition

The trip back downriver was uneventful, and over in only twelve words. By the time the *Metaphoric Queen* had docked the senator for Farquitt had already denied that her genre had anything to do with Herring's plan, and expressed 'great surprise' and 'total outrage' that someone had 'faked romantic troops' in order to attack the 14th Clown. For their part, Comedy had mobilised their 2nd and 6th Clown divisions to their borders and were demanding reparations from Farquitt, at the same time bringing pressure to bear on WomFic by threatening to withdraw all humour. Not to be outdone, Speedy Muffler had declared that the 'presence of untapped Metaphor' within his territory was 'unproven and absurd' and he had so far refused all offers of commercial extraction contracts, further commenting that individual senators were welcome to see him personally in his 'love train'.

'Looks like it's business as usual,' I said to Commander Bradshaw.

We were in the Jurisfiction offices at Norland Park, and I was having a lengthy debrief that same afternoon. I had entered the offices not as a bit-player or an apprentice, but on my own merit. Emperor Zhark had awarded me a gift of some valuable jewellery that he said had been buried with his grandfather, Mr Fainset doffed his cap in an agreeable manner and Mrs Tiggy-Winkle had kindly offered to do my laundry. It felt as if I was part of the family.

'So what are you going to do now?' asked Bradshaw, leaning back in his chair.

'I had a small mutiny back in my series,' I explained. 'My own fault, really – I was thinking of Thursday and not my books. It'll need a lot of tact and diplomacy to win them back.'

Bradshaw smiled and thought for a minute.

'The BookWorld is falling apart at the seams,' he said, waving his hand at the huge pile of paperwork in his in-tray. 'We've got a major problem with eBooks that we'd never envisioned. The Racy Novel/Farquitt affair will rumble on for years, and I'm sure we haven't heard the last of Red Herring. Ten Duplex-6s have gone missing, and everyone has escaped from *The Great Escape*.'

'How is that possible?'

'There was a fourth tunnel we didn't know about – Tom, Dick, Harry and *Keith*. There's a serial killer still at large, not to mention several character assassins – and that pink gorilla running around inside *A Tale of Two Cities* is really beginning to piss me off.'

He took a sip of coffee and stared at me.

'I'm down to only seven agents. You've proved your capacity for this sort of work. I want you to join us here at Jurisfiction.'

'No, no,' I said quickly, 'I've had quite enough, thank you. The idea that people actually do this because they like it strikes me as double insanity with added insanity. Besides, you've already got a Thursday – you just have to find her. That reminds me.'

I dug Thursday's shield from my pocket and pushed it across the desk. Bradshaw picked it up and rubbed his thumb against the smooth metal.

'Where did you get this?'

I explained how Landen had contacted the red-haired gentleman when Thursday failed to check in as planned.

'So that's why he was out of his book,' muttered Bradshaw. 'I'll see him pardoned at the earliest opportunity.'

Bradshaw looked at the badge, then at me.

'So, how do you think this story's going to end?'

'I don't know, sir.'

'Are you sure you're not her?'

'It's a tricky one,' I replied after giving the matter some thought, 'and there's evidence to suggest that I am. I can do things only she can do, I can see things that only she can see. Landen thought I was her, and although he now thinks I'm the written one, that might all be part of a fevered delusion. His or mine, I'm not sure. It's even possible I've been Owlcreeked.'

Bradshaw knew what I was talking about. 'Owlcreek' was a Biercian device in which a character could spend the last few seconds of their life in a long-drawn-out digression on what might have happened had they lived. I might at this very moment be spiralling out of control in Mediocre's cab, Herring's coup still ahead of me, and perfect in its unrevealed complexity.

'Carmine might actually be the Thursday I think I am,' I added. 'It's even possible I'm suffering the hallucinatory aftershock of a recent rewriting. And while we're pushing the plausibility envelope, the BookWorld might not be real at all, and I'm simply a carpet-fitter at Acme with a vibrant imagination.'

I shuddered at the possibility that none of this might be happening at all.

'This is Fiction,' said Bradshaw in a calm voice, 'and the truth is whatever you make it. You can interpret the situation in any way you want, and all of the scenarios could be real – and what's more, depending on how you act now, any one of them could *become* real.'

I frowned.

'I can be Thursday just by thinking I am?'

'More or less. We may require you to undergo a short narrative procedure known as a "Bobby Ewing" where you wake up next chapter and it's all been a dream, but it's pretty painless so long as you don't mind any potential readers throwing up their hands in disgust.'

'I can be Thursday?' I said again.

He nodded.

'All you have to do is *know* you are. And don't deny that you've had some doubts over the past few days.'

It was tempting. I could be her and do Thursday things, and never have to worry about falling read-rates, keeping Bowden in line or dealing with Pickwick. I could even have Landen and the kids. I looked around at the Jurisfiction office. The Red Queen was hopping mad as usual, Mr Fainset was attempting to figure out why Tracy Capulet had locked her sister in a cupboard, Lady Cavendish was drafting an indictment against Red Herring for 'impersonating a red herring when you're not one' and the Emperor Zhark was putting together an interim peace deal for the northern genres. It looked enjoyable, relevant and a good use of anyone's time.

Commander Bradshaw smiled and pushed Thursday's shield back across the table, where I stared at it.

'What do you say?'

'I can be Thursday,' I said slowly, 'I can work at Jurisfiction. But at a *fictional* Jurisfiction. I want to depict the real Thursday doing everything she really did. I want her series to feature the Book-World, and you, and Miss Havisham and Zhark and all the rest of them. *That's* where I'd like to be Thursday. That's the Thursday I can be. A *fictional* one. I'd like to help you out, but I can't.'

Bradshaw looked at me for a long time.

'I reluctantly respect your decision to stay with your books,' he said at last, 'and I understand you wanting to tell it like it is. Naturally we're very grateful for everything you've done, but even if Jobsworth and I sign off on a Textual Flexation Certificate to change your series, I must point out that you can't truly be Thursday without Landen, and even if you get his permission, you still have to get Thursday's approval before you even begin to *think* about trying to change your series. And as far as we know, she may already be . . . dead.'

He had trouble saying the final word and had to almost roll it around in his mouth before he could spit it out.

'She's not dead,' I said firmly.

'I hope so too. But without any leads – and we have none – it's going to be an onerous task to find her. Here in Fiction we have over a quarter of a billion titles. That's just one island in a Book-World of two hundred and twenty-eight different and very distinct BISAC groupings. Most of those islands have fewer titles but some – like Non-Fiction – have more. And then there are the foreign language BookWorlds. Even if you are right – and I hope you are – Thursday could be anywhere from the Urdu translation of *Wuthering Heights* to the guarantee card on a 1965 Moulinex Chefette.'

'But you're still looking, right?'

'Of course. We rely on telemetry from our many unmanned probes that move throughout the BookWorld, all textual sieves have been set to pick her up if she makes a move, and Text Grand Central are keeping the waste-gates on the ImaginoTransference engines on alert for a "Thursday Next" word string. There's always hope, but there's a big BookWorld out there.'

'If she's alive,' I said in a resolute tone, 'I can find her.'

'If you do,' said Bradshaw with a smile, 'you can change whatever you want in your books – even introduce the Toast Marketing Board.'

I started.

'You heard about that?'

He smiled.

'We hear about *everything*. Take the shield. Use her rights and privileges. You might need them. And if you change your mind and want to be her, call me.'

I picked up the badge from the table and put it in my pocket.

'Commander?' said the Red Queen, who had been hovering and stepped in when she saw that our conversation was at an end. 'Text Grand Central have reported a major narrative flexation over in Shakespeare. It seems Othello has murdered his wife.'

'Again? I do wish that trollop Desdemona would be more careful when she's fooling around. What is it this time? Incriminating love letters?'

The Red Queen looked at her notes.

'No – it seems there was this handkerchief—'

'Hell's teeth!' yelled Bradshaw in frustration. 'Do I have to do everything around here? I want Iago in my office in ten minutes.'

'He's doing that spin-off with Hamlet,' said Mr Fainset from across the room.

'*Iago v Hamlet*? They got the green light for that?'

'Shylock bankrolled their appeal and got Portia to represent them. They were seriously pissed off about the "Give me my .453 kilo of flesh" directive from Brussels – hence the anti-European subplot in *Iago v Hamlet*.'

'Get him to see me as soon as he can. What is it, Mr Fainset?'

'The Unread, sir.'

'Causing trouble again?'

'They're all over Horror like cheap perfume.'

I moved off, as tales of the Unread gave me the spooks. Most characters who were long unread either made themselves useful like Bradshaw or went into a downward spiral of increased torpidity. Others, for some unknown reason, went bad and became the Unread. They festered in dark alleys, in holes in the ground, the crevices between paragraphs – anywhere where they could leap out and ensnare a character and suck the Reading Light out of them. Even grammasites, goblins and the Danvers avoided them.

I moved away. Bradshaw was busy and my debrief was over. Thursday was missed, but Jurisfiction's work couldn't stop just so they could utilise their full resources to find her. It would be the same for any one of them, and they all knew it.

I walked across to Thursday's desk and rested my fingertips on the smooth oak surface. The desk was clean and aside from a SpecOps mug, a picture of Landen, a stack of messages and a goodly case-load in the in-basket, fairly tidy. I looked at the worn chair but didn't sit down. This wasn't my desk. I opened the drawers but could find little of relevance, which wasn't hard – I didn't know what would *be* relevant.

I stepped outside the Jurisfiction offices and found the frog-footman dozing on a chair in the lobby.

'Wesley?'

He started at his name being called and almost fell off the chair in surprise.

'Miss Next?'

'Where do I requisition a vehicle?'

His eyes lit up.

'We have a large choice. What would you like?'

'A hover-car,' I said, having always wanted to ride in one, 'a convertible.'

I picked up Sprockett, who had been waiting outside, and a minute or two later we were heading west out of HumDram/Classics in a Zharkian Bubble-drive Hovermatic. We arrived over Thriller within a few minutes, and flew slowly over the area in which the *The Murders on the Hareng Rouge* had come down almost a week ago. If Thursday had survived the sabotage, she would have landed somewhere within the half million or so novels along the debris trail.

If Thursday had survived, I reasoned, the cab had come down more or less intact. No one had reported the remains of a taxi falling to earth, and I wanted to know why. We flew up and down the area of the debris trail for a while, searching for even the merest clue as to what might have happened but seeing nothing but an endless landscape of novels. We were yelled at several times by cabbies annoyed that we were 'hovering about like a bunch of numpties', and on one occasion we were pulled over by a Thriller border patrol and had to explain why we were loitering. I flashed Thursday's badge and they apologised and moved on.

'What are we looking for, ma'am?'

'I wish I knew.'

I had a thought and took out my notebook to remind me what Landen had told me when I spoke to him in Fanfiction.

He had stated that Thursday had said: '*The circumstances of your confusion will be your path to enlightenment.*'

I stared at the sentence for a long time, then took my *Bradshaw's BookWorld Companion* from my bag and flicked to the map section at the back. And then, all was light. She had been contacting me, and my confusion was indeed the answer.

'Bingo,' I said softly.

40
Thursday Next

'... A trip to Text Grand Central is a must for the technophile, and a day spent on one of the main Imagino-Transference engine floors is not to be missed. A visit will dispel for ever the notion that those at TGC do little to smooth out the throughputting of the story to the reader's imagination. Tours around the Reader Feedback Loop are available on Tuesday afternoons, but owing to the sometimes hazardous nature of feed-back, exposure is limited to eighteen seconds ...'

Bradshaw's BookWorld Companion, 15th Edition

It took nearly an hour to find what we were looking for. Sand-wiched between Political Thriller and Spy Thriller, and well within the condemned book's debris trail, was Psychological Thriller. The whole 'Am I really Thursday?' stuff I had been labouring through over the past few days had all the hallmarks of a Psycho Thriller plot device, and made total sense of Thursday's 'confusion, enlight-enment' sentence.

Finding the genre, however, was harder. It was difficult to spot from the air as a sense of ambiguity blurred the edges of the small genre, and with good reason. Psychological was another 'rogue genre' where nothing could be taken at face value, trusted or even believed – a genre whose very *raison d'être* was to confuse and obfuscate. Often accused of harbouring known felons and offering safe haven to deposed leaders of other rogue genres, Psycho Thriller could never be directly indicted as nothing was ever quite what it seemed, a trait it shared with others that also had a tenuous hold on reality, such as Creative Accounting and Lies to tell your partner when (s)he finds underwear in the glovebox.

We found the genre by using our small onboard textual sieve to home in on a trail of confused Reader Feedback, and Sprockett expertly brought us in for a landing at the corner of Forsyth and Ludlum. We walked across a vacant lot to the unfenced border of Psychological Thriller. The weather, naturally, was atmospheric. On the Thriller side of the border the skies were clear, but across into Psychological there seemed to be an impenetrable wall of rain-soaked air. Jurisfiction had considerably posted signs along the border at regular intervals, warning trespassers to stay away or potentially suffer 'lethal levels of bewilderment'. Only a fool or the very brave ventured into Psychological Thriller alone.

'Ma'am?' said Sprockett, his eyebrow flickering alarm.

'Problems?'

'You find me hugely embarrassed.'

'What is it? You need winding?'

'No, ma'am. It's the damp. Humans might fear viruses and old age, two things with which cog-based life-forms have very little issue. But when it comes to corrosion, honey, magnets and damp, I'm afraid to say that I must warn you that a rebuild might be necessary, and spare parts are becoming scandalously expensive.'

'It's all right,' I said, 'just wait for me here.'

I stepped across. Inside Psychological Thriller it was raining, and night. The cold wind lashed my face, and drove the rain into every crevice of my clothes until within a very short period I was soaked through. The tops of the trees swayed dangerously in the wind, and every now and then there was a flash of lightning followed by a splintering crack and the sound of a tree falling with a muffled crash somewhere in the dark.

I moved on, occasionally sinking ankle deep in the marshy ground. After a few hundred yards I came to a small clearing of tussocky grass, pools of brackish water and broken branches. On the far side, partially immersed in ooze, were the remains of a Trans-Genre Taxi. The front was stove in, the engine torn out and the bodywork rippled and bent. Scraps of tree had been caught in the wing mirrors as it tore through the foliage on its way down. As I stared at the mangled wreck, the lightning flashed, and I could see that on the side was painted 'No tips' and, farther along, '1517'. It was Thursday's cab.

I hurried round to see whether anyone had survived. I was perhaps in too much haste, and swiftly sank up to my thighs in the fetid waters. I extricated myself with a considerable amount of grunting and swearing, and finally made my way to the taxi and peered in. The rear door was open, and the empty back seat scattered with papers, mostly about the geology under Racy Novel. The Mediocre Gatsby was still sitting in the front seat, impaled on the steering column. He had been killed by a bad case of Selective Nostalgia. For some peculiar reason all TransGenreTaxis were modelled on the 1950s Yellow Checker cab design, at a time when safety standards were non-existent and fatal accidents embraced by Detroit with an alarming level of indifference. The 'Hose down the dash and sell it to the next man' attitude pervaded all the way into the BookWorld, and not without good reason. In here, there was always a battle between nostalgia and safety, and nostalgia usually won.

I stood up, pushed the wet hair out of my eyes and tried to think what might have happened. As I stared in turn at the exterior of the taxi, the empty back seat and the remains of Mediocre Gatsby, I suddenly had a thought: the rear door had been open when I got here. I looked around to see where I might have gone if I had found myself unceremoniously dumped in the middle of a rainy swamp at night, possibly injured and very alone. I took the most obvious way out of the marsh and managed to find a path to higher ground. I followed the trail as best as I could, and after stumbling through the forest for a few hundred yards in a generally uphill direction I came across a doorway in a high brick wall, upon the top of which were the remains of a corroded electrified fence. Attached to the brick wall was a weathered wooden board telling me to keep away from 'The Wilfred D. Akron home for the criminally insane'.

If I had been real I would doubtless have been more nervous than I was, but this was Psychological Thriller, and Secure Hospitals for the Criminally Insane were pretty much ten a penny, and rarely secure. I found myself in a small and very overgrown graveyard, the lichen-encrusted stones leaning with a frightening level of apparent randomness. I moved through the graveyard towards a mausoleum built of brick and stone but in an advanced state of decay. If I had crash-landed here in the taxi, this is where I would have sought shelter.

The double doors were bronze, heavy, and streaked green with age. There was a hole about three foot wide in the middle, so both doors looked as if they had a semicircle cut from them. My foot knocked against something. It was Thursday's well-worn pistol, her name engraved on the barrel – the hole in the locked doors had been blasted out for access. I was getting close. I carefully climbed through the hole in the door, and wiped the rain from my hair and eyes. It was light enough to see, and below the broken roof-light was a table that had once held flowers, but was now a collection of dirty vases. There were a few personal items scattered about – a picture of Landen and the kids, a five-pound note, an Acme Carpets pass.

'It's difficult to know sometimes who you are, isn't it?'

I turned to see a small figure of a girl aged no more than eight standing in a shaft of light that seemed to descend vertically from the roof.

'Hello, Jenny,' I said.

'Did anyone figure you out?' she asked. 'Hiding in plain sight as the written version of you. How did the written Thursday feel about taking a back seat for a while? And where is she, by the way?'

'I'm really Thursday?' I asked.

'Oh yes,' replied Jenny with a chuckle. 'Doesn't it all seem so obvious now?'

Two days ago, I might have believed her.

'No,' I replied. 'You see, I spoke to Landen and he told me I vanished from the RealWorld as a good book-person might do, so don't give me any of your Psychological Thriller bullshit.'

'O-kay,' said Jenny, thinking quickly, 'how about this: you're actually just witnessing—'

'Don't even *think* of trying to Owlcreek me. And while we're at it, you're not Jenny.'

'Is she giving you any trouble?' said another voice I recognised.

'A little,' said Jenny, and Sprockett – or a reasonable facsimile of him – appeared from out of the shadows. I sighed. My mother would be appearing next, and then probably myself. It was all becoming a little tedious.

'Did you try her on the *You really are Thursday* twist ending?' asked Sprockett.

'She didn't buy it. I tried the *It's all in your last moment before dying* gambit, too.'

Ersatz Sprockett thought for a moment.

'What about the *You're actually a patient in a mental hospital and we've been enacting all of this to try to find out if you killed Thursday*? That usually works.'

'Goodness,' said faux-Jenny, 'I'd clean forgotten about that one.'

'And now you've told me,' I said, 'I'm hardly likely to go for it, am I?'

'Well done, Einstein,' said faux-Jenny to her partner in a sarcastic tone, 'any other bright ideas?'

Ersatz Sprockett looked at me, then at faux-Jenny, then tried to telegraph an idea across to her in a very lame portrayal of someone being in a shower.

'Oh!' said faux-Jenny as she twigged what he was talking about. 'Good idea.'

But I had figured it too.

'You wouldn't be thinking about pulling a Bobby Ewing on me, would you?'

And they both swore under their breath.

'Well,' grumbled Ersatz Sprockett with a shrug, 'that's me clean out of ideas.'

And as I watched they reverted to the strangely misshapen shape-changers who skulked around Psychological Thriller, hoping to trap an unwary traveller into thinking they had once been a homicidal maniac, but now had amnesia, and all their previous visions depicted in horrific nightmares were actually recovered memories. In a word, they were a pair of utter *nuisances*.

'Thank heavens for that,' I said. 'Let's get down to business. Where is Thursday and why didn't you report her presence here to Juris-fiction?'

'We send so many conflicting and utterly bizarre plot lines out of the genre that everyone ignores us,' said Shifter-once-Jenny sadly. 'I think Jurisfiction set our messages to "auto-ignore".'

'For good reason,' I replied. 'You're only marginally less trou-blesome than Conspiracy.'

'That's why Thursday asked us to transmit all those ambiguities direct to you. We were hoping you'd get here sooner than this. We peppered you with as much confusion as we could, but you didn't pick it up.'

If I'd been Thursday, I would have. Being confused over iden-tity had been a mainstay of Psychological Thriller for years. I had a lot to learn.

'I'm new to this.'

'You'll get the hang of it.'

'I hope not to. Where is she?'

'In that antechamber.'

I turned and followed a short corridor to where there was a small room off the main mausoleum. It was where the shape-changers usually lived as there were posters of Faceache on the wall. They had given over the one bed to Thursday, who was lying on her back. The room was lit by a gas lantern, and by the flickering jet I could see that she was in bad shape. There was an ugly bruise on her face, and one eye was red with blood. She moved her head to look at me, and I saw her eyes glisten.

'Hey,' I said.

'Hey,' said Thursday in a weak voice.

I placed my hand on her forehead. It was hot.

'How are you feeling?' I asked.

She gave a faint smile and shrugged, but winced when she did so.

'Landen?' she whispered.

'He's fine. Kids too.'

'Tell them—'

'Tell them yourself.'

I stood up. I had to get her to *Gray's Anatomy* as soon as possible. There was an umbrella in a stand at the door and I picked it up.

'Thursday? I'm going to fetch someone who can carry you out of here. My butler. I'll be ten minutes.'

'You have a butler?' said Thursday in a weak voice.

'Yes,' I replied in a chirpy voice in order to hide my concern, '*everyone* needs a butler.'

41

The End of the Book

'About the Author: Commander Bradshaw has been one of the stalwarts of Jurisfiction for over fifty years, and has been the Bellman an unprecedented eight times. Hailing from a long-unread branch of British Imperialist Fiction, he now divides his time between Jurisfiction duties, his lovely wife Melanie and continually updating the *BookWorld Companion*, which remains the definitive work on the BookWorld and everything in it.'

Bradshaw's BookWorld Companion

I flew the Hovermatic home from *Gray's Anatomy* two hours later, but Sprockett and I said nothing on the trip. I was quiet because I was thinking about Thursday, and what a close call it had been. She had a fractured skull, a broken femur, and eight breaks to her left arm and hand. There were multiple lacerations, a loss of blood, fever and a concussion. Henry Gray himself took charge and whisked her into surgery almost the moment I arrived. Within ten minutes the waiting room was full of concerned well-wishers, Bradshaw and Zhark among them. I knew she was in good hands, so I'd quietly slipped away as soon as I learned she was out of danger.

I was quiet also because I had averted a war and saved many lives today, and that's a peculiar feeling that's difficult to describe. Sprockett was quiet, too – but only because I had inadvertently allowed his spring to run down, and he had shut down all functions except thought, and was having a mildly erotic meditation about bevel gears and how nice it might be to have a fly-wheel fitted in order to give him a little more 'oomph' in the mornings.

The first thing I saw when I got back to my house was Bowden, dressed up as me.

'This isn't how it appears,' he said, in the same tone of voice he'd used when I found him looking through my underwear drawer the year before. He told me then that he'd 'heard a mouse', but I didn't believe him.

'How *should* it appear if you're dressed up in my clothes?'

'Carmine's goblin ran off with a goblinette, and she locked herself in the bathroom again. I'm standing in for her. *You.* I've just done a scene with myself. It was most odd.'

'How many readers have we got?' I asked.

'Six.'

'You can handle it.'

'Oh!' said Bowden, in the manner of one who is pretending to be disappointed but is actually delighted. 'If I must. But who will play me?'

'I will,' came a voice from the door. I turned to find Whitby Jett standing there.

'Whitby?'

'How's my little Thursday?'

'She's good. But . . . what about the nuns?'

'A misunderstanding,' he said. 'I hadn't set fire to any of them as it turned out.'

I stepped forward and touched his chest. I could feel that the guilt had lifted. He'd managed to move the damaging backstory on.

'I'm going to mix some cocktails,' announced Sprockett, and buzzed from the room.

'Make mine a Sidcup Sling, Sprokky, old boy,' said Jett. 'Bowden – where are my lines?'

'Here!' said Bowden, and passed him a well-thumbed script.

'Whitby?'

'Yes, Muffin?'

'Are you busy right now?'

'Only selling useless rubbish for EZ-Read. Why?'

'Nothing.' I smiled, but there was something. Whitby could play Landen beautifully.

He and Bowden both went off to play a scene in the SpecOps building, leaving me to sit at the kitchen table, trying to figure out whether I could have found Thursday earlier. If I'd had more experience, probably.

Pickwick stuck her head around the door and looked relieved when she saw me.

'Thank goodness!' she said. 'I can't tell you what a disaster it's been. They threatened to tape my beak shut if I didn't join them. Your father was the ringleader — along with Carmine, of course. She'll come to a sticky end, I can tell you.'

'She'll be fine,' I said, feeling magnanimous. Carmine had problems, but so did we all. 'Make the tea, will you?'

'Isn't that why we have a butler?'

I stared at her and raised an eyebrow.

'So . . . milk and one sugar, right?'

And she waddled into the kitchen to try to figure out which object was the kettle.

'May I come in?'

It was the character who played my father. He was quite unlike his usual abrasive self, and seemed almost painfully eager to be friendly.

'Hello, Thursday,' he said. 'Is . . . that chair comfortable?'

'Don't sweat it,' I said, almost embarrassed to see him like this. 'I'm going to make some radical changes to your character. It's very simple: do the new scenes or you can have a transfer. Take it or leave it.'

He thought about it for a moment, mumbled something about how he would 'look forward to seeing his new lines' and made some excuse before departing.

Pickwick came back in.

'The tea is in the jar marked "tea", right?'

'Right.'

The doorbell rang. It was Emperor Zhark.

'Good evening, Your Mercilessness,' I said, opening the door wide, 'come on in and have a cocktail. My man does a Gooseberry Flip so strong it will make your toes swell.'

'That's a figure of speech, right?'

'Not at all. Your toes really do swell – to the size of apples.'

'I won't, thank you. I'm actually here on business. Do you have an automaton living here, name of Sprockett?'

I think my heart may almost have stopped.

'What is it?' I asked. 'What's going on?'

'I am ready, sir.'

It was Sprockett. He had his overcoat on and had packed his oils and a spare knee-joint, just in case.

'Wait a minute,' I said, 'you can't take him away. He has a job with me. I'll sign any papers you want.'

'Ma'am,' said Sprockett, 'I am no longer in your employ. If you recall, you gave me glowing references and relieved me of my duties. Emperor, may we go?'

The Emperor moved to the door, but I wasn't done.

'Emperor,' I said, 'I don't wish to appear above my station, but I do feel that a simple work-permit violation could be overlooked on this occasion.'

Zhark told Sprockett to get in his car and turned back to me.

'Miss Next,' he said in a firm voice, 'your butler might be the perfect Thursday's Friday, but he is far too dangerous to be allowed to remain at liberty. All those Laws of Robotics you've heard of are pretty much baloney. Good evening, Miss Next, and I'm sorry.'

And he turned in a sweep of black velvet and strode up to his waiting limousine, leaving me shaking with frustration, until I had a thought.

'Wait!'

I ran up to the limousine's window.

'This crime,' I said, 'did it have anything to do with nuns?'

'And puppies,' said Zhark with a shudder. 'Frightful business.'

'You stay right here. Don't move. Understand?'

I think Emperor Zhark started to respect me just then. Not just as a Thursday, but as a person. Either that, or he was used to taking orders from angry women.

Whitby and Bowden were in the SpecOps office, talking about Hades. I'd found Carmine looking in the fridge for something to eat and she did a mid-read changeover with Whitby. I took him by the hand and pushed him into an adjoining room. I'll admit it. I was angry.

'What the hell do you think you're doing?' I demanded.

'A scene with Bowden. You told me to.'

'Not *that*. I'm talking about Sprockett and the incident with the nuns. What were you doing?'

He shrugged.

'Listen, Muffin, he approached *me*. Said he'd take on my backstory so you'd be happy. What am I going to do? Turn him down? I want you and me to be happy, Pumpkin, and we'll always be thankful to it for such a selfless act.'

'Not it, *him*.'

I stared at Whitby and shook my head, and he knew then that however much I liked him, I couldn't let it happen this way, and neither could he. He leaned forward and kissed me on the cheek, and I could feel my eyes fill with tears.

'Listen, Whitby, you'll find a way of getting rid of the backstory.'

'Yes,' he said, 'and when I do—'

'You'll know where to find me.'

He smiled a wan smile, and walked out of the door. I wiped my eyes and went and sat down in the kitchen to stare at the wall.

'Here,' said Pickwick, panting with the exertion, 'your tea.'

She pushed it across the table with her beak and I picked it up.

'Oh,' I said, 'it's gone cold.'

'It was meant to be hot?'

'No, actually, this is good. Thank you, Pickers.'

'That's a relief. What's for dinner? I'm starving after all that tea-making. It really takes it out of you.'

'I thought we would have a lamb risotto,' came a voice from the door. I turned to see Sprockett standing tall and as straight as a poker, every bit the perfect butler.

I ran across and gave him a hug. He was hard and cold and although outwardly emotionless, deep within him I could hear his cogs speed up as I squeezed.

'Madam, *please*,' he said, faintly embarrassed.

'Thank you, Sprockett,' I said, 'for everything.'

The automaton inclined his head politely but my eyes were fixed on his eyebrow to see what it would do. I wanted to establish what loyal friendship meant to him – whether a man of cogs, dials, chains and sprockets could *really* feel as humans feel.

But I was to be disappointed. He pressed a white-gloved finger to his eyebrow, blocking any movement. All I could see in his face was blank moulded porcelain, two lenses for eyes and a slot through which he spoke.

'May I ask a question, ma'am?'

'Of course.'

'Was it a compassionate act to take over Whitby's backstory to enable you and he to be together?'

'Yes.'

'I believe I have learned something of value here today, ma'am. But what made Whitby retake the backstory from me?'

384

'Because he knew it was the right thing to do.'

Sprockett buzzed for a moment.

'Does that sort of thing happen out there in the RealWorld, or is it just in books?'

I thought for a moment. Of the untidy chaos I had seen in the RealWorld; of not knowing what was going to happen; of not knowing what, if anything, had relevance. The RealWorld was a sprawling mess of a book, in need of a good editor. I thought then of the narrative order here in the BookWorld, our resolved plot lines and the observance of natural justice we took for granted.

'Literature is claimed to be a Mirror of the World,' I said, 'but the Outlanders are fooling themselves. The BookWorld is as orderly as people in the RealWorld *hope* their own world to be – it isn't a mirror, it's an aspiration.'

'Humans,' said Sprockett, 'are the most gloriously bizarre creatures.'

'Yes,' I said with a smile, 'they certainly are.'

Acknowledgements

Firstly, my thanks to Carolyn Mays and Josh Kendall and all the team at Hodder and Viking for their steadfast support and understanding during the final stages of the book, when events of a daughtering nature conspired to render the manuscript past the ideal delivery time.

My thanks to Dr John Wooten for his valuable contributions to the understanding of Nextian Physics, and for being at the end of an email if I had a query as regards the best way to mangle physics while still looking vaguely correct.

The illustrations were drawn by Bill Mudron and Dylan Meconis of Portland, Oregon, and they have, as usual, surpassed themselves in their depiction of the Nextian Universe. Bill can be found at *www.excelsiorstudios.net* and Dylan at *www.dylanmeconis.com*.

My apologies to the many, many authors who have used the 'hollow earth' notion as the setting for a book. It *must* have been done before, and I would expect the mechanics of how it functions would be universal, as the concept has a tendency to write itself. In case of unavoidable parallels, my apologies.

BookWorld Cartographers. My thanks to the following for submitting wonderful ideas to me about the possible shape and layout of Fiction Island: Alex Maunders, Robert Persson, Laura, Catherine Fitzsimons, Geoffrey Elliot-Howell, Michael O'Connor, Ellie Randall, Steve James, Elizabeth Walter, Derek Walter, Theresea

Porst, Sarah Porter, Dhana Sabonathon, Alex Clark, Loraine Weston, Elisabeth Parsons, Jane Ren, Birgit Prihodko and Helen Griin-Looveer.

I am also indebted to my new agents Will Francis and Claire Paterson, who have filled Tif's recently vacated shoes with an aplomb and unswerving professionalism that I know she would approve.

No thanks would be complete without special mention of Mari, whose constant and overwhelming support allows me to function as a vaguely sentient creature rather than a mass of quivering jelly. I would also like to thank Ingrid and Ian, for much support when we needed it, and my in-laws, Maggy and Stewart, for help and assistance on occasions too numerous to mention.

This book took one hundred and eight days to write between December 22nd 2009 and September 3rd 2010. It was written on a Mac Pro using Pages software. During the writing I consumed 32 gallons of coffee, 18 gallons of tea and walked 192 miles. The filing backed up to a depth of seven and a half inches and I received 1,672 emails and sent 380. The average daytime temperature was 7.2 degrees and I burned 1.2 tons of logs in my wood-burner. In that time I lost a faithful hound, but gained a fourth daughter.

Jasper Fforde
October 2010

GOWER PENINSULA

Socialist Republic of Wales

Not __always__ raining.

See your local tourist office for details.

TransGenreTaxis

AS USED BY THURSDAY NEXT

* GENERALLY SAFE *
* USUALLY CLEAN *
* MOSTLY POLITE DRIVERS *
* ALL CARS NOW WITH SEATS *
* BRIBES READILY ACCEPTED *
* OVERCHARGING RARE *
* NO EXTRA FEE FOR WINDOWS *
* AIRCON WHEN FUNCTIONING*
* HASTILY TRAINED DRIVERS*

TransGenreTaxis
2644

TransGenreTaxis

CALL FOOTNOTERPHONE 7177 CASH - ACCOUNT - BARTER

Fforde Ffiesta

Do you want to meet other people who like Fforde's books?
Do you have a silly sense of humour?
Do you want to speed-read 'To be or not to be'?
Do you have nothing better to do?
If the answer to any of these questions is 'perhaps',
then you could certainly do a lot worse than attend the

Fforde Ffiesta

Held annually at Swindon, UK. For details of the next Ffiesta, log on to:

www.jasperfforde.com/ffiesta.html

Where it all began – the first in the Thursday Next series

JASPER FFORDE

The Eyre Affair

Meet Thursday Next, literary detective without equal, fear or boyfriend.

There is another 1985, where London's criminal gangs have moced into the lucrative literary market, and Thursday Next is on the trail of the new crime wave's Mr Big.

Acheron Hades has been kidnapping characters from works of fiction and holding them to ransom. Jane Eyre is gone. Missing.

Thursday sets out to find a way into the book to repair the damage. But solving crimes against literature isn't easy when you also have to find time to halt the Crimean War, persuade the man you love to marry you, and figure out who *really* wrote Shakespeare's plays.

Perhaps today just isn't going to be Thursday's day. Join her on a truly breathtaking adventure, and find out for yourself. Fiction will never be the same again . . .

HODDER

JASPER FFORDE

Lost in a Good Book

For Thursday Next, literary detective without equal, life should be good. Riding high on a wave of celebrity following the safe return of kidnapped Jane Eyre, Thursday ties the knot with the man she loves.

But marital bliss isn't quite as it should be. It turns out her husband of one month actually drowned thirty-eight years ago, and no one but Thursday has any memory of him at all.

Someone, somewhere is responsible.

Having barely caught her breath after *The Eyre Affair*, Thursday heads back into fiction in search of the truth, discovering that paper politicans, lost Shakespearean manuscripts, a flurry of near-fatal coincidences and impending Armageddon are all part of a greater plan.

But whose? And why?

HODDER

JASPER FFORDE

The Well of Lost Plots

Pursued by a sinister multinational corporation and an evil genius with a penchant for clothes shopping and memory modification, literary detective Thursday Next is on the run. Not an ideal situation considering she's pregnant by her husband who is presently suffering a non-existence problem.

Taking refuge in the Well of Lost Plots – the place where all fiction is created – Thursday ponders her next move from inside an unpublished novel of dubious merit entitled *Caversham Heights*. But in Thursday's world, trouble is only ever a page away, and when a succession of Jurisfiction agents are killed, only one woman is up to the job of unmasking the villain responsible.

Will Thursday ever be able to enjoy the quiet life again, or is she about to lose the plot completely?

HODDER

JASPER FFORDE

Something Rotten

Literary detective Thursday Next is on a mission – and it's not just a mission to save the planet. If only life were that simple . . .

Unemployed following an international cheese-smuggling scandal, our favourite cultural crime-fighter is faced with a world of problems: Hamlet's not attending his conflict resolution classes, President George Formby is facing a coup led by dastardly Yorrick Kaine and, what's more, the evil Goliath Corporation are refusing to un-eradicate Thursday's husband, Landen.

Will she ever see Landen again? Is shopping the new religion? Can Thursday prevent Armageddon? And who will babysit her son while she does it?

Join Thursday on her toughest assignment yet, and enter a world where fiction is always much stranger than the truth . . .

HODDER

JASPER FFORDE

First Among Sequels

Literary Detective Thursday Next is officially off the case. Once a key figure in the BookWorld police force, she is concentrating on her duties as a wife and mother. Or so her husband thinks . . .

Unofficially, Thursday is working as hard as ever – and in this world of dangerously short attention spans, there's no rest for the literate.

Can Thursday stop *Pride and Prejudice* being turned into a vote-em-off reality book? Who killed Sherlock Holmes? And will Thursday get her teenage son out of bed in time for him to save the world?

HODDER

The first in the Nursery Crime series

JASPER FFORDE

The Big Over Easy

It's Easter in Reading – a bad time for eggs – and no one can remember the last sunny day. Humpty Dumpty, well-known nursery favourite, large egg, ex-convict and former millionaire philanthropist is found shattered beneath a wall in a shabby area of town.

Following the pathologist's careful reconstruction of Humpty's shell, Detective Inspector Jack Spratt and his Sergeant Mary Mary are soon grappling with a sinister plot involving cross-border money laundering, the illegal Béarnaise sauce market, corporate politics and the cut and thrust world of international chiropody.

As Jack and Mary stumble around the streets of Reading in Jack's Lime Green Austin Allegro, the clues pile up, but Jack has his own problems to deal with.

And on top of everything else, the Jellyman is coming to town . . .

HODDER

JASPER FFORDE

The Fourth Bear

The Gingerbreadman — psychopath, sadist, convicted murderer and cake/biscuit — is loose on the streets of Reading.

It isn't Jack Spratt's case. Despite the success of the Humpty Dumpty investigation, the well publicised failure to prevent Red Riding-Hood and her Gran being eaten once again plunges the Nursery Crime Division into controversy. Enforced non-involvement with the Gingerbreadman hunt looks to be frustrating until a chance encounter at the oddly familiar Deja-Vu Club leads them onto the hunt for missing journalist Henrietta 'Goldy' Hatchett, star reporter for *The Daily Toad*.

The last witnesses to see her alive were The Three Bears, comfortably living out a life of rural solitude in Andersen's wood. But all is not what it seems. Are the unexplained explosions around the globe somehow related to missing nuclear scientist Angus McGuffin? Is cucumber-growing really that dangerous? Why are National Security involved? But most important of all: How could the bears' porridge be at such disparate temperatures when they were poured at the same time?

HODDER

JASPER FFORDE

Shades of Grey

Hundreds of years in the future, after the Something that Happened, the world is an alarmingly different place. Life is lived according to The Rulebook and social hierarchy is determined by your perception of colour.

Eddie Russett is an above average Red who dreams of moving up the ladder by marriage to Constance Oxblood. Until he is sent to the Outer Fringes where he meets Jane – a lowly Grey with an uncontrollable temper and a desire to see him killed.

For Eddie, it's love at first sight. But his infatuation will lead him to discover that all is not as it seems in a world where everything that looks black and white is really shades of grey . . .

HODDER

JASPER FFORDE

The Fourth Bear

The Gingerbreadman – psychopath, sadist, convicted murderer and cake/biscuit – is loose on the streets of Reading.

It isn't Jack Spratt's case. Despite the success of the Humpty Dumpty investigation, the well publicised failure to prevent Red Riding-Hood and her Gran being eaten once again plunges the Nursery Crime Division into controversy. Enforced non-involvement with the Gingerbreadman hunt looks to be frustrating until a chance encounter at the oddly familiar Deja-Vu Club leads them onto the hunt for missing journalist Henrietta 'Goldy' Hatchett, star reporter for *The Daily Toad*.

The last witnesses to see her alive were The Three Bears, comfortably living out a life of rural solitude in Andersen's wood. But all is not what it seems. Are the unexplained explosions around the globe somehow related to missing nuclear scientist Angus McGuffin? Is cucumber-growing really that dangerous? Why are National Security involved? But most important of all: How could the bears' porridge be at such disparate temperatures when they were poured at the same time?

HODDER

JASPER FFORDE

Shades of Grey

Hundreds of years in the future, after the Something that Happened, the world is an alarmingly different place. Life is lived according to The Rulebook and social hierarchy is determined by your perception of colour.

Eddie Russett is an above average Red who dreams of moving up the ladder by marriage to Constance Oxblood. Until he is sent to the Outer Fringes where he meets Jane – a lowly Grey with an uncontrollable temper and a desire to see him killed.

For Eddie, it's love at first sight. But his infatuation will lead him to discover that all is not as it seems in a world where everything that looks black and white is really shades of grey . . .

HODDER

Jasper Fforde's first work for a younger generation of readers

JASPER FFORDE

The Last Dragonslayer

In the good old days, magic was powerful, unregulated by
government, and even the largest spell could be woven without
filling in magic release form B1-7g.

Then the magic started fading away.

Fifteen-year-old Jennifer Strange runs Kazam, an employment
agency for soothsayers and sorcerers. But work is drying up.
Drain cleaner is cheaper than a spell, and even magic carpets are
reduced to pizza delivery.

So it's a surprise when the visions start. Not only do they predict
the death of the Last Dragon by a dragonslayer, they also point
to Jennifer, and say something is coming. Big Magic . . .

HODDER

JASPER FFORDE

The Song of the Quarkbeast

As the background Wizidrical Power slowly builds after the Big
Magic, King Snodd IV of Hereford realises the man who
controls Magic controls almost anything.

But one person stands between him and his plans for power and
riches: Jennifer Strange, sixteen-year-old acting manager of Kazam.

It may involve a trip on a magic carpet at the speed of sound to
the Troll Wall, it may involve a second Quarkbeast sniffing
around town. It might also involve the mysterious Transient
Moose, and a powerless sorceress named Once Magnificent Boo.
But one thing is certain: Jennifer Strange and her faithful assistant
Tiger Prawns will not relinquish the noble powers of magic to
big business and commerce without a fight.

**HODDER &
STOUGHTON**